THAT THEY MAY FACE THE RISING SUN

John McGahern is the author of five highly acclaimed novels and four collections of short stories, and has been the recipient of many awards and honours, including the Society of Authors, the American-Irish Award, the Prix Etrangère Ecureuil and the Chevalier de l'Ordre des Arts et des Lettres. *Amongst Women*, which has won both the GPA and the *Irish Times* Award, was shortlisted for the Booker Prize and made into a four-part BBC television series. His work has appeared in anthologies and has been translated into many languages. He lives in Ireland.

'Memorable set-pieces (haymaking, market day, the laying out of a body) are strung like rosary beads on the elegant narrative which, like all truly great novels, celebrates the mystery and power of humanity.' *Mail On Sunday*

'*That They May Face the Rising Sun* is a tour de force . . . as a description of rural life, unfolding as majestically as the seasons, it is quite exquisite.' *Sunday Telegraph*

'This stately novel by one of Ireland's foremost writers is, as the title suggests, primarily about the rhythms and cadences of place . . . [it's] greatest pleasures come from the unflinching probity of his observations.' *The New Yorker*

'At last an Irish author has awakened from the nightmare of history and given us a sense of liberation which is not dependent on flight or emigration or escape.' *Guardian*

'The most perfect novel I've read in years. I saved the last 20 pages of the book for two weeks, unread: as long as I did not finish, I could stay in that world beside the lake.' *Newsweek*

'An extraordinarily subtle study of Irish family life, written with all his usual poise, precision and grace.' *New Statesman*

'Cloaked in the kind of wisdom that makes it translucent, not transparent . . . You have to sense, to intuit, to feel your way through the narrative, hear the intent behind the wonderful spin of voices.' *Scotsman*

'One of Ireland's most stupendous prose stylists.' *Independent*

JOHN MCGAHERN
That They May Face
the Rising Sun

faber and faber

First published in 2002
by Faber and Faber Limited
3 Queen Square London WC1N 3AU
Open market edition first published in 2002
This paperback edition first published in 2003

Typeset by Faber and Faber Ltd
Printed in England by Mackays of Chatham, plc

A CIP record for this book
is available from the British Library

ISBN 0–571–21221–2

4 6 8 10 9 7 5 3

To Madeline

The morning was clear. There was no wind on the lake. There was also a great stillness. When the bells rang out for Mass, the strokes trembling on the water, they had the entire world to themselves.

The doors of the house were open. Jamesie entered without knocking and came in noiselessly until he stood in the doorway of the large room where the Ruttledges were sitting. He stood as still as if waiting under trees for returning wildfowl. He expected his discovery to be quick. There would be a cry of surprise and reproach; he would counter by accusing them of not being watchful enough. There would be welcome and laughter. When the Ruttledges continued to converse calmly about a visit they were expecting that same afternoon, he could contain himself no longer. Such was his continual expectation of discovery that in his eavesdropping he was nearly always disappointed by the innocence he came upon.

'Hel-lo. Hel-lo. Hel-lo,' he called out softly, in some exasperation.

'Jamesie!' They turned to the voice with great friendliness. As he often stole silently in, they showed no surprise. 'You are welcome.'

'Ye are no good. I have been standing here for several minutes and haven't heard a bad word said about anybody yet. Not a bad word,' he repeated with mocking slowness as he came forward.

'We never speak badly about people. It's too dangerous. It can get you into trouble.'

'Then ye never speak or if you do the pair of yous are not worth listening to.'

1

In his dark Sunday suit, white shirt, red tie, polished black shoes, the fine silver hair brushed back from the high forehead and sharp clean features, he was shining and handsome. An intense vividness and sweetness of nature showed in every quick, expressive movement.

'Kate.' He held out an enormous hand. She pretended to be afraid to trust her hand to such strength. It was a game he played regularly. For him all forms of social intercourse were merely different kinds of play. 'God hates a coward, Kate,' he demanded, and she took his hand.

Not until she cried, 'Easy there, Jamesie,' did he release his gently tightening grip with a low crow of triumph. 'You are one of God's troopers, Kate. Mister Ruttledge,' he bowed solemnly.

'Mister Murphy.'

'No misters here,' he protested. 'No misters in this part of the world. Nothing but broken-down gentlemen.'

'There are no misters in this house either. He that is down can fear no fall.'

'Why don't you go to Mass, then, if you are that low?' Jamesie changed the attack lightly.

'What's that got to do with it?'

'You'd be like everybody else round here by now if you went to Mass.'

'I'd like to attend Mass. I miss going.'

'What's keeping you, then?'

'I don't believe.'

'I don't believe,' he mimicked. 'None of us believes and we go. That's no bar.'

'I'd feel a hypocrite. Why do *you* go if you don't believe?'

'To look at the girls. To see the whole performance,' he cried out, and started to shake with laughter. 'We go to see all the other hypocrites. Kate, what do you think about all this? You've hardly said a word.'

'My parents were atheists,' Kate said. 'They thought that all that exists is what you see, all that you are is what you think and appear to be.'

2

'Give them no heed, Kate,' he counselled gently. 'You are what you are and to hell with the begrudgers.'

'The way we perceive ourselves and how we are perceived are often very different,' Ruttledge said.

'Pay no heed to him either. He's just trying to twist and turn. Thought pissed in the bed and thought he was sweating. His wife thought otherwise. You'll get on good as any of them, Kate.' He took pruning shears from his pocket and placed them on the table. 'Thanks,' he said. 'They were a comfort. Pure Sheffield. Great steel.'

'I bought them from a stall in the Enniskillen market one Thursday. They weren't expensive.'

'The North,' he raised his hand for emphasis. 'The North is a great place for bargains.'

'Would you like a whiskey, Jamesie?' she asked.

'Now you're talking, Kate. But you should know by now that "wilya" is a very bad word.'

'Why bad?'

'Look at yer man,' he pointed to where Ruttledge had already taken glasses and a bottle of Powers from the cupboard and was running water into a brown jug.

'I'm slow.'

'You're not one bit slow, Kate. You just weren't brought up here. You nearly have to be born into a place to know what's going on and what to do.'

'He wasn't brought up here.'

'Not too far off, near enough to know. He wasn't at school but he met the scholars. Good health! And more again tomorrow,' he raised his glass. 'The crowd lying below in Shruhaun aren't drinking any drinks today.'

'Good luck. What's the news?'

'No news. Came looking for news,' he cried ritually and then could contain his news no longer: 'Johnny's coming home from England. He's coming home this Tuesday. Mary got the letter.'

Every summer his brother Johnny came home on holidays

from the Ford factory at Dagenham. He had left for England twenty years before and never missed a summer coming home.

'I'd be glad to run you to the station,' Ruttledge offered.

'I know that well, and thanks, but no, no.' He raised the hand again. 'Always go in Johnny Rowley's car. Jim is meeting Johnny at the airport and putting him on the train. Jim is taking time off.'

Jim was Jamesie and Mary's only child, who had been clever at school, had entered the civil service, where he had risen to a high position, and was married with four children in Dublin.

'There was a time Johnny spent the night with Jim and Lucy in Dublin.'

'Not any more. Johnny and Lucy don't pull. He's not awanted. It's better, better by far the way it is. I'll meet the train with Johnny Rowley. We'll have several stops on the way from the station. When we get to the house, Mary will put the sirloin down. You can't get meat in England. You'd just love to see Johnny's face and the way he says "God bless you, Mary" when she puts the sirloin in front of him on the table.'

The house and the outhouses would be freshly whitewashed for the homecoming, the street swept, the green gates painted, old stakes replaced in the netting wire that held Mary's brown hens in the space around the hayshed. Mary would have scrubbed and freshened all the rooms. Together they would have taken the mattress from the bed in the lower room, Johnny's old room, and left it outside to air in the sun. The holy pictures and the wedding photographs would be taken down, the glass wiped and polished. His bed would be made with crisp linen and draped with the red blanket. An enormous vase of flowers from the garden and the fields – roses and lilies and sweet william from the garden, foxglove and big sprays of honeysuckle from the hedges – would be placed on the sill under the open window to sweeten the air and take away the staleness and smell of

4

damp from the unused room. The order for the best sirloin would already have been placed at Caroll's in the town. The house couldn't have been prepared any better for a god coming home to his old place on earth.

'Johnny was the best shot this part of the country has ever seen. On a Sunday when all the guns gathered and they'd be blazing away, all Johnny had to do was to raise his gun for the bird to fall like a stone. He had two of the most beautiful gun dogs, Oscar and Bran, a pointer and a red setter. He had the whole world at his feet,' Jamesie said. 'He didn't have to lift a hand. All he had to do was go round and oversee what other men were doing. Yes, he could be severe enough and strict, too, in his own way . . . too exact when it wasn't needed. The whole country was leaving for England at the time and if any of them had a hope of Johnny's job there'd be a stampede worse than for a gold rush back from England. If anybody had told us what was going to happen we wouldn't have believed them. We'd have laughed.

'He went after Anna Mulvey. He and Anna were the stars in *The Playboy* that got to the All-Ireland Finals in Athlone the year before but neither of them was fit to hold a candle to Patrick Ryan. He had Donoghue the solicitor in town down to a T as – I forget rightly who it was . . . Patrick had the whole hall in stitches every time he moved. Johnny was wild about Anna. We were sure Anna left for England to get away from Johnny. The Mulveys were well off and she didn't have to go. Then when she wrote to Johnny that she missed him and wanted him to come to England I don't think his feet touched the ground for days. We wanted him to take sick leave and go and test the water and not burn all his bridges but he would-n't hear. If he'd heeded our words he could be still here.'

'Why would Anna write for him to come to England when she wasn't serious or interested?'

'She was using him. She could be sure of adoration from Johnny. She had only to say the word and she'd get anything she wanted.'

5

'That was wrong,' Kate said.

'Right or wrong, fair or foul, what does it matter? It's a rough business. Those that care least will win. They can watch all sides. She had no more value on Johnny than a dog or a cat.

'Poor Bran and Oscar. The gun dogs were beautiful. They were as much part of Johnny as the double barrel, and they adored him. The evening before he left he took them down to the bog with the gun. They were yelping and jumping around and following trails. They thought they were going hunting. I remember it too well. The evening was frosty, the leaves just beginning to come off the trees. There wasn't a breath of wind. You'd hear a spade striking a stone fields away, never mind a double-barrel. There was just the two shots, one after the other. We would have been glad to take care of the dogs but he never asked. I wasn't a great shot like Johnny but I would have kept the gun and the dogs. They were beautiful dogs. That evening a man came for the gun and another for the motorbike. He had sold them both. You'd think he'd have offered me the gun after all the years in the house. I'd have given him whatever he wanted.'

'Why didn't you ask to buy the gun?'

'No. I'd not ask. I'd die before I'd ask.'

'Why?'

'He might think I wanted the gun for nothing. I didn't mind the gun so much though it was a smasher. It was the poor dogs that killed me – and Mary . . . far worse. She adored the dogs.

'Johnny took the train the next evening. That was the move that ruined his life. He'd have been better if he'd shot himself instead of the dogs.'

'Wasn't it a courageous thing compared to what happens in most of our lives? To abandon everything and to leave in the hope of love?'

'No, Kate. You don't know what you're saying. He didn't know what he was doing. He'd have gone into a blazing house if she asked. Compared to what he saw in her he put no value on his own life. He thought he couldn't live without her.'

'Why was she using him if she didn't want him?'

'You must know, Kate. You're a woman.'

'There are as many different kinds of women as there are men.'

'Mary says the same,' he struck the arm of the chair for emphasis. 'Johnny'd have bought her drinks, cigarettes, God knows what, we don't know, and he gave her money. He had a lot of money when he went to England and he'd have given her the clothes off his back if she asked. He'd be at her every beck and call. We heard afterwards that Anna went to England after Peadar Curren and got burned. I suppose Johnny put her back on her feet after the gunk she got with Peadar and then she got rid of him. Johnny didn't come home that first summer but came without fail every summer since.'

'Was Anna mentioned when he came?'

'Never once. We don't even know how it ended. Then we heard she married a policeman in London who turned for her.'

'Converted to Catholicism,' Ruttledge explained. 'Turned his coat. I'd have turned my coat for you, Kate, but I had no coat to turn by that time, and you never asked.'

'Spoken like a true heathen. They'll all turn, Kate. If they have to pick between their religion and the boggy hollow, they'll all turn,' he laughed exultantly.

'We've all been in Johnny's place, except maybe not to the same extent,' Ruttledge said.

'Speak for yourself, Mister Ruttledge. I haven't been there,' Jamesie said.

'Then you haven't been far.'

'I've never, never moved from here and I know the whole world,' he protested.

'You're right, Jamesie. Pay no heed to him,' Kate said.

'What do you think, Kate?'

'I think women are more practical. They learn to cut their losses. They are more concentrated on themselves.'

7

'Enter lightly, Kate, and leave on tiptoe. Put the hand across but never press. Ask why not but never why. Always lie so that you speak the truth and God save all poor sinners,' he said, and greeted his own sally with a sharp guffaw.

A loud sudden rapping with a stick on the porch door did not allow for any response. 'God bless all here!' was shouted out as a slow laborious shuffle approached through the front room.

'Bill Evans.'

'It could be no one else,' Jamesie rubbed his hands together in anticipation.

Bill Evans did not pause in the doorway but advanced boldly into the room to sit in the white rocking chair. The huge wellingtons, the blue serge trousers and torn jacket, a shirt of mattress ticking, the faded straw hat were all several sizes too large. The heavy blackthorn he carried he leaned against an arm of the chair. His eyes darted eagerly from face to face to face. 'Jamesie,' he grinned with condescension. 'You are welcome to this side of the lake.'

'I'm delighted, honoured to be here,' Jamesie laughed.

Tea was made. Milk and several spoons of sugar were added to the tea and stirred. The tea and biscuits were placed on a low stool beside the rocking chair. He ate and drank greedily.

'How are you all up there?'

'Topping. We are all topping.'

'You are managing all right without Jackie?'

'Getting along topping. Managing fine.'

He had been schooled never to part with any information about what happened. There was much to conceal about Bill Evans's whole life. Because he knew no other life, his instinct to protect his keepers and his place was primal.

'Do you think will Herself get married again?' Jamesie asked jocularly, provocatively.

'Everybody says that you are far too nosy.'

'News is better than no news,' Jamesie answered, taken aback.

There are no truths more hurtful than those we see as partly true. That such a humble hand delivered it made it more unsettling. Though he pretended not to care, Jamesie knew that his curiosity was secretly feared and openly mocked. He became unusually silent.

Bill Evans finished the tea and biscuits. 'Have you any fags?' he demanded when he put the plate and cup away and rose out of the rocking chair.

Ruttledge gave him five loose cigarettes that had been placed in a corner of the dresser. 'A light?' Bill asked. Some matches from a box were emptied into his palm. Cigarettes and matches were all put together into the breast pocket of the large serge jacket. 'Not faulting the company but I'll be beating away now,' he said.

'Good luck, Bill,' Jamesie called out amiably, but Bill Evans made no answer.

Ruttledge accompanied him to the gate where he had left the two buckets in the hedge of fuchsia bushes.

'See if there's anybody watching in the lane,' he demanded.

Ruttledge walked out into the lane and looked casually up and down. Between its high banks the narrow lane was like a lighted tunnel under the tangled roof of green branches. 'There's not a soul in sight.'

'There's no one watching above at the gate?'

'Nobody. You were very hard on poor Jamesie,' Ruttledge said.

'That's the only way to give it to him,' he grinned in triumph. 'He's too newsy.' He lifted the two buckets out of the fuchsias and, gripping the blackthorn against one of the handles, headed towards the lake.

His kind was now almost as extinct as the corncrake. He had fled to his present house from the farm he first worked on. When he was fourteen years old he had been sent out from the religious institutions to that first farm. Nobody knew now, least of all Bill Evans, how long ago that was.

9

One cold day, several years earlier, they had gone away, locking him outside, warning him to watch the place and not to wander. They were an unusually long time away. Towards evening he could stand the hunger no longer and came to Ruttledge. 'Get me something to eat. I'm starving.'

'What's happened?'

'They went away,' he admitted reluctantly.

There was little food in the house. Kate had gone to London and Ruttledge was housekeeping alone. 'You're welcome to anything in the house but there isn't even bread. I was waiting till tonight to go to the village.'

'Haven't you spuds?'

'Plenty.' He hadn't thought of them as an offering.

'Quick, Joe. Put them on.'

A pot of water was set to boil. The potatoes were washed. 'How many?'

'More. More.'

His eyes glittered on the pot as he waited, willing them to a boil. Fourteen potatoes were put into the pot. He ate all of them, even the skins, with salt and butter, and emptied the large jug of milk. 'God, I feel all roly-poly now,' he said with deep contentment as he moved back to the ease of the white rocking chair. 'Do you have any fags?'

The small ration was taken from the shelf. A cigarette was lit. He smoked, inhaling deeply, holding the smoke until the lungs could no longer bear the strain, and then released the breath with such slow reluctance that the smoke issued first from the nostrils before gushing out on a weak, spent breath. So deep was his pleasure that watching was also a dismaying pleasure. For once, he was in no anxiety or rush to leave, and Ruttledge began to ask him about his life, though he knew any enquiry was unlikely to be welcomed. Already he knew the outlines of such a life.

He would have known neither father nor mother. As a baby he would have been given into the care of nuns. When these boys reached seven, the age of reason, they were transferred to places run by priests or Brothers. When he reached fourteen, Bill Evans was sent out, like many others, to his first farmer.

They were also sent as skivvies to the colleges; they scrubbed and polished floors, emptied garbage and waited at tables in the college Ruttledge attended. He recalled how small the boys were in their white jackets, the grey stripes of their trousers, their crew-cut heads, the pale faces tense and blank. No words were allowed to pass between them and the students. They brought huge trays of fish or meat, bowls of soup and vegetables, baskets of bread, and on Sundays glass siphons of red lemonade with silver tops. The place was so bleak that the glass siphons were like flowers on the table for the one festive day of the week. What went on in the kitchens behind the heavy oak partition was a hubbub of distant sound from which the occasional crash or cry or shout emerged. In his long black soutane and red burning eyes under a grey crew-cut, the dean of students was a sinister figure, never more so than when he smiled weakly. He walked up and down between the rows of tables or stood under the big crucifix between the high windows. He read out notices and issued warnings and with bowed head intoned the prayers of grace before and after meals. As he walked slowly up and down between the tables he read his Breviary, pausing now and then to cast an unblinking eye on any table where there was a hint of boisterousness or irregularity. Such was his reputation that cutlery was often knocked to the floor or scattered in the nervous rush towards correction. Then, with a chilling smile, he would pass on, returning to his Breviary, resuming the metronomical walk, until pausing to rest his gaze on an upturned salt cruet. Around him the boys in their short white coats hurried between the kitchens and the tables.

One morning a boy turned quickly away from a table and found the Dean unexpectedly in his path and went straight into him with a tray. Plates and bowls went flying. The soutane was splashed. Only the students who were seated close to the accident saw what happened next, and even they weren't certain. In the face of his fury it was thought that the boy broke the rule of silence to try to excuse the accident. The beating was sudden and savage. Nobody ate a morsel at any of the tables while it was taking place. Not a word was uttered. In the sobbing aftermath the silence was deep and accusing until the scrape of knife and fork on plate and the low hum of conversation resumed. Many who had sat mutely at the tables during the beating were to feel all their lives that they had taken part in the beating through their self-protective silence. This ageing man, who could easily have been one of those boys waiting at tables or cleaning the kitchens if he hadn't been dispatched to that first farm, sat at ease and in full comfort in the white rocking chair, smoking, after having eaten the enormous bowl of potatoes.

'You were sent out to that first farm when you were fourteen?'

'Begod, I was.'

'You worked for them for a good few years before you ran away to here?'

'Begod, I did.'

'They didn't treat you very well?'

For what seemed an age he made no attempt to answer, looking obstinately out from the white chair that no longer moved. 'Why are you asking me this, Joe?'

'Everybody comes from somewhere or other. None of us comes out of the blue air.'

'You'll be as bad as Jamesie soon,' he answered irritably.

'Weren't you in a place run by Brothers and priests before they sent you to the first farm?' Ruttledge ignored the rebuke. A troubled look passed across Bill Evan's face as swiftly as a shadow of a bird passing across window light and was replaced by a black truculence. 'Before the priests and Brothers weren't you with nuns in a convent with other small boys? Weren't you treated better when you were small and with the nuns?'

This time there was no long pause. A look of rage and pain crossed his face. 'Stop torturing me,' he cried out.

Taken aback by the violence and ashamed now of his own idle probing, Ruttledge answered quickly, 'I'd never want to do that. I'm sorry there's so little food in the house.'

'The spuds were topping, Joe. They have me packed,' he said rising stiffly from the chair, leaning on the rough handle of the blackthorn. 'They left me in charge and could be home any minute now. I'd want to be above when they get back.'

Now, several years later, Ruttledge watched him toil slowly down to the lake with the two buckets. Every day since he and Kate had come to the house, Bill Evans had drawn water from the lake with the buckets. In the house, Kate and Jamesie were talking about him still.

'I told you, Kate, you are too soft,' Jamesie argued. 'The decenter you treat the likes of him the more they'll walk all over you.'

'What else has he ever known?'

'You'll be the one to suffer but you could be right in the long run,' Jamesie yielded in his agreeable way. 'What was done to him was wrong and they could never have luck. When Jackie was drawing to the creamery Bill had to ride on the trailer behind the tractor in rain and wet, get down at gates and throw those heavy cans up on to the trailer. When the cans were full he was barely able. They'd put a stronger man to the pin of his collar. As soon as the can touched the trailer, Jackie would lift his foot off the clutch and turn up the throttle. Bill had to run and scramble up on the trailer after the cans. There were times when he fell. Jackie would kick him if he had to stop the tractor and climb down. Christ hadn't much worse of a time on the road to Calvary except Bill always came home alive with the cans of skim. It got so bad that Guard Murray had to warn Jackie.'

'It's hard to understand. Couldn't he have waited a few seconds for him to climb back on the trailer?'

'Ignorance. Pure ignorance. There's no other way to describe it. One day I was watching them turning sods. There were two other men in the field with Jackie that I won't name. I was watching through the hedge. Bill's job was to trample the sods into place with the big wellingtons. Every time they'd pass close with the plough to where he was stepping the sods they'd knock him with a kick or a shove into the furrow and kill themselves laughing. It was their idea of sport.'

'Couldn't you do something?'

'What could you do? If I went into the field they'd turn on me unless I went and knocked him into the furrow as well. That was the year he ran away. He never did a better act. Nobody knew how he got away. He must have walked and got lifts. He was gone two years. He'd be gone still but a crowd up for the All-Ireland stopped at a pub outside Mullingar for a drink on the way home. They didn't even recognise Bill. He had got fat and was in boots and ordinary clothes. They couldn't believe when he gave them this great welcome. He had his hand out of course for cigarettes. The place was a farm as well as a pub. He was a kind of a potboy and got to drink all the leftovers. They should have kept their big mouths shut. Jackie and two other men got into the Ford Prefect one Sunday and drove up to Mullingar and brought him back.'

'Did they force him?'

'Nobody knows. He could even have been delighted to see them. He could have given them the same welcome as he gave to the All-Ireland crowd. The next Sunday he was back at Mass with his hand out for cigarettes as if he had never been away.' Jamesie had risen to leave.

On the way out through the porch, Jamesie's whole attention became fixed on the four iron posts standing upright in their concrete base in the small garden between the house and the orchard.

'Lord bless us, but Patrick Ryan is a living sight. He starts everything and finishes nothing.'

'One of these years he'll be back,' Ruttledge said.

'We have all been scourged,' Jamesie said sympathetically.

'When we came first it was hard waiting for him and never knowing whether he'd turn up or not. Watching that empty road around the lake all day until you knew for sure by evening that he wasn't coming. Now it doesn't matter.'

'Still, you'd like it finished,' Jamesie said. 'Those four posts standing there on their own are a living sight. All they need is a crossbeam and a rope and a crowd and a cart and a man to hang.'

'Where is Patrick these days?'

'The last I heard he was around Dromod putting up a garage for diggers and dozers. He could be gone from there by now. His poor cattle are about the hill.'

'I've often wondered why he keeps cattle at all.'

'For the name. The name of cattle and land. Without the cattle and the land he'd be just another wandering tradesman. I know Patrick all my life. His poor brother, who's as gentle as a lamb, has been bad for several weeks in Carrick and Patrick hasn't once called to see him. They say poor Mrs Logan and the dog are lost for him ever since he went into hospital.'

They walked together between the steep banks of the lane. The banks were in the full glory of the summer, covered with foxgloves and small wild strawberries and green vetches. The air was scented with wild woodbine. Before they saw Bill Evans they saw the slow puffs of cigarette smoke behind a screen of young alders. He was seated on an upturned bucket at the water's edge, the other bucket by his side, drawing in the cigarette smoke as if it were the breath of life, releasing it to the still air in miserly ecstasy. Around him was the sharp scent of the burnished mint. Close by, two swans fished in the shallows, three dark cygnets by their side. Farther out, a whole stretch of water was alive and rippling with a moving shoal of perch. Elsewhere, except when it was ruffled by sudden summer gusts, the water was like glass. Across the lake, at Jamesie's gate, a man had backed his tractor out into the lake and was fishing from the raised transport box, the engine running.

'Cecil Pierce, as sound a Protestant as ever walked, can drink pints as good as any Catholic,' Jamesie identified the man fishing from the transport box. 'At your ease, Bill,' he whispered as they passed Bill Evans.

'Not doing too badly at all, Jamesie,' he answered.

'Give our love to Mary,' Kate said when Jamesie lifted his bicycle out of the ditch.

He paused and turned to bow low, 'I never liked yous anyhow,' and cycled away.

The heron rose out of the reeds and flapped ahead as if leading him round the shore, but then swung high out over the lake to make its own way to that part of the shore where two round piers stood close to the water's edge. Hidden in a wilderness of trees and crawling briars behind the piers were the ruins of the house where Mary had grown up and from where she crossed the lake to marry Jamesie.

When the Ruttledges turned the corner away from the lake they came on Bill Evans standing between his two buckets of water. He was not smoking. He had been waiting for them. They each lifted a bucket. Usually his slow, arthritic walk uphill from the lake entailed a stop every ten or twelve paces. Now, freed from weight, he easily kept pace, using the blackthorn vigorously to propel himself in a crab-like, sideways climb. They continued past their gate until he hissed, 'Ye are far enough.'

'You'll be ready for the dinner now?'

'I'll be ready,' he grinned wolfishly.

'Will there be anything left?'

'Begod there will. There'll be lots,' he said, but the sudden look of anxiety in the eyes belied the assertiveness.

Across the lake Jamesie was resting after climbing the steep hill away from the lake, he and his bicycle silhouetted against the sky. Cecil Pierce sat slumped in the raised transport box out over the water as if he had fallen asleep while holding the fishing rod, the engine of the tractor throbbing peacefully away.

*

'Bill Evans was the one person we met the first time we came in round the shore,' Ruttledge said.

'I remember the storm,' Kate said. 'We were in the Shah's car, following Jimmy Joe McKiernan's battered little red Ford. The waves were washing across the lake wall, pouring down the windscreen, blinding the windows. The wildness could only be heard. The road was spattered with foam, the Shah shaking with laughter behind the wheel as the car rolled from rut to rut. "If it's away from it all yous are trying to get, this royal avenue is as good as any moat." When he laughs like that you hardly hear a sound. He just sits and shakes like a huge ball of jelly. He believed it was all a wild goose chase.'

'We had spent the whole day looking at places. Empty houses, falling-down houses, one house on the mountain, its floor covered with rat traps, new bungalows full of children. Dreams in tatters with the "For Sale" sign at the gate.'

'And the small children peering up at us from the floors. Where were they all to go?'

'To England. To the towns. A mother told me they'd buy a house in the town if they sold. Her husband had already a job in the cement factory. Jimmy Joe McKiernan hardly said a word all day. He'd mention a price or the acres of land or the family name.'

'Your uncle, the dear Shah, was silent as well. Once I said it would look better if one of us travelled with Jimmy Joe. "That'd be only mixing things up, Kate. Jimmy Joe is well used to being on his own," he laughed. I had no idea he was referring to the years in jail. "Jimmy Joe has as much interest in houses and lands as I have in the moon." "What interests him?" I asked. "Freeing Ireland," was the answer. "But Ireland is free?" "In Jimmy Joe's book there's a part that's not free."'

'The Shah always hated politics,' Ruttledge said. 'I don't think he's ever voted.'

'I didn't know what he was referring to. I was good at giving the impression I understood when I hadn't a clue – it's not a very admirable quality but I didn't care. I was falling in love with the place.'

A green gate hung from the ash tree then. From the gate a path ran between two rows of alders to the small stone house with an asbestos roof. In the grove, old moss-covered apple trees stood under the great oaks. The garden and the whitethorn hedge were completely wild. An ugly concrete porch had been tacked on to the house as a windbreak and was coming dangerously loose from the stone walls. A line of stone outhouses stretched past the house. In the middle of the rusting hayshed stood a heeled-up cart.

A kettle hung from a blackened bar above the ashes in the fireplace. There was a small table with unwashed mugs and a heavy glass sugar bowl and a big aluminium teapot. A dishevelled bed stood against the wall in the tiny lower room, a stripped iron bed and a plywood wardrobe in the upper room. Beside the fireplace was a wall cupboard filled with large rounded stones. When the cupboard was opened the stones rolled out in all directions around the floor.

'They told me they'd tidy up the place,' Jimmy Joe McKiernan complained. 'Anyhow you're seeing what you're getting.' He had his own quiet authority.

'This isn't a house,' the Shah said, running the place down. 'The most you could call it is an address and you'd want to be hard up. It's no more than a site!'

'People lived here,' Jimmy Joe said. 'It was a house and home to them but I won't argue. I can't pretend it's in great shape. The place is a site, if you want, a site above a lake, on twenty acres.'

Within the deep walls of the window on the lake, a butcher's calendar of the year before was hung. Above the tables of the months and days was a photo of two boys wheeling bicycles while driving sheep down a country lane between high stone walls. Helping them were two beautiful black-and-white collies. *High-class beef, mutton and lamb at best prices. Large and small orders equally appreciated.*

An X was drawn through each day of every month until October was reached. On the twenty-second of October the march of Xs across the days came to a stop. The twenty-third of October was the first clear day and all the remaining days of the year were unmarked. 'That was the day he died,' Jimmy Joe said.

A shop bill lay open in the window sill: *a dozen of stout, a bottle of Powers, tea, butter, two loaves, a half-pound of ham, a Mass card, two telephone calls.*

'That was the bill for the wake,' Jimmy Joe McKiernan told them. 'They wouldn't have many people. She was a cousin of my own. Once he died she wouldn't live here on her own and went to live with relatives. They had cattle on the place but had trouble with fences and neighbours. Now they want to sell.'

Jimmy Joe McKiernan had spoken more in the short time they'd spent in the house than in the whole of the rest of the day they had spent looking at places.

'The one thing she is determined about is that the place must not go to any of the neighbours. That's why it was never put in the *Observer*. You are the first to see the place.'

'It's not a great reference for anybody coming in,' the Shah said.

'That's for the people coming in to decide. I'm just being straight.'

'I know that, Jimmy Joe,' the Shah said appreciatively. 'Some of the other crooks would have you believe you were entering paradise.'

'You are speaking about my colleagues?' Jimmy Joe asked ironically, playfully.

'A good crowd of boys,' the Shah jeered.

'A few months ago I was the undertaker. Now I'm the auctioneer. I suppose that's life,' Jimmy Joe McKiernan said quietly, as if he felt he had spoken too much.

The small fields around the house were enclosed with thick whitethorn hedges, with ash and rowan and green oak and sycamore, the fields overgrown with rushes. Then the screens of whitethorn suddenly gave way and they stood high over another lake. The wooded island where the herons bred was far out, and on the other shore the pale sedge and stunted birch trees of Gloria Bog ran towards the shrouded mountains. On most of the lake the storm ran and raged but directly underneath the hill a strip of water was as calm and unruffled as a pond. Swans and dark clusters of wildfowl were fishing calmly in the shelter.

'"If you want it, Kate, keep quiet. Jimmy Joe isn't a rogue but like the rest of them he has to get the best price he can," the Shah warned when I told him how much I liked the place.'

'I was having a bad time on the side of that hill,' Ruttledge said. 'It was the only possible place that we saw that whole day. I knew you liked it. I had grown up among such fields. I had escaped through an education that would hardly have been possible a generation earlier. Now I was face to face with all those dreams we have when we are young. I knew these rushy fields, the poverty, the hardship. On that hill I realized that this could be the rest of my life. It was far from what I had dreamed or hoped for. "What do you think?" Jimmy Joe asked me suddenly. "It's a possibility," I answered. "What are places like this worth now?" "The value of anything is what people are willing to pay," he said with that quiet smile. "Your uncle tells me you live in London. How do you find England?" "We have jobs. The life is easy and comfortable. We'd hardly be looking at places here if we were entirely happy." "What do you find wrong with England?" "Nothing but it's not my country and I never feel it's quite real or that my life there is real. That has its pleasant side as well. You never feel responsible or fully involved in anything that happens. It's like being present and at the same time a real part of you is happily absent." "Would you find this place real?" "Far too real." "Would it be the quiet and the birds that'd interest you?" I hadn't noticed until then that small birds, wrens and robins and finches, were indeed singing in the desolate branches. And at that moment, as if on cue, a pheasant started to call in a nearby field. No, it wouldn't be to listen to the birds. They say we think the birds are singing when they are only crying *this is mine* out of their separate territories. "Have you ever lived in England?" I must have asked aggressively enough because I remember resenting the reference to the birds. He didn't seem to mind and spoke openly. "I spent one winter in the East End around Forest Gate and West Ham. We were trying to spring some men of ours who were in Pentonville. A gang of criminals from the East End was in the same wing of the prison. We were trying to use them in a breakout. Nothing came of the plan. We wanted to use them. They wanted to use us. We also discovered that they were planning to double-cross us during the breakout." "What were they like?" I asked. "The East End gangsters? They were like rats. They cared about nothing but their own skins." He had the idealist's contempt and distaste for the purely criminal. "What would you have done with the gang if there had been a breakout and they tried to double-cross you?" "We'd have shot them. We planned to shoot them anyhow. They knew too much." "Whether there was a double-cross or not?" "They knew too much. We knew we were being watched." He spoke without feeling or rancour. "Anyhow nothing came of the plan. We just got out in the nick of time." The calm with which he said "We planned to shoot them anyhow" added to the chill on that wet hillside.'

'Bill Evans was standing in the lane in those huge wellingtons when we got back to the cars.'

'I don't remember the two buckets but they must have been somewhere,' Ruttledge said. 'A rope was tied around the heavy overcoat. On his head was a shiny black sou'wester hat. "Do they smoke?" he asked.'

'It was then that the Shah reached down into one of his pockets and threw a fistful of coins into the air. Some of the coins clattered on the bonnet of the small Ford and rolled among the stones and leaves of the lane. Bill Evans scrambled after the coins like some kind of animal.'

'I was taken aback by the way he threw the coins,' Kate said.

'He meant no harm. When we were small whenever he came to our house he did the very same, sometimes with sweets instead of coins. It was a way of expressing power. The whole country was very poor. The Shah then bought the place for us.'

'I was afraid he'd lose it with all his haggling,' Kate said.

The asbestos roof was replaced with black slates, new rooms added, a bathroom, a well for water bored. Once the price and contract had been agreed, the Ruttledges returned to London, leaving the Shah to oversee the work. This he undertook with proprietary zeal, rolling round the lake several times a week in the Mercedes. Jimmy Joe McKiernan had said that relations between the old woman and his immediate neighbours were poor. This and everything else he had stated so casually on that first wet stormy day around the lake turned out to be true. They got on as badly with one another as they did with the old woman. 'They were like that as far back as I remember,' Jamesie had said. 'Give no help or hand to anybody. Grab everything in sight. On our side of the lake people couldn't do enough for one another and got on far better. Here they were always watching out for themselves. When people are that way there's never any ease.'

They coveted the childless old woman's fields, and she in her turn was determined that they would never own those fields.

The addition of rooms to the house, the new roof, the drilling of a well for water – with the lake a stone's throw away – the coming and going of the large Mercedes, were all carefully observed, and resentment fuelled an innate intolerance of anything strange or foreign.

When the Ruttledges came from London in the spring they were shunned by near neighbours, but they were too involved with the place to notice. Would the move succeed or fail? If it failed they would return to London.

Jamesie came to the house in the very first days, pretending to be casually passing. They began to talk, and he welcomed them to the place and was invited in. A few evenings later, he arrived unexpectedly with Mary, bringing fresh eggs, small bags of potatoes and carrots and parsnips. 'For the house. For the house,' he insisted, in the face of their protestations that what he had brought was too generous. 'Just for the house. To wish the house luck.'

Then John Quinn came. In clouds of smoke, he turned his old white Beetle under the alder tree at the gate so that it faced down towards the lake. When he got out of the car he propped a heavy stone against one of the back wheels before strolling confidently up the little avenue.

John Quinn was a tall, powerfully built, handsome man, wearing a well-cut suit, his thick grey hair brushed back. As soon as he spoke there was an immediate discrepancy between the handsome physique and the cajoling voice.

'I came to wish new neighbours good luck and success and happiness. It does the heart good to see a young pair happy and in love starting up their lives in a new place. It lifts the heart. It does the heart good.'

He was invited in and offered tea or whiskey. With a lordly wave of the hand he refused both.

'I'm not here to waste your good time or waste my time. I'm here for a purpose. I'm here on a little business. I know your poor uncle well, better known as the Shah, as fine a man as ever entered the town and got on like no other. The little business that brought me is that I have been noticing Mrs Ruttledge walking the roads and seeing that you got a tall fine-looking woman for yourself when you were abroad I thought you might be able to do as good or nearly as good for a neighbour. I'll keep my account short. The first poor woman died under me after bringing eight children into the world. After they were all reared I married again. The Lord God has said in the Holy Book "'Tis not good for man to live alone," and I have always taken that Commandment to heart. I don't mind admitting that the second round of the course was not a success.'

'What went wrong?' was asked politely in the face of all that was proffered as fluently as a door-to-door salesman pretending straight-faced openness.

'What God intended men and women to do she had no taste for. What was meant to be happy and natural was for her a penance. John tried everything he knew to turn her round and make her happy. On a beautiful day like this day, the sun shining in heaven, I took her out for a row on the lake to make her feel better in herself. The lake lovely and calm, hardly a breeze, just the odd fish jumping, the birds singing for all they were worth, the mountains lovely and blue in the distance, the swans sailing around and every sound a happy sound, and do you know what she said to me? "You wouldn't be thinking of throwing me in now, John, would you?" Wasn't that a strange sort of love talk? John here rowing like a boy and the lake all peaceful and the mountains so blue and so distant. Soon afterwards she beat back to her own place. As we were married in church and she still lives, I have to forage for myself if I do not want to live alone. That's the little business that has brought me. Since you have done so well for yourself abroad you might do as well or nearly as well for a close neighbour. Your lovely woman is bound to have women friends of her own. And if she could place one of them in my house she'd have a friend of her own close by. We'd be great neighbours and the two houses would get on wonderfully well together and all visiting and helping one another and happy together.'

Kate excused herself and left the room and John Quinn rose to leave.

'That's the little business that brought me now. I'm hoping you'll be able to give a neighbour a helping hand. I put all my cards out on the table. There's nothing underhand about my way of doing business.'

Ruttledge walked him to the battered white Beetle parked

24

outside the gate. He removed the stone from the back wheel before getting into the car.

'If things manage to work out now, please God, we could have wonderful times together and everybody will be happy.'

When he let in the clutch, the car rolled downhill, gathering speed. The engine coughed and spluttered into life close to the lake in clouds of smoke and continued to batter slowly out along the shore like a disabled boat attempting to make it back to harbour.

'I was sorry to leave,' Kate said. 'I couldn't bear to be in the same room with him. Very few people have that effect.'

'I was wondering if he was real while he was talking,' Ruttledge said.

'Oh, he was real all right. He was looking me up and down as if I were an animal. What are we to do about the extraordinary request?'

'We'll do nothing,' Ruttledge said. 'We'll find out about him.'

It was obvious the Shah knew a great deal more about John Quinn than he was willing to tell when he was asked about their visitor the following Sunday.

'Oh, John Quinn,' he wiped his knuckles on his eyes and shook at the mention of the name. 'Oh John's a boy. Women and more women,' he said but would not add to the detail. 'When he was young he was the law around and loved to settle fights in bars, taking both men outside and beating them good-looking. "Putting a little manners on people," he would say.'

'He said he had dealings with you.'

'Everybody has dealings with John Quinn. That's all there is to John.'

'How do you deal with him?'

'You don't. But he can always unearth these silly women,' and shaking with amusement he indicated with a wave of the hand that to be a provider of such low detail was valley upon valley beneath him.

When they next met, Jamesie and Mary's attention was fixed on every word as the visit was described. 'I thought I heard everything till now. John Quinn is a living sight. He'll try anything. He never misses a chance but I never thought I'd see the day when he'd be trying to get people to forage for women for him in England,' Jamesie said.

'His first lookout would be to see if there was any chance to get in with you, Kate,' Mary said.

'That's the way these fellas are,' Jamesie said. 'They'll try anything. "Fuck them. What can they do but refuse?" is how they think about other people. They'll just go on to someone else. They have no value on people, only what they can get out of them. When he came about our place first he borrowed our little mule of the time and when he brought the mule back his breast was all skinned. "The borrowed horse has hard hooves!" When he came again he was refused. I think he was the first person we ever turned away but it was like water off a drake. "What can they do but refuse!" My father was fond of that mule and we weren't able to work him for months afterwards.

'John Quinn was tall and good-looking and strong, as fine-looking a man as you'd meet in a day or two days. His older brother Packy still lives in the homeplace and is as different from John as difference can be, quiet and decent. John used to plough for hire. On a headland he was able to swing the plough around without backing from the horses. He'd drink a bottle of stout or two but never more, he was always too careful, especially if he had to pay. He never went with girls or women when he was young, though he could have had his pick. He'd sweet-talk them plenty and flirt and dance, but all the time John Quinn was looking out for John Quinn.

'The Sweeneys were ripe for plucking. Their place was the sweetest place around, the same limestone fields as you get at the old Abbey – you know them yourselves, where you can see the shapes of the old monks' cells in the grass – and they had money when no one had money. The place was known as the beehive. Margaret was an only child like her mother before her. Her father Tom Sweeney had married into the place from the mountain. He was no beauty but a great worker and it was him who planted the big chestnut tree in the middle of the yard and ringed it round with the wall of whitewashed stones and the iron hoops. Her mother was a big easy-going woman and she adored Tom Sweeney, ugly as he was – there's no telling with people – and they both adored the ground Margaret walked on. They were simple, decent people and nothing mean or small about them. They were just that bit innocent. Tom Sweeney would be the first to go to the help if any neighbour was in trouble. Anybody who called to the house would be welcomed and given food and drink – they had always great poitín Tom got from the mountain, far far better than any whiskey – but they never went out much to people or bothered with other houses. They were content with their own company, and those sort of people are the most lost when anything happens. They have no one to turn to.

'I suppose Margaret was spoiled. She'd have been given everything she ever wanted but that was about to all change when John Quinn came with his team of horses to do their spring ploughing. Many girls better looking than Margaret wanted John Quinn but they didn't have limestone fields and a house and place to walk into.

'Her father was against him from the first, though John Quinn was dripping with sweetness. He was in dread that everything he had built about the beehive was about to be trampled underfoot. Mary the mother, though, was all for John Quinn from the very first and the place was hers.'

'What could they have done anyhow? Margaret was wild about John Quinn. All they could have done was shut the door against their only child and the poor things weren't about to do that,' Mary said.

'All around the lake were invited to the wedding. Even Mary here went and she hadn't long left school at the time. No expense was spared. All kinds of meat and drink were bought in. It was all the talk around the lake for weeks ahead of the wedding. There was going to be music. Packie Donnelly from the crossroads was alive then and he was the best fiddle player we ever had about the lake. He got a cousin of his own to come from Drumreilly, Peter Kelly, who was a smasher on the melodeon. Poor Tom Murphy was coming as well from Aughoo. He was a martyr for the drink but could make a tin whistle talk. On the wedding morning, when it was seen that the day was going to be without rain, a long trestle table was set up under the chestnut tree in the yard.'

'Margaret went to the church with the father and mother in the pony and trap,' Mary said. 'I saw them going. She was wearing a beautiful dress of blue silk that fell to her ankles the mother had made, as good as any dressmaker. She wore a blue hat with white flowers and white shoes. John Quinn was in a brand new grey suit with a white flower in the buttonhole. He was full of himself and he was shining.'

'He had Stratton the tailor scourged for fittings for that grey suit. Stratton would never make anything for him again. Probably he was never paid for the suit after all the fittings,' Jamesie said. 'As soon as John Quinn got into the trap to drive with Margaret and the mother and father back from the church to the house, he took the reins from Tom Sweeney. In that sweet false voice, he said that Tom had done more than his share up to now and it was his time to sit back and put his feet up and take his ease. What could poor Tom Sweeney say? John Quinn took up the place of two people in the trap. Then he got the whip and waved it to the people who passed along the road and then whipped the fat brown pony till it galloped. Tom Sweeney used to talk to that pony. "What hurry is on you? We'll be home as it is far too soon. She's not used to that treatment." He might as well have been talking to the wind for all the heed John Quinn paid.

'A few neighbouring women and children had stayed behind preparing the house and setting tables. They had scattered the whole yard with flowers and they must have been surprised to see the wedding trap come into the yard ahead of everybody, the pony lathered in sweat, Tom Sweeney ready to cry. By the time the crowd arrived he had untackled the pony and given her water and was rubbing her down, with him still in his good clothes.

'Then the crowd gathered from the church. They all were waiting for the bridegroom to carry the bride across the doorstep into the empty house and for the feast and the music to begin, but John Quinn had another surprise in store. "Now Margaret, before we go into the house there's a little thing I want to show you over here on the shore". Everybody was around them in the yard and the words could be heard clear. "We'll go in. There's nothing to see in the lake that we haven't seen before."

'He opened the gate and though she was a big enough girl he picked her up and carried her like she was a feather. I remember seeing one of the white shoes fall off her foot on to the grass. I think someone picked it up and brought it back to the house. "It won't take a minute. Excuse us, good friends and neighbours, for there's just this little thing we have to do first that won't hold up things at all." You know how sweet and humble he talks.

'Everybody thought that John Quinn was only acting the fool and they kept on talking and laughing and chatting away. "It wouldn't be John if he didn't do things different. He's a holy terror. It wouldn't be John if things happened like for everybody else," and they began to wonder what strange thing he had to show Margaret over on the shore. He was not known then as he is known now.

'They reached the top of the slope where the rock field slopes down to the shore. There's little earth and in places the rock is bare. In dry spells the grass there turns red on that part of the shore.

'They stood for a while in full view. Though the yard had turned quiet as a church what they were saying couldn't be heard. They were too far off. John Quinn put the blanket he had brought down on the rock. Margaret looked as if she was trying to break away but he could have held her with one hand. It was over before anybody rightly knew. He lifted the blue dress up over her head and put her down on the blanket. The screech she let out would put your heart crossways. John Quinn stood between her and the house while he was fixing his trousers and belt. He must have been afraid she'd try to break back on her own but she just lay there on the ground. In the end he had to lift her and straighten her dress and carry her in his arms. The mother and father stood there like a pair of ghosts. Not a word was spoken.

'Once the rush to get away started, you never saw the like. A few went up to the old pair before leaving but most just cut for the road. What could they say? It was clear that Margaret didn't even want to face back to the house after what had happened. By the time he carried her into the yard the whole place had emptied. There might never have been a wedding except for the scattered flowers and the long trestle table weighted down with all sorts of food and drink under the chestnut tree. The musicians were the last to leave without playing a note. Poor Tom Sweeney walked them all the way out to the gate at the road without uttering a word. He tried to give them a fistful of money but none of them would take as much as a penny. When he kept pressing the money, all Packie Donnelly – who was as decent a man as you'd find as well as a great fiddle player – all Packie did was to put his arm round poor Tom's shoulder and hold him tight to show that they understood everything and wanted nothing and that no fault or blame was attached in their minds to him. In those sort of cases sympathy is nearly the hardest thing of all to take and Tom Sweeney who hadn't said a word up to then started bawling like a child. What could they do but look at one another and say how things could turn out all right yet in the end and hurry away? It's a terrible thing to see an old man bawling. People always say that things will turn out all right in the end when there's never a chance of them turning out right.'

'He must have been out of his mind.'

'Not one little bit out of his mind, Kate.'

'How could he have done what he did otherwise?'

'There's a method in everything John Quinn does. It's all thought out. In those days when a man married into a place he had little shout. He was expected to take a back seat. Some were not much more than servants. From the minute John Quinn took the reins into his hands on the way from the church till he brought Margaret as far as the rock, he was showing who was going to be boss and that everything was going to be under him from that day out.'

'You'd think he'd be ashamed, if nothing else.'

'Not one little bit. He'd glory that it was in full view. It was said he didn't let Margaret wear knickers in the house so that he could do her there and then whenever he wanted, against the table or the wall and all the better if it was in front of the old pair.

'They lasted no time. They faded away. Tom Sweeney never let a morsel of food pass his lips for weeks before he died. Margaret had the eight children, and then she got bad. One morning Johnny was out with the gun he saw her walking in her nightdress in her bare feet in the dew before it was fully light to see if the coolness would ease the pain. In the end the schoolchildren didn't want to pass the gate on their way to school because they were frightened by her cries. When they laugh over his cavortings and carry-on, they should not forget the full story,' Jamesie said.

'He can't be blamed for her death?'

'No. It could have happened anyway. The place had been a little paradise. The animals would nearly talk to you they were that well looked after. Tom Sweeney grew every sort of vegetable – beans, peas, lettuce, parsnips, you name them – he had hives; the apple trees were pruned into shapes like bowls or cups and he was a master thatcher. He grew his own straw and thatched a seventh of the roof every year. The seven years could be seen side by side in the different shades of the straw in the thatch, from golden brown to what was nearly black with rain. John Quinn planted nothing but potatoes and cabbage and maybe turnips. He put a tin roof over the thatch and sold the bees and the hives. I don't think he ever put a spade in the vegetable garden. The fruit trees went wild. There were several cats around the place. They used to line up in a row when Tom Sweeney was milking. I'm afraid the cats got short shrift. Anything not drawing to John Quinn's mill wasn't going to last long about a place.

'In fairness he was good enough with the children. He turned himself into a middling cook after the mother died and had always a big pot of something tasty bubbling by the fire. The children were all strong and good-looking, wonderful workers, and John showered them with praise so that they'd try to outdo one another. Naturally he didn't forget himself either when he was handing the praise around and he learned to sew and to cobble.

'At the time there were terrible beatings in the schools. Some of the teachers were savages. People were afraid to speak out but John Quinn wasn't afraid. There was a Missus Kilboy who was a terror with the cane. She'd swipe you round the legs as well as murder your hands; and if you tried to cover your legs with your arms, the arms and back would get it as well.

'None of the children ever forgot his appearance at the school. He knocked very politely before lifting the latch and coming into the classroom, the heavy hobnailed boots loud on the hollow boards. His voice was dripping with politeness. "Excuse me now, children, for interrupting your lessons but I have just a few little words to say to your mistress here that won't take long."

'Naturally the children were delighted and sat up in the desks, all full of ears. "Sorry to be taking time away from the lessons, Mistress, but my two little girls came home crying from school yesterday evening. Their hands were so swollen they weren't able to hold their spoons to eat the dinner. They were still crying when it was time for them to go to their bed. You might have noticed now, Mistress, that they weren't at school today."

'What could she say? John Quinn had her cornered. The children were drinking in every word. John Quinn's voice couldn't have been sweeter. He was like a cat purring over a saucer of milk.

'"Now, Mistress, if this ever happens again I'm afraid it'll go a lot further than this and it could be that when the courts are finished with the case you could be looking for another position. That'd be a pity to happen in a small place like this where everybody is happy and getting on well together. It can bring in bad feelings between people. And sometimes these are hard to forget. Now my pair of little girls are coming back to school tomorrow and nothing like that must ever happen again. Don't as much as lay a hand on those little girls. That's all I have to say for now. I won't take another minute away from the good lessons."

'As he went with the hobnailed boots back down the hollow boards between the rows of desks, he spoke to the children. "Excuse me now, children, for interrupting your lessons but I had a few little important words that had to be said to your mistress. Now go back to your books and work hard and pay heed to everything your mistress tells because that's how you'll learn to get on well in the world and be happy and make your poor parents happy. Excuse me now, children. I'll not take another minute from your lessons."

'Missus Kilboy hadn't said a single word throughout. As soon as John Quinn left she went to the Master's room and they both went out into the porch where the children couldn't see or hear. They were a long time in the porch and when Missus Kilboy came back the children could see she had been crying.

'None of the Quinns were ever beaten after that but they weren't given much attention or schooling either. The teachers were afraid of John Quinn and that was their way of dealing. He came back to the school more than once to complain that his children were being overlooked and cold-shouldered but there was nothing he could prove. Let nobody try to best the guards or the doctors or teachers. They have their own ways of getting back at you.

'It didn't seem to hold any of the Quinn children back. They were strong for their years and as soon as they got to fourteen or sixteen they all hit for England. They got on the best there. A few of them are said to be millionaires and they all think the world of John Quinn. Many more normal parents aren't thought nearly as well of or as honoured by their children.

'He didn't bother much with women while he had the children. He was too busy and too well known around, and to go into a houseful of small children with John Quinn at the head of affairs wasn't much of a draw for any woman. When the children were thinning out he started. He got them from newspapers and magazines and agencies. He got women from all over. You'd be surprised at how many poor people are going round the world in search of a companion and John Quinn was the boy to find them: "Gentleman Farmer with Lakeside Residence" was his calling card. I seen severals. There were no beauties but they say he got money from some of them and I saw them buy a world of groceries for the house while John waited next door in the pub with his bottle of stout.

'Missus O'Brien he definitely sold. He had her for several months until he tired of her and a replacement no doubt was lined up. She was a great housekeeper who had worked for a rich family in the North. They thought a sight of her and keep in touch with her to this very day. She was a little bit innocent, that's all that was wrong with her. She'd believe anything you'd tell her and she adored John Quinn. However he engineered it, he got her to marry Tom O'Brien, who was hardworking and looking for a woman, and money changed hands. They were wonderfully happy and still are. In no time she had the place shining, with hens and geese about the yard, and they got a bathroom and washing machines and the whole show. John Quinn wasn't one bit pleased it turned out so well – he's like your dog – and felt he should have got more money. Those rich people she worked for visit her every year and take her and Tom O'Brien out to a big meal and drinks in the Central in town.

'The strange thing is that she is still as sweet as ever on John Quinn. A few months back Tom O'Brien was in hospital and in no time John Quinn was around. She was delighted to see him and had the welcome of the world. John was in his element, being fed royal, his eye out for whatever else was going. It was the neighbours who ran him, warning him not to darken the place again till Tom got out of hospital. She wasn't one bit pleased when she got to know what happened. If anything was to happen to Tom he'd be in there like a shot in the morning and as sure as day she'd have him.'

'Would the priest not have some say?'

'None. Early on he called to the house but he was wasting his breath. Nobody could best John Quinn. He delights in taking every woman he has up into the front seat of the church, genuflecting and allowing her into the seat first, kneeling in adoration. You'd have to die at the performance. Then as soon as Mass is over he takes the woman up to the candleshrine. They light two small candles. The two of them together light a third candle and then set the candle on the spikes between their own two candles. The third candle is for a wish, "Always wish for something good and happy for yourself, Maura. There's no use in a star falling and no one seeing it and no one making a wish. Always wish something for yourself." You'd nearly die. If John Quinn was ever an actor our Johnny and even Patrick Ryan would be only trotting after him. And the ladies lap it up – good-o.'

'And that's the sort of church you're trying to get me to return to,' Ruttledge said.

'The fellow doesn't go to church for religion,' Mary said dismissively. 'He only goes to see shows like John Quinn. It'd be a poor lookout if people were to follow him to church.'

Jamesie enjoyed the chastisement, but then countered, 'We go to the door of the church anyhow, which is more than can be said for some others present whose names will not be mentioned,' he intoned loftily.

'Why did John Quinn marry if he could have all those other women without benefit of ceremony?'

'I'm surprised at you asking. There could be only one reason. He thought she had money. Maybe as well he was finding it that bit harder to get women. Like the rest of us he's getting no younger. His name as well was probably going ahead of him. He was getting too well known.'

'And *had* she money?'

'I think she had but John didn't get his hands on any. She wasn't that foolish. She may have parted with some things but she didn't part with money.'

'That fella,' Mary said with disapproval but went on to say, 'John always had horses. He had a white stallion then. When the odd mare used to come to the house he'd order the wife out to the yard to watch the performance. "Natural and healthy, what God intended," he'd say. The flat-bottomed boat he keeps below in the reeds is a living danger. Of course he had her out in the boat. He could be trying to get the money out of her. I'm sure she wasn't far from the truth when she asked was he thinking of throwing her in. A lot he cared about the birds and the blue mountain and the swans sailing.'

'Why would he regale us with the poetry?'

'Because he thought it would suit, that it would go down well. It might help get Kate here on his side. John would watch mice at a crossroads,' Mary said with the same dismissiveness as she described Jamesie's churchgoing.

'Anyhow it wasn't long till she left. The brother took her back. I don't think John got a farthing, which was a God's charity. They were decent, quiet people who minded their own business. They had no idea what John was like. Somebody was telling me not long ago that the poor thing isn't all that well.'

'If anything were to happen to her, John will be marching up the aisle again. Mark my words,' Jamesie said.

'He'd be trying anyhow whether he'd succeed or not. He's a pure disgust,' Mary said.

'Look how he's beating around. See how he's round to Kate looking to get women from England.'

'He'll not get very far with Kate,' she said.

'The poor fella is only doing his best. He's contributing to the race. Like the rest of them he's only trying to find his way to the boggy hollow,' Jamesie rubbed his hands together, slyly looking out of hooded eyes.

'You, you, *you* – are a pure disgust as well!' Mary said, and added, 'No wonder Lucy can't stand this fella!'

Lucy was his daughter-in-law, and Jamesie went quiet as if struck. She was one of the few people he had never been able to charm; it was a deep sore. 'Some of these ones would want you tailor-made. Some of these ones are just too precise,' he said, and they were all too fond of him to say another word until he recovered and a path was found out of the silence.

The Shah rolled round the lake with the sheepdog in the front seat of the car every Sunday and stayed until he was given his tea at six. Some days during the week he came in the evenings as well. On dry Sundays he loved to walk the fields, and to look at the cattle and sheep and the small wooded island out in the back lake where the herons nested, and to look across the lake to the acres of pale sedge of Gloria Bog, which ran like an inland sea until it met the blue of the lower slopes of the mountains where his life began, the stunted birch trees like small green flowers in the wilderness of bog.

When it was raining or there was little to be done, he was content to sit in the house. Often he sat in silence. His silences were never oppressive and he never spoke unless to respond to something that had been said or to say something that he wanted to say. Throughout, he was intensely aware of every other presence, exercising his imagination on their behalf as well as on his own, seeing himself as he might be seen and as he saw others. Since he was a boy he had been in business of some kind but had never learned to read or write. He had to rely on pure instinct to know the people he could trust. This silence and listening were more useful than speech and his instinct was radar-sharp. His manners had once been gentle and hidden with everybody but to some extent the gentleness had been discarded as he grew in wealth and independence. With people he disliked he could be rough. People or places that made him ill at ease or uncomfortable he went to great lengths to avoid. When caught in such situations his manners would turn atrocious, like a clear-sighted person going momentarily blind. Where he blossomed was in the familiar and habitual, which he never left willingly. The one aberration of his imaginative shrewdness was a sneaking regard for delinquents, or even old villains like John Quinn, whose activities excited and amused him, as they tested and gave two fingers to the moral world.

All his family, dominated by the mother, had been hard-working, intelligent, humorous, sociable. Across from the three-roomed cottage, the whitethorns had been trained to make an arch into the small rose garden, and a vine of roses covered the whitewashed wall when few houses on the mountain had more than the bare necessities. They also kept bees, had a small apple garden, ground coffee from dried and roasted dandelion roots; and when they got some money a room would be added to the house rather than building another outhouse to keep more fowl or animals.

He alone in the family escaped school. A dedicated but ill-tempered schoolmaster, who had been instrumental in his older brother and sister becoming the first to win scholarships out of these mountains, had given him a bad beating during his first year at school. No amount of coaxing or threats could get him to return. At twelve, he made his first shillings by borrowing the family horse to draw stones to make a road to the new national school where his sister taught. His first job was in a local sand and gravel pit, where he learned to weld and fix machinery; soon, he was driving a sand lorry for the pit, and then purchased an old lorry of his own, drawing merchandise to and from the Belfast and Dublin docks. On the potholed roads it was more important to be a good mechanic than a driver, and by his early twenties he had four lorries of his own. At the outbreak of the war he switched into tillage contracting and made serious money.

Seeing compulsory tillage about to disappear with the ending of the war, he sold out early, preserving and increasing the money he had made. For a few years he had a sawmill before buying the railway station, its land and buildings and some miles of track, when the small branch line was closed. In the middle of a long recession it went cheaply and he had to borrow very little. A bank manager he knew from the town card school gave him the loan, which he quickly repaid by dismantling and selling off the track, rails and sleepers and buildings that he didn't want. At thirty, he owned a small empire and had no debts at a time when only the old established traders, the priests, the doctors, the big farmers had money and all the trains to the night boats were full. From such a position many men of his age would have expanded; he contracted. The only regular employment he gave was to a young boy, taciturn and intelligent, from a house close to his own on the same part of the mountain. Whenever he needed other workers he employed casual labour. When what was left of the railway line was broken up and sold off or stored, he began to buy old lorries, tractors, farm machinery to sell for spare parts and to put down fuel tanks. And when the four small railwaymen's cottages that had come to him with the station became vacant, he installed bachelors he knew who had grown too old to work their mountain farms and wanted to move into the town. He charged them no rent and in return they helped about the sheds and in the big field of scrapped machinery on the edge of the town, while they were able. They were all silent, withdrawn people who spoke little, but seemed to understand one another perfectly and to get on well together without talking. When they died or had to go into the Home, he replaced them from the same stock, much as he replaced the black-and-white sheepdogs he was attached to. He did not drink or smoke and his fondness for cards was profitable. His luxuries were the new, expensive cars he liked to drive and the big meals he enjoyed every day in the hotel. With thick curly brown hair, an alert, pleasant appearance, his manner easy and assured, he was attractive to women in spite of an unconcealed, long-held determination to avoid marriage as he had avoided school. When he had the lorries on the road, he had several girls, all of them small and pretty; and then after a few years there was just the one girl, small too and pretty, Annie May McKiernan, and for nine years they went out together, meeting on the same two evenings every week.

He called for her in his big car where she lived with her parents and brother on their comfortable farm. They went to dances and films and the local plays. Gradually, he became almost another member of her family, helping her brother with the machinery on the farm, driving her parents to the seaside at Strandhill and Bundoran and later to Manor-hamilton Hospital.

When her father and then her mother died, he was as helpful and as present about the house as any member of the family, but soon afterwards her brother wanted to marry and bring a young woman into the house. Pressure was put on Annie May and on her suitor of many years. As they exchanged presents that Christmas while sitting in the big car, she said, in her placid way, 'Aunt Mary wants me to go out to her in New York. You know, if something doesn't happen soon I think I'll go out to America around Easter.'

It would not have been possible for her to be more direct, and he understood perfectly. There must have been an inter-minable silence, but the same negative resourcefulness that had frustrated every attempt to force him to go back to school won out over affection and scruples.

'You know, Annie May, with the way this country is going I doubt but America will be the end of us all yet.'

No door was ever closed more softly or with more finality. She did not go to New York at Easter but married old Paddy Fitzgerald, a cattle dealer, in an arranged match.

The only change afterwards in the Shah's life was that he went to the local cinema on his own and took to visiting the houses of his sisters and brother more often, especially on Sundays.

Only his fellow card players in the poker school ever had the temerity to test the wall of stolidity he presented to the world.

'Did you see that Annie May McKiernan got married to old Paddy Fitzgerald?' was slipped in with seeming casualness as cards were dealt.

Feet sought other feet beneath the table. His reaction could not be predicted. There was none. All the cards were played and the winnings gathered in.

'I'm afraid you missed out there,' was risked as new hands were dealt. 'You didn't move quick enough when you had the chance.'

'If she had waited another few years she'd have been safe,' he said at last.

The whole table erupted in laughter, but he did not even smile as his gaze travelled evenly from face to face and back to his hand.

'Diamonds are trumps,' he said, and the intensity of the game resumed. 'Let the best man win.'

He and Ruttledge had always got on well together, and it did no harm that they shared the same first name. When Ruttledge abandoned his studies for the priesthood, his uncle had been supportive at a time when the prevailing climate had been one of accusation and reproach. 'Let them go to hell,' the Shah had said, and offered money for further study – he who had never been to school long enough to learn to read or write – before Ruttledge decided to go to

England, joining the masses on the trains and the boats.

Not until some time after they had come to live by the lake, Kate having returned to London to find new tenants for her flat, did he learn how deep his uncle's dislike of marriage ran, how ideal he considered his own single state to be.

He couldn't have been better company the previous Sunday, wishing Kate a safe journey to London with obvious affection. The very evening of the day Kate left, Ruttledge was surprised to see the Mercedes roll up to the house. The Shah remarked on the gardens and the improvements to the place, but not until he was seated comfortably was the purpose of the visit revealed.

'It must be a great relief to you, now, that Kate is in London,' he offered in a tone of heartfelt congratulation.

'I wouldn't exactly call it relief.'

'Tell us more,' the Shah said indulgently and began to shake in silent laughter.

'She has business in London but I don't feel any relief that she's gone.'

'I know,' the Shah agreed, wiping away tears with his fists. 'I know full well. We all have to make those sort of noises from time to time.'

'They are not exactly noises.'

'That'll do you now. That'll do,' he raised his hands for silence and relief.

'I thought you liked Kate. I thought the two of you got on.'

'Kate is the very best. You couldn't get better than poor Kate.'

'I don't know what you are on about, then.'

'Listen,' he said. 'If you talk to the wall tonight – answer me this while you're at it – is the wall going to answer you back? Am I right or wrong?'

'You're right. Except I haven't much interest in talking to the wall.'

'Now you see,' he said contentedly, though it wasn't clear what had been seen, and when Kate returned he welcomed her back as if he had missed her every single day she had been away.

So regular were his habits – turning each day into the same day, making every Sunday into all the other Sundays – that when any small change occurred it was very noticeable. Only a few months before he had asked diffidently if he could have his meal early. He always ate silently, with such absorption that to be in the same room was in itself a silent, pleasurable participation in the single ceremony. Unusually, that evening he ate hurriedly, without enjoyment, and rose early from the table.

'There must be something important on this evening,' Ruttledge remarked as he and Kate saw him to the car, Kate petting the sheepdog.

'There's a removal,' he said hurriedly.

'Who's dead?' Ruttledge asked without guile.

'Missus Fitzgerald,' he said, immediately turning red.

What had happened had taken place so long ago and was now so remote that Ruttledge would not have made any connection with the name but for his obvious discomfort. 'Wasn't she an old flame of yours?' he asked intuitively.

'That'll do you now,' he said, and let the sheepdog quickly into the car before getting behind the wheel. He was still red with embarrassment when he let the window down to say his usual, 'God bless yous,' as the big car rolled out towards the alder tree and down towards the lake and shore.

'It's strange,' Kate said, 'to show so much emotion going to her funeral when he could have married her when they were young. He was fond of her. His deep embarrassment was there to see.'

'He wanted to be on his own. He didn't want to be married,' Ruttledge said. 'The priest, the single man, was the ideal of society, and with all the children we saw looking up at us from the floors of those bungalows, who can blame him?'

'Don't you think we are happy?' she asked so seriously that he paused, and drew her close.

43

'We are different. I don't think we should worry it too much. We wanted to be together. We weren't afraid.'

The four iron posts standing uselessly upright in their concrete bases had for long been an affront to the Shah.

This Sunday as they walked the fields he remarked, 'They are a holy sight. Do you think will that Ryan ever finish?'

'He probably will – some day.'

'If I was you I'd get in someone who'd finish the job properly. I'd run him to hell and not let him near the place again,' he urged.

'I couldn't do that. He did a good deal of work here when we had nothing.'

They walked the fields until they found the sheep and lambs in the shade on the side of the hill. The cows were lying with their calves in a circle like wagons a few feet from the water in the small field where old potato ridges were still marked on the grass. A little way off the old Shorthorn stood on her own under broken whitethorns that came down to the shore.

'She's about to calve. It's not a great time – out on all this grass.'

'She's a long time with you now. A great old lassie,' he said.

The cow stood still as the Shah put out his hand to feel her bones. 'She's well shook,' he said. 'She'll have to be looked at again before night. She could calve at any time.'

They turned away. The surface of the water out from the reeds was alive with shoals of small fish. There were many swans on the lake. A grey rowboat was fishing along the far shore. A pair of herons moved sluggishly through the air between the trees of the island and Gloria Bog. A light breeze was passing over the sea of pale sedge like a hand. The blue of the mountain was deeper and darker than the blue of the lake or the sky. Along the high banks at the edge of the water there were many little private lawns speckled with fish bones and blue crayfish shells where the otters fed and trained their young.

'I can never look at the blue of the mountain now without thinking of John Quinn,' Ruttledge said.

'Oh John,' the Shah shook gently. 'You wouldn't want to be depending too much on John unless it was for women you were looking. John is a boy.'

The meal was served when they returned to the house. He ate alone, with the sheepdog by his chair, and no one spoke. The only sounds were the knife and fork on a plate or a stirring spoon and the small birds on the green bank outside the window. Kate and Ruttledge left the room and returned without attracting his attention. When he rose from the table he said, 'That was great. God bless and keep you, Kate.'

They saw him to the car. The sheepdog leaped into the front seat and placed his front paws on the dashboard. He turned under the four iron posts and let the windows down to call out, 'God bless yous,' as he passed the porch. They watched the light flash on the glass and metal as the car appeared and reappeared in the breaks in the big trees as it went slowly out around the shore.

They continued looking for a long time at the evening sparkle on the lake until a dark figure appeared in a pale space, walking slowly, disappearing behind the trees. When the figure moved across the last clear space, it could either turn uphill or enter the fields along the shore. So even was the slow pace that Patrick Ryan emerged into the shade of the alder above the gate at the expected moment.

'Talk of the devil,' Ruttledge breathed as soon as he recognized the figure in the dark suit.

He came at the same slow, studied pace up the short avenue to the porch. The dark suit was neatly pressed, the white shirt ironed, the wine-coloured tie carefully knotted and the black shoes shone beneath the thin white dust of the road. He was five feet, six inches in height, with broad shoulders, a remarkably handsome head, sixty-five years of age, erect and strong.

Ruttledge knew that his first words would have been pondered carefully, and waited in front of the porch instead of going towards him.

'I have been meaning to come round several times but there's been people hanging out of me for months,' Patrick spoke slowly and deliberately.

'That doesn't matter. You are welcome,' Ruttledge said, and led him into the house.

'Where is she?' he demanded when he was seated in the white rocking chair. 'Is she here?'

'In the house somewhere.'

Kate came into the room. She had changed into a blouse of pale silk and brushed her hair. 'You are welcome, Patrick.'

'It's great to see you, Kate,' he rose from the chair with natural easy charm.

It was cool and dark within the house after the brightness of the porch, the green bank outside the large window glowing in the hidden light.

'You'll have a drink – it's a while since you were in the house,' Ruttledge said as he took out a bottle of Powers.

'I bar the drink,' Patrick Ryan raised his hand dramatically. 'I completely bar the drink. There's too much fucken drink passed around in this country.'

'You'll have tea?' Kate said.

'No tea either. I came on a mission. I want this man to drive me to Carrick.'

'That's easily done.'

'I suppose you have all heard that our lad is bad in Carrick?'

'Jamesie told us that Edmund is poorly,' Ruttledge said carefully.

'With Jamesie around, this place will never lack a radio-TV station,' he said sarcastically.

'We'd be lost without Jamesie,' Ruttledge said.

'I suppose he told you that I was never in to see our lad. He probably has it spread all over the country.'

'He just mentioned that Edmund was poorly and that old Mrs Logan and the dog are lost since he went into hospital.'

'They are casting it up that I was never in to see him when I only heard today that he was in hospital. When you are working here and there all over the country you hear nothing.'

'When do you want to leave?' Ruttledge asked.

'We'll go now, in the name of God.'

'Would you like to come?' Ruttledge asked Kate, though he knew Patrick Ryan wouldn't want her and she was unlikely to come.

'No, thanks.'

'I'll be back tomorrow,' Patrick Ryan said, but Kate made no response. In the porch he stood looking across at the four iron posts standing in their concrete bases and said, 'I heard they are talking about that as well.'

'If it wasn't that it would be something else. There's no hurry,' Ruttledge said.

'We might as well stop them talking, lad. The people around this lake were always known to be a holy living terror for news and they'll never die while Jamesie lives,' Patrick Ryan laughed lowly, suddenly in much better humour. 'There was a boy of the Reagans down on holiday from Dublin. The Reagans were all doctors, lawyers, teachers, that kind of crowd and the boy was delicate. I heard not long ago that he's a diplomat in Chicago. He wanted to visit an uncle, the Master in Kesh, and they thought him too delicate to walk or cycle, so they harnessed up an old quiet pony they had. I'm not telling a word of a lie, lad, but the mile by the lake took longer than the other five miles to Kesh. They were all out. They wanted to know who he was, where he was from, who he was staying with – though they all knew the pony and cart well – and where was he going and what was he doing in this part of the country. It was like having to pass through customs and excise. They got in between the shaft of the cart and the pony's shoulder so that the poor gossen couldn't move until they had extracted every word of flesh. If he had a loudspeaker to broadcast the details, hours could have been saved, but they all had to find out for themselves. It was dark by the time he got to Kesh and they were beginning to be worried. I'm telling you, lad, those people will never die while Jamesie is cycling around.'

'Jamesie is marvellous,' Ruttledge said.

'He's a pure child, lad. He'll never grow up,' he said dismissively. 'There's been a big clear-out since young Reagan came round the lake in the pony and cart. The country was walking with people then. After us there'll be nothing but the water hen and the swan.'

They passed the wide opening down to the lake where earlier Cecil Pierce had sat fishing from the transport box with the tractor running. 'Cecil has gone home to do the milking. He was fishing here all day,' Ruttledge said.

'No better sort than poor Cecil,' Patrick Ryan said. 'I never heard a mean word about anybody from Cecil's mouth. You'd think that crowd up in the North would learn something, lad, and get on like Cecil and us.'

'It's different up there.'

'How could it be different?'

'They are more equal there and hate one another. There were never many Protestants here. When there are only a few, they have to keep their heads low whether it suits or not, like the Irish in England when a bomb goes off. Cecil would want to keep his head low whether they were many or few. He is that kind of person.'

'They are a bad old bitter crowd up there. They'll eat one another yet,' Patrick Ryan said belligerently.

'Johnny is coming home from England this week,' Ruttledge said to change the subject.

'God bless us, has that come round again?' Ryan said, and then brightened to mimic Jamesie with affectionate malice. '"Meet the train with Johnny Rowley's car . . . There'll be drinks, you know, rounds . . . rounds of drinks, stops at bars, shake hands and welcome . . . Welcome home from England

48

. . . no sooner in the door than Mary has the sirloin on the pan."' He laughed in the enjoyment of his power and mastery. He had a deadly gift.

'That's almost too good, Patrick – it's wicked.'

'"He's a sight, a holy sight,"' he mimicked Jamesie again, warmed by the praise, and then changed briskly into his own voice. 'After all that performance he'll spend the next two weeks avoiding Johnny at every stop and turn as if he had grown horns. They never got on. For two brothers they couldn't be more unlike.'

They drove through a maze of little roads until they reached the main road close to Carrick. In places, the encroaching hawthorns brushed the sides of the car. Some of the cottages were newly painted and pretty, with gardens and flowers. Others were neglected, uncared for.

'You can always tell the old bachelor's burrow. None of them ever heard tell of a can of paint or a packet of flower seed. The country is full of them and they all had mothers.'

He spoke of the people he had worked for. Many were dead. He spoke of them humorously, with a little contempt, as most of them had been poor. 'I never took a penny, lad. They hadn't it to give.'

When he turned to speak of the rich houses he had worked for, his voice changed: it was full of identification and half-possession, like the unformed longing of a boy.

'Most of the people in this part of the country will never rise off their arses in the ditches. You have to have something behind you to be able to rise.'

Rise to what? came to Ruttledge's lips, but he didn't speak it. 'I suppose they'll move around in the light for a while like the rest of us and disappear,' he said.

'They wouldn't like to hear that either, lad,' Patrick Ryan replied trenchantly. 'All the fuckers half-believe they are going to be the Big Exception and live for ever.'

The spires of the churches on the hill rose above the low roofs of Carrick, and on a higher isolated hill across the town stood a concrete water tower, like a huge mushroom on a slender stem. The long stone building had been the old workhouse and was now part of the hospital. Age had softened the grey Victorian harshness of the stone.

The open wards they walked through were orderly and clean. The men in the military rows of beds were old. As they passed down the brown linoleum-covered corridor, many were in their own world, a few engaged in vigorous conversation with themselves. Others were as still as if they were in shock. Sunday visitors gathered around certain beds in troubled or self-conscious uselessness, but they formed a semblance of company and solidarity against those who lay alone and unvisited.

'It'd make you think, lad,' Patrick said sourly. 'There's not a lot to it when it all comes down.'

They found Edmund in a tiny room on his own, a drip above the bed attached to his arm, in deep, drugged sleep.

'Our lad is bad,' Patrick Ryan said.

'We'd be better to let him sleep.'

Patrick Ryan put the bottle of Lucozade they had brought firmly down on the bedside table, and without any warning he took Edmund by the shoulders and began to shake him violently.

'Let him rest. You can see he's very sick,' Ruttledge said, but his words only increased Patrick Ryan's determination.

'We'll bring him to his senses in a minute, lad.'

'Watch the drip!' Ruttledge called in alarm as the tubes and bottle trembled.

When Edmund woke he was frightened. At first, he did not know where he was. 'Patrick,' he said out of his disturbed sleep when he recognized his brother's face, and offered his trembling hand.

'Are you all right?' Patrick Ryan demanded.

He made no answer. Either he didn't understand or his attention was distracted by Ruttledge's presence at the foot of the bed. With great effort he reached back to an old

50

tradition of courtesy, 'Joe,' he called to Ruttledge and with difficulty again reached out a trembling hand. 'You were very good to come. How are yous all around the lake?'

'We are well, Edmund. How is yourself?'

He wasn't given the opportunity to answer. Patrick filled a glass from the Lucozade bottle. 'Drink this,' he ordered. 'It'll do you good.' He held it to his lips but Edmund was too weak to drink. Much of the yellow liquid ran down his white stubble.

'Leave it be,' Ruttledge said in anger and took the glass from his hand. 'We are doing more harm than good.'

For a moment Patrick Ryan looked as if he was about to turn on Ruttledge. Instead he turned back to Edmund. 'Go back to sleep now, lad,' he commanded. 'You'll be all right.'

Edmund looked towards Ruttledge in mute enquiry. The face was as regular and handsome as Patrick's but far more withdrawn and gentle and it was now refined by illness. Ruttledge hardly knew him. They had met over the years by chance on the roads. Each had made the usual polite enquiries of the other but past that point conversation never began, falling back on that old reliable, the unreliable weather. As with many diminished people, Edmund's response was to rephrase each thing the other person said in the form of a question, often with an expression of great interest, even charm. In its humble way it gave the other every encouragement to continue. Many did not know or care that they were responding to nothing but an echo. Others mutely acknowledged that this was his simple way. Only a few were openly contemptuous.

'Have you nothing to answer but repeat the words after me?' his exasperated brother had demanded more than once.

'Nothing to answer? Nothing at all to answer.'

No matter how much Patrick railed, Edmund remained safe within these echoes and repetitions. Now he was on the cliff-face of a silence that required nothing.

'You must be tired,' Ruttledge said gently.

'Not too tired. You were very good to come. You were both very good to come.'

51

'We'll go now. You can go back to sleep,' Patrick said.

'Goodbye, Pa,' Edmund used a family name for Patrick that Ruttledge hadn't heard him called in years. 'Remember me to all of them around the lake.'

'They are all asking for you,' Ruttledge said. 'They are waiting for you to come home.'

'You can go back to sleep now,' his brother repeated, but Edmund was already sleeping. A nurse came into the small room and when Patrick engaged her in conversation about the patient, Ruttledge went out to the corridor to wait.

'We were wrong to wake him,' Ruttledge said as they walked through the wards and down the long pale green corridor.

'Our lad isn't long for this world, I fear,' Patrick Ryan answered vaguely.

At the car, Ruttledge asked, 'Where would you like me to leave you?'

'I never left this town yet without leaving them money. I'm not going to start doing anything different now.'

'Where would you like to go?'

'We'll call to see how Paddy Lowe is getting along, in the name of God.'

A young girl was serving behind the counter in Lowe's Bar. Except for a party of two girls and five men of different ages who were on their way home from a football match, the bar was empty.

'Where's Paddy?' Patrick asked the girl as she was drawing the glasses of beer.

'He's out on the land,' the girl answered.

'Me and Paddy are great friends,' Patrick Ryan said, but the girl was not drawn further into the conversation. As soon as they raised the glasses of beer, all Patrick's attention veered to the crowd returning from the football match. 'I'll dawnder over to see where this crowd is from,' he laughed apologetically, and approached their table with a theatrical slowness that engaged the attention of the table even before he spoke. 'Did yous win?' he asked with charm. They had lost. The match had been played in Boyle and hadn't been even close. Their team was Shannon Gaels. 'Ye must have a crowd of duffers like our crowd,' he said amiably.

'They are not great but it's a day out,' a man said. 'Only for football we might never get out of the house.'

'You can say that again.'

'Over and over,' another man said.

There was more talk and some laughter. When Patrick Ryan rejoined Ruttledge at the counter, he was a man restored and refreshed.

'They are all from Drumlion,' he confided. 'Their frigger of a team lost. We might as well drink up and go now, in the name of God. Don't forget to tell Paddy Lowe I was in and was asking for him.'

'Who will I say . . .?' the girl enquired politely.

'Tell him the man who wore the ragged jacket called. Once he hears that he'll know. '"For none can tell the man who wore the ragged jacket."'

'The man who wore the ragged jacket,' she repeated, puzzled and amused at his confidence and theatricality.

'"And when all is said and done, who can tell the man who wore the ragged jacket?"' he repeated. The men who had been to the football match shouted out to them. Ruttledge waved. Patrick Ryan stood at the door and shouted, 'Up us all! Up Ceannabo!'

'"May we never die and down with the begrudgers,"' they chorused back and pounded their glasses on the table. One man cheered.

'God, you could have a great evening with that crowd,' Patrick Ryan said as they got into the car. 'I can tell you something for nothing, lad. Only for football and the Mass on Sunday and the *Observer* on Wednesday, people would never get out of their frigging houses. They'd be marooned.'

They drove out of town and were soon back in the maze of small roads. Except for the narrow strip of sky above the bending whitethorns they could have been travelling through a green wilderness.

'I'll be round tomorrow. We'll finish that shed,' Patrick Ryan said as they drove slowly, Ruttledge blowing the horn loudly at every blind turn of the road.

'There's no hurry.'

'You were anxious enough to get building done once,' Patrick Ryan said.

'That was a long time ago.'

'You've got on a sight since you first came round the place, lad.'

'We managed. Most people get by in one way or another.'

'Some get on a sight better than others. What do you put that down to – luck? Or having something behind you?'

'They all help,' Ruttledge said.

'Do you miss not having children?' Patrick Ryan asked aggressively as if sensing the evasion.

'No. You can't miss what you never had. It's not as if there aren't enough people in the world.'

'Was she too old when you started?'

'No, Patrick. She wasn't too old,' Ruttledge said quietly but with an edge of steel. 'Where do you want to be left? Or do you want to come back to the house?'

'Drop me in the village,' Patrick Ryan said.

There was nothing stirring in the small village. A few cars stood outside the two bars. A boy was leaning over the little bridge, looking down into the shallow river, and he lifted his head as the car drew up beside the green telephone box. The priest's cows were grazing with their calves in the rich fields around the roofless abbey.

'You'll see me in the morning,' Patrick Ryan said as he closed the car door, and went jauntily towards the Abbey Bar.

At the house Ruttledge called to Kate that he was back, changed quickly into old clothes, remembering that he had completely forgotten to look at the Shorthorn.

The cattle had left the ridged fields by the shore, their shapes still visible on the short grass. Two fields away he found them grazing greedily. At a glance he saw the old red shorthorn was missing. Anxiously, he went in among the cattle. She wasn't there; neither was she in any of the adjacent fields. She was their last surviving animal of the stock they had first bought. It would be hard to lose her now through carelessness.

He searched the obvious places quickly. He said to himself as he grew anxious that it was useless to panic or rush. Nothing could be done now but to search the land methodically, field by field. Having searched every field, he found her finally in a corner of the young spruce plantation that had been set as a shelterbelt above the lake. At her back was a ditch covered with ferns and briars and tall foxgloves. She was lying on her side when he parted the branches. She tried to struggle to her feet but recognizing him fell back with a low, plaintive moan for help. 'My poor old girl,' he spoke his relief at finding her. She repeated the same low call. She wanted help.

The little corner of the shelterbelt was like a room in the wilderness. He could tell by the marks and shapes on the floor of spruce needles that she had been in labour for some time. The waterbag had broken. Afraid his hands were not clean enough, he felt lightly without entering the cow and found that the feet and head were in place. The Shorthorn began to press. The womb dilated wide. The feet showed clearly but did not advance. She fell back and moaned again.

'We're not going to lose you after all these years,' he spoke reassuringly, without thought.

He had hardly said the words when he heard a sharp cough. He turned and found Jamesie staring at the cow. The spruce wood behind him was almost in night. He had crept up without a sound. 'Hel-lo. Hel-lo,' he called in a hushed, conspiratorial voice.

'You're an angel of the Lord.'

'Have you felt the calf?'

'The calf is coming right. She's making no headway though.'

'Get the calving jack,' he said.

As Ruttledge turned to go to the house, he saw the soft ropes hanging from Jamesie's pocket. He must have been watching the cow covertly the whole evening: he came prepared and didn't expect to find Ruttledge there. At the house Kate put aside what she was doing and got warm water, soap, disinfectant, a towel. The jack was made of aluminium and light to carry. They hurried to the plantation.

'Jamesie, it's great that you're here,' Kate whispered when they entered the darkness of the small room beneath the spruce branches.

'Kate,' he smiled.

Both men scrubbed their hands and arms. Kate held the towel. Jamesie drew out the feet. Ruttledge slipped on the loops and drew them tight above the hooves. When he got the jack in place he ratcheted quickly until a strain came on the ropes. He then waited until the cow began to press. Each time she pressed he increased the strain.

'That's a great girl,' Jamesie said. 'Look how she's pressing. There's many an old cow that would just lie there on her side and give you no help at all.'

The long tongue and the nose appeared. At one moment there was a terrible strain on the ropes and the anxiety and tenseness were so near at hand they could almost be touched and felt, and the next moment the ropes went slack as the calf came sliding out on to the floor ahead of the quick ratcheting, covered in the gleaming placenta. Jamesie called out, 'It's a bull, a savage!' as he plucked the veils of placenta from the nostrils and turned the calf over. Quickly Ruttledge lifted the navel cord and immersed it in a cup of disinfectant. Bellowing wildly, the shorthorn struggled to her feet.

'Careful, Kate, not to stand in her way. You never can tell.'

The Shorthorn's whole attention was fixed on her calf as if it was her first calf all over again, the beginning of the world. Between wild loos she began to lick the calf dry. So vigorous were the movements of her tongue that they moved the calf along the ground in spite of its inert and sprawled weight.

When she nosed the calf over on its other side, she was undeterred in the vigorous licking by the spruce needles that were sticking to the bright curtain of slime. With the same loud, exhorting cries – so wild that they sounded threatening – she nosed him to his feet. He tottered on the long wobbly legs, fell and rose before sinking on his knees in spite of her impatient urgings. His head was large, the shoulders heavy and thick, his coat a light chocolate brown, with white markings on the deep chest and the legs.

'He's a monster,' Jamesie said in admiration. 'The old lassie would never have landed him on her own.'

'It's wonderful she's safe . . . that they are both safe.'

'These new jacks are great,' Jamesie said. 'I often saw six men pulling with ropes, using the trunk of a tree to hold the strain, the poor cow bursted.'

'Don't tell me, Jamesie. Look how excited they are to meet one another.'

'Money, Kate. Money.'

'I suppose we should leave them to one another,' Ruttledge said.

'He'll suck when he gets hungry. They know their own business best.'

There was a great feeling of relief. She was safe with her calf for another year. The relief was like peace.

'How did you come to be here, Jamesie?' Kate asked suddenly as they went towards the house. It hadn't occurred to her to ask until now.

'The sleepy fox, that's how, Kate,' he said defensively. 'You'll be sick of the sight of me. Twice in the same day.'

'That could never happen.'

'You must have been here all the time. You must have been watching while I was looking for the cow. You are something. You were watching me all that time? Why didn't you call?'

In response, he gave a sharp guffaw. 'Where did you leave Patrick Ryan?' he asked.

'How did you know I was away with Patrick?'

'I saw him go round the shore. I saw the car head for Carrick. I knew well what Patrick wanted. He wanted to go to the hospital. I knew the cow was sick. I didn't expect you home so soon. Better men than you failed to get Patrick out of the town.'

'I left him in the village. He didn't want me.'

'Don't tell me. I know too well.'

With difficulty they persuaded him to enter the house. 'Twice drinking whiskey in a house the same day. I'll be the talk of the country.'

'Not every day the old Shorthorn calves.' Ruttledge gripped his shoulder in a sign of gratitude and affection.

The drinks were poured. They spoke of the visit to the hospital, Edmund's great courtesy, the difference in character between the two brothers with the same father and mother and the same upbringing in the same small place.

'Would never harm a fly, "How are yous all round the lake. You were very good to come." I can hear his voice,' Jamesie said.

'Patrick shouldn't have shaken him awake,' Kate said.

'No, Kate. You can quit. Patrick never had value on Edmund. He just wanted to say that he made the visit in case it could be upcasted. All he cared about was that he was seen talking to Edmund. When the parents were going, it was Patrick this and Patrick that and Edmund wasn't even noticed. The sun shone out of Patrick.'

'That's not right.'

'Right or wrong, Kate? There's nothing right or wrong in this world. Only what happens. I'll be beating away,' he said, draining the whiskey and refusing the offer of more. 'Mary's over in Mulvey's on her Sunday *ceilidhe*. She warned me not to be late. We'll come back home across the bog together. She wouldn't cross that bog on her own even if it was the end of the world.'

They walked to where he had left his bicycle down by the lake. The moon was high above the lake. Scents of the wild mint and honeysuckle were sharp and sweet on the night air. The full trees stood high and still, dark and magnificent against the moonlit water.

'I doubt but poor Edmund will ever go these roads again,' Jamesie said quietly as he prepared to cycle away. 'I doubt he'll ever see the lake again.'

Late that night they walked through the heavy dew to the plantation. The calf had sucked and was sleeping by the mother. She let out a sharp, anxious moo as they approached through the branches. When they spoke to her she was quiet and gave the sleeping calf a few sharp, casual licks as if to show her pride. They appeared now as if they had been together for ever. The black cat followed them over the fields. As they retraced their steps she made little runs and darts across their path, a ruse to get herself lifted from the wet grass and carried. Eventually Ruttledge picked her up, and she rode back to the house on his shoulder.

The warm weather came with its own ills. The maggot fly had struck, each stricken sheep or lamb standing comically still as if in scholarly thought. Then suddenly they would try to bite back at the dark, moistened patch of wool tantalisingly out of reach. They were run into the shed. A bath was prepared. The infected sheep and lambs were picked out and the parts dipped in poison. The fat white maggots writhed underneath the wool and on the ground around the bath. The sheep and lambs bounded free, rid of their deadly guests.

From the plantation the Shorthorn guided her stumbling calf down to the herd by the water's edge. They all gathered dutifully to sniff and snort and poke the new calf while the mother stood proudly by. When the cows returned to their grazing, the calves approached their new companion in the expectation of frolics and play but he just sank wearily to his knees, exhausted after his long journey. Ruttledge was surprised to hear voices when he reached the house and stood to listen. Patrick Ryan had come. He and Kate were talking.

'I hear Edmund isn't well.'

'He's finished.'

'He could get well again.'

'No, girl. He's finished.'

Patrick Ryan was seated at the table, his cap beside his hand on the tablecloth. He was eating a boiled egg and buttered toast with a big mug of tea. Kate faced him across a separate table where she was putting together frames for the hives. She often resorted to such tasks when Patrick Ryan was in the house.

'I'm in heaven here with a great boiled egg,' he greeted Ruttledge with sunny amiability.

'We've been talking about Edmund,' Kate said.

'It's no use. I told her our lad is finished. There's no use talking or pretending otherwise,' he asserted darkly. 'I suppose ye were hardly expecting to see me?'

'We are glad to see you,' Ruttledge said. 'We expect you, Patrick, when we see you.'

'There's no surer way as far as expecting goes.'

'Was there much fun in the village last night?'

'It went on too late. Somebody gave me a lift to the corner of the lake. We sat too long in the car – discussing. Fuck all these late-night discussions. They never go anywhere. There was a moon as big as a saucepan when I had to climb the hill to the Tomb. I think it must have been six weeks since I last slept in the house. Anyway there was no little woman there to give out.'

'That was good,' Ruttledge said.

'You wouldn't know. She wasn't there anyhow. This woman here is looking to her bees. If people were as busy and organized as the bees we'd have paradise on earth.'

'The bees can be rough too in their way. They make short work of the drones,' Kate said.

'That's what should be done with our layabouts as well,' he said vigorously, taking his cap from the tablecloth. 'We better be making a start. Are you ready?'

'As ready as I'll ever be.'

'We'll proceed, then, in the name of God.'

The timbers, the angle irons, the long nails, the nuts and bolts, the sheets of iron had lain about in the shed since they had been bought two years before. They took a long time to find and arrange in order.

Patrick Ryan worked slowly but meticulously. He measured each beam several times before drawing the line with a set square and a stub of a pencil and checked again before taking the saw.

Late in the day they heard a heavy motor come slowly in round the shore and turn uphill towards the house.

'It looks as if we may have a visitor, lad,' Patrick Ryan said with excitement as they lifted their heads from the measuring and checking.

'It's the Shah,' Patrick Ryan groaned with obvious disappointment when the new black Mercedes entered the shade, towing a covered cattle trailer. The two men knew one another too well. 'You better go and attend to him. He's unlikely to leave me any washers. I wonder what the hell he's doing with a cattle trailer,' he said sourly.

Ruttledge went towards the car. The Shah made no attempt to get out. The window was down. The sheepdog was sitting upright in the passenger seat, his paws on the dashboard, barking and wagging with excitement.

'Aren't you getting out and letting the dog out?'

'I'm waiting,' he said darkly.

'For what?'

'To know what to do.'

'To do with what?'

'This consignment,' he answered irritably.

'A consignment of what?'

'As if you didn't know,' he said more irritably and struggled from the car. The sheepdog followed him out. Ruttledge petted the dog while the Shah took the pins from the trailer door and swung it open dramatically.

The trailer was full of boxes. Ruttledge started to laugh

quietly. The mood and its reason fell into place. A few months before he had done an assignment for a wine company. A payment in wine had been agreed.

'They should have delivered all this to the house here,' Ruttledge said. 'They weren't told to dump it on you.'

'They said the lorry was too big to get in round the shore,' he said angrily. 'If I knew what they were carrying I'd have run them to hell.'

'You could nearly start up a pub with this,' Ruttledge said.

'There are several taverns in the town operating with far less,' the Shah said disagreeably.

'I suppose we better get it into the house out of harm's way.'

'Unless you want to dump it in the lake. I'm glad you can see the funny side of it anyhow. I suppose it pays to have a sense of humour when you're giving the party.'

Kate hadn't heard the motor's approach and was surprised to see the car and cattle trailer outside the porch. She went towards the Shah in welcome but was taken aback by his abruptness. 'What are all these boxes?' she asked.

'I suppose your man didn't tell you either,' he said accusingly. 'You should ask him. He appears to know it all.'

'Tell me what?'

'About these boxes he's ordered for himself. He must be planning to have one whale of a time. It'll be no time now till you see the whole place going up in smoke.'

She looked towards Ruttledge.

'You remember the work I did for the wine company?'

'Of course.'

'They left it with this man in the town instead of delivering it here to the house.'

'I never thought it would come to so many boxes,' she said.

'They won't go to loss,' Ruttledge said humorously.

'You can say that again,' the Shah said. He had been watching Kate's face intently and was reassured by her manner.

They began to carry the boxes into the house. The Shah stayed by the trailer, opening and shutting the door as if to guard against anybody seeing the shameful cargo. Ruttledge carried the boxes through the porch and into the spare room. Kate found the boxes heavy and put them down in the porch. When all the boxes had been carried in, she saw the Shah staring at her little stack of boxes.

'Am I doing something wrong?'

'Can't you put them where nobody will see them? Can't you put them where your man is putting them, where they'll be out of sight?'

Ruttledge said quietly under his breath. 'If they are too heavy leave them alone. I'll carry them into the room. We couldn't have done worse if a cargo of fallen women had been delivered to the railway sheds.' He was having difficulty presenting a straight face to the world and was glad to hide behind the carrying.

The Shah closed the trailer door and dropped the pins into place with a firmness in which anger and relief were mixed. Patrick Ryan had not looked their way. With a pencil and metal tape he was studiously measuring and marking the various lengths of wood.

'I see you have that drunken sally back working. If he gets wind of this cargo he'll never leave from around the place,' the Shah said as he entered the house, somewhat mollified to see that the boxes had been removed and put away.

'He doesn't like wine,' Ruttledge said.

'I suppose he's no sooner here than he'll be gone again. I've been telling you for a long time that you should run him to hell from around the place and get a proper tradesman.'

'He's all right. He'll do for now.'

At first, the Shah had been taken by Patrick Ryan's easy charm, his effrontery, his mimicry, a delinquency he was partial to, but eventually he went too far and the Shah withdrew and watched him as coldly as if he were evaluating a hand of cards. On his way out to the lake one evening he gave Patrick a lift from town. Patrick was the worse for drink and in foul humour. In this mood he was given to lecturing people.

'You have gathered a sight of money. What do you think you'll do with it? You can't take it with you. The shroud has no pockets. Have you made decisions?'

Patrick Ryan could not have staggered into a more dangerous territory. The Shah continued to drive in silence; he had not been spoken to like that in years. His money was a source of pride and satisfaction and a deep security. He did not speak at all until the car reached the two bars in Shruhaun beside the little river and the roofless abbey. He stopped the car at the stone bridge while Patrick continued his lecture.

'I'm not stopping here. I've had enough of the bars for one day, bad luck to them. I'm going on to the lake.'

'Out!' the Shah said while looking straight ahead.

If Patrick Ryan had been more sober and more watchful he would not have been so taken by surprise.

'There's no need to take things so seriously. What were we doing but a bit of aul ravelling? They're no cause to get so het up.'

'That's enough. Out.'

When Patrick Ryan saw that his attempt to smooth things over would not work, his mood swung round again. 'I can tell you something for nothing. You may have money but you're as thick and ignorant as several double ditches.'

'Out, I said. I'm not one bit interested in what you think.'

'He should be run to hell,' the Shah repeated now as he entered the house. Once he was seated he asked for tea but would have nothing to eat. He was going down to the hotel as soon as he got rid of the trailer.

'You are a great girl, Kate. We have no doubt about you – unlike your man here,' he said as he took the tea, returning to the subject of the wine.

'What doubts?'

'Who's giving the party?' he demanded half-humorously, anxiously, disapprovingly.

'What party?'

'Someone has to be giving the party with a cargo like that

in the house. I never saw the man giving the party yet that lasted long.'

'Visitors come. There are times for celebration. It will last for years,' Ruttledge said.

'It'd be some party all on your own. I wouldn't be surprised if it ended with Kate here throwing you out.'

'She may well do that anyhow.'

'And she mightn't be too far out,' he started to shake gently, his good humour restored.

They walked him to the car and trailer. Kate gave the sheepdog a biscuit, which he carried with importance to the front seat.

'I'm sorry it was dumped on you. It should have been delivered here,' Ruttledge apologized.

'Anyway it's safe now. It's hid,' the Shah said.

As he turned the heavy trailer in the space between the house and the bare iron posts, he raised a slow hand in a version of an episcopal blessing to a grinning Patrick Ryan, who was all mock attention beneath the posts. Patrick answered with a blasphemous sign of the cross – on forehead, on both shoulders, on breast, in mock gratitude, and then raised his own hand in a smart military salute as the car and trailer swung around. The performance was superb, but its intended victim did not even glance in the mirror as the car and trailer crunched past the porch and out the gate to go slowly round the shore. Patrick had been acting for himself. There was no response or applause to drown out the empty echo, and he turned away in disgust.

'A worse thing could not have been left at the sheds,' Ruttledge said to Kate as he prepared to rejoin Patrick Ryan. 'I'm sure he'll be counting now to see if we've sold any cattle.'

'What was the Shah doing with the trailer?' Patrick Ryan asked when Ruttledge returned. 'He's unlikely to be heading into the cattle business at this stage.'

'Some things for the house were delivered to the railway by mistake.'

Jamesie would have been on fire to know what had been delivered, but Patrick Ryan was incurious about the things around him and asked no further.

'He may be your uncle and he may have made his weight in money but let me tell you something for nothing, lad: he's still as thick and as ignorant as several double ditches.'

'I'm fond of him,' Ruttledge affirmed simply. 'He was kind when I was young. That goodness is still there even if it sometimes doesn't show too well.'

Patrick looked hard at him for a moment, but Ruttledge stood unflinchingly, and after a long pause he turned away to mark the angle of a beam.

They were able to raise the heavy beams and, using ladders, bolt them to the top of the iron posts. As they worked in the heat and silence, Bill Evans was the only visitor they had on his way to the lake for the buckets of water. He stayed chatting with them until Patrick Ryan threw him cigarettes, and then he went into the house for tea and food and more cigarettes.

'He may well be happier than any of us, lad. He doesn't know any differ,' Patrick Ryan said.

'Who can tell?' Ruttledge asked lightly.

'*Who can tell, when all is said and done, and who can tell the man who wore the ragged jacket,*' he sang softly. 'It's a conundrum, lad. That's what it is.'

'Would you swap with him?'

'No, lad. I would not swap with a lord. We all want our own two shoes of life. If truth was told, none of us would swap with anybody. We want to go out the way we came in. It's just as well we have no choice. If there was choice you'd have certain giddy outfits having operations to get themselves changed into other people like those sex change outfits you see in the newspapers.'

They never knew whether he would come from one day to the next until his dark figure appeared in the spaces between the trees in around the shore or at the alder at the gate or standing in the doorway of the room. They worked often till dark. Once the heavy crossbeams were bolted into place, they started to cut the frame to hold the roof. When they had finished work for the day and eaten, he always sat on in the house, reluctant to go home.

'I'll be glad to run you to Carrick to see Edmund,' Ruttledge offered several times as a way out of the long, closed evening.

'I know that well,' he answered. 'I know that well but Edmund's days are done. Our lad was easygoing like my father. My mother spent years in America and was hard. She lost an eye when she got hit in the byre with a horn while tying a cow and nearly all the money she brought back with her was lost trying to save the sight of the other eye. She was very hard. In my turn I was probably too hard on Edmund. In the end what does it matter? I could see Edmund was finished the minute he woke. He's hanging by a thread in Carrick. We'll not see him again.'

'Would you like to take a run into town?' Ruttledge offered on other evenings.

'No, lad, no. We'd take to the drink if we went to town.'

'We could have one or two and leave it at that. We don't have to go wild.'

'You should know by now that your Irishman can do nothing by halves. He has to go the whole hog.'

'There's a few things that have to be got for the house.'

'You go to town, lad, if you have to run for messages,' he said. Kate looked up from her ironing with alarm. 'Why don't you put that away so that we can have a proper chat, girl?'

'We can talk away while I'm ironing. It's more pleasant.'

'It's hard to whistle and chew meal. Do you think will you ever make that drawing you do pay?'

'I don't think so, Patrick.'

'Why do you keep at it, then, girl?'

'It brings what I see closer.'

'Does it mean that nobody would want those drawings if you tried to sell?'

'That's possible. An aunt of mine painted and drew all her life. She was good but never sold a drawing or a picture.'

'She must have plenty of washers, then.'

'Her husband was a lawyer.'

'He kept the show on the road. I suppose they had no children either.'

'They had two girls.'

He would become more and more frustrated but could not attack openly and they could not get on. What he wanted was complete attention and his moods were unpredictable, always changing. 'Don't tell me about the people of this part of the country. I've ploughed their fields, built their houses, laid them out, slept in their beds, sat at their tables. They're as ignorant as dogshite. All they want is to get as much for themselves and to give as little back as they can ever manage. And the older they get – when you'd think they'd have some sense – the greedier the cunts become.'

'That's too hard. There are many decent people round here.'

'There's a few,' he admitted reluctantly. 'They are far from the normal.'

'What about Mary and Jamesie?'

'Mary's the best in the world,' his face brightened. 'There's none better than Mary. Jamesie would give you the shirt off his back. Once I was coming to borrow their mule. He had the mule tackled and was putting out topdressing. As soon as he saw me come he had the mule untackled in seconds. He declared before God that he was doing nothing with the mule. The mule was there for me to take.'

'What about yourself? You aren't too bad either,' Kate said firmly.

'You should know me well enough by now,' he laughed and grew light. 'I don't count. I'm just a sort of comedian to the crowd. Do you think when you made those drawings of me, Kate, do you think you got any nearer to the beast?'

'You have an interesting face but you know that yourself. I don't think I ever got it right.'

68

'Maybe it's just as well that it wasn't laid out for all to see,' he said defensively, but his pleasure was obvious.

'You gave us a great deal of help when we came first,' Ruttledge said when they were alone laying out the timbers for the roof.

'It was nothing, lad,' Patrick Ryan said. 'What else would I have done?'

'The first time I gave you money you threw it to the wind. We had to search for the notes in the bushes.'

'I disremember, lad. I've done many things in my time that are best forgot but I've never taken money from neighbours.'

'You were here the first day the priest came to the house,' Ruttledge said.

'I disremember that as well.'

'You went into hiding. When the car pulled up at the gate you told me to go and invite him into the house and be in no hurry out.'

'It's beginning to come back. Go on, lad.'

'I brought him in and made him tea. Kate was in the town. He wasn't looking for you at all. We talked about the weather and cattle and the land. After a long time he asked, "I suppose you are wondering what brought me here?" "It did cross my mind but that doesn't matter. It's nice that you are here," I said. "Whatever about that," Father Conroy said, "I'm not here on my own account. I believe in living and letting live. The man up in Longford is very interested in you and why you left the Church and has me persecuted about you every time he comes. He's coming on Thursday to give Confirmation and one of the first things he'll ask me is, Have you been up to see that man yet? And this coming Thursday I'll tell him in no uncertain terms I *have*, and that's the whole of my business here."'

'He's straight and direct,' Patrick Ryan said. 'Himself and the Bishop don't pull. They're like chalk and cheese.'

'He drank the tea black without sugar. He wouldn't even take a biscuit,' Ruttledge said.

'I'm surprised he took the tea. He must have been upset. He generally takes nothing in houses. He lives on fruit and bread and milk and water. For a man with such an interest in cattle he never touches meat. I suppose that's why there's not a pick on him for such a big man.'

'As soon as we came out of the house he spotted you by the sheds and headed your way at once,' Ruttledge laughed. 'Even before he got close, you started pulling money from your pocket. The day was wild. The wind took a fiver and stuck it on a whitethorn.'

'I should have kept out of sight. I mustn't have expected him to leave the house so soon,' Patrick Ryan said. 'I owed him washers. I hadn't paid any dues for a couple of years.'

'After you paid him what you owed he saw the fiver stuck on the thorn and reached into the bush. "I think God meant that for me as well."'

'He has an eye like a hawk, especially where there is money. You have a good memory, lad.'

'It was that same day I tried to give you money. You threw it back in my face and it all went on the wind. We had to search for it in the bushes.'

'I never cared about money,' Patrick Ryan said.

When the crossbeams were bolted to the four iron posts, they used scaffolding planks to walk between the ladders. The heavy roof beams were angled and cut and fixed into place. They started to cut the rafters. The work was clean and pleasant. High up on the planks there was a cooling breeze from the lake. The noise of distant traffic on the road became part of the insect hum and the sharper singing of the birds. A wren or a robin would alight on one of the roof beams and look down on them as if they were sheep or cattle and fly back into the bushes. They had become so used to working together spasmodically over the years that they were often silent. When they talked, it was generally Patrick

Ryan who wanted to talk, and it was often mordant and funny, about people he had worked for or known. Now and again out of the silence would come without warning a seething, barely restrained urge to strike out and wound over a mislaid tool or a piece of wood. These violences would come and go and appeared both to fulfil and to exhaust themselves in their very expression.

'Johnny must be home by now,' Ruttledge remarked as they worked. 'He should be over on his visit any of these days.'

'I know, lad. I should have gone over to see him but I hate the sight of going though we were great friends. His was the worst case this part of the country ever saw. He left when he had the whole world at his feet.'

Once they started nailing the rafters, the frame to hold the roof took shape. Each new rafter formed its own square or rectangle, and from the ground they all held their own measure of sky; in the outer rectangles leaves from branches of overhanging ash and sycamore were mixed with the sky.

'What are you looking at, lad?'

'At how the rafters frame the sky. How the squares of light are more interesting than the open sky. They make it look more human by reducing the sky, and then the whole sky grows out from that small space.'

'As long as they hold the iron, lad, they'll do,' Patrick Ryan laughed sympathetically. 'There was a time when people were locked up for saying less than that. If you came out with a spake like that they'd think you had gone off like one of the old alarm clocks.'

A few mowers were starting up in the early meadows.

'I could mow for you this year, Patrick, when I get the mower out. I'm mowing for Jamesie,' Ruttledge offered as they worked.

'No, lad, no. I have plenty of clients who have asked. My meadows won't be fit for weeks yet and it would make no great differ if they were never mowed.'

71

Wisps of cloud trailed across the blue. Whenever the hammering stopped, the steady motor hum of insects met the shrilling of the small birds and the harsher cries of gulls and crows closer to the shore.

An approaching car was heard. They paused on the ladders to watch it move through the breaks in the trees.

'God almighty, this place is getting like O'Connell Street,' Patrick Ryan said when the car turned uphill from the lake.

A green Vauxhall came to a stop beneath the alder tree at the gate. Two burly middle-aged men got out.

'Trouble,' Patrick Ryan said. He quickly descended the ladder and hurried towards the gate as if he didn't want the men to come any closer. No handshakes or pleasantries were exchanged. The three men moved out into the lane until they were hidden by the high banks.

Ruttledge rearranged the planks and tidied the cut ends of the beams and rafters into a small heap for firewood. He was used to people looking for Patrick Ryan. Often he had seen him gather up his tools and leave with them in the middle of work. It had been galling once. Now he had come not to care. There was very little work that couldn't just as easily be left undone.

When they reappeared from behind the high banks of the lane, the two burly men got straight into the green Vauxhall and Patrick Ryan came slowly back to the shed. He was not in a good mood and stood staring up at the pattern of beams and rafters in sour abstraction.

'The longer you live the more you eat,' he said.

'What's wrong?'

'We should have put on the creosote.'

'We can still put it on from the ladders.'

'It'd be a sight easier if we'd had the wit to put it on before the timber left the ground.'

As they nailed the last of the rafters into place, Patrick Ryan appeared troubled or absentminded and made a number of small unusual errors.

'Who were those men?'

72

'A couple of certified thicks from the arsehole of Drumreilly. When they want anything done they think the only work in the world is their work.'

'Did they threaten you?'

'Put it this way, lad, they didn't offer me oranges,' he said.

The cans of creosote were taken from the shed and the dark liquid poured into two smaller paint cans. Ruttledge brought out two pairs of rubber gloves and offered them to Patrick Ryan.

'No, lad. You put on the gloves. My hide is too hard.'

'That stuff is dangerous. You can smell the fumes.'

'I've been plastering and painting all my life and never wore nothing. I'm not doing anything different now.'

They were high on the ladders, brushing the creosote into the raw timber, when Kate came from the house in a white beekeeper's suit and hat and veil. In her gloved hands she carried a brass smoker and a yellow hive tool. The smoker had been lit and breathed a pale smoke when she pressed the fan-like bellows.

'What's she up to now?'

'With that gear on you hardly need two guesses.'

'What can she be doing with the bees?' he asked aggressively.

'I don't know. We can ask her on the way back.'

He poured out creosote roughly, and as it ran across the beam it sprayed out in all directions from the violent brush strokes. One cheek bulged while his jaw worked slowly up and down as if he was eating his tongue. He was in foul humour again.

Kate was a long time in the orchard. When she reappeared she looked dishevelled and her long fair hair was flying about her face, smoke blowing from the brass nose of the smoker she carried awkwardly. She would have passed by quickly but Patrick Ryan called, 'How is the bees?'

'They're angry.'

'Were you afeard?'

'No.' She was taken aback by the mocking aggressiveness of the tone, and stopped. 'I could have gone through the hives but there was no point. They were boiling up. I *was* afraid.' Small beads of sweat glistened on her forehead when she looked up. One side of her neck was red and chaffed where she had been stung beneath the veil.

'What cause has the bees to be riz on a fine day the like of this in Ireland?'

'They didn't want me around. It wasn't a good idea.'

'What wasn't?'

'To go near the hives.'

She waited but Patrick Ryan went back to pouring the creosote out on the timber, spreading it roughly around with the brush. When a spray of the dark liquid fell dangerously close to where she stood, she moved quickly on without glance or word. The two men worked in silence, pouring the creosote, spreading it with the brush, moving the ladders.

'This creosoting from the ladders is one slow feck of a job,' Patrick complained as he moved the heavy ladder along the beam one more time. 'I'm away with myself out to the orchard here to cut a button.'

'I'd be careful of the hives,' Ruttledge warned.

'The bees won't bother me. My hide is too hard.'

'I'd still be careful.'

'No, lad, no. The bees won't bother me.'

He disappeared into the orchard, his cap worn jauntily back to front. His shoulders and back beneath the dirty white shirt were large and powerful but so perfectly proportioned that their strength was concealed.

Ruttledge continued creosoting. There was a mindless pleasure in brushing the dark liquid into the wood in the heat and the light breeze from the lake. In the far distance, the bucket of a mechanical digger clanged and pushed and clanged again.

Patrick Ryan's re-emergence into this slow mindlessness was like the eruptions of air that occur in the wheaten light of mown meadows in a heatwave. Dried grass and leaves, and even bits of sticks, are sent whirling high in a noisy spinning cylinder of dust and violent air, which then as quickly dies, to reappear like a mirage in another part of the meadow. With one hand he held up his trousers as he tried to run. His free hand swung his cap in a wild and furious arc as he attempted to beat away his tormentors. Whirling round to face the attacking bees, he beat out to left and right, but it was to no avail: he swung the cap round his head in a smaller despairing arc as he turned again and ran. The barely manageable trousers were bunched awkwardly around his ankles and with every fighting step he threatened to fall over. At the foot of the ladders he turned and stood. With his cap he beat away the single bees that zoomed in like dive-bombers. There was nothing Ruttledge could do. He had to beat away stray bees that came at him high on the ladder. A bee became entangled in his hair. Only very gradually did the attacks cease. At the foot of the ladders Patrick Ryan was slumped low but his breathing was growing easier. 'Double fuck those for fucken cunts of bees,' he cried out.

A buzzing came from his hair. With his cap he pummelled and crushed his head until the buzzing stopped. Ruttledge helped him search his shirt and trousers. There were even bees in his shoes. When Ruttledge shook free a number of bees trapped beneath the collar of his shirt, he called out angrily, 'Why didn't you kill the fuckers?'

'There was no need.'

'They should be all killed. They shouldn't be let around any house. I was sitting there with my trousers down thinking about the world to come when they came down on me like a fucken cloud.'

'Are you in much pain?'

'I tell you, lad, I wouldn't swap the pain for a place in heaven,' he grinned savagely. 'It'll pass. Everything does if you can wait long enough.'

'There's Blue in the house.'

'It'll do no good. We'll give them no heed. They'll go in their own time.'

'We'll dodge into the house for a break. They'll be more settled when we come back. I could do with a drink of water,' Ruttledge said.

It was cool within the house. The dark light was restful. No matter how Kate pressed Patrick Ryan, he would not allow her to examine or treat the stings.

'Not a blessed thing will do any good. Pay them no heed. Treat yer man if he wants,' he brushed all offers aside.

'My few stings are nothing,' Ruttledge said.

'Give me a good glass of whiskey instead,' Patrick Ryan said. A large glass was poured. He wanted neither water nor lemonade. 'Yer Irishman's morphine. May we all meet up in heaven. Am I having no company?' He raised his glass in salutation.

'It's too hot and I'm not in pain.' Ruttledge poured himself a small measure as a gesture and added much water. Kate had tea.

The pain forced Patrick Ryan to move and shift as he drank but his humour was improving by the minute. 'They came down on me like a cloud,' he said. 'The noise was worse than the darkness. No matter where you ran or turned they were around your head and you couldn't beat them away.'

'I'm sorry. I should have warned you,' Kate said. 'I never saw them so angry. I couldn't handle them, even with all the gear.'

'It wasn't your fault, Kate. Yer man here warned me but I paid no heed.'

He constantly moved and shifted on the chair as he spoke. He talked as if talk itself could ease the pain. He drank quickly and appeared not to notice when Kate refilled his glass.

He talked of a mowing accident that happened when he was a child. A man had been mowing a meadow with a young horse when the blade cut through a nest of wild red bees. The young horse was nervous. They say the bees can smell fear. They lighted on the poor horse. The man was luckily flung clear when the horse bolted. In no time the horse made bits of the shafts and traces before dropping down stone dead. Patrick Ryan had never laid eyes on the man or set foot in the meadow but he could see the man sitting on the single-bar mowing machine and the young horse and the big trees of an enclosed meadow as real, as real as if he had been there.

'The past and present are all the same in the mind,' Kate said. 'They are just pictures.'

'Are you sure you haven't been drinking, Kate?' Ruttledge asked.

'It must be the aspirins and the Blue,' she said and winked.

Patrick Ryan was so concentrated that the little exchange passed unnoticed.

'There were red bees and black bees. We used to raid the nests in the meadows and suck the honey. The red bees were the wickedest. The rotary mowers and the bag stuff took all the nests out of the meadows,' Patrick Ryan said as he rose gingerly. 'If we have any more of that painkiller we'll be falling from ladders. We'll go back to work in the name of God and his Blessed Mother.'

Outside, the bees were still flying around but they were no longer attacking. Patrick Ryan kept changing his weight from foot to foot on the rungs of the ladder but he never complained, all the time keeping up a flow of jokes and stories as if speech alleviated pain. In the silences, he whistled and recited nonsensical refrains and blasphemies. Solicitous enquiry was brushed aside.

'They are nothing. In another hour they won't even be heard tell of. They'll be clean forgot.'

A sudden sharp cough and a loud deliberate scraping of shoes on the gravel drew their eyes to a man wheeling a girl's bicycle towards the house, a cane basket on the handlebars. A pattern of knitted wool like a tea cosy covered the saddle. His head was bent low as if he was more animal or circus clown than man, his shoes lifting slowly to make exaggerated, comical steps over the gravel. His suit was a worsted blue. A red tie hung low. The bottoms of his trousers were stuffed into dark socks. His grey hair was darkened with oil and combed flat out across a receding hairline. As he wheeled the bicycle closer, his walk became slower and even more exaggerated, like an animal pawing uncertain ground.

'Johnny's home! Johnny's home from England!' Patrick Ryan cried.

Under the iron posts Johnny drew himself to his full height, pushed the bicycle away, where it wheeled perilously around before falling short of one of the posts, clicked his heels together, and saluted. 'Reporting for duty,' he called out.

The pain inflicted by the bees was cast aside as Patrick Ryan hurried down the ladder to go towards his old friend. 'Johnny. You never lost it, me oul' comrade.' They clasped hands high like athletes in victory and then held them still as if about to begin a trial of strength.

'They're all fucked,' Johnny sang.

'Except our Ellen,' Patrick Ryan took up as they danced round and round with clasped hands held high.

'And she's, and she's, and she's,' they sang out as they swung. 'And she's in Castle – Castlepollard,' they sang as they came to a breathless stop and cheered.

'You're welcome home. Welcome home from England.'

'Great to be home. Great to see yous all so well.'

'You're welcome home, Johnny,' Ruttledge took his hand.

'Great, great to see you. Herself is well?'

'She'll be delighted to see you.'

'I heard only yesterday,' Patrick Ryan said.

'It was all alphabetical,' Johnny said. 'Jamesie met the train per usual in Johnny Rowley's car. We stopped at several bars. When we got home Mary hopped the sirloin on the pan and it was like butter. Jamesie fell asleep at the Stanley and burned his forehead while we were eating. The scutching Mary gave him would do your heart good. In short, it was all quite alphabetical and couldn't be done any better. I borrowed Mary's bicycle here to cycle over to see yous all. It's great to see everybody looking so well.'

'You are still at Ford's in Dagenham?'

'Still at Ford's. In the canteen, hoovering up, keeping the toilets clean. You'd hardly call it work.'

'It must be better than being on the line,' Patrick Ryan said.

'The line was terrible. It did the old ears no good,' he indicated a pale plastic hearing aid attached to his left ear. 'That's how I got moved to the canteen.'

'You made the mistake of your life when you left here. You were in paradise and didn't know it. You went and threw it all away.'

'Maybe I did make a mistake,' Johnny assented blankly as if blankness alone could turn aside the judgement. 'Anyhow it's done now.'

'Patrick shows none of us any mercy,' Ruttledge said by way of comfort.

'I tell the truth and ask no favours.'

'The truth isn't always useful.'

'Tell me what is.'

'Kindness . . . understanding . . . sympathy maybe. I'll tell Kate Johnny is here. She'll want to get a few things ready.'

'Tell her to go to no trouble. I only cycled over to see that you are all well.'

'Go in,' Patrick Ryan said roughly to Ruttledge. 'And tell her we'll not be in for a while.'

'They're still here?' Johnny said when Ruttledge had gone.

'As large as life.'

'I never thought they'd last out. Every year I came home expecting to find them gone.'

'They're expanding,' Patrick Ryan gestured ironically towards the four iron posts holding the squares and rectangles of wood. 'I think we better make up our minds that they'll be here now like the rest of us till the hearse comes. They even bought more land, as if they hadn't enough.'

'I heard. Are they making any better shape of it?'

'They'd pass. You know yourself that you have to be born into land. That brother of yours kept them afloat in the beginning. Everything round the place are treated like royals. There's a black cat in there with white paws that'd nearly get up on its hind legs and order his breakfast. You'd not get thanked now if you got caught hitting it a dart of a kick on the quiet. The cattle come up to the back of the house and boo in like a trade union if the grass isn't up to standard. They reseeded meadows and had to buy sheep to crop the grass. They even got to like the sheep. There's no more stupid animal on God's earth. There's an old Shorthorn they milk for the house that would nearly sit in an armchair and put specs on to read the *Observer*. The bees nearly ate the arse off me an hour ago. She draws all that she sees. She even did a drawing of me.'

'What was it like?'

'You wouldn't hang it up on a wall now,' he said with a laugh. 'You wouldn't know whether I was man or beast.'

'She probably wears the britches. In England it's the women that mostly wears the britches. The men are too washed out to care.'

'Let me tell you. They'll all wear the britches wherever they're let. I've seen it all in house after house. That pair in there are different. They never seem to go against one another. There are times when they'd make you wonder whether they are man and woman at all.'

'Strange to think of all the people that went out to England and America and the ends of the earth from this place and yon pair coming back against the tide.'

'People had to go. They had no choice. You went and had no need to go.'

'I know. I know. I know.'

'You'd be on the pig's back now, lad, if you'd stayed.'

'We'd all be rich if we knew the result of tomorrow's races.'

'All around could see at the time and yet you couldn't see.'

'All around didn't count. We better, I suppose, in the name of God, go into the house.'

'Wait a minute,' Patrick Ryan said and proceeded to gather his tools – a spirit level, metal measuring tape, set square, a saw, a hammer, various chisels – into a brown hold-all.

'Another thing that brought them here was the quiet. Will you listen to the fucken quiet for a minute and see in the name of God if it wouldn't drive you mad?'

As if out of a deep memory of timing and ensemble playing, both men flung themselves into a comic, exaggerated attitude of listening, a hand cupped behind an ear, and stood as frozen as statues in a public place.

In the held minute, the birds seemed to sing more furiously in their branches. Bees laboured noisily between the stalks of red and white clover. Cattle lowed down by the lakeshore. Further away, cars and lorries passed on the main road and from further away still came the harsh, heavy clanging of a mechanical shovel as it cleared a hedgerow or dug the foundations of a house. As suddenly as they launched themselves into this burlesque of listening and stillness, they danced noisily free, cheered, clapped their hands and, taking one another's raised arm, danced awkwardly round and round an iron post.

They were both out of breath and Johnny looked distressed, sweating profusely but wonderfully revived in spirit. 'We better go in before we do any more damage,' he fought for breath as he laughed.

'If we stay out here any longer they might think we're talking about them,' Patrick Ryan said.

They went noisily into the house.

'You're welcome home, Johnny.'

'Great to be home, Kate. Great to see yous all well.'

A damp tea towel covered squares of sandwiches. She took the towel from the yellow platter and placed it on a chair between the two men. Ruttledge poured rum from a dust-covered bottle into a glass and added blackcurrant concentrate.

'Rum and black,' Johnny said as he took the glass. 'You shouldn't have gone to so much trouble. A whiskey would have done just as well.'

'The bottle nearly waits for you from one year to the next. Very few around take rum except maybe one or two at Christmas.'

'As soon as I walk into the Prince of Wales they hop up the rum and black on the counter before the regulars have even time to lift their glasses,' Johnny said.

'I don't know where you got the taste,' Patrick Ryan said. 'You even drank rum before you left.'

Ruttledge poured Patrick Ryan a large glass of whiskey and added water from the brown jug. Kate shook her head to his silent enquiry. He poured himself a whiskey and drank with the men.

'Good health.'

'And more again tomorrow, with the help of God, as Jamesie says.'

'Good luck and cheers.'

'"Lord, son, don't cheer in here or we'll get put out," as Pee Maguire said to his English son-in-law after buying him his first pint down in the pub,' Patrick Ryan joked.

As none of the men had reached for the sandwiches, Kate handed the platter around while the glasses were being refilled.

'These sandwiches are beautiful, Kate,' Johnny said.

'It's great to see you home, Johnny,' Kate repeated.

'Johnny here was the best shot this part of the country ever saw,' Patrick Ryan said. 'When all the guns were going left and right all he had to do was raise his gun for the bird to fall like a stone.'

'Nowadays I wouldn't hit the back of a house,' Johnny said. 'A few summers ago I took up Jamesie's gun against a few grey crows. I couldn't hit a thing.'

'It would still come back with practice.'

'I doubt that. It's gone,' he said simply. 'Patrick here was the best this part of the country has ever seen in the plays. He was the star.'

'I would have been nothing without the others,' Patrick could not hide his pleasure. 'All of us were good. The two of us played off one another. There was many who said you couldn't pick between us.'

'In Athlone when we won the Confined Cup it was Patrick who was singled out. I was sometimes mentioned in dispatches but I never won anything.'

'It's matterless who won or didn't win. We all won in Athlone and weren't sober for a whole week.'

Warmed by the rum and whiskey and the memory of the lost halls, both men felt an intensity of feeling and affection that the passing day could not long sustain.

'How is England?' Patrick Ryan demanded roughly.

'England never changes much. They have a set way of doing everything there. It's all more or less alphabetical in England.'

'Not like this fucken place. You never know what your Irishman is going to do next. What's more, the chances are he doesn't know either.'

'Everybody has their own way. There are times when maybe the English can be too methodical,' Johnny said.

'No danger of that here. There's no manners.'

'Some people here have beautiful manners,' Kate protested.

'Maybe a few,' Patrick Ryan admitted grudgingly. 'But there's no rules. They're all making it up as they sail along.'

'Are you still in the same house in England?' Ruttledge asked.

'The same house. On Edward Road. A room on the top floor. Sometimes it's a bit of a puff to climb the stairs but it's better than having someone over your head. I had a room in Fairlop once and there was a Pole in the room overhead. Lord bless us you'd swear he was on death row, up and down, up and down, even in the middle of the night, it'd nearly start you walking yourself. The room on Edward is a good-size room with a big window. You can watch the lights come on in the Prince.'

Suddenly, as if he was seeing Johnny's high room for the first time and able to look all the way down Edward Road from the big window to the Prince of Wales, Patrick Ryan was drawn to the room in the same way he was drawn to strangers and started asking about the room and the house and the people in the other rooms.

'I'm sure I told it all before. I'm going on five years in the room on Edward Road,' Johnny said.

'Go ahead. There's nothing new in the world. And we forget. We'll hear it again,' Patrick Ryan demanded.

There was a table in the room, a high-backed chair, a single bed, an armchair for reading and listening to the radio, a gas fire in the small grate. On the mantel above the grate he always kept a pile of coins for the meter on the landing. A gas cooker and a sink were in the corner of the room inside the door. He didn't have a television. He saw all the TV he wanted in the canteen at work and at weekends in the betting shop or in the Prince of Wales.

'Mister Singh owns the house. He's an Indian and drives a Merc and owns several houses. All the rich Indians drive Mercs. On Thursday nights he collects the rents personally. If there's anything wrong – a broken gas ring, an electric socket – you tell Mister Singh on Thursday night and it's fixed pronto. The Indians are a very alphabetical people. Mister Singh doesn't drink, very few Indians drink, it is forbidden in their religion. A Jock and a Taffie have rooms in the house but all the rest are Irish and all but two of the Irish are Murphy Fusiliers. Mister Singh rents only to single men: no marrieds, no women, no coloureds.'

'Mister Singh must be coloured himself,' Kate said.

'That makes no differ, Kate. It's business. Mister Singh said to me once, "Even in Ireland you don't mix robins with blackbirds." There was a pufter there for a while, English, but he ran into trouble with the Fusiliers. The Fusiliers only sleep in the house. A minibus collects them early. They work a lot around the airport and in tunnels. Most of them go straight from work to the pub without a change of clothes. They work at weekends as well. I don't think any of them ever darkens a church. They make big money. A few of the married men are careful enough because they send money home but most let it go in smoke. Some of them get badly hurt from time to time. I heard a few were killed. They stand by one another then and take collections. A lot complains about the Fusiliers but I can find no fault. They used to give me their money to hand to Mister Singh on Thursday night and now I collect for the whole house. It suits all round. The Fusiliers are all big strong men.'

'I can't see them and the pufter making much hay together,' Patrick Ryan grinned.

'I don't know what happened,' Johnny said firmly. 'There was a good-looking black-haired lad from the Galway Gaeltacht in the Fusiliers that the pufter tried to get friendly with. Anyhow he was taken away in an ambulance. The police were around. Mister Singh didn't like that. Anyhow nothing came of it. The Galway lad left soon afterwards as well. The canteen in Ford's is an easy number, clearing the tables, keeping the floors and the toilets clean, taking the bets down to the betting shop for the men on the line.'

'How is the hearing?'

'I often hear more than I want,' he said.

'Still, anything must be better than the fucken assembly line.'

'The noise was terrible but you get used. Time passes quickly on the line. You have no time to think. You're too busy. Time is often slow enough around the canteen. But I know I'm lucky to be there at all.'

'I suppose the evenings are hard enough to put round as well,' Patrick Ryan said.

'They're all right. As long as you have a plan,' Johnny said. 'I sometimes take a light kip. Once I get up I wash and shave and change into new clothes. That's the one thing I hold against the Fusiliers. They never change their clothes from morning till they fall into bed. If the darts team is playing away I go down to the Prince early. There's always plenty of transport. If we're playing at home I go down around eight-thirty and when there's no game I dawnder down at nine. They all know me in the Prince. Saturdays and Sundays I lie in late. I always have a few bets on Saturday after going through the *Post*. Sundays I never miss evening Mass at St Ann's. Father Wrynn is the priest there. He's from Drumshambo. I wait behind after Mass and if he's not busy we have a long chat about home. We always have the joke how there's no getting away from the Drumshambo wind no matter how far you travel.'

'I knew Father Wrynn's poor father and mother well,' Patrick Ryan said with feeling. 'At that time you had to be rich to have a priest in the family. The Wrynns weren't rich but they worked every hour God sent. They thought they were entering heaven the day Father Wrynn was ordained.'

'The son isn't a bit religious. I talk to him nearly every Sunday,' Johnny said. 'Anyhow all the priests in England are sociable. They are not directly connected to God like the crowd here.'

'Father Conroy isn't like that,' Ruttledge intervened.

'Father Conroy is plain. The priests had this country abulling with religion once. It's a good job it's easing off,' Patrick Ryan said.

'At Christmas I go up on the train to Josie Connor in Birmingham. I always bring the turkey and a few bottles of Powers. We go over everything that ever happened round the lake. Anne and Josie are pure fourteen-carat. They always write to me well before Christmas. It'd be a lonesome oul Christmas Day looking down a deserted Edward Road with the Prince closed all day and a few people going by carrying presents.'

'All the Connors were decent, as decent as ever wore shoe leather. Even when they lived on the edge of the bog they'd give you what they didn't have for themselves,' Patrick Ryan said emotionally from the whiskey. 'And Anne's crowd, the Dohertys, were near enough the same cut of cloth. They'd give you as well what they didn't have for themselves.'

A fat bullfinch came into view and began to peck at the small wild strawberries on the bank. The black cat was sleeping in the window but tensed when its attention was drawn to the small bird's darting movements as it hopped about like a mechanical toy among the ferns and grasses.

'That's a great cat,' Patrick Ryan said sarcastically. 'She'd like if she was handed the bird and given a knife and fork.'

'Half the pleasure of the wild strawberries is watching the finch,' Kate said. 'I'm glad the cat is in the house.'

'I'd side with Kate,' Johnny said. 'I must have shot every game bird that ever moved. Now I'd sooner see them flying around.'

'I wouldn't,' Patrick Ryan said. 'I'd shoot the lot.'

'How is Bill Evans this weather?' Johnny asked.

'As large as life. He still goes to the lake for the buckets of water.'

'That's one man who has earned his place in heaven,' Johnny said.

'Jesus Christ had nothing on Bill Evans except Bill was never put up on a cross. He has had a better time since his Master Packie died. You wouldn't call it heaven now but it's a big improvement on what went before,' Patrick Ryan said.

Johnny and Patrick exchanged cigarettes, sharing the single match Johnny had struck. Patrick Ryan's face lit in a strange childlike peace as he reached into the flame, as if they were in possession again of that old warm world that was once theirs together. It could not last. As soon as he took the last quick draw on the cigarette, he thrust the butt towards Ruttledge without preamble or warning.

'Throw that out on the street for me, lad.'

Ruttledge did not speak or move. The air filled with the tension of uncertainty. The low murmur of summer outside the house that had gone unheeded entered the room, the blundering of a big black fly against the window on the bank from which the finch had disappeared was suddenly loud.

Ruttledge rose slowly and bowed. 'At your service, sir,' and took the smouldering butt and opened the door of the unlit brown Raeburn and threw it in. He was too familiar with these demands to be hurried. He had seen him make supplicants who needed his skills carry his coat and tools as abjectly as slaves.

'You wouldn't have made a bad actor, lad,' he laughed uncomfortably as Ruttledge closed the door of the stove; but the room stayed silent.

'I should have put out an ashtray,' Kate said.

Johnny had already slapped his quenched cigarette into his pocket. 'Thanks for everything,' he rose and placed his glass on the table. 'It's great to see yous all so well after another year.'

'Thanks for coming over,' they answered. 'It was great to see you again.'

'I'm going. I'll not be back for a while,' Patrick Ryan said, his anger still raw from the unsatisfactory confrontation. 'You'll have plenty of time to finish the creosoting. That way you'll not have to worry about the rain on the timber.'

'That'll be all right.'

'What'll be all right?'

'Everything. The creosoting – everything,' Ruttledge answered.

'It won't be all right but it'll have to do,' Patrick Ryan said.

'Would you ever think of coming back for good when you retire from Ford's?' Kate asked as they saw them to the gate.

'I don't know, Kate. You get used to England. When you cut your stick and make your bed you have to lie on it,' he said.

'It wouldn't work out,' Patrick Ryan said. 'He'd know nobody here now.'

'Be sure and remember us to Mary and Jamesie.'

'Will do,' he responded jauntily, his English accent showing.

88

'I suppose you have many calls to make.'

'Not too many, Kate. Just a few and there are fewer every year. That's why it's great to see everybody so well.'

Patrick Ryan picked up his bundle of tools. Johnny wheeled the girl's bicycle. The two men seemed to fall into spirited conversation as they went downhill to the corner of the lake. Twice they paused. There was the clear ring of laughter in the voices.

Once all the timbers were creosoted the frame stood like a dark, ungainly skeleton high on the four posts. As Ruttledge was tidying up, Kate passed outside the ladders to check that the hive roofs hadn't been dislodged in the disturbance of the previous day. The bees were working quietly.

On Sunday the black Mercedes rolled round the shore, bringing an enormous box of chocolates wrapped with blue ribbon for Kate and a small metal box with handles. The metal was the colour of grass and mud and looked like military surplus.

'I see the cathedral is coming along,' the Shah said as he eased himself out of the front seat.

'Probably it'll stay that way for a while now. He's gone again. God knows when he'll be back.'

'I told you long ago he should be run.'

'I'd say yes to that,' Kate said.

'Now you're talking.'

He handed Kate the chocolates and she thanked him, protesting that it was too much.

'That'll do you now,' he said. 'It's not one bit too much.'

'What's in the strange box?' Ruttledge asked.

'I'm going on a bit of a holiday and leaving this here,' he announced as he placed the metal box on the table. He had never gone on holiday, unless three days many years before on Lough Derg counted as a holiday. From time to time he would recall how much he had suffered: the cold, the wet, the lack of sleep, the never-ending circle of prayer in bare feet, the hunger, the sharp stones. 'If hell is anything like it I'm sticking to the straight and narrow.' The one hot Sunday or two he drove to the ocean at Bundoran every year to wallow in the waves and lie in the sun until he was burned pink hardly counted as holiday.

'I'm going to Donegal, to Burtonport,' he said. 'I'm bringing Monica and the children. The poor thing needs taking out of herself.'

Monica was his favourite niece, a tall, dark-haired, intelligent woman with four children. Her husband had been a successful businessman, extrovert and popular, an overweight, gentle giant of a man. They had made a striking couple. 'He was warned and gave no heed and paid the price. He just keeled over,' the Shah said with some satisfaction, as he too had been warned about his weight. The difference was that he had started to eat grapefruit in the morning, the one meal he never cared for, as someone told him they reduced weight. He bought them by the boxful. They did not affect his weight but they allowed him to enjoy the enormous meals he ate in the Central with a clear conscience. 'I told him about the grapefruit but all he did was laugh. He learned.'

The couple had been close. In spite of the sudden loss, Monica had taken over the parts of the business she could handle while bringing up the children and sold off other parts she felt she couldn't manage on her own.

'She's doing middling,' he admitted reluctantly. 'There's too many around her. She needs to get away.'

'What have you in the box?'

'Money.'

'Why isn't it in the bank?'

'There's enough money in the bank,' he said defensively. 'The tax man has a habit of peeping into banks.'

'What are you going to do with it?'

'Leave it here till I get back,' he said, and placed a key beside the box.

'How much is there?'

'There must be near thirty thousand,' he admitted reluctantly.

'We are going to count it,' Ruttledge said decisively. The Shah protested, but Ruttledge was determined: he would not allow room for suspicion.

In the bedroom, with the curtains drawn, they counted out the money like a pair of thieves. The metal box contained more than forty-three thousand pounds.

'You could buy a house and land with this. You could get married. You could start a life. You could go to Africa or America,' Ruttledge said as he prepared to put the box away. 'It's there like strength.'

'It's better than the other fella having it, anyhow,' the Shah agreed uncertainly; and Ruttledge decided not to protest or joke any further.

There was no time to walk the fields. The time had disappeared in the slow counting.

He ate in silence from a large white plate: sausage, rasher, grilled halves of tomato, mushrooms, onion, black pudding, a thin slice of liver, a grilled lamb chop. From another plate he drew and buttered slices of freshly baked soda bread. By his chair the sheepdog sat in patient expectation. As always, the movements of the Shah's hands were delicate.

'Is it all right?' he enquired politely when he finished.

'Of course,' Kate nodded and he gave what was left on the plate to the sheepdog.

With an audible sigh of satisfaction he reached for the slice of apple tart, the crust sprinkled with fine sugar. He poured cream from a small white jug. He drank from the mug of steaming tea. 'God bless you, Kate,' he said as he rose and reached for his cap. 'You'll not see me now for a while.'

'Have a great time in Burtonport.'

'I doubt if it'll be great,' he said, 'but we'll be there anyhow.'

With little warning the weather broke, not in the usual summer showers but in a sustained downpour, with rumbles of distant thunder and quick lightning flashes above the fields and lake. The black cat grew agitated and cowered in a corner by the cooker, protected by the rocking chair. Out in the wet air the sound of water rushing towards the lake was loud in all the drains. When the storm ended, the broken weather continued with high winds and showers.

The days disappeared in attendance on small tasks. The fly struck the lambs a second time. An old sheep was found on her back, two small lambs by her side: if she had remained as she was their life was gone. When righted, she staggered around in a circle and fell a number of times. Once she regained her balance, she checked that the lambs were hers before allowing them the joyous frenzy of their suck. Weeds had to be pulled in the garden; carrots, lettuce, onion, beets, parsnips were thinned; the beanstalks supported, the peas staked, the potato stalks and the fruit trees sprayed. These evenings they ate late. In the soft light the room seemed to grow green and enormous as it reached out to the fields and the crowns of the trees, the green banks and the meadow and trees to enter the room with the whole fullness and weight of summer.

'It's ages since we've seen Mary and Jamesie,' Kate said one evening. 'Why don't we walk round the lake? Johnny must have gone back to England by now.'

Below the Ruttledges' stood the entrance to the house where Mary had grown up on the edge of the lake, its stone walls and outhouses hidden in the tall trees. In the middle of the living room an ash tree had taken root where they had played cards and said the Rosary in the evenings before raking the ashes over the red coals; but it was still easy to see what a charming, beautiful place the living house had been, a stone's throw from the water. The blue of the pieces of broken delph in the shallows of the lake out from the piers even spoke of prosperity and ease. Cherry and apple and pear trees grew wild about the house, and here and there the fresh green of the gooseberry shone out of a wilderness of crawling blackthorn. Hundreds of daffodils and white narcissi still greeted each spring by the lake with beauty, though there was no one near at hand to notice.

As a schoolgirl Mary had fallen in love with Jamesie and had eyes for no other man. He used to come round the shore on his battered bicycle. She was always waiting. Their courtship could not have been more different from the harsh lesson Johnny had received.

On their marriage she moved to Jamesie's house across the lake. Jamesie's father left the upper room where he had slept since his own marriage, to take up Jamesie's single bed in the lower room, across from where Johnny slept beneath the window.

Vases of flowers appeared on windowsills and tables. There were touches of colour in bedspreads and chair coverings she brought with her from her own house. Linen for the beds was washed and aired and ironed and changed regularly. The meals were suddenly delicious after the old rough cooking. The house had always been cleanly kept but now it sparkled.

For years she had waited for him. Now she was with him. This was her new life, but in her joy she discovered a fresh anxiety. She had to leave that other house she also loved, her father and her young brother. In spite of their insistence that they could manage, she baked bread for the two houses and brought the loaves around the lake a couple of times a week.

Every Thursday her father drove into town in the pony and trap. When he had the shopping done he went to Hoy's Hotel, which was owned by his cousin, and drank several glasses of their best whiskey, an eighteen-year-old White Powers, while engaged in agreeable conversation with Mister Hoy about politics and the political party to which they both belonged. Then the pony took him home. Unless there was wind or heavy rain he was always seen to be asleep in a corner of the trap as they passed between the two bars in Shruhaun. There was so little traffic on the roads, his nature so unassuming and easygoing, his little weakness so well known, that this quiet passage drew no more attention than affectionate smiles of recognition. No one even shouted a mischievous greeting. Generally, he woke coming in round the shore, the pony's pace quickening in anticipation of being released from the trap and watered and given hay and oats. If the quick change of pace hadn't woken him, he would be quickly shaken awake by the rutted road.

On Thursdays, no matter what the weather, she could not resist going out to the brow of the hill with the two dogs about the time the pony was due to turn in round the shore. She would breathe with relief as soon as the trap appeared and the pony started to gallop. She followed it all the way to the house till their dog began to bark: 'That will surely wake him now if he's not awake already. I wish all people knew their business as well as that brown pony.'

When Jamesie teased her about going out to the brow of the hill, she was silent: she was beginning to understand that to be without anxiety was to be without love and that it could not be shared. She was content and happy that her first and older love, who had never spoken a harsh word to her in all the days of her girlhood, was safely home and sleeping off his Thursday in the big bed with the broken brass bells.

Then the world she had left, little by little, began to disappear. On a wet soft evening in October, veils of mist and light rain obscuring the hills as well as the water, the pony trotted safely home from the Thursday outing to the town, but the life in the trap had died somewhere along the road. She had been too young to feel her mother's death. This was her first great loss, and she was inconsolable.

'No man had a luckier life. A good wife. Children that worked and were no trouble. Not a day sick. Then, to slip away after several glasses of White Powers after a good chat about politics with Ned Hoy, do you think the rest of us are likely to get out so easy? Can you tell me an easier way?' Jamesie tried to reason her out of her grief.

In a year the house was closed. Her brother Tom had a girl from Kesh who had gone out to an aunt in Boston. They had been writing to one another. At Halloween he left for Boston and they were married there. He gave Mary the choice of anything she wanted from the house. She took only a few things for his sake.

On a mild October Saturday, when the nuts were ripe on the hazel trees, the auction was held on the shore. A great crowd gathered. Everything was sold: the mowing machine, the plough, the heavy red dresser, all the cattle, the pony, the harness, the trap. She didn't attend or even go to the brow of the hill to look across at the crowd gathered. She asked Jamesie to bid for all the brown hens and the red Shorthorn she used to milk for the house. When Jamesie arrived triumphantly home with the small cow and the crate of clucking hens, they seemed like poor scattered things from a broken world. By morning she was too busy to dwell on it any further. She was pregnant and had the house and three men to care for. The birth was difficult but she was strong and recovered quickly. The boy was christened James after his father and grandfather though Jamesie offered to name the child after Mary's own father.

Because of the boy and the expectancy of other children, it was decided to add an extra room to the house. Patrick Ryan was starting to build at the time and was as much around the place during the building as the men who lived in the house. Johnny and he were acting in plays at the time and often acted out their parts as they worked.

The Ruttledges felt that the spirit of that roofless house by the water's edge had never died but simply moved to the other house across the lake they were walking towards. From the lake gate they climbed to the brow of the hill. From there the pass ran along a low mossy bank down to the house in its ragged shelter of trees, alder mostly, lilac and a few ash, none of them large. The sheepdog and red terrier, Ruff and Bobby, met them at the second iron gate, barking fiercely; but when they spoke the dogs wagged and nosed their recognition and escorted them down to the house. The brown hens were behind the netting wire. There were many flowers, nasturtiums, sweet williams, lilies, climbing roses. The wall of the house and outhouses had been freshly whitewashed, the doors painted a deep red, window frames a brighter, harsher green than the softly glowing green of the meadows. The room Patrick Ryan built at a right angle to the old house was slated. Sheets of asbestos had replaced the thatch on the original three rooms. On the black windowsills stood little wooden boxes of flowers, velvety pansies and geraniums. The door of the house was open but the silence was so great that the clocks could be heard ticking within. They knew that they had been recognized by the barking of the dogs and were being waited for. They knocked playfully and knocked again.

'Come in if you're good-looking.'

'We're not. What will we do?'

'Too bad. You'll have to stay outside.'

'Pay no heed to yon omadhaun. He'd disgrace a holy saint,' Mary came towards them with two hands of welcome and kissed them both on the mouth.

'Kate,' Jamesie demanded with his enormous hand. 'God hates a coward. The brave man dies but once.'

'I'm a weak woman, Jamesie.'

'You're not one bit weak.' She gave him her hand. When she cried 'Careful, Jamesie,' he released his gently tightening grip with a low cry of triumph. 'You are one of God's troopers, Kate. You are welcome.' He bowed to Ruttledge like a formal clown. 'I never liked you anyhow.'

'I am honoured,' Ruttledge bowed in return.

After the glaring light of evening on the lake, the room with the one small window looking south was dark even with the door open. They did not see the grandchild Margaret seated on a low stool between Mary's chair and the yellow cooker with the shining rail. She was a beautiful dark-haired child, with very pale skin and eyes the colour of sloes. Ruttledge lifted her high in affection and welcome to see how she had grown since the summer before.

'You can't be doing that any more. She has boys,' Jamesie teased.

'I have no boys.'

'Lots of boys. All nice and cuddly. Very nice-mannered boys,' he thrust his tongue out provocatively and pretended to hide his head under his arms while she cuffed him officiously.

'The other three went with the parents on their holiday but Margaret came to us. Isn't that right?' Mary said, stroking her hair with affection, and the child nodded gravely as she leaned closer.

'Where did they go to?' Kate asked.

'They went,' Jamesie said authoritatively, but couldn't remember. 'They went – you know – out there – somewhere foreign,' he said with a great sweep of his arms.

Both the child and Mary began to laugh. 'Out there, somewhere,' Mary repeated mockingly. 'They took a house for three weeks near Florence. Do you have any idea where Italy is?'

'It's out there – somewhere,' he said defensively and shook his fist at Margaret.

'Do you have any earthly idea where Italy is? I declare to God he doesn't know the difference between Florence and Mullingar. You couldn't take him anywhere.'

'They're all out there somewhere anyhow. We are not a bit bothered about them,' he said grandly, recovering his poise. 'Have you any news?'

'No news. I suppose Johnny is back in England by now.'

'Long back.'

'And poor Edmund is gone. He was buried yesterday. May the Lord have mercy,' Mary said softly.

'I never heard. I'd have gone to the funeral if I'd known,' Ruttledge said, taken aback. 'I was fond of Edmund.'

'We were all fond of Edmund. You'd have heard if you were at Mass,' Jamesie said gently. 'That's what you get for not going to Mass.'

'You could have told me,' Ruttledge said.

Jamesie felt the reproach and became uncertain: he was always uncomfortable when appearing in any mean or poor light.

'He wanted to go for you,' Mary said carefully, 'but Patrick didn't want. He said you weren't needed.'

'I should have paid no heed. Patrick would sicken your arse. He wants his own way in everything,' he rested his hand briefly on Ruttledge's shoulder. 'I should have said nothing and just gone over. He'd never have known.'

'Don't worry. I was fond of Edmund but it makes no difference now.'

'There was no wake. He went straight from the hospital to the church. All that was bothering Patrick was all the important people that turned up, doctors and big builders and politicians, people he worked for. He was pure silly buying them drinks and shaking their hands and looking them straight in the eye and brushing the odd tear away. You'd swear it meant something. Up in their arses he'd go if he was let. He had no time for me and he'd have no time for you either if you were there.'

'You should know Patrick by now. He wasn't going to behave any different,' Mary said as if she felt the blame to be excessive. 'I suppose if the truth was told they *did* turn up because of Patrick. Who knew poor Edmund?'

'We knew him,' Jamesie responded angrily. 'There are times when the truth is the wrong thing.'

'We don't count,' she replied firmly.

'Lies can walk while the truth stays grounded,' Ruttledge said.

'Patrick had no value on Edmund. When he was alive he let the roof of the house fall to be rid of the poor fella.'

'They say the only people missed Edmund was the dog and old Mrs Logan. The dog is pining since the day he went to the hospital, comes and goes between the gate and the house looking for him, and the poor woman is lost. She took him in when the roof fell. He did everything for her around the place. They cared a sight for one another.'

'Did she go to the funeral?'

'The poor thing wasn't fit,' Mary smiled a sweet, inward-looking smile. 'Anyhow Patrick wouldn't want her. There's another person who died, John Quinn's second wife. John turned up at the funeral though he wasn't wanted. They didn't let him into the house but he marched up the chapel with the coffin and knelt in the front seat and shook hands with everybody and went into the solicitor afterwards to see if there was any window through which he could get his hands on money.'

'John is a sight. It'll be no time till he's marrying again. God never closed one door but he opened another.' Jamesie rubbed his hands together gleefully and made a similarly playful gesture towards Mary that he had enough of talking and needed a drink. She answered with a ritualistically disapproving gesture as she went slowly to the press and took out a bottle of Powers. Kate asked for tea but Mary persuaded her that they would both have a light hot whiskey. While they were being made the small airy room filled with the scent of cloves and lemon. Margaret had a large glass of lemonade.

'Good luck and more again tomorrow and may we never die.'

'And Johnny has gone back to England after another summer,' Ruttledge said.

'The train from Dromod. Two drinks in the bar across from the station waiting for the train that you'd be as well without. There's nothing to celebrate seeing someone going. Margaret's father met the train, left him at the airport.'

'I hate to say but I wasn't sorry,' Mary said. 'I had Johnny for most of the whole day every day.'

'He was very good company when he was over on his visit.'

'All these fellas know how to play when they are out,' Jamesie raised his hand. 'There's a big differ between visiting and belonging.'

'Even when he wasn't talking it was hard seeing him, remembering all that happened,' Mary said. 'He thought he could not live without her. At this table he used to put his head down in his arms and cry without crying. There he was a few days ago doing the crosswords or marking the racing pages if he wasn't talking.'

'Anna Mulvey must have been beautiful to have set anybody so far astray?'

'No. There were plenty better looking but she was far ahead of what's beautiful. Tall, with long black hair, long back, sharp face. All the Mulveys had a swing and an air. *The Playboy* it was that brought them together. Anna had never any interest in Johnny. She was even two-timing him with Peadar Curran when *The Playboy* was still on. He had me nearly driven out of my mind when she tried to break it off. Walking up and down, talking, talking, not able to eat, not able to sit for a minute,' Mary said.

'There were times we got afraid. We didn't know what he'd do if he got to know about Peadar.'

'Then he did get to hear,' Mary said.

'Hugh Brady went and told him when he should have packed him with lies like everybody else. He frightened poor Brady into telling. Johnny went straight from Brady to Anna and she swore she had nothing to do with Curran or any other man. Johnny was like putty in her hands. He went back and devoured Brady for spreading rumours and lies. It was a God's charity. Omadhauns like Brady are a living danger.

'Peadar Curran went to England. That was one torment less for Johnny. There was nothing much special about his going. Everybody was going to England. He may have gone as well because the business with Anna was getting too warm for comfort. Peadar was always careful.'

'Anna was seeing Johnny but only to keep him pacified.'

'Anna was the next for England. We thought it was to get away from Johnny. The Mulveys were well off and she didn't have to go. She went after Peadar.'

'How did Johnny take her going?'

'What could he do? By then he was grasping at every straw. She promised to write.'

'Anna got a land in England. The good Peadar had another woman. Then Anna started writing to Johnny. Johnny was delirious for those letters.'

'Instead of waiting for the post to come to the house he'd go round to meet the postman. He'd stop him on the road and make him search through the letters. Then when she wrote that she missed him and wanted him to come to England I don't think his feet touched the ground for days.'

'Then he shot the poor gundogs, Oscar and Bran,' Mary said quietly. 'I used to feed those dogs. They were beautiful.'

'Far better if he'd shot himself or rowed out into the middle of the lake with a stone around his neck,' Jamesie said.

'All this because Anna happened to be in *The Playboy*?'

'She was probably the worst of them as far as the acting went but you couldn't take your eyes off her while she was on the stage.'

'Johnny used to get me to read out her lines for him when he was practising his part,' Mary said.

'Can you remember any of them?'

'Not a single line, except it was terrible old eejity stuff,' Mary smiled. 'Especially when you'd compare it to what was happening under your eyes.'

'*It's Pegeen I'm seeing only, and what'd I care if you brought me a drift of chosen females, standing in their shifts itself, maybe from this place to the Eastern world*?' Ruttledge quoted.

'That's it. Terrible eejity stuff,' Mary said.

'When it was new it had power enough to get people very exercised and excited,' Ruttledge said.

'It's easy to get people excited,' Jamesie said dismissively. 'Was I like that when I was going round the lake on the bicycle trying to get at you, Mary?'

'You hardly cared. You were far too interested in everything else that was going on. I was the big booboo. What did I ever see in him, Margaret?' She put her hand on the girl's hair.

'Did you see my Jamesie?' he mimicked, rubbing his hands together. 'Those were the days, Mary. You loved me then.'

'Love,' Mary repeated. 'Love flies out the window.'

'When someone falls like Johnny, it guarantees suffering,' Kate said.

'Isn't that what courting is all about? It's finding out,' Mary said. 'Those too bound up with themselves will get their eyes opened.'

'Even the clever ones can get nabbed. While they're circling and beating about,' Jamesie said. 'Is that how this fella was nabbed, Kate?'

'No,' she laughed. 'We worked for the same firm in different departments, on different floors. We hardly spoke. I never thought about him in any way in particular other than it was unusual to have someone Irish working in the firm.'

'Robert Booth was Irish. He gave me the job,' Ruttledge said.

'You'd never think of Robert as Irish,' Kate said. 'He went to acting school to get rid of his accent.'

'Don't let him sidetrack you, Kate. We want the low-down on how he was nabbed. We want the feathers,' Jamesie said.

'Don't tell him, Kate,' Ruttledge warned playfully.

'One day our copying machine wasn't working and I went down to his floor to do some copying. We knew one another's names and we probably would have exchanged a few words from time to time. Out of the blue he said, "You have very nice legs, Kate."'

Jamesie cheered as if a goal had been scored, while Margaret wagged her finger at him with the solemnity of the pendulums of one of the clocks.

'Sexy. He was the sleepy fox lying in the grass, all that time waiting to pounce,' Jamesie said.

'He'd disgrace you,' Mary said.

'Don't tell him, Kate,' Ruttledge said. 'It'll be all over the country.'

'Pay no heed to him either. It's a charity to show them up,' Mary said.

'You can't get on without us either,' Jamesie asserted.

'Then we met in the lift on the way out of work – I think I might have engineered that – and he invited me for a drink. It was November, it was raining. We went to the Old Wine Shades, a wine bar near the river, not far from the office. We had a bottle of red wine – I hardly ever took a drink then – with a plate of white cheddar and crackers.'

'I don't know how you can drink that red wine. It tastes like pure poison. Yer man here was trying to get behind the fence.'

'I think I was doing the same, Jamesie.'

He gave a small cheer of approval.

'And then that was Him who was married to Her. Margaret will be heading out into all this soon. All those boys, nice and cuddly.' The granddaughter gave him a light blow and he pretended to hide behind the shield of his huge arms.

'Margaret must think us all a terrible crowd of donkeys,' Mary said and drew her into the crook of her arm. 'What would her father and mother say?'

All through the evening the pendulum clocks struck. There were seven or eight in the house, most of them on the walls of the upper room. The clocks struck the hours and half-hours irregularly, one or other of them chiming every few minutes.

'Are any of those clocks telling the right time?' Ruttledge asked, looking up, when he felt it was time to leave.

'What hurry's on you?' Jamesie countered quickly. 'Isn't the evening long? It's ages since ye were over.'

Unnoticed, Mary had made sandwiches with ham and lettuce and tomato, cut into small squares. As they were handed round, Ruttledge joined Jamesie in another whiskey. Kate and Mary had tea with Margaret.

'I keep those clocks wound,' Mary said. 'I don't know how to set them. We should get the little watchmaker to the house one of these days to clean and oil the parts and to set all the clocks. Jamesie's father was a sight for clocks. He'd go to hell if there was one at an auction. He was able to set them perfect. I just keep them wound. You get used to the sound.'

'Who cares about time? We know the time well enough,' Jamesie said. 'Do you have any more news now before you go?'

'None. Unless the Shah going on holidays qualifies for news.'

'The Shah gone on his holidays. Lord bless us,' Jamesie said in open amazement.

'Did he ever go on holidays in his life before?' Mary asked, the more sharply amused.

'Once, to Lough Derg years ago. This time he's gone in the same direction but to an hotel beside the ocean.'

'He must be surely ravelling in spite of his money. He won't know what to do with himself.'

'He went with Monica, that cousin of mine who lost her husband. The four children are going as well. He's taking them.'

'I'd praise him for that,' Jamesie said.

Ruttledge lifted the little girl high and gave her coins and asked her and Mary to come round the lake on a visit. The child, holding Mary's hand, Jamesie and the two dogs walked them all the way out to the brow of the hill.

'I'll be over with the mower as soon as there's any stretch of settled weather,' Ruttledge said.

'Whenever it suits,' Jamesie answered with the most studied casualness, though for him it was the most important news in the whole of the evening.

Three days before the planned end of the holiday the Mercedes was back in round the shore followed by Monica's large red Ford. The eldest boy travelled with the Shah, the girl and two younger boys with their mother. The old man and the boy were chatting as the Mercedes rolled past the porch and getting on wonderfully well together.

'This man is going to be an aeroplane pilot,' he said expansively, and put his hand proudly on the boy's shoulder outside the porch. The boy was already taller than the stout old man. All the children were casually, expensively dressed; they were bright-looking, confident.

Their mother was wearing a simple green dress, the first time since the funeral they had seen her out of black. She was tall, with a natural elegance, and her face was humorous and kind.

'You came home a little early?'

'We did,' the Shah answered defensively, while Monica raised her eyes to the ceiling in eloquent silence. 'We had long enough.'

They all had tea with fresh apple tart. By the time tea was over the younger children discovered the black cat. The eldest boy stood beside his mother's chair as if he was now the support and hope of an ancient house.

'What was the hotel like?' Ruttledge asked his uncle when they were alone together outside the house.

'Good enough. It was right beside the front. You had only to cross the road to get to the ocean. Every day I had a dip. I tried to get Monica to go in but she wouldn't hear.'

'Was the food good?'

'Good enough.'

'They didn't mind your leaving early?'

'They were decent. They gave money back. Not that it would have mattered. The Northerners are all good business people.'

'How did you find Monica?' Ruttledge asked, wanting to know how she was recovering from the death.

'I noticed she's that little bit fond of the bar. She was in it every evening. That or she's on the lookout for men,' he started to shake.

'I find that hard to believe.'

'There's nothing worse than widows. Even priests will tell you that.'

'Do you want me to put the box quietly in the boot of the car?' Ruttledge wanted to change the conversation.

'No. Leave it. I'll be out on Sunday,' he said, and Ruttledge saw how strained he was.

'I suppose it'll be a while before you go away again,' he said sympathetically.

'Wild horses wouldn't drag me. You'd wonder what all those silly fools are doing rushing off to places.'

'Maybe it renews and restores a sense of their own place?'

'Then they're welcome to it,' he said dismissively.

'Still, it was a very decent thing for you to do,' Ruttledge said with feeling, knowing how much it had cost him.

Within the house Monica spoke of the days in the hotel. 'You know, he did his very best. It must have been hard. He spoiled the children. He couldn't do enough for us.' At first her shoulders shook with laughter but then the laughter appeared only in the smile. 'At eleven each day he went for a swim. He changed in his room into a faded pair of old trunks that must have been in fashion at the time of the Boer War. If he'd pulled on a dressing gown or even a raincoat it wouldn't have been too bad but he marched through the hotel in nothing but the trunks and an old pair of sandals, carrying a towel – through the hotel lobby and out into the middle of the road, with cars honking and people splitting themselves – and then into the ocean like a whale.

'You know, you don't notice how big he is in his clothes but in the trunks he was like a walking barrel. I kept well out of sight after the first day. A crowd gathered. Eamon here came to me and said, "You know, Mother, if Uncle was a funny man we could make money out of him."'

'It's all true,' the boy said. 'There was a bigger crowd every day.'

'Be careful,' Monica warned. 'I think I would have died if I had been in the lobby but all he did was wave to the people like a cardinal. He was so unbothered and so much himself that people began to take to him in the end. Before we left I saw him get all sorts of looks – people laughing and amused – but also attracted. People are funny. They look down from all sorts of heights and then if the looking down has no effect they get unsure.

'He may have ignored the crowd but he misses very little. After the children were in bed and Patrick here was in charge I used to go for a walk along the front on my own. On the way back I went into the hotel bar. I had to force myself the first evening. It was what Paddy Joe and myself used to do at the end of the day whenever we went on holiday and I wasn't sure if I could bear to walk in without him. I wasn't even sitting down when his lordship was there like my shadow. I was glad of his company. You'd never be bored with him. And it stopped those men coming up and offering drinks, which is the worst of being on your own. One night I had a second brandy. I saw him staring at the glass in an odd way and I asked if there was anything wrong. "You could get used to it, Monica," he said in that way of his that makes it sound like the end of the road. All that family hated drink. Only very late in her life did my mother take a drink. Lord bless him: he did his very best and he couldn't have been nicer with the children and they are all fond of him except when he appeared as Funny Man.'

'Or throwing his money up in the air,' the boy added.

'They didn't like that. I had to make them pick up the coins. When we were growing up we were glad to gather coins no matter from what quarter of heaven they fell.'

'Mother is always talking about how things were when she was growing up,' the boy screwed his face into an expression of distaste.

'In fairness, he'd have stayed the whole week in the hotel and never said a word, even though it was killing him, but you should have seen the look on his face when I said that maybe we were there long enough: it was deliverance.'

Outside the porch the Ruttledges witnessed the formal end of the holiday, the thanks, the praise, the promises, the handshakes, the final kiss. All the children were travelling with Monica and she was the first to drive away after inviting the Ruttledges to her house for an evening.

'We'll come when you have time to get settled. We'll come as soon as you are ready.'

The Shah let down the window as the big car rolled slowly past the porch. 'I'll be out on Sunday. Things should be more or less back to normal by then.'

On Sunday he took the metal box away.

'Are you sure you don't want to count?' Ruttledge asked playfully when he handed over the box. 'I could have helped myself to thousands.'

'That'll do you now,' he said. 'That's enough out of you for one day. I don't know how on earth you put up with him, Kate.'

Then the settled weather came, the morning breeze from the lake lifting and tossing the curtains on the open windows to scatter early light around the bedroom walls.

A sharp clawing sound came from behind the curtain where a window was open. The din of birds was already loud about the house but the low motor hum of the small insects had not yet begun. The traffic was barely moving on the distant road.

The clawing was followed by a loud falling into the room, and then stillness. There was a sound of something heavy being dragged along the floor towards the bed. Most mornings the black cat came through the window into the room. Usually she came soundlessly, except when she brought mice or small birds and woke the room with the racket of her play. The sound was heavier and more alarming than a cat coming in with her prey.

Kate slept through the noise. She even moved her face lower into the pillow as if in search of deeper sleep.

With a single leap, the cat was on the foot of the bed, claws digging into the white cover as she fought not to be dragged down by the weight she carried. Not until she had secured her grip on the edge of the bed did she advance to leave the animal beneath Kate's raised shoulder. Then the cat sat straight up and began to purr. It was a young hare she brought, its brown fur stretched out on the white cover, the white of the belly glowing softly in the darkness. All her attention was fixed on the sleeping woman.

When she was wild and starving, Kate had brought her food. She would watch from behind a tree, not leaving the safety of the tree for the food until the woman left. Eventually, she came, dragging her body low along the ground, provided Kate stood some distance away. Until one day she ate from the plate and sat and cleaned her face instead of running back for cover.

Though she was now tame and belonged more to the house than the fields, she never lost her wildness completely. She must have come on the leveret when it was sleeping in its form in the long grass or hunted it down when it tried to escape through the thick waves of the meadow.

Tired of sitting on the bed without any reaction from the sleeping woman, the cat seized the young hare again and advanced until she was able to drop the leveret across Kate's throat.

Ruttledge was trapped in the fascination of watching. He could have reached across and lifted the young hare, but he felt powerless, as if he were part of a dream.

Before he could move, her own hands came from beneath the bedclothes and groped about her throat as if the hands had the separate life of small animals. Feeling the warm fur, they suddenly went still, and with a cry she sat up, flinging the small hare loose.

'What a thing to do!'

The cat retreated to the corner of the bed in the face of the outburst and stood her ground. Ruttledge switched on the bedside lamp.

'How did it get here?'

'Your cat brought it in. She brought it in through the window.'

'Why didn't you stop her?'

'I didn't know what she was going to do.'

Released from the tension of her fright, Kate suddenly reached for the cat. 'Oh, you villain! What is the poor animal?'

'A young hare – half-grown.'

The flesh was still warm. A trickle of bright scarlet ran from the nostrils. There was a thin red stain along the white cover of the bed, like a trail. He lifted and put the leveret out of sight on the floor.

'Why did you do that to me?' The cat reacted to the tone of the voice and purred louder than ever and came forward to be lifted and prized.

Outside there wasn't a cloud in the sky. The ripe heavy grass in the meadow was stirring like water beneath the light breeze. Over breakfast they heard on the radio that ridges of high pressure were moving slowly in off the Atlantic. As they went about the tasks of the morning, from every quarter came the sounds of machinery starting up and the whine of rotary mowers, like low-flying aeroplanes in the meadows. There was a sense that the whole of this quiet place was becoming deranged.

Ruttledge was ready for cutting. As he swung the mower round to connect to the drive shaft, he felt some apprehension but no excitement. He had not grown up with machines and got none of the pleasure he saw young men take in their power; neither would he ever be as skilful and confident in their use. He knew the basic mechanics and the danger of the blurring speed of those small blades. The morning wind from the lake that lifted the curtains had died. The water was like glass, reflecting the clear sky on either side of a sparkling river of light from a climbing sun. Not a breath of wind moved on the meadows. The only movement was the tossing of the butterflies above the restful grass. The idling tractor stilled the insect hum but not the clamour of the crows or the shrieks of the lake gulls. Once the mower was in gear and turned up to full throttle it drowned every sound. In a cocoon of noise and dust and diesel fumes and the dull, reflected heat from metal, he sat at the wheel while the tractor and mower circled and circled the meadow, the grass falling in front of the blurring whine of the blades. Out of a corner of an eye he saw hares escaping and a hen-pheasant leading her small band of young across the swards towards the dubious safety of a deep drain. When all the meadows were cut they looked wonderfully empty and clean, the big oak and ash trees in the hedges towering over the rows of cut grass, with the crows and the gulls descending in a shrieking rabble to hunt frogs and snails and worms. In corners of the meadows, pairs of plump pigeons were pecking busily at grass seed. No pheasant or hare had been killed or maimed. With the sea of grass gone, the space between the house and the lake suddenly seemed a different land.

'I'm hurrying,' Ruttledge said as he had tea and a sandwich in the house. 'I know Jamesie will be on edge once he hears the mower.'

'What time do you think you'll be finished?'

'His meadows are small: by teatime.'

'I'll be over around six.'

He travelled round the shore. All the gates from the road to the house were open. The pair of dogs met the tractor at the last gate, escorting it down to the house. The brown hens lay sprawled in the dust and shade behind the netting wire. A pair of boots was drying in front of the open door. The green gate to the meadows had been pushed wide from the whitewashed wall of the outhouse. Ruttledge left the tractor running on the street, the mower raised.

'Are yous ready?'

A sound of laughter came from within.

'Good soldiers never die,' Jamesie shouted out but did not appear.

It was dark and cool within the cave of the house after the hot sunlight. Jamesie sat at the table by the window in his stocking feet with a copy of the *Observer*. Mary and Margaret sat quietly together at the unlit stove. After the greetings and welcomes, Jamesie said, 'Why don't you turn the bloody thing off out on the street and we'll have tea or a drink or something?'

'No. We'll start. How much do you want cut?'

Jamesie and Mary looked to one another quickly before turning to Ruttledge. 'What do you think?'

Ruttledge refused to be drawn. 'It's up to you. I can mow it all if you want.'

'Mary?' Jamesie turned.

'There's no use asking me. You know yourself what you want.'

He was in crisis, having always had the meadows cut in three parts: it was against his instinct to risk it all in the one throw. In bad summers he would spend weeks struggling with hay, but cut in three portions all of it would never be lost. While he knew that the machines had taken most of the hardship from haymaking, he couldn't quite believe that they had taken most of the risk and excitement and drama as well.

'What did you do?' he asked anxiously.

'I knocked all mine.'

'Cut it all to hell,' Mary said suddenly. 'Otherwise we'll be sick looking at it for the whole summer.'

'What if it pours?' Jamesie demanded.

'The forecast is good,' Ruttledge said gently.

'Fuck it,' Jamesie said suddenly. 'Cut it to hell. We'll live or die.'

'Good!' Mary said vigorously. 'I wouldn't like to count the summers I was sick of the colour of hay.'

The meadows must have once been tiny, not much more than gardens. Hedges or ditches had been removed and now ran as shallow drains through the small meadows. Wherever they dipped sharply Jamesie had marked them with old nylons tied to the top of poles like flags. In places the meadows ran along the river and the edges of the bog. On these stretches he kept watch. Ruttledge was uneasy to have him so close because he knew the danger of a blade flying loose or catching a small stone to whirl it from the thick grass like a bullet, but Jamesie could not be persuaded away.

'Here you can't see the river from the grass. Lord bless us, if the tractor went in we'd be the talk of the country for weeks.'

No stone or blade flew and by evening all the small meadows were mowed. A huge flock of crows descended on the swards, and some pigeons but no gulls. The meadows were hidden from the lake. Away to the west the sky was turning red.

Ruttledge was surprised not to find Kate in the house. 'She said she was coming over.'

'Something must have held her up,' Mary said.

'I couldn't look at whiskey. I'll have water or a beer,' Ruttledge protested when Jamesie pounded a bottle of Powers down on the table like a challenge and unscrewed the cap, the three swallows on the gold label poised for flight.

'You're no good. Useless,' he said as he poured a large whiskey and raised his glass with a challenging flourish.

The cold beer was delicious in the tiredness. The tiredness itself was deeply pleasurable after the jolting and heat and dust and concentration on the disappearing ground. Mary put a large platter heaped with sandwiches on a chair.

'These are wonderful, Mary. Did any word come from Italy?'

'Yesterday,' she smiled the sweet smile that was all her own and took a postcard from the windowsill. 'There's nothing in it. Read away.'

Ruttledge was expecting to see a crowded beach or a café with tables under awnings or an old church on the card, but it was a reproduction of Giotto's *Flight into Egypt*. Joseph with a bundle on his shoulder was leading the donkey carrying Mary and the Child. Against the deep blue of the sky and the pale hills hovered two angels with outspread wings and haloes of pale gold. The blue of Mary's robe was lighter than the lightest blue of the sky. The robes of Joseph, the child and the angels were as brown as earth. The trees on the pale hills were flowers. The whole had an extraordinary and deeply affecting serenity: it was as if they had complete trust in the blessed light as they travelled to a place or state where nothing cast a shadow.

By the time he handed it back, Jamesie and Mary were laughing at Ruttledge's absorption in the postcard.

'What's so funny?'

'I'd say the mother picked it. Jim just wrote. It's more like what you'd get for Christmas,' Mary said when the laughter died.

'The card is beautiful. It must have been a long journey for Jim,' Ruttledge said.

'Before he went to school, he had me and the Granda tormented with questions. We had no idea at first how good he was,' Mary said. 'Once he went to school he turned quiet. He used sit here at the corner of this table doing his exercises. We knew he was good but what is *good*? This fella here couldn't wait to quit school. I was just middling.'

'Don't heed her,' Jamesie said. 'She was by far the best in her class. I was never any good.'

'That doesn't mean anything. It doesn't mean a single thing. I was far from what Jim turned out to be. We didn't know he'd turn out to be Margaret's father then, either.' Mary smiled at her grandchild. 'We knew nothing.'

'Jamesie here always took a week from the roads to cut the turf and set the potatoes. We had the bank we still have on Gloria though it's never used now. There was no hardship with the wheelbarrows then like when I was young. We had the mule and the cart with rubber tyres. All Jim had to do was catch the sods his father pegged out of the boghole and put them on the cart. The mule took them out on the spread

114

where they were heeled up. I think Jim would far sooner be at school than on the bog but he never complained. Most people kept their children from school then when they were needed. No heed was passed.'

'It was always cold on Gloria,' Jamesie said. 'You wouldn't be cold down in the boghole but on the bank you'd be blue. The only shelter on Gloria is those poor little lone birch trees. People used to cut out little houses in the banks to shelter or get away from the showers. We used to be weak watching for Mary. There was always a *fear gorta* on Gloria. We'd be middling until we'd spot her bicycle coming in the lane and then we'd nearly die. We'd go pure weak.'

'One day we saw Master Hunt's car come in the bog road. Of course this hawk here was the first to spot it and was watching and wondering what the Master could be doing on the bog.'

'Sleepy fox,' he cried.

'We didn't think he could be coming for us when he stopped the car out on the road. In those days unless you were somebody as forward as John Quinn you were afeard to go near a priest or a teacher and didn't expect them to come near.'

'Master Hunt was as decent, as straight a man as ever wore shoe leather. He wasn't like the savages we had for masters.'

'We were finishing the tea. After chatting for a while he said he wanted a word with us on our own. When we walked a bit out towards the car he told us that he had come on only one or two others as good as Jim in all his years of teaching. He felt sure he'd win a county scholarship the next year but not if he was kept from school.'

'We were only delighted. The only reason we kept him from school is that we never thought it mattered,' Jamesie said.

'Master Hunt brought the results himself. He had never been to the house before. His hands were shaking when he handed us the letter. You'd think he was the child that had won the scholarship.'

'Well, in a way he had,' Ruttledge said.

'Nothing would do this omadhaun but make the Master sit down. Though it was morning he opened a fresh bottle of whiskey. I declare to God the pair finished the bottle.'

'What did Jim say? He must have been in heaven.'

'He got to say nothing with this fella ravelling on with Master Hunt. I was afraid the Master would drive into a ditch with that much whiskey. Master Hunt wasn't used to whiskey.'

'He was very apt,' Jamesie said defensively. 'He was a big strong man.'

'When the Master left, Jamesie got on his bicycle and cycled all over the country full to the gills as he was with whiskey.' Mary laughed maliciously, but her eyes were full of deep affection. 'They called him First-in-the-County for a long time afterwards.'

'They were jealous,' he said.

'You should have known enough about people by then not to blow. You were long enough in the world to know.'

'What was it but the truth,' he said. 'There were a few who were glad.'

'A rare few,' she responded.

'To hell with them,' he said. 'Nobody counted but Jim and Master Hunt.'

'You'd have been better to let them find it out for themselves. Jamesie here can keep nothing in,' Mary said wistfully.

'Mary was never the same again after Jim went away to college that September,' Jamesie had said many times before. 'Her heart was broken. She was never to be the same again. The life left the place.'

'What does Margaret here think hearing about her father when he was young?' Ruttledge asked.

'Father never talks about when he was young. Only Mother does,' the child said matter-of-factly.

'They'll all come down for Margaret as soon as they get back from abroad,' Mary said, and the child drew closer to Mary.

Outside on the street Jamesie looked anxiously down at the fallen meadows and then at the sky where a jet was chalking a path on the cloudless blue of evening. He felt anxious and exposed: the whole country would laugh at his greed if the heavens opened.

'I'll be over early in the morning,' Ruttledge said. 'There'll be no rain.'

'Please God. Whenever suits,' he said almost absently as Mary and Margaret waved from the doorway. The casualness was studied; he would not know ease again until his meadows were safe.

Along the shore a boy was fishing out on the stones, casting a glittering spoon out over the water and then reeling it slowly in. The heron rose out of the reeds and flapped ahead before swinging away towards the farther shore. A glaring red sun was sinking below the rim of the sky.

'We were expecting you over,' Ruttledge said to Kate.

'I couldn't get away. The Shah arrived. He wanted to talk to you about something. Then I had Bill Evans and it was too late.'

'Had Bill any news?' Ruttledge asked idly, tiredly: Bill Evans never had news.

'Big news,' Kate said. 'One day every week from now on he is going to town on the bus. He'll get a meal and be generally tended to.'

'He must be in heaven.'

'In pure heaven.'

The next morning a white mist obscured even the big trees along the shore. Gossamer hung over the pear and plum and apple trees in the orchard and a pale spiderwebbing lay across the grass in the fields. A robin was trapped in the glasshouse and set free before it became prey for the black cat. The heavy mower was uncoupled from the tractor and replaced by the tedder. The very quiet and coolness of the morning was delicious with every hour promising later heat. When the sun had burned away the mist and dried the dew on the swards, the tedding began. The tedder was new and working perfectly, turning the flat neat swards into a green stream of grass and when it was done the spread grass lay like a raised green floor to the sun. Then the tractor and tedder went slowly round the lake to Jamesie.

The dogs met the tractor as it came down to the house. They were all in the meadows. Jamesie and Mary were shaking out the heavy swards with pitchforks while Margaret played with the dogs.

'Those pitchforks aren't a great sign of faith in the machines,' Ruttledge said as they gathered around the running tractor to watch him move the tedder into its working position and connect the drive shaft.

'We were just putting in time,' Jamesie said defensively.

'Which would you prefer – to be in Italy or in the meadow?' Ruttledge asked Margaret when the tedder was set for working and he was warning her not to come too close to the tines.

'In the meadows,' she answered and drew closer to Mary.

On the television forecast of the night before, the map of Ireland was shown covered with small suns, like laughing apples. Soon after midday all the small meadows were tedded. By evening the mown grass rustled like hay to the touch. The next morning they were swept into rows. The swept ground between the rows had already turned golden. Because of Jamesie's anxiety Ruttledge went round the shore to bale his meadows first. Kate came with him to help stack the bales. Though the balers were a familiar sight in meadows for years, Jamesie watched in a kind of disbelief as the cumbersome red machine gathered in the loose rows and spat them out in neat tied bales. In a break in the baling, when Mary came with a can of sweetened tea, all his anxiety and lack of trust surfaced.

'If the thing was to break down now we'd be able to get up what's left with the forks.'

'What about my poor meadows?'

'You wouldn't care a frig.'

'I'd care but there's not much I could do.'

'Please God, it'll hold,' he said.

The bales were too heavy for the child but the two women and Jamesie were able to stack them almost as quickly as the baler spat them out. Two bales were placed sideways, sufficiently close to be crossed by two other bales but far enough apart to allow air to circulate. The stack was completed by a single bale on top, the uncut side turned upwards to cast the rain. When they were all stacked, they stood like abstract sculptures in swept empty space.

Then they all followed the tractor and baler round the shore to work in Ruttledge's meadows, the two dogs trotting ahead. By evening, when the sun had gone round behind the house, all the meadows were baled and stacked under the long shadows of the trees stretching out into the lake. When the last bale was lifted to crown the last small stack, Jamesie gave a loud cheer. The sound was of triumph and heartfelt relief.

'All that work done in a few hours,' he repeated over and over. 'Several men and horses would need days and not get it done.'

'It's safe now,' Kate said gently.

'Not in the shed yet,' Jamesie warned.

'If there was rain we could take it in tomorrow. What could it do but heat in its own sap now?'

Inside the house a reading lamp with a green shade was lit on the big table. On the red-and-white squares of the table-cloth stood a blue bowl filled with salad and large white plates of tongue and ham, a cheeseboard with different cheeses, including the Galtee Jamesie liked wrapped in its silver paper, a cut loaf, white wine, a bottle of Powers, lemonade. There was a large glass jug of iced water in which slices of lemon floated.

'A great house. A pure feast. A lamp lit in the middle of the summer,' Jamesie said. 'Wasteful. Wasteful. Children dying in Africa.'

'A lot he knows about Africa when he didn't even know where Italy is! Men never quit about the lights and they'd drink as much whiskey in a day as would light a house for a year.' Drinks were poured. They were more tired than hungry after the work and heat. The soreness and tiredness became delicious in the drowsy glow of alcohol. Nobody wanted to sit at the table.

Margaret stood by Jamesie's chair and he touched her hair and pulled at her ribbon. For the rest, they were content to sit and watch the light. The child stayed by his chair until the black cat came cautiously into the room. As the light faded, the sky beyond the dark shapes of the trees softened to a glow, and the room became enormous as it reached out to the fields and the trees in the long, velvety light of the sky.

'In weather like this but a little later Jamesie's father died,' Mary said quietly. 'They were building the hayrick in the yard where the hayshed is now. The father was sick in bed but couldn't stay away from the window. "They are putting it up wrong," he'd cry out in a rage. Why worry yourself about them? It'll be their lookout, I'd say, and try to coax him away from the window. But he'd not be five minutes back in bed in the lower room when he'd be back with his nose pressed to the glass like a bold child.'

'Were they putting up the rick wrong?'

'Not at all. They were putting it up different to the way he put it up. The string of curses was terrible: it'd fall, let in rain, rot, there wouldn't be a mouthful for the cows. I'd coax him back to bed again but in no time he'd be back at the window with his nose pressed to the glass. This went on for the whole of the day. I was getting food for the men. Part of the time I had a job to keep a straight face. When they came into the house to eat he went down to the room and banged the door shut and never appeared again until they left.'

Jamesie sat in absolute silence while Mary spoke. When she finished he added, 'My father was thick and ignorant but he adored Mary. He didn't want her in the house at first but by the end he adored the ground she walked on.'

'He wouldn't talk to me when I first came into the house but by the end he wouldn't even take a drink of water from the hand of anybody else.'

'A week or so after the rick was built I was putting out topdressing with the little mule. Nothing would do my father but come out to help. It was weather like this, wonderful weather. He should have been in bed but you could tell him nothing. I passed no heed. Then he called me over. His graip, he said, was stuck. I could have laughed out loud. A child could have lifted the graip. It wasn't stuck at all. He hadn't the strength. It was then I saw there was something badly wrong. It was as much as I could do to get him back to the house. He only lasted three days.'

'I had to stay with him,' Mary said. 'He'd get all worried if I tried to leave for even a few minutes. In the end he just faded. It was as peaceful as anybody could want.'

'He seems to have been more like Johnny than Jamesie,' Ruttledge said.

'Far more. That's why the two were never able to get on. I don't know where they got Jamesie. He wasn't a bit like any of them.'

'The cuckoo!' he cried.

'Where do you think Johnny is at this minute?'

Jamesie drew back his sleeve but had difficulty telling the time in the muted light. 'In the Prince. He's bound to be in the Prince at this time. Unless the darts team are playing away.'

'People we know come and go in our minds whether they are here or in England or alive or dead,' Mary said with a darkness that was as much a part of her as the sweet inward-looking smile. 'We're no more than a puff of wind out on the lake.'

A loud knocking came from the porch with the sound of Bill Evans's stick on the floor, the heavy brushing of his wellingtons in the slow walk. 'God bless all here,' his glance flitted from face to face until it fastened on the lighted table and stuck. His eyes wolfed the table.

'It's not often we see you twice in the same day,' Kate said. Margaret left Jamesie to stand close to Mary. The black cat raced from the room.

'I hadn't much to do above and I battered down to see how you were all getting along with the hay.'

'We have it all safe. You're too late,' Jamesie said ironically.

'You'll eat something?'

'Begod I will, Kate, quick,' he said, and when he was seated in the rocking chair with a large plate of sandwiches by his side, he said grandly, 'You're all very welcome to this side of the lake.'

'We are all very glad to be here,' they answered, suppressing their laughter.

'Did ye cut up there yet?' Jamesie teased.

'No.' Bill Evans felt at a disadvantage. 'The meadows aren't ready yet.'

'Anybody who hasn't his meadows cut this evening is lost.'

'You were always a sight for blowing, Jamesie,' he said.

'That's right, Bill. Give it to him,' Mary said.

'I'm well able to put him in order. I've been watching his capers for years,' he said, and Jamesie responded with a light cheer.

'Bill is going to the town soon,' Ruttledge said.

'Every Thursday. The bus will be coming to the gate,' he boasted.

'Good man, Bill,' Jamesie said agreeably.

'A whiskey, Joe, before I go,' he demanded.

'You're not used to it, Bill,' Ruttledge said, but poured him a moderate whiskey, adding plenty of water.

He downed it in one swallow. 'Another, Joe.'

'No Bill. It would only get you into trouble,' he said, and walked him to the gate. He had no buckets and turned straight uphill, the stick reaching out in the crab-like, sideways walk.

The night air was sweet with cut grass and meadowsweet and the wild woodbine. A bird moved in some high branch and was still. The clear yellow outlines of the stacked bales were sharp in the ghostly meadow under the big moon and the towering shapes of the trees. Headlights of a passing car from across the lake were caught like little moons in the windows of the porch as it travelled towards Shruhaun. They had all risen to leave when he got back to the house.

'You must be tired. We'll run you round the lake in the car.'

'No. We'll walk. We had a powerful evening. Who wouldn't want to walk on a night the like of that?' Jamesie said.

'The night is perfect but it's been too long a day. Sit in the car.'

Ruttledge knew not to take the words at face value. They were glad to sit in the car and be driven, Mary and Margaret holding the two dogs in their arms. Jamesie's head started to droop towards his chest as they drove.

Kate's intuition was right that there was something on the Shah's mind. He praised the cleaned meadows and the stacked bales when he rolled up to the house in the big car at his usual time on Sunday, but his mind was elsewhere. He could hardly wait to unburden himself.

Clearing his throat loudly he announced, 'I'm thinking of retiring,' as if he couldn't quite bring himself to believe his own words.

'There's nothing wrong with you, is there?' Ruttledge was equally surprised.

'No,' he laughed defensively.

'Why do you want to retire?'

'There comes a time. There are some old cunts going around who think they'll never disappear. I wouldn't want to be one of those.'

The silence of the room was strange. To think of the Shah as retired was as difficult for the Ruttledges as it was for himself but Ruttledge knew that it would have been carefully considered and thought through.

'What would you do with the business?'

'I'd sell.'

'Who would you sell it to?'

'Whoever'd buy. Whoever'd come up with the washers. That's no six marker.'

'What would happen to Frank?'

'Frank will have to do like the rest of us. Well, what do you think?' he asked out of a silence that had grown uncomfortably long.

'Wouldn't you miss it? It has been most of your life. What would you do with yourself?'

'I'd have plenty to do,' he bristled. 'I wouldn't mind having nothing to do.'

'You shouldn't rush into anything, that's all I'd worry about. You should wait till you're sure.'

'We'll not rush. That's one thing we'll not be doing anyhow,' he laughed, his confidence returning.

'What will happen to those men in your cottages?'

'Nothing will change in their direction. They'll come to no harm. The cottages will stay as they are. Well, what do you think about it all, Kate?'

'It's a big move. What does Captain here think?' and at the sound of his name the sheepdog left the sofa and went to Kate. His master appeared reassured and pleased as a child by both the move and the words.

'He knows who to go to. He's no fool.'

'Bones!' she said playfully, and the dog barked.

'Have you discussed this with anybody else?' Ruttledge asked.

'No. I mentioned a few words to that woman down in the hotel – but no, I didn't go over it with anybody.'

'There's nothing wrong with your health?'

'Not that I know of but the mileage is up.'

'I find it hard to get used to the idea.'

'I find it hard to get used to it myself,' he admitted with rueful humour. 'The time comes though when we all have to move over.'

'Why don't we leave it for a while? If you feel the same in a few weeks we can talk,' Ruttledge said.

'That's what we'll do,' he said with obvious relief. 'It's been on my mind for a good while now. It'll not go away.'

'I think you should give Frank Dolan his chance at it if you decide to sell. He's worked for you all his life.'

'Will he be able for it? Will he have the washers?'

'We can go into all that when you make up your mind for certain.'

They walked the fields. They looked at the stacked bales in the shaved meadows, already a rich yellow in the sun, and at the cattle and the sheep. They stood on the high hill over the inner lake and watched a heron cross from the wooded island to Gloria Bog. The day was so still that not even a breath of wind ruffled the sedge that was pale as wheat in the sun. The birch trees stood like green flowers until the pale sea merged with the far blue of the mountain.

'That distant blue means good weather.'

'Talking of that blue and that neighbour of yours, I hear he's going to take the plunge again.'

'The mountains so lovely and blue in the distance?' Ruttledge echoed. 'He's been plunging ever since I came about the place.'

'This time it's going to be in the church with all the blessings and a big reception afterwards in the hotel. I'm told yous all are going to be invited.'

'Who is the lucky woman?'

'Some fool of a widow from up the country, Meath or Westmeath, with a grown family and a big farm of land. A fine, fresh woman, I'm informed.'

'Where did he find her?'

'In the best of places: the Knock Marriage Bureau.'

'Where the Virgin appeared to the children?'

'That'll do you now but you'd think the priests and nuns would have something better to do than running a bucking shop,' he was shaking, wiping the tears away with small fists.

'Where did you hear this?'

'From that woman who owns the hotel. It's all booked. I warned her she better get her money beforehand.'

'Are you sure you're not making this up?'

'Not a word,' he shook silently. 'There's no fool like an old fool.'

The mower, the tedder, the baler were put away for the year. An old buckrake the Shah had given Ruttledge years before was taken out. With its ungainly weight of solid metal and the sharply pointed steel pins it looked and was antique but was perfect for drawing in the square bales.

As soon as Ruttledge entered the street with the big buckrake on the tractor he saw that Jamesie's shed was already almost half full. Margaret came leading the mule by the bridle up from the meadows, six bales stacked on the small cart with the rubber wheels, Jamesie following behind. The brown hens paraded proudly around in the dust inside the netting wire. The box of pansies glowed on the windowsill beside the geraniums. Mary stood at the door.

'You should have told me you had started. I'd have come over,' Ruttledge said.

'We were doing nothing and started to jog along on our own. We hadn't a thing else to do.'

They unloaded and stacked the few bales, untackled the mule and let him loose in his field.

'If he had manners he could run with the cows,' Jamesie said. 'Since he hasn't any manners he has to stay on his own. The very same as with people who can't hold their drink.'

In the house Jamesie called for the bottle of Powers and derided Ruttledge when he refused whiskey.

'It's too early. I couldn't look at it now.'

'I'd drink it any hour of the day or night and thrive,' he boasted.

'Of course you would,' Mary echoed sarcastically as she poured him a whiskey.

'Have you any news?'

'No news. Came looking for news.'

'You came to the wrong place. We are waiting for news.'

Margaret laughed sharply at the repetitive foolishness of the play but instead of continuing the banter Ruttledge said, 'I have big news,' and the room went still. 'Very big news.'

'What? What?' Jamesie cried. 'You're only acting. You have no news!'

'I have very big news,' Ruttledge repeated.

News was the sustenance of Jamesie's interest in everything that lived and moved around his life. Years before it had been arranged that they would come over to the Ruttledge's for an evening, which was unusual in itself because of his dislike of formal arrangements. Early in the day, Ruttledge had gone into the town to get provisions for the evening and ran into Jamesie by accident. They went into Luke's and chatted pleasantly for a half an hour or so.

'I'll not say goodbye as I'll be seeing you this evening,' Ruttledge said casually as they parted.

'You won't,' Jamesie answered bluntly.

'Why? Is there something wrong?' Ruttledge asked in alarm.

'Not a thing wrong but you'll have no more news this evening. I have all your news for a while,' he answered simply.

Ruttledge didn't quite believe it until the evening disappeared without sight of Jamesie or Mary.

Now Jamesie could not bear Ruttledge's mischievous withholding.

'You have no news. You are only acting the fool,' he accused.

'You may be acting the fool but he isn't,' Mary said.

'I'm telling you he has no news. There hasn't been news around here in years.'

'John Quinn is getting married again,' Ruttledge laid it out like a trump card on a green table.

'You're lying. Who told you? Somebody's been packing you.'

'The Shah told us.'

'How does he know? He's in the town.'

'The Shah's not lying. He wouldn't care one way or another. He thinks all who marry are fools.'

'He could be right there,' Mary said.

'Missus Maguire who owns the Central told him. They are great friends.'

'I know. I know. He drives her to Mass every Sunday. They are like an old married pair.'

'The wedding breakfast is already booked for the Central. We are all going to be invited.'

Jamesie was silent a long time before deciding that Ruttledge wasn't playing or lying, and then instead of saying anything he cheered.

'Where did John find the omadhaun of a woman who'll have him?' Mary asked.

'Out of the Knock Marriage Bureau.'

'He could have. It gets better and better,' Jamesie said. 'There's notices up on the church door about the Bureau. John would try anything. He's been getting and sending a sight of letters in the post. He's been going places lately.' Jamesie rubbed his hands together in glee as if he believed it for the first time.

'One thing sure is that John Quinn isn't paying for a wedding reception for half the country,' Mary said.

'Maybe the wife is paying. Maybe she has money.'

'Then she's even a bigger fool.'

'And it could all turn out a pack of lies,' Jamesie said.

'We better make a start at the bales unless we intend to get married ourselves,' Ruttledge said.

The buckrake could be lowered or raised with the lift at will and it was easy to sling the bales on to the long spears. As the bales rose in the shed, Jamesie and Mary stayed behind and Ruttledge worked the meadows on his own. Sometimes Margaret rode with him between his knees and steered the big tractor. The bales rose towards the roof of the shed in stairs. In some ways the heaviest work fell to Mary. She took the bales from Ruttledge and then lifted them to Jamesie higher up, who took the binder twine in his enormous hands and swung them lightly into place. With the man's cap turned back to front to keep the hayseed and dust from her hair, she looked wonderfully boyish whenever she smiled, but by evening she was visibly wilting. When Ruttledge suggested that she had more than enough done for the day and he and Jamesie would be able to finish on their own, she would not hear of giving up.

'What is it but another small while? I wonder what the poor old father would make out of the shed now if he ran and put his nose to the window?' she laughed.

'He'd go out of his mind,' Jamesie said. 'He'd think the world had gone mad.'

'We may all be the father at the window yet,' Ruttledge said.

'And that's life!' Jamesie shouted down from the stifling heat of the hayshed.

'I suppose when we are lying below in Shruhaun, Margaret will be talking about us the way we are talking about the father,' Mary said.

'She'll be talking nice and sweet to her young man. She'll be saying they were decent enough people, God rest them, but they never went to school and they had no money and never learned manners but they weren't too bad. They were decent old skins when it was all added up,' Jamesie said.

'I will not,' Margaret stamped her foot.

'That's right, Margaret,' Mary said. 'He's had his own way for far too long. Joe here went to school and is an educated man, not like that comedian up on the hay who has enough to say for ten scholars.'

Jamesie cheered the speech defensively and Ruttledge said, 'Don't you see where it got me, Mary?'

'An important job with the government,' Jamesie shouted down, and they stood and laughed before swinging back to work.

They were gathering in the last few stacks when a big green car drove in on the street. The car wasn't a substantial statement, like the Shah's heavy Mercedes, but it was a statement of sorts – brand-new, expensive, an open sun roof and silver wheels that looked like the spokes of the sun. Music was playing from speakers in the car.

'Margaret's holiday is over,' Mary turned to the child, who drew closer to Mary and looked apprehensive. The parents were the first to emerge from the car, Jim in casual golfing clothes and Lucy in a summer dress. The children looked subdued. They were at an awkward age and stood on the street without moving towards Margaret or she to them. For a still moment the scene appeared frozen in uncertainty, until Jamesie shouted out and with nimble quickness came down the rows of bales.

'You're welcome. Welcome.' He shook everybody by the hand, but did not kiss or embrace. In an instinctive move to harness his excitement, he swooped to lift the three grandchildren one by one and then pretended he was no longer able. 'You are all growing up past me and this poor old fella is going down,' he pulled his doleful clown's face so that they all laughed. By then he had regained his old watchful, humorous presence. In contrast, Mary's face was mute with devotion as she waited to receive her son's kiss as if it were a sacrament.

'Is he still treating you badly, Mother?' her son joked.

'Sleepy fox,' Jamesie cried but Mary remained silent.

'How are you, Gran? Great to see you,' Lucy said effusively as the two women kissed.

'You are as welcome as ever anybody could be,' Mary said, but all the uncertain pauses of her heart were audible in the simple string of words.

'You're welcome,' Ruttledge shook their hands in turn.

'Helping Mom and Pop with the hay? The extended family. How is Kate?' Lucy asked with a breeziness that had the effect of a voice singing out of tune though well intentioned.

'She is well. She'll be sorry to have missed you. How was Florence?' Ruttledge asked.

'Fantastic. Just fantastic,' Lucy said. 'The experience of a lifetime.'

'We were glad enough to get home,' her husband added quietly.

'How did Margaret behave herself?' the mother asked, smiling forcefully down at the child.

'Margaret was wonderful. She lifted us all in the meadows,' Ruttledge said, feeling out of place. 'She gave us heart.'

'It must be some weight off this man's mind to get the hay in the shed. He used always go a bit bananas about this time of year,' their son laughed.

'Pay no heed. I never heard. They'd all have you circling if you paid them heed,' Jamesie answered jauntily while engaged with the three children who had been joined by Margaret and the pair of dogs. 'They'd have you so that you wouldn't know whether you were coming or going.'

'He has an answer for everything. He's a character,' Lucy said in glorious condescension.

'A quare hawk,' her husband echoed, but defensively, uncertainly, and laughed.

'A poor old fella. A decent poor skin. May the Lord have mercy on his soul,' the subject himself answered, still engaged with his grandchildren.

The flurry and excitement of the arrival died away. The brown hens returned to their pecking in the dirt, raising a yellow eye sideways from time to time to inspect with comic gravity the strangely crowded street. From within the house one of the clocks began to strike an earlier hour. A blackbird landed with a frenzied clatter in the hedge beside the hayshed. Completely alone though a part of the crowd, Mary stood mutely gazing on her son and his wife as if in wonderment how so much time had disappeared and emerged again in such strange and substantial forms that were and were not her own. Across her face there seemed to pass many feelings and reflections: it was as if she ached to touch and gather in and make whole those scattered years of change. But how can time be gathered in and kissed? There is only flesh.

To Ruttledge, Jim was a quiet, courteous man without the vividness or presence or the warmth of his parents. He had the habit of attention and his face was kind. It was as if he had been prematurely exhausted by the long journey he had made and discovered little sustenance on the new shores of Kildare Street and Mount Merrion. Already he had gone far but was unlikely to advance much further without luck. The people who could promote him to the highest rung would have to be interacted with and could not be studied like a problem or a book.

His wife would want his advancement and certainly she herself would be a hindrance to what she sought. When she first met the Ruttledges she expected them to be bowled over by her personality since they were already friendly with her parents-in-law. They found her exhausting. She drew all her life from what was outside herself, especially from the impression she imagined she was making on other people, and her dark good looks and sexual attractiveness helped this primal conceit. She accepted mere politeness as unqualified endorsements but was quick to dismiss anybody who allowed signs to show that they found her less than entrancing. Her sense of importance and confidence could only be kept alive by the large, closely bound family to which she belonged and to which her husband had been inexorably annexed.

'I'll get in these last bales and leave you to your evening,' Ruttledge said.

Once all the meadows were empty and clean he refused to turn off the engine. He waved to everybody and blew a kiss to Margaret, who turned away as pleased as she was embarrassed.

'I hope you have a great evening,' he shouted down.

'God bless you for all the help,' Mary said.

'You know I never liked you anyhow,' Jamesie shouted.

'Isn't he terrible? But you have to admit he's a character,' Lucy smiled, waving like a queen.

Jim smiled quietly as he waved.

The next morning was heavy and still. The radio said that thundery showers in the south would cross the whole country by evening. Very early in the morning they started to draw in the bales, the wheels of the tractor making bright streams through the cobwebbed grass. Kate insisted on helping. She wore old gloves against the hard binder twine but hadn't the strength to lift the heavier bales.

'Are you sure you want to be doing this?'

'As long as I'm useful.'

'You are great use. Those bales are heavy though. There's no use getting hurt.'

They worked steadily. Not until the bales rose high would the lifting become hard and slow. While it was still morning they saw Jamesie and Mary come through the open gate under the alder tree. They were wheeling bicycles and wearing caps with the peaks turned back. Their two dogs were already following trails through the meadow. Their hearts lifted. A weight of heavy repetitious work stretching into the evening rain was suddenly halved and made light.

'A poor old pair slaving away against starvation in the winter,' Jamesie called out.

'Why aren't you attending to your guests?'

'They're gone. They went last night. In that car Dublin is only two hours away.'

'We thought they'd stay a few days.'

'No. They went,' Jamesie said carefully. 'Jim had to be back at work. The house is too small.'

'Poor Margaret was lost,' Mary said. 'She didn't want to go at all. All she wanted was to be in the meadows with us again today.'

'When you see a child like her you wish for happiness.'

'Then wishing you'll be. She'll have to batter it out on her own like the rest of us,' Mary said.

'There's nothing worse than seeing a lone man in a meadow,' Jamesie said, and burst out laughing when he spotted the gloves Kate was wearing. 'God bless you, Kate. You came prepared for winter,' and displayed his own enormous welted hands with pride: 'Pure shoe leather!'

The drawing in started to go very quickly. The two women went into the house and brought out a jug of sweetened tea.

'The Shah was right. John Quinn is getting married,' Jamesie said, resting on the bales.

'He was like a hen on a hot griddle until he found out,' Mary said. 'It was a sweet charity someone got to hear something for once before he did. As soon as you were gone he got Jim to drive him down to Shruhaun. Lucy was fit to be tied. She thought they'd never come back.'

'We had only two drinks.' Jamesie said. 'The place was packed. There was a great welcome for Jim. John Quinn was there like a cat with cream, people congratulating him and slapping him on the back, buying him drinks. It'd nearly make you die. He got her out of the Knock Bureau all right. Her family is dead set against the match. That's why the wedding is here. She has three sons, a big farm and money. We're all going to be invited. He's not going to send out anything as ignorant as invitations. John himself is coming round on all the good neighbours and inviting us all personally. You can expect a visit. We had a most wonderful time.'

'Had Jim drinks?' Ruttledge enquired.

'Just the two but Lucy was wild. She bundled everybody into the car the minute they got back,' Mary laughed. 'I'd say your ears were well warmed on the way back to Dublin if you could hear.'

'I'll recover,' he said. 'Some of these ones are just too precise. They think the whole world revolves round their whatnot.'

As the stacks disappeared from the meadows and the shed filled, the sun coming and going behind the dark, racing clouds, they were able to stack the last loads at their ease, chatting and idling. The birds had gone quiet. The hum of the insects was still. Swallows were sweeping low above the empty meadows. The wing beats of swans crossing between the lakes came on the still air and they counted seven in formation before they disappeared below the screen of trees. For such elegant creatures of the air and the water, their landing was loud and clumsy.

They were lingering and tidying up, with hours of space and weather to spare, when Bill Evans came through the gate and lumbered over to the packed shed. He was wearing the huge wellingtons but no overcoat, wide braces crossing the shirt of mattress ticking. The braces were connected to the voluminous tweed trousers with nails instead of buttons.

'Ye got on great,' he praised.

'Anybody with meadows yet to mow is late,' Jamesie said provocatively.

'There'll be plenty of weather yet,' he defended his own house stubbornly.

'That's right. Give him no heed, Bill,' Mary took his part. 'When will the bus start taking you to town?'

'Every Thursday from now on,' he said importantly.

'They'll wash your whatnot when they get you to town,' Jamesie said. 'You'll never be the same again.'

'You're a pure disgust, Jamesie. They will run you out of the parish yet. It's a wonder Mary has put up with you for so long,' he responded ringingly.

'What else can I do, Bill? I'm stuck with him now,' Mary said.

'That's all that is saving him,' he grinned.

The two women left to go into the house and he followed them as trustingly as a child.

'Lord bless us,' Jamesie said. 'They treat him worse than a dog and yet he'd die on the cross for them if you said as much as a word. He'll have great times in the town. He'll devour everything in sight. He'll eat and drink rings round him. He'll fatten,' Jamesie said in glee. 'Sometimes I think he's as happy as anybody.'

The words hung in the air a moment without meeting agreement or disagreement: it was as if they both knew secretly that there was no certainty as to what constituted the happiness or unhappiness of another.

'Would you change places with him?'

'No.'

'Would he change places with you?'

'Like a shot.'

'I doubt it. Nobody will change lives with another. Anyhow it's not possible.'

'I'd change. I'd love to have been de Valera,' Jamesie said.

'Then you'd be dead,' Ruttledge said, and from the expression on Jamesie's face he saw that he felt that his words were no joke at all.

By early evening they were looking down at the complete emptiness of the meadows under the stillness of the big trees. All over the country for a week or more these reaped meadows would give back their squares and rectangles of burned yellow light amid the green of hedges and pastures. A number of times Ruttledge suggested that they finish and go into the house but Jamesie continued to dawdle and fuss over the last few rows as if he was waiting for the rain. When it came, in the complete silence of the trees and the birds, the first sparse drops were loud on the iron.

'Isn't Patrick Ryan the most hopeless man?' Jamesie said as he looked across the lake at the bare hill where Patrick's few cattle were grazing. 'Not a blade of grass cut yet and all that good weather gone. A most hopeless man and he couldn't care less if there wasn't a dry day between now and Christmas.'

The surfaces of the lake between the trees were now pocked with rain. Water was splashing heavily down from the big sycamore leaves on to the roof of the shed.

'I'm going to enjoy this rain. I'm going to sit with a glass in my hand at the window and watch it pour down,' Jamesie said as they prepared to run towards the house.

The ground softened quickly and the drains were loud with rushing water. When the rain stopped, it was followed by broken weather, wind and light showers racing over the face of the lake.

On a showery Sunday the Shah came grim-faced to the house and said that he had made up his mind.

'Have you spoken to anybody since?'

'Just that woman in the hotel.'

'What did she say?'

'Much what you said yourself. She's made a will. The children will take over the place but not till she decides and how long they'll last is another matter,' he said. 'One thing sure is they'll never fill her shoes.'

'What did she think of giving Frank Dolan his chance?'

'She thought it was fair enough. If he can come up with the washers. What do you think?'

'It doesn't matter what I think.'

'Well, what *do* you think?'

'He's worked for you all his life. He's as much entitled to the place as anybody. That said, people don't always get what they're entitled to.'

'You can say that again,' he said with relish.

'You can always take it to an auctioneer.'

'No,' he said in alarm. 'That crowd of crooks. They're not all like Jimmy Joe McKiernan. You'd be annoyed as well with people beating round the place and the taxman snooping.'

'There are times when they are necessary,' Ruttledge said.

'Will the other fella be able for it though? Will he have the washers? Will he be able to pay?' he asked, and it was clear to Ruttledge that his mind was made up.

'I don't know. You'll have to find out first if he wants the place.'

The Shah found this unbelievable: he couldn't imagine anyone not desiring the place.

'There are people who don't want responsibility,' Ruttledge explained.

'What'd happen if some other man walked in?' he asked.

'He could be out on his ear,' Ruttledge said.

'Now you're talking. Now you see,' he declared confidently.

'What are you going to do?'

'That's what I'm asking.'

'You'll have to have a word with him. The two of you will have to talk.'

The Shah stopped, dumbfounded. Close by, the berries of a rowan were starting to redden. On the branches of a whitethorn a small bird, a robin, was singing. A single crow lighted silently in the bare field.

'We don't talk,' he said.

'He must be with you twenty years by now.'

'A good deal more than that but we still don't talk,' he said stubbornly.

It was Ruttledge's turn to be dumbfounded. He had assumed that people who were so close for so long talked with one another. Now he had to acknowledge that in all the times he had seen them together never once had he witnessed even a brief conversation. From time to time they made statements that were intended to be overheard, sometimes with their backs turned or delivered sideways but never face to face. These communications were received in silence and then they went back to whatever they had been doing.

Their ways and habits helped. The Shah liked to rise early. Frank Dolan seldom got out of bed before midday but would work late into the night. They were agreeable to their many customers but always separately. The customers they disliked soon learned not to come about the place. However it was communicated – and it was as sure and quick as radar – there was never the slightest disagreement about the unwanted customers. Whether they met Frank Dolan or the Shah they were unceremoniously shown the door. If the other happened to be close by, they would generally lift their heads from whatever they were doing to observe what was going on but never to comment or take any part.

'What do you want me to do?' Ruttledge asked.

'Would you have a word with him?'

'Are you sure? Are you sure you wouldn't be better going on as you are for a while longer?'

'No. It's time to make a move and nobody else but Frank knows anything about the place. It wouldn't be much use to anybody else. They wouldn't know how to get on with the people.'

'I take it you are not selling your house or the cottages or the fields. Just the business?'

'I'm bad but I'm not that bad. I'm not putting out every light in the house in the one go,' he shook gently for the first time that day, restored to his old self. 'Frank is due for a big awakening,' he said with gusto.

'He may not want the responsibility,' Ruttledge warned.

'Then we can go to your auctioneer and he'll get an even bigger awakening. Some of these fellas think life is a picnic.'

Not many days later John Quinn came to the house in a new second-hand green Vauxhall. He parked beneath the alder tree where he had parked the old white Beetle years before. This time he placed no big stone beneath the tyre to ensure it didn't roll towards the lake. In a new dark pinstripe suit, he could have been a distinguished politician or businessman.

'It's wonderful to see a young couple happy and getting on so well in the world and going from strength to strength and turning their backs on nobody and bringing everybody else along with them,' he began as he entered the house.

'I'm afraid, John, we are not all that young any more,' Ruttledge said.

'All in the mind. It's all in the mind. You are as young as you feel. I myself intend to be a permanent twenty-two or twenty-three till night falls. I come with good news and I won't be staying long,' he said when he was offered a chair. 'I have work to do and you have your work to do and I don't want wasting good time or good neighbours' time.'

All through the brief visit he remained standing but his eyes were restless about the room and only paused when he looked at Kate. His small eyes and a few missing teeth were the only blemishes in his handsome head. 'The Lord God has said, 'Tis not good for man to live alone, and John Quinn always took this to heart,' he continued smoothly, softly; 'and when the mountain doesn't go to Mohammed then Mohammed must go to the mountain. So John went to the Marriage Bureau in Knock where Our Lady appeared to the children. Everything was vetted and proved to be above board. They found me a most respectable person. She lost her good husband after bringing up her family and like myself did not think it good to live alone. There is a small trouble with her family but that will pass given time. Young people sometimes find it hard to understand that older people need the same little things and comforts and enjoyments that they need. So we are having the wedding here among good friends and neighbours instead of in her part of the country, which would be more according to the book. So it's no wild goose errand that has brought me here but to invite you to join with us in our happiness,' and he named the date and time of the wedding and the reception at the Central Hotel.

The Ruttledges congratulated him and wished him happiness and thanked him, saying they would be delighted to attend his wedding.

'We are not now in our first bloom and have no reason to wait and whether young or old the summer is the best time for marrying. I'll be going now and leaving you to your good work and not wasting any more of your time.'

He would take neither tea nor whiskey in celebration of the happy occasion and made a point of repeating that they were busy and he was busy and no one should stand too much on ceremony or politeness. Too much politeness was sometimes a big hold-up to people's business in this world.

They both walked him to the green Vauxhall under the alder tree.

'We hope you'll both be very happy.'

'Happiness makes happiness. When people are happy they help one another and get on well together.'

He didn't start the engine but released the hand brake to let it freewheel down to the lake. Approaching the lake, he put it into gear. It shuddered a moment before starting.

'He was saving on juice,' Ruttledge said.

'Ah,' Kate shook her shoulders with distaste.

'This time he could meet his match,' Ruttledge said. 'You'd never know. There must be villains in the female line as well.'

'Of course, but I bet they take good care to steer clear of one another,' she said.

The time came when the lambs had to be sold. Every year without fail Jamesie accompanied Ruttledge on the drive to the factory. Early on the arranged morning he entered the house rubbing his hands together. He knew it wasn't a day they welcomed.

'We are going to gather the money. We are going to be rich. We'll lie in clover and speak the truth without fear or favour.'

'You look like a prince,' Kate said.

'Prince of the bogs and the rushes,' he answered defensively, but he was shining. His loose grey tweeds were worn but spotless and in the open-necked shirt he looked even more elegant than in his Sunday clothes. The leather of his boots was pale in places where the black dye had been washed away by wet grass.

'Would you like anything before starting?'

'No. Not today. We're as well to be making tracks. There could be a long queue.'

The trailer was already hitched to the car and backed up to the door of the shed. The sheep and lambs had been enclosed

141

in the small field next to the shed and were easily penned. The fat male lambs were picked out and carried to the trailer. Borderline lambs were weighed on a metal scale in the corner.

'Salvation,' Jamesie said when an underweight lamb was marked and let free.

'A very temporary salvation.'

'Tell me what other kind there is?'

'A long life on grass.'

'You think that's permanent? They are going where they should be going. To a good Sunday table,' he said.

'Five months old. It's a short journey.'

Jamesie rapped the roof of the trailer in quiet satisfaction as they got into the car. 'They'll never see the lake again.'

To Jamesie everything they passed was of intense interest: the fields well kept, the neglected fields, the grazing cattle, ramshackle houses, houses that shone, houses in ruin. A long, slow-running commentary rose out of the avid looking. He praised where he could, but most people were allowed their space without praise or blame in a gesture of hands that assigned his life and theirs to their own parts in this inexhaustible journey.

As they passed the roofless Abbey at Shruhaun, he made the sign of the cross, quickly and hurriedly, like sprinkling water.

The bars in Shruhaun were closed but vans were delivering bread and newspapers to the side doors. He craned back to try to discover who was taking in the bread, frustrated by the vans. Once they reached the outskirts of the town he ordered Ruttledge to slow.

'I saw the day when every man around thought that woman was the light of heaven,' he said of a big woman crossing the street. 'A pure wilderness of a woman now.'

'You'll find the light of heaven hasn't travelled far. It's come to rest on some other young women.'

'Two detectives – in the alley – watching,' he sang out as the car and trailer went slowly past Jimmy Joe McKiernan's bar.

'They're always there.'

'Night and day.'

'And it's a waste of time. Nobody they want is going to roll up to the front door.'

'I know. I know. I know full well. Everything goes on round the back,' he protested. 'The world knows he led the big breakout from Long Kesh – didn't he get his arm broke? – and a whole lot else but they can't arrest him. They have to be seen to be watching, that's all. Everything that is done they do in the North. They don't care a straw as long as it doesn't travel down here. All for show.'

'I think it's wrong,' Ruttledge said. 'There shouldn't be two laws.'

'I have nothing against Jimmy Joe McKiernan. As plain and decent a man as there is in the town. He's not for himself like all the others.'

'You don't mind that he'd shoot you?'

'He'd do that only if he had to. He'd only do it if you stood in the way of the Cause. Jimmy Joe wouldn't harm a fly unless it stood in his way.'

'I don't see much difference between getting shot in a bad cause or a good.'

'You're getting too precise, Mister Ruttledge. He's not going to shoot you or me. We don't count,' Jamesie was uncomfortable with the argument. 'There's not a soul stirring round Luke's,' he said as they passed Luke Henry's bar. Jamesie always wanted to flee unpleasantness and disagreement.

'We'll have a drink in Luke's on the way home,' Ruttledge said, recognizing his anxiety.

'Please God,' he said fervently, relieved. 'The Empire of the Shah,' he said caressing the words as they came to the end of the town and saw the sheds and diesel signs and the cottages and the huge yard packed with the scrapped lorries and cars and tractors and machinery behind the high wire fence. 'Does he know the end of his money?'

'He enjoys having money,' Ruttledge said, and then saw the small round figure in the arched entrance of the main shed, with his fist firmly fixed on his hip, the sheepdog sitting by his side. 'He hasn't a great deal of use for money. It's just the having of it that gives him pleasure.'

'Lord bless us, he is up already with half the town still asleep. What is he going to do with it all?' Jamesie said in wonderment as soon as he spotted the round figure by the sheepdog.

'It'll go to somebody or other. It has nowhere else to go,' Ruttledge said laughingly. 'It was gathered from people and just goes back to other people.'

'I know you're not a bit interested in his money and Kate doesn't care,' Jamesie said cautiously. 'I'd praise you both for that. There's no worse sight than watching people wait to fill dead men's shoes when they should be going about their own business.'

'I know, Jamesie. I know.'

Once they passed beyond the town he no longer knew any of the people who lived on the farms or in the roadside bungalows. His fascination did not lessen but he was silent now, looking to left and right, as if he was afraid he might miss something important along the way.

'Dromod,' he cried out when the stone station and the bar across the road came into view. 'Every single summer. Meet Johnny off the train with Rowley's car. Put him back on the train.'

'It's a pretty station,' Ruttledge said.

'It's all right. It'll do,' he said dismissively. In itself it held no other interest.

On the wide road to Rooskey he was bewildered by the number of cars and trucks and the speed at which they passed. As they crossed the Shannon by the narrow bridge in Rooskey, he asked Ruttledge to slow again so that he could feast his eyes on the white pleasure-boats below.

'Foreigners and people from Dublin. Plenty of money.

Drinks. Riding,' he rubbed his hands together in mock celebration of their moneyed pleasures.

'Would Lucy and Jim like to own one of those boats? They
could afford –'

'No,' the very idea was disturbing. 'No. She might but Jim
wouldn't want. No,' he said definitely, with relief. 'They'd
want to go out foreign. To Italy or somewhere. They'd have
no taste for this place. They know too much about places like
round here.'

They drove through bog and scrub. The floodwaters of the
river lowlands had withdrawn to leave sedge as pale as ripe
wheat. A match could strike it into sweeping flame. Then
they started to climb. Far below, a narrow inlet of the
Shannon sparkled. They passed a school and a church with
a big bell, sitting silent on the grass, white houses, old trees,
and once they began the descent they entered the limestone
fields and stone walls of Roscommon. Here and there slender ash trees stood alone among the grey stone walls and the
sheep and cattle and the occasional field of horses. They
went through sleepy villages, circled the spires and chim-
neys of Roscommon town on the ring road that took them
past the cattle mart.

'At home you see nothing. See nothing,' Jamesie sighed, as
people and places flew past.

As soon as they eased in behind the queue of cars and
tractors drawing trailers outside the factory, he raised his
wristwatch to the window light. 'An hour and ten minutes
since we left the house – five minutes quicker than last year.
Do you mind the year the wheel came off the old trailer and
we thought we'd never make it and the lambs roaring?
Those men in the ESB van saved our lives. They lifted the
trailer as if it was a feather. They were toppers and wouldn't
even take the price of a drink. All of them were in a tug-of-
war team.'

'I remember. I don't know what we'd have done.'

The queue moved slowly. Big lorries entered by a different

gate. Occasionally, farmers left their cars and went to chat at the open windows of cars they knew. After a half-hour or so they reached the gate. Ruttledge told the man in the small wooden office the number of lambs in the trailer and was handed a docket and paper disks with the number 126. At the pens he reversed the trailer. Farmers helped run the frightened, huddled lambs from the trailer. The disks were fixed on the wool. It was all very quiet and orderly except for the bleating of the lambs. Ruttledge left Jamesie in the pens and went to park the car and trailer. He drove quite a distance out the road for home before he found a space. He took his time walking back. When he reached the pens, he found Jamesie agitated and wildly anxious. The lambs had been moving quickly and he was afraid Ruttledge wasn't going to return in time.

'I thought you'd never get back.'

'I had to go a distance to park. There's plenty of time.'

'Very little time. They'll be going in any minute.'

They had several minutes more to wait and in that time his anxiety evaporated completely. A man in a white coat took and checked Ruttledge's docket against the numbers and wrote him a receipt. When a pair of young men came to drive the lambs towards the chutes, the whole flock turned and ran towards the men.

'Fucken pets,' they cried out in frustration as they pushed, hushed, kicked, lifted the lambs towards the final pens.

'Your lambs are getting a bad reference,' Jamesie said slyly, but Ruttledge by now had detached himself from the lambs, the way people have to separate themselves from whatever is hopeless and inevitable.

'They were well treated,' he answered. 'They had no reason to fear people.'

'Too well treated, those men think,' Jamesie replied, watching Ruttledge carefully.

'Let them think away.'

They watched the final gate close on the lambs, where two more men without time to raise their heads were pushing lamb after lamb into a shoot covered with hanging strips of thick black rubber, and then they turned away.

As they made their way to the offices, they saw an old red lorry unloading lambs directly into a pen on the factory floor. There was a constant hiss from the water hose as the white-clad workers moved about like ghosts in the clouds of steam and the clanging of metal and cries and shouts. Another old lorry drew up. The driver climbed down. With obvious surprise and anger he recognized the first lorry, and when he saw the driver he advanced on the other man. This was his territory.

The workers unloading the lambs, the men checking their numbers, the men driving the lambs through the pens stood rooted in their places. Violence seemed a hair's breath away. When they were only a few feet apart, he stopped. Both men were in their forties, small and burly, physically a fair match. Suddenly, the first driver started to sing.

'Take my hand. I'm a stranger in paradise. All lost in a wonderland.'

The other driver was taken aback at first, and then a slow, cunning smile spread across his face. He too knew the song and could sing.

'If I stand starry-eyed. That's the danger in paradise. For mortals who stand beside an angel like you,' he began.

'I saw your face. And I ascended. Out of the commonplace into the rare.'

'Somewhere in space I hang suspended,' the other sang confidently now, and raised his hand, which was clasped and held.

'Until I know there's a chance that you care,' they sang together as they danced round and round in their awkward boots with hands held high in front of the spellbound floor, and then stood to face one another.

'And tell him that he need be a stranger no more!' they roared, and stamped their feet like stags.

When they finished, the entire factory floor applauded. Waving, they climbed back into their separate cabs.

'You see nothing at home. Nothing,' Jamesie complained.

'You see the birds and the sky and the tracks of the animals,' Ruttledge said teasingly.

'Nothing. You see nothing. People are far more interesting. You see more in one day out than at home in a month.'

'I thought they were going to hammer one another.'

'The singing and dancing was a clever way out. I'd say there'd be less singing if it happened again. A clattering match or a tyre lever.'

'Johnny and Patrick Ryan were singing and dancing round the iron posts like that when Johnny was home.'

'Johnny and Patrick could sing better in their day than yon pair,' Jamesie said loyally. 'I'd praise the pair though for not coming to blows anyhow.'

They went down a long corridor past offices into a room with a glass-viewing wall where a dozen or so farmers were gathered. At the end of the room a man and a girl sat in a high glass office. The hung lambs moved on a slow line, headless already, disembowelled, skinned. Men with power hoses washed each carcass down. The swirling steam softened and made ghostly the whole scene. They were then lifted on to a separate line where they were weighed and graded on a huge digital scale. Each farmer could tell his own lambs when the number showed in big electronic red digits above the scale. In the steam and water, the men in white rubber aprons and white rubber boots and white caps worked without pause in dance-like silence. They could have been athletes dressed as doctors or nurses in a great swirling hospital of the dead.

In the glass office the girl printed out the weights and grade as they appeared on the scale. She then spoke each farmer's name and number into a microphone and handed down a printed slip through a small hatch in the glass. She called, 'Ruttledge 126,' and he went and was handed his slip. The farmers were almost as silent as the workers moving within, all their attention fixed on the red digital numbers above the scale. Jamesie's eyes never stopped moving from face to face to screen to carcass to the silent workers. He too was completely silent.

'They are very young, the workers,' Ruttledge said to one of the watchers at the glass wall.

'Like footballers. Few last more than a couple of years – the damp, all the lifting; it's a young man's game.'

'What do they do then?'

'What does anybody do who needs work?' the man smiled grimly. 'Go on the buildings or to a different factory. Head for America or England or do without.'

At a busy inner office a woman tapped the details on the slip into a machine that produced an itemized account complete with deductions. She then wrote a cheque, had it countersigned by the only man in the office, and gave the cheque and account to Ruttledge in a brown envelope. The whole atmosphere was efficient and friendly and casual, the stream of men coming and going with their slips.

'Nearly all the women in that office are married,' said Jamesie, who had been busy looking at their hands while Ruttledge's slip was being processed. 'It's a sight how the world is going. You drive in with a trailer of lambs and an hour later leave with them all in a cheque in your hip pocket,' he remarked as they drove away with the empty trailer.

Soon his eyes were feasting on the fields of short, rich grass in their walls of lichened limestone, the slender ash trees, a huge chestnut, some elevated strips of bare rock, like promontories in a sea of grass.

'A few fields of this land would be worth a whole farm around the lake.'

At an empty bar-and-grocery outside Roscommon town they had ham sandwiches with a creamy pint of stout. A woman sliced the ham and made up the sandwiches from a loaf so fresh the bread was warm. Jamesie was enjoying the strange bar and looking forward to the rest of the journey. Ruttledge was relieved the morning was over.

'Have you noticed how the journey home always seems to go faster?' he asked, when the pleasure boats came into view as they crossed the Shannon by the narrow Bridge at Rooskey.

'Of course,' Jamesie answered readily. 'You never know rightly what you are facing into when you're setting out. You always know the way home.'

There was a space for the car and empty trailer outside Luke's, and Jamesie practically danced into the bar in front of Ruttledge. Luke was sitting behind the counter, his chin resting on his joined hands. Except for a family of tinkers drinking quietly in a corner, the bar was empty. Jamesie went straight up to the counter.

'Are you vexed yet, Luke?' he demanded.

Luke leaned slightly forward to say in a mock, confidential voice, 'I'm not vexed yet, Jamesie.'

'Why aren't you vexed, Luke?'

'It's not time yet.'

'When will it be time?'

Luke stared studiously at the electric clock among the wreaths of plastic flowers. 'At two minutes to four I'll be very vexed but I'll expect you to be gone out of the town before then.'

'Good man, Luke! You never failed us yet,' Jamesie cried approval, and by now the tinker family had dropped their own quiet conversation. All their attention was fixed on the two men at the counter.

'A pair of Crested Tens and two pints of stout, Luke,' Ruttledge called.

'The man who made the money is buying,' Jamesie rubbed his hands vigorously together. Through the bar window they could see all the way across the street to where a man was laying out trays of potted plants on a long trestle table. Jamesie wandered over to talk to the tinkers.

'Mister and Missus McDonough. You are most welcome to the town,' he said expansively, holding out his hand. They were delighted. Neither seemed to mind that they lived closer to the town than he did and were in the bar and the town long before he arrived.

'Good health, Luke.'

'Good luck and a long life,' Luke said. 'I see your friend has left you.'

'He'll be back,' Ruttledge said.

Ruttledge picked a time when he was fairly sure of finding Frank Dolan alone to see if he was interested in taking over the Shah's business. At six the scrapyard would be closed. The Shah would be enthroned at his table in the Central. The men who waited about the sheds and scrapyard all day would have retired to their cottages. The little shops were already closed or closing as he drove through the town.

He found Frank Dolan in the main shed. He was in one of the deep pits examining an old JCB, the sheepdog lying close to his head on the edge of the pit. Recognizing him at once, the dog ran forward.

'He know, he knows,' Frank Dolan said of the sheepdog as he climbed the steps out of the deep pit. He was as besotted with the dog as his master was.

'If anybody else had walked up like that he'd have devoured them. In another hour there won't be sight or light of him round the place. He'll have disappeared to meet Himself coming from the Central. Isn't that right?' he caught and roughed the dog playfully, who growled in turn and caught and held Frank Dolan by the wrist. When the dog released his hand, he wiped it with a cloth and offered Ruttledge a little finger in a gentle, comic apology for the oil- and grease-stained hands.

The two men were friendly. They had known each other a long time without ever having been close. Frank's grey eyes were humorous and sharply intelligent and over the years he had acquired a striking resemblance to his master, so much so that he was sometimes taken for his son by inexperienced commercial travellers. This was seen by both as highly compromising.

There was little similarity of feature but they had grown alike in the way they moved and stood and talked and listened. Through night classes and reading and the practical work of the shed, Frank had become knowledgeable and skilled. The Shah knew little about the newer machines; what he could do well was rough welding, meet customers he liked and buy and sell shrewdly. Each stayed well clear of the other's territory.

'His lordship asked me to have a word with you on a small business matter,' Ruttledge said when pauses began to occur in the polite conversation.

Immediately, Frank Dolan assumed an apprehensive formality.

'It's nothing unpleasant,' Ruttledge hastened to say. 'Is it all right to talk here?'

'We'd be safer further back.' He was reassured but still apprehensive. He and the Shah shared a dislike of anything new or strange entering their world.

They moved through a clutter of old engines, cars, tractors, machines, tools, benches, Frank Dolan patting the dog's head as if for comfort. From the back it was possible to see how enormous the shed was, all the way out to the huge rounded arch.

'He wants to retire and is thinking of selling. Would you be interested?'

Frank Dolan's face registered shock, washed clean of its everyday watchful expression, and was replaced by an intensity of feeling that was close to innocence. Ruttledge still hadn't any idea what his response might be.

He looked long and seriously into Ruttledge's face as he answered, 'I would be very interested,' with a mixture of iron dignity and humility.

Ruttledge hadn't been expecting anything as straightforward and uncomplicated. 'He's not too hard in what he's asking,' he said and told him the price the Shah had agreed.

Frank Dolan looked steadily into Ruttledge's face but did

not make any comment on the price. 'The big question: Can it be afforded? Can I get money?' he said as if thinking aloud to himself out of unnerving silence. 'To be interested is the easy part.'

'Only you could know that, Frank.'

'How?' he asked bluntly and without guile.

'Do you have any savings or property?'

He had no property but had considerable savings, much more than Ruttledge would have guessed. 'How though will the rest be got?' His tone changed, asking humbly, almost hopelessly.

'The way everybody else gets that sort of money. Apply for a loan. You must know all this yourself. I shouldn't be telling you.'

'I don't,' he said simply. 'Would you help me?'

'Of course I would – as far as I'm able – but wouldn't you be better with people closer to yourself?'

'Who?'

'Your family . . . relations . . . friends.'

'They can be the very worst,' he laughed. 'You'd be better on your own than with some of that crowd.'

'I'll help you if you want. I told his lordship that he should speak to you about this himself but he wouldn't hear. Anyhow it's done now.'

'That's him all over,' he said with open confidence. 'In some ways he's the most terrible coward you could meet in a day's walk. He's a great show till something awkward turns up. Then he runs to other people. He'll face nothing.'

Ruttledge smiled at the accuracy of the description that went beneath the surface and said, 'God knows you have been observing him long enough to know. With all that I'm very fond of him.'

'We all are – except betimes – but you wouldn't want to let on,' Frank Dolan said with emotion.

'I'll tell him, then, that you *are* interested and we'll go ahead from there,' Ruttledge said.

'If you wait another half-hour you'll meet him coming from the hotel. Soon you'll see the dog going to meet him. You and me won't exist then.'

'I'll tell him another time. There's no use rushing anything with him. I hope it will all turn out lucky.'

'Please God,' Frank Dolan said as he walked him to the car, and for the first time it struck Ruttledge that there was something of an unorthodox monastic community about the ramshackle scrapyard and pumps and sheds and the small cottages. There wasn't a woman anywhere in sight or in any of the small houses.

There were many days of wind and rain. Uneasy gusts ruffled the surface of the lake, sending it running this way and that. Occasionally, a rainbow arched all the way across the lake. More often the rainbows were as broken as the weather, appearing here and there in streaks or brilliant patches of colour in the unsettled sky. When rain wasn't dripping from leaves or eaves, the air was so heavy it was like breathing rain. The hives were quiet. Only the midges swarmed.

The hard burnt colour of the freshly cut meadows softened and there was a blue tinge in the first growth of aftergrass that shone under the running winds. The bullfinch disappeared with the wild strawberries from the bank. The little vetches turned black. The berries on the rowans along the shore glowed with such redness it was clear why the rowan berry was used in ancient song to praise the lips of girls and women. The darting swifts and swallows hunted low above the fields and the half-light brought out the noisy blundering bats.

There was little outside work. The sheep and cattle were heavy and content on grass. Radish, lettuce, scallions, peas, broad beans were picked each day with the new potatoes. In the mornings Ruttledge worked at the few advertising commissions he had until they were all finished. Then he read or fished from the boat. Kate read or drew and sometimes walked or cycled round the shore to Mary and Jamesie.

Even more predictable than the rain, Bill Evans came every day. All his talk now was of the bus that would take him to the town. For some reason it had been postponed or delayed for a few weeks but each day he spoke of the imminent arrival of the bus. They were beginning to think it as illusory as one of the small rainbows above the lake, when a squat, yellow minibus came slowly in around the shore early on Thursday morning and waited. In the evening the bus climbed past the alder tree and gate, and went all the way up the hill.

He had always been secretive about what happened in his house or on the farm unless there was some glory or success that he could bask in; it was no different with the welfare home.

What he was forthcoming about was the bus and the people on the bus and the bus driver, Michael Pat. Already, he had become Michael Pat's right-hand man: the two of them ran the bus together and he spoke of the other passengers with lordly condescension.

'I give Michael Pat great help getting them off the bus. Some of them aren't half there. They'd make you laugh. Michael Pat said he wouldn't have got on near as well without me and that I'm a gift. He's calling for me first thing next Thursday. I sit beside him in the front seat and keep a watch.'

If a strange bird couldn't cross the fields without Jamesie knowing, a big yellow minibus coming in round the shore wasn't going to escape his notice, but he didn't want to seem too obviously curious. He took a couple of days before cycling in round the shore. The Ruttledges knew at once what brought him and told him what they knew. They were inclined to make light of Bill Evans's boasting.

He held up his hand in disagreement, knowing several people on the bus. 'Take care. He may not be that far out. With people living longer there's a whole new class who are neither in the world or the graveyard. Once they were miles above poor Bill in life. Some of them would have tossed him cigarettes after Mass on a Sunday. Now they are in

155

wheelchairs and hardly able to cope. The bus takes them into town. It's a great idea. They get washed and fed and attended to and it gives the relatives looking after them at home a break for the day. People fall very low through no fault of their own. Compared to some of the souls in that bus, Bill Evans is a millionaire.'

The bus was a special bus, with safety belts and handrails and a ramp for wheelchairs. The following Thursday Bill Evans sat in the front seat beside Michael Pat and waved and laughed towards the Ruttledges as the bus went slowly down to the lake. Under the 'No Smoking' sign he sat puffing away like an ocean-going liner. The faces that appeared at the other windows were strained with age and illness and looked out impassively. Many did not look out at all.

The Shah tried but could not conceal his impatience when he arrived at the house on Sunday. 'Have you managed to get in to see that man yet on that business?'

'Did you not hear? Did he not tell you?'

'You must be joking. He'd tell you nothing. You might as well be dealing with a wall.'

'I was in. You had gone to the hotel. The place was practically closed.'

'Why didn't you come down to the hotel? Herself is always asking. You could have had something to eat after your trouble.'

'It wasn't any trouble.'

'Did you get a word out of him at all? It must have been like pulling teeth.'

'He was agreeable and sensible. He had plenty to say.'

'Well?' he demanded impatiently.

'He wants to buy the place if he's able.'

'Aha,' he said with satisfaction. 'He's not as green as he's cabbage-looking. Has he the washers?'

'He has savings, more than I thought he could have. I can't see him ever getting fat on what you'd pay.'

156

'That'll do you now,' he shook with pleasure at this picture of his shrewdness. 'He gets paid well enough. He'd live on air. How is he going to come up with the rest? Did he get round to that?'

'He'll have to try and get a loan.'

'Who'll give *him* a loan?'

'He'll have to go to a bank.'

'What'll the bank say when they see him? They could run him to hell.'

'I'd say he has every chance of getting the loan but are you sure you want to go ahead and sell?'

'Why would I want to change?' he demanded.

'The place has been your life. Once you sell, it won't be yours any more. You'll no longer have any say. He'll be able to sell it on to someone else or tell you he no longer wants you round and there's not a thing you'll be able to do. I'm not saying he's likely to do any of these things. In fact, I think it's most unlikely, but once you sell you're gone. Now is the time to be sure.'

'I'd love it if he told me he didn't want me near the place. I'd be out the door before he had time to turn.'

'As long as you know,' Ruttledge said.

'I know full well. Too many hang on till they're staggering round the place. There's a time for everything. That boy is going to get some land. It'll take some of the sleep out of his eyes.'

'I'll go ahead, then, with the sale if that's what you want.'

'Go full ahead. And take care! You may find that the banks may be in no rush to hand out loans when they see the boy they have on their hands,' he started to shake silently.

'As long as you are sure?'

'I'm certain. It's time.'

The ground had become soft and unpleasant for walking and they did not go further than the hanging hill above the inner lake from where they were able to count the sheep. Several swans were sailing on the lake amid dark clutches of

157

wildfowl. The occasional lone heron flew between the island and the bog. Nothing was sharp. The lanes of watery light that pierced the low cloud from time to time seemed to illuminate nothing but mist and cloud and water. The sedge of Gloria Bog and the little birches had no colour. The mountains were hidden. From this hanging hill the Shah had always looked across the lake and bog towards those mountains. Increasingly, the way he stood, his right hand resting firmly on his hip, his feet wide apart, reminded Ruttledge of the way his grandmother had stood at her half-door in old age. She had been a good-looking, vigorous woman even then, with a great sense of fun. The way she stood was like a symbol of her independence and spirit when her other advantages had disappeared.

'The rain comes down. Grass grows. Children get old,' the Shah said suddenly. 'That's it. We all know. We know full well and can't even whisper it out loud. We know in spite of them.'

At that same time Kate was offered tempting work in London.

Every summer Robert Booth came from London. When the Ruttledges first moved to the lake, other visitors had come from London, but over the years they dwindled until Robert Booth was their only serious connection with that busy world to which they had both once belonged, a world that was growing increasingly distant.

Robert Booth came from humble origins in the North of Ireland, a small draper's brilliant son. Scholarships took him all the way to Oxford, where his studies were interrupted by the war. After the war he returned to take a double-first in history and classics and then entered the law to discover that it wasn't acceptable to practise at the Bar with a thick regional accent; so he took himself to acting school where he acquired the accent that would serve him for the rest of his life, its only flaw being that it outdistanced what it sought to emulate.

He was reasonably successful as a barrister but felt too exposed, too much on his own: he was an outsider who always wanted to be on the inside. When offered a partnership in a young advertising firm by people he had known at Oxford, he abandoned the law with relief. Within the firm he rose steadily. He had interviewed Ruttledge when he applied for a copywriter's position in the firm a few years after arriving in London. He already knew Kate and Kate's father. At her marriage he had been one of the two witnesses. He had been against their decision to leave London, and without the freelance work he put their way after they left, the first years by the lake would have been more difficult. From time to time he had been able to arrange for Kate to return to her old position in the firm for short periods.

In those years he came on the bus, which dropped him at the end of the road. Ruttledge met the bus and they walked slowly round the shore, Ruttledge carrying his suitcase, Robert Booth using a rubber-topped walking stick to help him through the potholes and loose stones.

In later years Ruttledge met him each year at the hotel by the river in Enniskillen and drove him to the house. He waited by the hotel bar where he had a view of the entrance. A wide lawn sloped down to the Erne, where pleasure-boats were tied up at a wooden dock. Further down, the new theatre stood beside the high stone pillars on which the railway once had crossed the river.

A large black car drew up at the entrance of the hotel. A tall, elegant, middle-aged woman in tweeds got out from behind the wheel and walked to the passenger side to open the door for Robert and hand him a travelling case from the back seat. He used his walking stick to lift himself slowly from the seat. The couple stood for a minute smiling and exchanging words. The woman's dress and manner spoke of golf and bridge and dinner tables, children at good schools or university, books perhaps, but strict conformity within a class of money and comfort. They embraced. She had been leaving him at this hotel for years but Ruttledge had never met the wife of Robert Booth's brother. All his various social lives were kept within separate compartments and were never allowed to cross. Robert stood politely in the entrance as the car drove away. As soon as it banged on the cattle grid over the entrance, he raised his walking stick and turned and entered the hotel.

''A very great pleasure,' he said.

They had a drink at a table in the near-empty bar and Robert talked of his stay at his brother's weekend cottage in Donegal, the people they both knew in London. As they walked to the car, Robert said politely how much he was looking forward to seeing Kate again. Ruttledge knew Robert and yet he hardly knew him. He knew only what Robert Booth chose to reveal, which was very little, or let slip involuntarily. He was a secretive, complicated man and much was hidden, Ruttledge suspected, from himself as well as from most other people.

The friendship had been always intertwined with business. It was unlikely that one would have survived without the other. Robert Booth looked better now than when Ruttledge first knew him. Time had softened his ugliness and slowed his ungainliness.

The road was wet with summer showers as they drove towards the border, the fields and houses neater and better tended than in the South. Many had flower gardens. At the checkpoint they sat in a queue of cars behind a ramp until a green light allowed them into the armoured and sandbagged compound. All around was a wilderness, small fields of rushes and sally and scrub with the occasional isolated house. Above them stood the bare slopes of the mountain.

Ruttledge had asked Robert Booth once how he had found the class system when he first arrived at Oxford, he who now seemed so at ease within its mazes.

'It was quite easy,' Robert Booth answered agreeably. 'When we were growing up we felt superior to the Catholics.

The first step is always the hardest. After that it is easy.' Ruttledge doubted if that could be admitted so openly and confidently now.

A young soldier carrying a machine gun read the car number into a wire grille in a camouflaged steel hut and waited until someone working the computer within the hut gave the all-clear. Another soldier stood close by on guard. They both wore boots and combat dress and had a look of drilled efficiency. Ruttledge handed the soldier his driving licence. He was friendly and personable as he took and checked the licence. Ruttledge gave his name, his trade, his date of birth, his address.

'What is the purpose of the visit?'

'To pick up a friend who is coming on a short holiday.'

'Where has he come from?'

'From London.'

'Good day,' Robert Booth said in his officer's accent.

'Have a good holiday, sir,' the soldier saluted smartly after handing back the driving licence. He did not ask to look in the boot.

'A very pleasant young man,' Robert Booth said as they drove across the ramps leading out of the compound, where other cars entering the North were waiting to be checked.

'They all are. They are well trained.'

'I'm told it's quite difficult to get into today's army. They no longer require cannon fodder,' Robert Booth said.

'Two soldiers were killed here. A bomb was put in a car and pushed downhill. The soldiers saw too late there was no one behind the wheel.'

'Will it ever end?'

'You should know that better than I do. You come from the place.'

'If it came to an all-out conflict our people would render a very bloody account of themselves but they would probably lose,' Robert Booth said, making it clear he wanted the subject pursued no further.

Kate got on well with Robert Booth. A part of her family came from the class he had so assiduously joined. He never brought presents and after an exchange of pleasantries he was shown his room. The visit was then as predictable as a timetable. He washed, walked around the lake, read a newspaper. The way he crackled the pages as he read created a space around the rocking chair. They knew him well enough to ignore him completely. They would have been rebuffed if they had enquired if there was anything they could do. His mood changed noticeably when he put the newspaper aside: the time for drinks was drawing close.

'It is a very great pleasure to be here,' he raised his glass and laughed his most agreeable laugh. Over dinner he told many stories. Like many very sociable people, he would never discuss people he worked with or anybody they knew in common unless they had been written off. Only when he spoke of paintings did something like feeling enter his voice.

Kate asked about a Turner watercolour he owned that she admired. He had purchased it for a small sum when he was young.

'It's in Japan. At a Turner exhibition,' he laughed triumphantly. 'Before Tokyo it was in Sydney. It does give me pleasure to think of all those people looking at it.'

The next morning after breakfast he walked down to the lake. Later he sat in the white rocking chair on the porch and read. While he was reading, Bill Evans came. Ruttledge heard the loud knocking on the glass from within the house and when he reached the porch Robert Booth was about to open the door.

Instead of following Ruttledge into the house, Bill Evans stood stubbornly outside and asked, 'Does he smoke?'

'He doesn't but I have cigarettes within.'

'Where is he from?' he demanded when he was finally seated.

'From London. You've seen him several times before. Don't you remember him from last summer?'

'Begod, now I do.' A look of cunning crossed the sharp features. 'Hasn't he some big job?'

'Yes. In London.'

'Would yous be getting anything out of him?'

'He's a friend. Sometimes he gives us work.'

'Is it paying work?'

'Yes.'

'Yous would want to be getting something out of him,' he said as he put his cup away and took hold of his stick.

Ruttledge saw him to the gate, and as he was returning to the house he noticed that Robert Booth had stopped reading and was following Bill Evans with his eyes as he lifted the two buckets out of the fuchsias and headed towards the lake.

'He looks like something out of a Russian novel,' he said.

'He's all ours, completely home-grown and mad alive. They were scattered all over the country when I was young. Those with English accents came mostly from Catholic orphanages around Liverpool. The whole business wasn't a million miles from the slave trade.'

'It's not a pleasant story.'

'Any of us could have found ourselves in his place.'

'But we didn't,' Robert Booth said firmly.

At lunch he asked for a glass of wine, which was unusual, though occasionally they had seen him drink heavily into the late afternoon.

'We've had a very long association now. I was going to bring it up last night at dinner but decided to wait,' he began.

The head of layout and design was retiring. They had decided to split that department in two and to offer Kate one of the positions. The people who knew her were certain she could do the job well. He wasn't able to put an exact figure on her salary but it would be considerably more than she had been paid in the past. They would have written but it was known he was coming on this visit.

'The decision was completely unanimous, I'm glad to report.'

'It's very flattering,' Kate said.

'It shouldn't be all that great a move. Haven't you kept that flat?'

'It is rented now but that wouldn't be a problem.'

'What is the problem?'

'Leaving here.'

'There's another thing,' Robert Booth said. 'The people that run the firm now know and like you both, but there's a whole new generation coming up. Naturally, they'll want their own friends. People tend to forget quickly once you are no longer there.'

A second bottle of wine was opened. Excitement and holiday entered the afternoon. The prospect of London in all its attractiveness was laid out in squares and streets and parks, shops and galleries, the winding river and the endless living stream of its people. It could be enjoyed with the lulling wine without the sharpness of the knowledge that it would only become their same lives again in different circumstances in a different place.

'I'd also like to say it would give me a great deal of personal pleasure if you were both to move back to London.'

'And it would be one of the pleasures of London to see you more often.'

'This place could be kept on as a second home.'

'We'll have to think all of that out.'

'Of course you would have no difficulty finding a position,' he turned to Ruttledge. 'With us there's no staff position open now but there will be.'

'I doubt if I'd want a regular job again,' Ruttledge said. 'It all depends on Kate.'

'Remember. People forget,' Robert Booth said.

Ruttledge changed into old clothes and went into the fields. After the wine and the heady excitement he was glad to lose himself in the mindlessness of the various tasks.

Returning to the house, he saw Jamesie come through a gate at the back and stand for a moment. Almost nonchalantly, Jamesie moved along the cart path, bending low to pass the big window on the bank. Once past, he stood and listened intently, like a bird or an animal. Then he began to check the sheds, examine tools left lying around, test the posts of the unfinished shed, shaking his head in silent disapproval as he surveyed the skeleton of the roof. He entered the orchard and then the glasshouse. He spent a long time examining the herbs and flowers, picked and ate a ripe tomato, chewing studiously, and then headed out to the land towards the cattle and sheep. He had to pass very close to where Ruttledge stood. He was chewing on a long stalk of grass.

'Hel-lo,' Ruttledge called softly as he passed.

He whirled around, startled. 'Blast you anyhow. Why hadn't you the manners to show yourself?'

'I was taking a leaf out of your book.'

'It was a poor leaf, then,' he answered and held out his hand.

'Why didn't you go into the house?'

'The big Englishman is there. He's asleep in the porch, a book on his knee,' and he imitated a deep snoring sound.

'He wouldn't mind.'

'No, no. I'll be beating away. The robins don't mix with the blackbirds.'

There was a heavy, sweet perfume in the air. It came from wild woodbine that had climbed an old hawthorn close to the house and was still putting out pale yellow flowers in the high branches.

Robert Booth was asleep in the porch. Ruttledge entered the house by the back. The black cat was sitting on Kate's knee, the white paws opening and closing on the blue denim.

'Fats goes to London!' she said laughing as Ruttledge entered the room, and the cat hearing the tone purred louder.

'She'll not like that.'

'I'm not sure I'd like it either. It's lovely to be asked.'

'What do you think?'

165

'I don't want to think just now.'

'I caught Jamesie prowling round the house, inspecting everything. He even tasted your tomatoes in the glasshouse.'

'Why wouldn't he come in?'

'He saw we had a visitor and wouldn't.'

Robert Booth felt refreshed when he woke. He showered, changed, went for a long walk round the shore and was in particularly good form when he returned to a dinner of steak and salad and wine. The steaks were cooked over a fire of dried oak on an iron grill the Shah had made for the fireplace in the small front room. As they cooked, grease dripped from the raised grill and flared in the red embers. Robert Booth sat in silence with a whiskey, watching the fire and the lights from the fire play on the white walls. At the table he came to life.

He told stories they had heard before but they were still all interesting because Robert Booth was interesting, and they stayed up late.

In the morning they could see that he had already left them; in spirit he was already in Dublin. 'Write me or call if you have any questions,' he said as he embraced Kate. 'Thank you for a wonderful visit. I hope I'll be seeing you very soon in London. It was a very great pleasure.'

'Thanks for coming. Thanks for everything.'

'Are you staying in the Shelbourne?' Ruttledge asked as they drove to the station, passing green hedges and green fields and the odd farmhouse among the new bungalows.

'Yes, but going out to dinner this evening,' and Ruttledge did not ask further.

They arrived early at the small railway station because Robert disliked being pressed for time and did not mind waiting. When they checked the time of the train, he removed a book from his case.

Robert Booth walked to a green bench beside the flowerbeds and opened the book. He did not look around at the other passengers waiting for the train. He would not welcome conversation or any interference. His life had already entered another of its closed compartments.

Ruttledge went to an assistant manager he was friendly with in the bank about getting Frank Dolan a loan. 'There should be no problem,' Joe Eustace said in his agreeable way after Ruttledge stated his business.

Within a week Joe Eustace had the loan approved, subject to an interview Frank Dolan would have to undergo in Longford. That town was chosen because it was both close and far enough away for nobody to know their business.

'He'll have to say he intends to expand the business and employ more people. That's bank policy: it looks better for the bank when they have to face the politicians and the bank likes nothing more than lending money to a thriving business. He'll have to say all that so that it goes in the report. Once he gets the loan he can do whatever he wants as long as he makes his monthly payments.'

'Why can't you do the interview yourself? That's what we did years back when I got the loan.'

'You were already a customer. We had more power back then as well. Now head office has the power. I know the man who's doing the interview and I have put him in the complete picture. The loan is in the bag. It's all arranged. It's just a matter of going through the motions and him saying the right things.'

Ruttledge wanted to drive Frank Dolan to Longford but he insisted stubbornly that they go in his old Toyota since it was on *his* business they were going. The exhaust was gone, as was the ignition key: the engine was started by crossing two sparking wires.

'What does any of them do but go?' he said to Ruttledge as they battered towards Longford. Frank Dolan had a new haircut, was spruced and shaven, dressed in his dark Sunday suit and white shirt and wine-coloured tie. His nervousness gave vividness to his pleasant, sensitive face.

'Do you want me to speak about the business of expansion and employing a young lad or two – or do you want to do that yourself?'

'I haven't the slightest intention of expanding anything or employing anybody,' he answered.

'I know that but we have to say otherwise if we want to get the loan.'

'I've been thinking that over. We could be setting a trap for ourselves. We could be going in away above our heads.'

'It's nothing like that,' Ruttledge explained with some exasperation. They had been through this twice before. 'Once you get the money you can do whatever you want as long as you make the payments. Until we get the loan we have to agree to whatever *they* want.'

'You're sure it's as simple as that? You're sure it's not some trap?'

'Certain. Absolutely certain,' Ruttledge answered. 'Is it the payments that have you worried?'

'Not one little bit,' he said. 'If they couldn't be managed we might as well not be in business at all.'

The bank in Longford was an impressive Victorian stone building in the middle of the town. They entered as the heavy door was about to close for the day. They were asked to wait for a few minutes while the last customers were being attended to. They were then led inside the counter and into a large office at the back. The bank official was a tall, athletic man. He stood to shake their hands and he and Ruttledge spoke warmly of Joe Eustace before he invited them to sit.

Ruttledge explained the background of the application, adding that while the business was profitable it had ceased to expand in recent years. Frank Dolan was a much younger man than the present owner and was anxious to expand the business and employ some young people. As the business thrived and expanded, he would certainly require further loans.

'That seems highly satisfactory,' the official said as he

wrote, remarking that the bank would require the deeds once the transfer was completed, and then began to read back to Frank Dolan what he had written. All the bank official needed was his agreement.

'Oh no. Oh no,' Frank Dolan spoke. 'I'd not want sight or light of those fellas round the place. They are dear bought. They'd annoy your head. You'd have to show them everything. It'd be far easier to do the thing yourself.'

The official looked up, puzzled and somewhat amused.

'We spoke about it on the way up,' Ruttledge intervened. 'Frank is, I think, unnecessarily worried about having to take on too many young people. I told him he'd be free to do that at his own pace.'

Frank Dolan's face was pale. All his attention was fixed on the bank official.

'I know there can be difficulties with young people and of course you'd be free to expand as you see fit,' the official said helpfully, but Frank Dolan had now discovered his own voice and would not be contained.

'No,' he said. 'I'd cut back. In my opinion Mister Maguire has been stretching himself far too much. I'd cut back. I'd do far less than we are doing now.'

There was silence in the room. Outside the iron-barred window hung the dark fruit and rough leaves of an elder tree. Ruttledge made a couple of attempts to rescue the interview. The official did his very best. The disaster had all the fascination of watching a vehicle set out on a predictable journey and then without warning see a wheel come loose and roll unpredictably along until it wobbled and fell flat. When they rose it seemed that they had been no more than a moment in the room, but the big electric clock on the office wall told that they had been more than an hour there.

Out in the busy evening street they felt as unreal for a time as if they had just emerged from a cinema, the shadows they had been part of more real than the substantial buildings and the passing traffic. Frank Dolan looked as if he had gone into shock, he who had been so articulate such a short time before in talking himself out of the loan.

'I think we went down,' he said.

'We didn't do too well. Would you like a drink or not?' Ruttledge wanted to soften the raw taste of failure with some little act or ceremony before they left the town.

'I don't drink,' Frank responded bluntly.

'I know. I was thinking of tea or coffee – or a glass of water.'

'Well in that case I'm taking you. It was my business that brought you to the town,' he insisted.

'Maybe we'll leave it for another time. There'll be a better time,' Ruttledge said.

The noisy Toyota battered slowly home. The rows of pleasure-boats moored along the Shannon at Rooskey appeared to lift Frank Dolan's spirits briefly.

'I suppose it was a day out anyhow,' he said hopefully.

'It was a day out. It was a very interesting day.'

When it was considered carefully, all Frank Dolan had done was to be too honest and too self-expressive. Each quality alone was dangerous enough: combined together they were a recipe for disaster.

'We are not giving up. We'll find some way. There has to be some way,' Ruttledge said when Frank Dolan pulled in beside his own parked car at the narrow bridge in Shruhaun.

'What will we say to his lordship if he asks anything?' Frank Dolan said.

'We'll say nothing.'

'What if he puts two and two together? He's as quick as lightning in that way.'

'Tell him I'm looking after everything,' Ruttledge said. Frank Dolan was now downcast and uncertain after the strength of his performance in the bank. 'Don't worry about it. We'll think of something.'

As soon as Kate saw Ruttledge, she said, 'The meeting didn't go well?'

'No. It could hardly have gone worse. We entered the

meeting with the loan as good as guaranteed and left without a prospect of a loan. Frank talked a blue streak. He talked himself out of the loan.'

'Usually he is careful and watchful.'

'Not on this occasion. I think he felt he was getting into something above his head, that he was being trapped into the loan under false pretences. All he had to do was keep his mouth shut but he talked as if speech had just been invented.'

'What are you going to do?'

'I don't know. We'll have to deal with the Shah first. He'll be like a bloody lion if he finds out what happened.'

Very late that evening the Mercedes drew up outside the porch. He had left the sheepdog behind.

'Well?' he cleared his throat as soon as he was seated. 'What happened?'

'Nothing much,' Ruttledge said cautiously.

'You don't have to tell,' he said. 'He went to Longford and made a holy show of himself. Once they got a look at him they wouldn't entertain him for a minute. They threw him out.'

'Nothing like that happened,' Ruttledge said. 'He made a show of nobody.'

'You're not pulling wool over my eyes. He shouldn't even have been let out. Did you get the loan or not? Yes or no?'

'We didn't.'

'Aha, I knew it,' he said triumphantly. 'I knew it the minute he stepped out of that wreckage of a Toyota. I have been watching him all my life. You can't deny he didn't go and make a hames of everything.' His intuition had grasped what had taken place.

'He's not used to dealing with banks or institutions. That's all that was wrong.'

'He should never have been let out. Is he able for the job?'

'That's unfair. Of course he's able. He's just not used to dealing with banks.'

'You can say that again. I'm not going to be giving him forever.'

171

'He won't need forever. We'll get that loan some other way,' Ruttledge said.

'What do you think of all this, Kate?' the Shah demanded good-humouredly, and he began to relax. 'That's a most beautiful cake.'

'I like Frank,' Kate said.

'I'm glad there's somebody that likes him,' he said.

Ruttledge was getting cash for John Quinn's wedding when Joe Eustace called him into the inner office in the bank. 'I heard about the interview in Longford. The whole bank has. The telephones have been buzzing.'

'Because of what happened?'

'What else? Not every day a man goes into a bank with a loan secured and walks out an hour later having talked himself out of it – big.'

'He was too straight, too honest.'

'I hear he spoke straight out that he was going to do far less than the previous man. There's no way the bank could run with that. We'd be accused of giving loans to people to stay in bed.'

'There must be some way he can get a loan. He's decent and intelligent. The bank is sure of its money.'

'I've been thinking,' Joe Eustace said. 'And I don't see many ways. The only way I can see is for you to take out and guarantee the loan in his name.'

'There must be some other way.'

'I'll ring around. I'll ask about it. If we can come up with anything, we will,' Joe Eustace said in his helpful way.

On the morning of the wedding, Bill Evans arrived at the house early. He was in his Sunday clothes, scrubbed and combed and polished. 'Where's the Missus?' he asked.

'She's getting ready. You're a bit early,' Ruttledge said and handed him a packet of cigarettes.

'Begod, it's better to be early anyhow than rushing at the last minute,' he responded complacently and lit up a cigarette. 'John Quinn getting married in the church. Who'd ever think to see the day. It's a holy living terror.'

'I suppose you'd hardly take the plunge if you were in John Quinn's place?'

'Begod I wouldn't,' Bill laughed out loud. 'I'd have far too much sense. I'd stay single and enjoy myself.'

The dress Kate was wearing she hadn't worn in years. The surprise must have showed.

'Do I look all right?'

'You look beautiful.'

'Not too young?'

'On the contrary. Bill came early.'

'You look powerful, ma'am.'

'You're looking great yourself, Bill.'

'We'll have a great day.'

Though they left early, Mary and Jamesie were already waiting out of sight at the corner of the lake. Mary wore a suit, Jamesie was in his Sunday clothes, and their excitement was such that it overflowed in grimaces and awkward movements. Jamesie shrugged his shoulders and pretended to hide, as if they had been caught in something shameful. Amid jokes and laughter, they squeezed into the car.

'You're a pure imposture, Jamesie,' Bill Evans said.

'That's right,' Mary encouraged. 'Give it to him, Bill. Give it to him good-o.'

'Good man, Bill. You're dressed to kill. You'll land a woman for yourself today,' Jamesie said.

At the church they stood outside on the gravel to watch the other cars arrive. Jamesie was vivid with excitement, continually greeting people, and when Patrick Ryan drew up in an expensive car that dropped him at the church gate he was all eyes. 'Could be the Reynolds that have those big diggers and earth removers.'

'There's no need for you to be so nosy,' Mary scolded. 'You know poor Patrick always had that weakness,' and she kissed Patrick warmly when he joined them to ask if they had room in the car for going to the hotel.

'We'll make room. We'll manage.'

'Good man, Patrick. You won't be left behind,' Jamesie thrust out his hand.

'I'll sit on the women's knees if they can't trust to mine,' he sallied amid laughter. 'Bold Bill,' he took Bill Evans's hand. 'They're all getting married but you and me,' but Bill Evans hardly heard. He was eyeing all the people arriving for the wedding as intently as a dealer measuring cattle, to ascertain how many cigarettes they were worth.

John Quinn arrived in a cavalcade of big cars, all with English registrations belonging to his children, decorated with long fluttering white streamers. They had driven from their homes outside London across England and Wales to Holyhead, crossed on the car-ferry to Dublin and driven down to the Central Hotel in town, where they had rooms booked for a week.

A hush fell on the people standing about on the white gravel as John Quinn emerged from the front car, a brand new Mercedes as large as the Shah's. He stood erect as a man half his age and waved like a politician. Children emerged from the other cars, small girls in First Communion dresses, boys in blue and grey suits. Not a single one of John Quinn's children had stayed away. They all came to the wedding, bringing their wives and husbands and children. Gathered together outside the church door before making their way to the altar, they made a formidable and striking picture of youth and strength and solidarity. John Quinn was at their living centre, in a tailor-made pinstripe suit with a white rose in the buttonhole, thriving on the attention. Together they all filed into the church to await the bride. She came late. Only the whisperers at the church door saw her arrive, a handsome, determined-looking woman in her late fifties, wearing a stylish navy-blue costume and a veil with a spray of white lilies in her hair. In spite of her vigour and good

174

looks the bride appeared vulnerable as she walked up the aisle on her white-haired brother's arm past all the curious heads that turned, but she appeared to grow in confidence during the ceremony. Afterwards she looked excited and happy when confetti was thrown and the photographs were taken. Father Conroy moved from person to person on the gravel, shaking hands. Some who needed Masses said or owed him dues gave him money. When he reached Ruttledge, he caught his elbow and guided him over to the wall. They seldom saw one another but had remained friendly ever since that first visit.

'I didn't expect to see you here,' he said.

'We were all invited – all the good neighbours around the lake. Naturally, I came. Are you going to the hotel?'

'No. He has his own views on marriage as he has on most things. While I have him on *my* ground I'm taking the happy pair into the sacristy for tea and advice. I take every couple into the sacristy for tea and advice. I know most of them would like something stronger than tea after their ordeal, and the sort of advice I dole out is probably not what they are looking for. Advice and tea, though, is what they all get.' With that, he left Ruttledge, who soon afterwards saw him leading the newly married couple towards the sacristy door.

They all piled into the car to drive to the hotel, the four men squeezed together into the back, Mary sitting with Kate in front. As they drove, Patrick Ryan began to tease Bill Evans about the food being prepared in the hotel kitchen. 'I can smell it already. The chickens roasting . . .'

'Stop it, Patrick,' Bill Evans called out as if in pain.

'The skin brown, roasted bread crumbs with little bits of onion in the stuffing, covered with brown gravy, small roast potatoes, fresh green peas . . .'

'Stop torturing me, Patrick.' The cry was terrible.

Patrick Ryan laughed carefully, lowly, maliciously, as if testing the air, but he did not continue. The rest of the car was silent. The hair stood up on the back of Ruttledge's neck. The cry cut through the years to the evening he was questioning Bill Evans after he came starving to the house: 'Stop torturing me.' It was the same unmistakable cry that had to be bowed to then as the silence in the car respected it now. Bill Evans could no more look forward than he could look back. He existed in a small closed circle of the present. Remembrance of things past and dreams of things to come were instruments of torture.

A few people had come into the bar from the wedding. They waved or smiled to one another when glances met but kept to their separate tables. Many more wandered about the hotel corridors and gardens because the big dining room was still closed. Mary and Kate left the bar to go to the Ladies. When they returned to the table, it was clear they had come on something strange. In a conspiratorial whisper Mary spoke so low and so quickly that they had to interrupt her.

'John Quinn has taken her upstairs.'

'Where?'

'To the son's bedroom. He got Liam to give him the keys. No. She didn't want to go. They say she didn't know right what was happening but you can be sure she knows by now. Kate and me saw it with our eyes. They were all laughing like donkeys when he lifted her in his arms as if she was a child.'

'Maybe she won't allow . . . she won't let him?'

'O-ho,' Mary laughed. 'He'll do it with soft sweet-talking and if that doesn't work, he'll do it with strength. Only for Knock and the Church were mixed up it would have been done long before. It must have killed him to wait this long.'

'Maybe she's just dying for the hog,' Patrick Ryan said provocatively, coarsely.

'On an occasion like this?' Kate asked coldly.

'It's better for herself if she wants it,' Jamesie said quietly. 'Whether she likes it or not she'll have to open the door.'

'She'll get the rod,' Bill Evans said suddenly.

'Good man, Bill,' Mary said, and a quiet descended.

A bell rang in the hotel corridors. Everybody rose from the tables, some finishing their drinks while standing.

For a country wedding it was small but the tables were so cunningly arranged that they disguised how few were present. There was no long raised table and no flowers other than in vases. John Quinn and his bride and her party sat with his family at a single large table at the head of the room. There were no set places and people kept to their own small groups. As no priest was present there was some hesitation until the religious postman rose and recited grace with joined hands and closed eyes. The mushroom soup was home-made. Roast chicken was served with large bowls of floury potatoes and carrots and mashed turnips. There was plenty of crisp breadcrumb stuffing and a jug of brown gravy. Instead of the usual sherry trifle, a large slice of apple tart was served with fresh cream.

Nobody ate more than Bill Evans and he didn't speak from when the meal began until it ended other than to give abstracted monosyllabic answers to enquiries. Occasionally, he sat back and surveyed the room in dazed, contented wonderment, with his knife and fork held absently in his hands before setting to again.

'Lord bless us, where is he putting it?' Jamesie asked from time to time in one of his loud stage whispers, but Bill Evans was paying no attention, completely absorbed in eating.

'He's stacking it in the bank. He'll be drawing on it for weeks like yer otter,' Patrick Ryan said.

Despite the good food, the real focus was on John Quinn's bride. Whatever had happened or had not happened, all were agreed that she looked subdued by John Quinn's side at the big table. When the choice of drinks was offered, it emerged that John Quinn's children were hosting the meal, not the wife as had been rumoured. There was general relief and everybody drank more easily. The speeches were mercifully brief, John Quinn's the longest, every word so predictable that it was heard in a conspiratorial silence, with the occasional wink or raised glass.

When it ended, the speech was greeted by vociferous applause and at some tables a pounding of feet on the floorboards. John Quinn smiled and bowed and raised his wife by the arm to receive the applause, which prolonged the clapping and shouting and pounding. His wife seemed to be easier now and to have regained her composure, but she refused to be drawn into an embrace and held her distance in such a way that John Quinn was neither yielded to nor rejected.

'Do you know what I'm thinking?' said Mary, who had been studying it all quietly. 'That woman may be more than he bargained for.'

'She's going to have to start getting up very early in the morning if she's going to best John Quinn,' Patrick Ryan said.

The tables were cleared away for dancing. There were no musicians but the hotel had a jukebox with old dance tunes. The groom and his bride led the dancing in a slow waltz. Bill Evans was almost immobile with food and drink and sat staring out at the dancing through rings of cigarette smoke as impassively as a Chinaman.

Mrs Maguire was making the rounds of the wedding party, enquiring if everything had been to their satisfaction, and seeing the Ruttledges she sat and spoke with them. When she left, after talking with Jamesie and Mary, they decided that they were ready to leave. Patrick had already left their table. Away on the far side of the room they saw him in conversation with the bride's brother.

'Should we ask Patrick if he wants a lift?' Kate asked.

'He'll not want,' Jamesie said. 'He'll go round on everybody. He'll have a world of lifts before the night is out.'

'You know, that Missus Maguire is a great friendly manly woman. Herself and the Shah are great friends. It'd be a terror if the two went and got married,' Jamesie said jauntily as they drove out of the town.

'They're not daft like you and John Quinn,' Mary said sharply. 'Isn't that right, Bill?'

'Yes, ma'am,' Bill replied absently, freed of all concerns.

'What would they be getting married for?'

'We all know,' Jamesie rubbed his huge hands together.

'You're a disgrace!'

'All make their way,' he sang.

'I think people are sexual until they die,' said Kate, who was driving as she had hardly anything to drink.

'God, Kate, you're a caution,' Mary broke down in laughter.

'She's right,' Jamesie said. 'You can see children jigging as soon as they can walk. The old crowd have it in their heads and if they have it anywhere else they are clever enough to keep it under cover.'

'You see, you are only putting things in his head, Kate.'

'We had a most interesting day. Will the bride sit or will she run?' Jamesie asked.

'She'll run if she has sense,' Kate said.

Jamesie and Mary insisted on walking all the way into the house from the lake gate. 'It'll clear the heads,' Mary said.

Bill Evans hadn't said a word during the drive home. They drove him past their own gate to the top of the hill so that he had only a short walk down to the house.

'How do you feel?' Ruttledge asked when he got him out of the car. 'Will you be all right?'

'Topping, topping,' he answered tiredly. 'I feel all rolly-polly.'

John Quinn's marriage celebrations lasted a week. The bride waited until the big cars carrying John Quinn's children passed through Dublin and Holyhead and were well on their way to their various homes around London. All that week she lived with John Quinn in the house by the lake but spent little time there other than the nights and the mornings.

The cars would arrive early to take them away for the day. It was always late night or early morning before they were left back again. The days were spent over meals in hotels, in bars and visiting relatives. John Quinn's wife found the atmosphere charming: such a large family, getting on so well together in the excitement their interest in one another generated; they, in turn, were delighted by the solid respectability of his new wife after the succession of ladies he had paraded over the years.

To the relatives they visited John Quinn's children brought offerings of whiskey and chocolates and fruit. Growing up so hard and poor, they had received small kindnesses from many of these people. Now they enjoyed returning these kindnesses in the ease of their prosperity and were too tactful to ruin it with loud display. Their conduct was a direct counter to their father's behaviour.

Many of the relatives would not have wanted John Quinn. He would have owed them money or have tried to take advantage of them in some other way. They were content to pretend to 'Let it go with him. It'll all sort itself out' for the sake of peace and the family. Alone, they kept him at an iron distance, but when he appeared with the children they allowed that distance to lapse.

Most of these houses would know few visitors. Some would see no faces other than when they went into town to shop or look in on the cattle mart or attend Sunday Mass. Such a visit as John Quinn's family would be a huge break and excitement in the sameness of the days. Even in the poorest houses, whiskey, set aside for such rare occasions, would be offered. Tea would be made. A hunt would be started to search out sweets or biscuits or some small delicacy for the children. In their fierce pride, John Quinn's children, in turn, would have ensured that more was brought to the house in offerings and gifts than could be given back.

The welcome disruption of the everyday the visit brought was nothing compared to the richness it provided for weeks and months. 'A terror how old villains like John Quinn could have such decent good children while decent people are as likely as not to get children bringing nothing but trouble. Study how an old blackguard like that after burying two wives and having all sorts of other women could sail out at the end of his days and get a respectable, well-preserved, presentable woman from, of all places, Knock where the Virgin appeared, when men who would make far better husbands were left with two hands hanging. Some poor women can go badly astray when it comes to this love business.'

Already, the new wife had come to realize that she had made a mistake, but was keeping her own counsel.

On the last evening the family gave a dinner in the Central, with toasts and all kinds of wishes for long lives and much happiness to the new couple, and afterwards there were drinks and a singsong in the bar till late. They all said goodbye to one another that night in the Central, with promises to see one another when they came again the following summer, if not before that, when, as they hoped, the happy couple would visit them in London. The next day, while the convoy of cars was crossing England, the wife packed all her personal belongings while John Quinn was away out the land fencing and attending to cattle, and walked to Shruhaun.

A tall, fair-haired young man came by car to the village an hour earlier. He had a single pint of stout in the bar. Though he was polite and answered readily enough to the small talk of the bar, he didn't volunteer either where he was from or what business had brought him to Shruhaun. As soon as John Quinn's wife walked in the door, he rose and put his glass back on the counter and went and took the two suitcases she had been carrying. They left without a word. There were only a few in the bar at the time. Nobody thought to get the registration number of the car but they guessed by his appearance and by the way he went towards her that he was one of her sons.

Jamesie had great belief in two spoons he used for casting from the shore, an elongated piece of rough beaten copper Johnny had made before going to England and a red and silver spoon with a tiny amber eye he had found years ago hooked in a piece of driftwood. It was the long copper spoon he was using from the shore the day after John Quinn's family had returned to England. With each cast he drew closer to the iron-roofed house under the great chestnut tree in the yard. Very few fish were ever caught in this part of the lake and the morning was too bright, but fish weren't much on his mind. Not far away from where he sent the spinning copper out on the water was the bare rock to which John Quinn had led his first bride. Around the edges of the rock the sparse grass had turned red. There were clusters of wildfowl out on the lake and the swans were sailing around and feeding close in to the shore. Everywhere birds were singing. When Jamesie moved between the rock and the house, the old sheepdog came to the gate of the yard, gave a few half-hearted barks and went away. He could see hens pecking about in the dust of the yard around the big chestnut tree. If he advanced any further along the shore, he would begin moving away from the house. He knew he had only to wait.

The old sheepdog came first. While continuing to cast and reel in the copper spoon, Jamesie was able to observe John Quinn's approach. He was still dressed in his wedding suit.

'John Quinn is one happy and contented man this bright morning,' Jamesie sang out as he drew close while reeling in and lifting the copper spoon from the water.

'It's lovely to see good neighbours innocent and at peace and looking for something good for the table,' John Quinn said.

'You must be one happy man to be safely married again to a fine woman,' Jamesie was all smiles as he turned the attention around.

'I do my best to be happy and not live alone, as the Lord intended – "Tis not good for man to live alone, He himself has said" – but I don't mind admitting that we have had a little setback that I'm hoping and praying will only be very temporary.'

182

'A setback?' Jamesie enquired incredulously. 'A setback for John Quinn?'

'Yes, Jamesie. You could call it a setback but I'm hoping it'll be only temporary, no more than a hitch or a small hiccup. It's down in a holy writ that what God has joined together no man can put asunder. I was away on some cattle business yesterday evening and when I came back I found she had left for her own part of the country. All she left behind was a note and it wasn't a love note.'

'Was there no signs or warnings?'

'No signs. No signs worth remarking. We had a most wonderful week, the children taking us everywhere and all happy and getting on wonderfully well together. Except one night when we were most content and peaceable after the usual love performance she turned to me and said, "John, I think I've made a big mistake." Women get strange notions like that from time to time, like children, and have to be humoured. I told her what you have to tell them on such occasions and when I heard nothing more thought it was the sweet end of that figary and we were back to happiness again.'

'Still, you must have had a great week in spite of everything, John Quinn?' Jamesie had known him over a lifetime. John Quinn had circled and wheedled and bullied many in search of advantage. Now he was being circled expertly.

'The children have done well for themselves and got on well in the world and wanted to do as good for their old father. They came in a great show of strength. Nothing was too much for them or too good. They brought us everywhere. Then we had the nights to ourselves. I don't mind telling you, Jamesie, it was like being young again. It was youth come back again and it wasn't wasted. We had the strength but not the know-how when we were young.'

'She was a fine woman,' Jamesie said.

'As fine as was ever handled, Jamesie, hadn't to be taught a thing and was more solid and wholesome than a young woman. You could tell she had an easy, comfortable life and never got much hardship. She was as ripe as a good plum picked when it was about to fall off the tree. It was most beautiful. It was like going in and out of a most happy future.'

'You're a terror, John Quinn. A pure living holy terror,' Jamesie cheered and John Quinn luxuriated in the rapt attention.

'Then this little slip-up came along and sort of went and spoiled everything but please God it'll be soon rectified and everything will be back happy and everybody getting on wonderfully well together again.'

'I don't doubt it. I can't see John Quinn letting anything go without an almighty struggle. I don't doubt it for a minute.'

'Even now I'm negotiating for a happy outcome. Once you marry you know you have rights as well as duties. It can't be put away like a pair of old boots. It's my belief anyhow that she won't be got back to this part of the country. My plan is very plain and simple and I tell you man to man, Jamesie: if the mountain won't go to Mohammed, then, it was always said, Mohammed has to go to the mountain.'

Jamesie went straight from John Quinn to the Ruttledges. There were no games of stealth, of ghosting into the house to listen. The trolling rod was left in the fuchsia bushes at the gate and he whooped and called out as he came in the short avenue and rapped with his palm on the glass of the porch. He could have been a small crowd returning victorious from a football match or a spectacular cattle sale. Kate was alone in the house and went to meet him in the porch. Ruttledge heard the commotion and came in from the fields.

'Finding it much easier now, thanking you very much for your most kind enquiry,' he called out mockingly as he threw himself down in the armchair, but then could contain his news no longer. 'Gone!' he laughed out. 'Gone. Out the gap. Gone!'

'Who's gone? What's gone?'

'A drink in the name of God before I die. John Quinn's

wife has gone. Skipped it before the children were right back in England, gone and left him, stranded as long as he ran. Hit it for her own part of the country.'

Over whiskey and water he went over the story at his ease, occasionally choking as he drank into his speech but more often banging his glass down to hoot with laughter. 'I heard going to the boggy hollow described as many things in my time but never as "going in and out of a most happy future". Lord bless us. John Quinn is a living sight. He could think or do anything. He said it was like being young again and she tasted like a ripe plum picked from the tree. I'd give good money to know what the plum thought.'

'You're a disgrace, Jamesie. You were leading him on.'

In answer, he cheered.

'Did she give no sign or warning?' Ruttledge asked.

'Oh yes. Oh – yes, but those like John Quinn are too bound up with themselves to heed. When they had done the love performance one night and were most happy and peaceful, she turned to him in the bed and said, "I think I may have made a big mistake."'

'That's the end. Imagine having to go to a place like Knock to find someone like John Quinn,' Kate said.

'Lots go and won't be stopped,' Jamesie laughed. 'Nature starts jabbing them. This tangle is far from over. Mark my words. John Quinn won't be got rid of so easily.'

'What can he do?'

'Plenty. He'll set the land for as high a price as he can ever get and head for Westmeath. "If the mountain won't come to Mohammed then Mohammed has to go to the mountain." John Quinn may act daft but there's not much daft at the back of the acting.'

'He'll be turned away?'

'He won't be easily turned. Whether she likes it or not she married him. John Quinn is a bit of a lawyer as well as everything else. He'll be a sweet-talking John Quinn and butter wouldn't melt in his mouth until he gets his head in again. She'll have her work cut out if she intends to stay clear.'

'What about her sons?'

'They're all married with houses of their own. They won't want to be too involved after she's gone and done a caper like that. They'll have wives. If you make your bed you lie on it. Isn't that what's said? There's a lot going for John Quinn and no better man to play his cards. He won't come back with his hands empty. She'll have her work cut out.'

They walked him to the gate, where he retrieved the rod and copper spoon from the fuchsias, and then down to the water and part of the way round the shore. The sloes were already ripening on the blackthorn. Patches of yellow were appearing in the thick wall of green along the shore. There was rust on the briar leaves. Certain grasses and early vegetables were dying back.

The lake was an enormous mirror turned to the depth of the sky, holding its lights and its colours. Close to the reeds there were many flies, and small shoals of perch were rippling the surface with hints of the teeming energy and life of the depths. The reeds had lost their bright greenness and were leaning towards the water. Everything that had flowered had now come to fruit.

They would not be in London at Christmas, a time they had particularly liked in London. Kate wrote to Robert Booth. She had delayed writing. The indulgence of delay had been to keep the door open for as long as possible. She wrote how grateful she was, how grateful they both were. A door had been held open at a time when most doors were starting to close.

'It's extraordinary how different it is to be young,' Kate said quietly. 'Dressing up for a party, the excitement of who you might meet, your whole life possibly changed by a single meeting.'

'You were going into your life then,' Ruttledge said. 'Now you are in the middle of that life.'

Kate wrote to Robert Booth, closing the door, and it was not a pleasant sound even though she herself was doing the closing.

'Has that man said anything further to you about buying that place?' The Shah became more pressing on Sundays and he started arriving more often now in the late evenings.

'No, but I am fairly sure it'll be all right. We are trying to find a way round a few things,' Ruttledge answered with deliberate vagueness.

'He won't get forever. Not many would be so backward given a chance the like of that.'

Ruttledge had talked to Joe Eustace in the bank again. They went over every possible way of obtaining a loan until they were forced to return to the plan of last resort: Ruttledge would have to take out the loan and then transfer it with legal safeguards.

'If there was another way we'd have come up with it by now,' Joe Eustace said. 'That interview is still the talk of the bank: the man who swore to do less.'

Ruttledge went to check that Frank Dolan still wanted to buy. When he looked coldly at the square, not for the first time was he amazed at how much the Shah had come to acquire. The place was worth several times more than the asking price.

He found Frank sorting small engine parts under a powerful spotlight on the long bench at the back of the shed. He stood for a long time watching in silence until Frank noticed him and turned the metal hood of the lamp towards the wall.

Frank Dolan looked at him slowly, enquiringly; stubbornness and independence showed on the face.

'You are still interested?'

'I most certainly am.' Everything else was so cautious and covered that Ruttledge was as surprised by the forthrightness as relieved.

'I think I have found a way. I'll be back in a few days,' Ruttledge said.

Frank Dolan made no enquiry as to what had been found. In pauses, they talked for a while of business and the town and then Frank Dolan walked Ruttledge to his car. He did not turn off the sharp spotlight at the back of the shed. He would be working late, preferring to work when nobody was about.

'You're not going in to see him?' he indicated the blue light of the TV in the station house. 'I'm sure he'd like to see you. He'll be like a lion if he gets to hear you were in.'

'It's a bit late and he's not likely to hear,' Ruttledge said.

'You'd be surprised the things he's able to pick up.'

'What's the humour like this weather?'

'Rough – that's if you paid it any heed.'

Later, when the Ruttledges were talking over the whole business, Kate asked, 'If there's no risk why are you so reluctant to take out the loan?'

'It's generally a bad idea to do business with people you are close to. It's just that I feel there should be a simpler way.'

'There is,' she said. 'Why doesn't the Shah give him the loan? Remember all the money we had in the house when he went to Donegal? And that's probably only a fraction of what's there.'

Ruttledge stood frozen in amazement that something so close and so obvious hadn't occurred to him.

'It's true that we can't see what's under our noses.'

'I think it's even more simple.'

'How?'

'You were always careful never to ask him for anything. Even reluctant to accept things he offered.'

'We didn't need for much,' he said stiffly.

'That's true but there were times that weren't all that easy.'

'We managed,' he answered defensively.

'I know,' Kate said and continued to look at him without speaking.

'It seems we can never know ourselves,' Ruttledge admitted out of the silence. 'But will he agree to give Frank the loan?'

'I don't see why not. He wants him to have the place. You know that. It's even obvious to me.'

'People act strangely when money's involved. It goes deeper than sense or reason.'

'All you can do is ask.'

Armed with information from the bank about interest rates, monthly and quarterly repayments, Ruttledge went to see the Shah as he was finishing his evening meal in the Central. He was eating alone in the alcove overlooking the dining room, rosy with contentment, eating slowly and concentratedly, oblivious of the other diners. Slow to recognize Ruttledge, he laughed and gestured towards a chair, apologized and called the waiter in practically the same movement. 'Give this man whatever he wants, Jimmy. He'll need something.'

'I don't feel like eating. I'll have tea. A pot of tea.'

'You might as well have something stronger. Whiskey, wine, stout,' he pressed. His abhorrence and fear of alcohol did not extend to his power as host. He kept a huge cupboard of drinks in the station house and loved to serve large measures to visiting relatives – especially those he disliked – about which there was a definite element of spreading bait for garden snails.

'Tea is what I want.'

'How is Herself?' he asked after Kate.

'She asked to be remembered to you. We've both been going over that business of the sale and the loan.'

'Well?' he demanded, all concentration in an instant.

'Every way I look at the business it makes sense for you to give him the loan. You have plenty of money.'

'I'm not too short,' he admitted.

'You won't even have to give him money. Instead of making payments to the bank, it'll just be a matter of Frank making the payments to you.'

'I wouldn't want to be going to him every month with my hand out,' he said.

'That won't happen. There'll be an agreement. He'll have to pay the money into an account in the bank in your name every month or three months. Once the agreement is signed, the two of you won't even have to say a word to one another.'

'What if he's not able for it?'

'Not able for what?'

'To make the payments.'

'The place and business would revert to you just as it would to the bank if they gave the loan. There's no way you can lose.'

In the bank, Ruttledge had agreed with Joe Eustace that a fair rate of interest should be midway between the current bank rate and the lending rates. Frank Dolan would pay less than if he had borrowed from the bank and the Shah would get a higher interest than if his money were on deposit there.

'It'll do better than that. I'll give it to him for even less,' he said expansively when the proposition was put.

He spoke as if he had been set free from anxiety and constraint. All the time he had wanted Frank Dolan to have the place but it had remained hidden because of the fear that he might be seen as unmanly or unbusinesslike or even perhaps of going outside the family.

'You can give him any rate you want. But I'd leave it. It's fair at that. There's no use going overboard,' Ruttledge said.

'Leave it so, then,' he agreed readily. 'But will he be up to it at all?' He began to shake slowly at the thought.

'You realize that once you sign the place over he can have you out on your ear at any time?'

'I'd be delighted to go in the morning,' he said.

'Many think that and then are hurt.'

'I'd glory. I'd sit in the station house and look across. I'd be at my pure ease.'

'Then you are all right,' Ruttledge said.

'Will he be able for it though?' he asked again.

'Of course he will. That is unless he takes to the drink in a big way or something like that.'

'Oh Lord,' he said. 'That'd be the last straw.'

When Ruttledge told Frank Dolan that the loan had been secured and that it was the Shah who had advanced the money, he went stone silent. Only when pressed if he still wanted to go ahead did he respond.

'I certainly do. They complain about him a lot but he's far from the worst. They are a lot worse themselves,' he said.

September and October were lovely months, the summer ended, winter not yet in. The cattle and sheep were still out on grass, the leaves turning.

The little vetch pods on the banks turned black. Along the shore a blue bloom came on the sloes. The blackberries moulded and went unpicked, the briar leaves changed into browns and reds and yellows in the low hedges, against which the pheasant could walk unnoticed. Plums and apples and pears were picked and stored or given around to neighbours or made into preserves in the big brass pot. Honey was taken from the hives, the bees fed melted sugar. For a few brilliant days the rowan berries were a shining red-orange in the light from the water, and then each tree became a noisy infestation of small birds as it trembled with greedy clamouring life until it was stripped clean. Jamesie arrived with sacks of vegetables and was given whatever he would take in return.

When the All-Ireland finals in Croke Park were live on television, Ruttledge walked round the lake to watch the match with Jamesie. Jamesie poured whiskey and Mary made tea and sandwiches. The irregular striking of the clocks from every quarter of the house throughout the match served as a cool corrective to the excited commentary. The team Jamesie supported nearly always won, his support completely based on which of the teams he thought most likely to win and provide a triumphant, satisfying ending to the year. Once they lost, it was as if his judgement had been impugned.

'No use,' he thrust out his hands. 'They should have been ashamed to turn out. It wasn't worth even looking at.'

When the match ended and was talked over for a while, Ruttledge and Jamesie, accompanied by the two dogs, walked out to the lake.

'Thanks for the game. It was great fun,' Ruttledge said.

'The right team won this year anyway,' he remarked complacently.

'We'll watch it again next year.'

'With the help of God,' Jamesie said firmly as they separated.

The shore was dry, the fallen leaves rustling against his tread. Not until he reached the alder at the gate did he see the Mercedes stationed in front of the porch. Once he entered the house, he could hear his uncle chatting happily with Kate.

'Will he be able for it, Kate? That's the sixmarker!'

They were discussing the sale and transfer of the business. As he listened to the two voices he was so attached to and thought back to the afternoon, the striking of the clocks, the easy, pleasant company, the walk round the shore, with a rush of feeling he felt that this must be happiness. As soon as the thought came to him, he fought it back, blaming the whiskey. The very idea was as dangerous as presumptive speech: happiness could not be sought or worried into being, or even fully grasped; it should be allowed its own slow pace so that it passes unnoticed, if it ever comes at all.

The leaves started to fall heavily in frosts, in ghostly whispering streams that never paused though the trees were still. They formed into drifts along the shore. Jamesie could now see everything that went on around the Ruttledges from the brow of his own hill. Traceries of branches stripped of their leaves stood out against the water like veins. Under each delicate rowan tree lay the pale rowan stones, like droppings. In the cold dry weather the hedges were thinned for firewood, the evenings rent with the whining rise and fall of other chain saws similarly working. In this new weather, sounds travelled with a new cold sharpness.

The streetlights were already lit in the town when people gathered for the late Saturday shopping. The Ruttledges generally went with Jamesie and Mary and had a drink in Luke Henry's after the shopping was done. One Saturday night they met up with Patrick Ryan in the bar. As they had not met for a long time he was at his most charming but would not go home with them. He had driven into the town with other people and they were waiting for him somewhere else.

Into another Saturday evening in Luke's John Quinn walked.

'It's a beautiful thing to see good neighbours out enjoying themselves and getting on peaceable and well together as if they belonged to the same happy family and having a little sociable drink together at the end of the shopping,' he greeted the bar. 'A bottle of stout, Luke. It's good for the health and even better with a little raw egg.'

'We could get you that too, John,' Luke glanced mischievously beyond the partition where the groceries were sold.

'I know that, Luke, and thank you but there is a time and a place for everything, even the raw egg in the little glass of stout.'

'You have let the land, John?' Jamesie enquired innocently.

'Yes, Jamesie, I have let the land on the eleven months at a fair rent to a good decent man who'll look after it as if it was his own until I'm in a position to take it back. Yes, I've been up in Westmeath quite a bit, a great rich part of the country with very industrious hard-working people. We're getting on far better now than could be expected but of course these things take time and can't be rushed. But I expect to be going up there permanently before too long. If everything works out as God intended the two of us could be still as happy as larks in the clear air moving between the two places and even crossing for stays to the children in England, who took a great shine to her and she to them. Of course it's much better and happier if these things are settled agreeably and peaceably but of course when you get married there's a matter of the law as well and people have rights,' he warned darkly. 'Anyhow, either way I expect to be moving permanently for a time to Westmeath in the not too distant future. And so I have let the land.'

'We wish you health and happiness and long life, John.'

'Not faulting any of the company, I'll be leaving you now. When a man is deprived of his helpmate there are many things he has to attend to on his own.'

There was talk and laughter as soon as he left the bar, all of it concentrated on his dealings, but no discussion as to why he exercised such a fascination.

'There's not a whit of difference between John Quinn and any of us. He's perfectly normal except that he's that bit slightly oversexed,' one man argued. The remark was met with much ribald banter. Luke Henry turned his face to the shelves to hide his amusement.

In the car on the way home, Kate asked, 'Does John Quinn believe his own speeches?'

'John Quinn doesn't care what he says or does. All he cares about is himself and what goes down, what works.'

'If the speech stood in the way of John winning it'd get short shrift,' Jamesie answered seriously and quietly.

'The women would get short shrift as well if they didn't come up with the goods,' Mary said.

'You can say that ten times over,' Jamesie added.

Jamesie's good spirits seemed inexhaustible, but they were taken away in late November. There were no shouts from the alder at the gate when he came to the house, no rattling of the glass in the porch. They had never seen him look so low. He held a letter in his hand.

'Read this,' he thrust a letter into Ruttledge's hand.

The black cat with the white paws was sleeping against a cushion in the rocking chair. Reaching out his great hand, he lifted her unceremoniously on to the floor and sat heavily down.

Ruttledge saw that he was upset, nakedly so. The letter was from Johnny. As Ruttledge read, the only sounds were water filling an upstairs tank and the ticking of a clock.

The letter was short, its burden clear. Ford had demanded redundancies in their Dagenham plant. The union wasn't able to protect the likes of Johnny any longer. They had negotiated a lump sum as severance payment and a small pension. He wanted to return home and live with Mary and Jamesie as they had lived before he left for England.

'What are you going to do?'

'We don't know,' he said in anguish.

'Do you want him home?'

'Mary,' he thrust out his hands. 'Mary says she'd go out of her mind if he was back in the house again. She hasn't slept a wink since the letter came.'

'What do you feel?'

'If he was to come home, if he was in the house, we'd have to leave. It's hard enough for the fortnight he comes every year. If he was in the house for good . . . I don't know what we'd do. We can't turn him away like a dog either.'

'Have you told Jim?'

'Jim's in Dublin. He wouldn't want to know. What does he do at any time but pick up Johnny from the airport, leave him back. Jim wouldn't want to know. Johnny and Lucy never got on. What do you think, Kate?'

'I don't know what to think, Jamesie. It's a real dilemma.'

They could not live with him and they could not be seen – in their own eyes or in the eyes of others – to refuse him shelter or turn him away. The timid, gentle manners, based on a fragile interdependence, dealt in avoidances and obfuscations. Edges were softened, ways found round harsh realities. What was unspoken was often far more important than the words that were said. Confrontation was avoided whenever possible. These manners, open to exploitation by ruthless people, held all kinds of traps for the ignorant or unwary and could lead into entanglements that a more confident, forthright manner would have seen off at the very beginning. It was a language that hadn't any simple way of saying no.

'If that's how you feel, you should be open and straight about it from the very beginning,' Kate said after Jamesie had spoken. 'It wouldn't be fair in the long run to Johnny either. It'd be hell for everybody.'

'What are we to do?'

'Write to him.'

'What can we say? Mary hasn't slept since the letter came. There hasn't been a tap of work done round the place.'

'You'll have to speak straight.'

'We wouldn't know what to say. We wouldn't know where to begin.'

'He'll write it for you,' Kate said, looking carefully at Ruttledge. 'Then it can be copied and sent. That's his trade,' she smiled. 'That's what he gets paid for.'

'Would you write it? Would you do it for us?' Jamesie asked.

'Of course I would. But wouldn't it be better to get Jim to write? He'd write it just as well or better.'

'No,' Jamesie thrust out his hand in a sign that his anxiety was lifting. 'Jim wouldn't want to be involved. He's in Dublin. It's not his business.'

'Then I'll write it,' Ruttledge said. 'I'll write it and bring it round the lake this evening.'

'The educated man for it,' Jamesie said in relief. 'It was Mary who said to cross the lake. "They'll come up with something," she said. The educated man can think of anything. He's not like you and me, Kate,' he rubbed his hands gleefully together.

'That's because he had to go to school longer than you and me. He had to go because he was slower,' Kate laughed.

'Shots! Shots, Kate!' he laughed in pure delight now.

'You'll need a whiskey after that,' Kate said with affection.

'God never loved a coward, Kate,' he replied in kind.

He began to relax and expand as he drank. Anybody walking into the room would have found it hard to imagine the anxiety, the blackness of a few minutes before. 'Did you ever hear of the crowd who couldn't write and had to send a letter to America?' he asked.

'No.'

'In those days if you couldn't write you went to the schoolmaster, who charged a fee like a lawyer. When he had it all down on paper, the master read the letter back to them. They seemed satisfied enough but didn't say much and he asked if they'd like to add a PS. They wanted to know at once if there'd be an extra charge for the PS. When told there wasn't they said, "Go ahead. It'll look better. Write this PS: *Please excuse bad writing and spelling.*" You'd love to see the master's face – it could have been old Master Glynn – when that comeoutance was delivered. "Please excuse bad writing and spelling,"' he repeated. 'Lord bless us but there were some awful poor people going about then.'

'Maybe they knew well what they were doing,' Ruttledge said.

'That'd be even better, but no. They didn't know. They heard it read out in other letters and wanted to get as good a value as the other crowd. They didn't want to be left behind.'

They walked him past the alder tree down to the lake.

'I'll write the letter and bring it round this evening.'

'God bless you,' he said with emotion.

'There won't be any charge.'

'That's all right. Never had any intention of paying anyhow,' he replied as he walked away.

Ruttledge roughed out a simple letter, explaining the

situation clearly but softening it enough to give Johnny room, suggesting that when he thought about the idea more he'd see how hopeless it was from his own point of view. Without a car or telephone and far from town he'd be stranded now beside the lake. Everything was more or less gathered in for the winter. They sent him their love and were already looking forward to seeing him next summer, like in all the other summers.

Late that evening he walked around the lake with the drafted letter. It was cold along the shore. Except for the holly and small oaks all the trees were completely bare. The palest of moons was above the lake. Wildfowl scattered from the reeds. The heron rose and flapped lazily out along the shore. There must have been many herons here since they first came to the house but the same bird seemed to lead them out whenever they left and to rise again to lead them in when they were returning home. It would be a hard and a lonely place for Johnny to come home to, he reassured himself as he walked.

They were all in the house, a blue light flickering in the window. Inside the netting wire the brown hens were already closed in for the night.

They were watching *Blind Date*. The two dogs were seated in armchairs and looked possessively at Ruttledge as if he might cause their removal. Mary rose at once to kiss him but Jamesie stayed glued to the screen, watching an attractive young girl in a provocative dress standing beside the hostess of the show in front of a large audience. Behind a screen sat three youths. The screen hid them from the girl but not the audience. Whichever youth the girl picked would spend a week with her in a luxury hotel, with a chauffeured car and candlelit dinners. To help the girl make her blind choice, each boy in turn had to answer questions put to them by the hostess about their hobbies, occupations, the cooking and music they liked, their sexual preferences. Even the most pedestrian question contained a sexual innuendo. Each answer was greeted with catcalls and laughter. The salacious enjoyment of the audience was obvious in both the responses to each question and the girl's reactions, particularly when the answer revealed a disparity between the boy's perception of himself and how he was perceived by the girl or the audience.

Mary was annoyed by what she took as Jamesie's discourtesy but Ruttledge assured her that he was glad to watch.

'This fella is like a child,' she said. 'He goes wild for eejity stuff like this. You wouldn't know whether the crowd or him was the worse disgrace. Cattle round a bulling cow in the middle of a field would be more decent.'

At last, the girl made her blind choice. The boy she picked came out nervously from behind the screen to huge applause while the cameras searched out every reaction the boy and girl betrayed at this their first meeting. The hostess turned to question them but by now Jamesie had lost interest. He reached out and turned the set off.

'I'm happy to watch it to the end,' Ruttledge said.

'No, no,' he raised his hand. 'They are just a crowd of eejits. Mary, pour us a drink.'

'It's all just a cover-up for sex,' Mary said contemptuously as she reached for glasses and the bottle of Powers. 'They all want it and they're all afraid. That's why they are killing themselves laughing. Soon they'll be watching it on television instead of doing anything themselves.'

'Oh they'll do it too,' Jamesie protested. 'They'll want to practise what they see.'

'You'd think he'd have more sense – and the age he is!' Mary said.

'Good soldiers never die,' he said as he raised his glass. 'Good health. Good luck. More again tomorrow. The crowd lying below in Shruhaun aren't drinking any drinks today.'

'I wrote this to Johnny,' Ruttledge said as he placed the letter on the table. A silence fell as complete as the blankness of the television screen. Mary took the letter and read it in the silence of the ticking clocks while one of the dogs turned round in the chair and sighed as he dropped into a more comfortable rest. After Mary had read the letter, she handed it at once to Jamesie, her eyes fixed on his face.

'You. You read the letter.'

'No. No. The eyes are too poor. Read it out loud.'

'The eyes can see plenty when they are not wanted to see. You, Joe. You read it for him.'

'Change anything you want. Change the whole thing or don't send it at all,' Ruttledge said as he read.

'It's perfect,' Mary said. 'We'll change nothing. I'll copy every word out as it stands.'

'What if he doesn't take to it?' Jamesie asked anxiously.

'It's matterless whether he takes to it or not,' Mary said fiercely. 'He can't come home. We'd all have to leave.'

'You don't want him coming home thinking everything will work out. It wouldn't even be fair,' Ruttledge said.

'A pity these things ever have to come up between people,' Jamesie's eyes went from face to face.

'This fella would never face anything unless there was someone to stand behind him with a stick,' Mary said with an edge. 'I haven't slept since the letter came and he's been wandering round in a haze.'

'Like a kittymore's hen,' he tried to joke but she would not be deflected.

'This fella gets all excited every summer when Johnny is coming. The place is done up. The best sirloin is ordered. Then what does he do when Johnny *does* come home? He disappears. Who has to put up with him? Listening to the old stories that everybody around has long forgot. You'd think the place hadn't changed since he left. It's easy for you to talk,' Mary accused.

'He was too old when he went to England,' Jamesie said defensively.

'It's a hard story,' Ruttledge said.

'He might as well have tied a stone round his neck and

rowed out into the middle of the lake,' Jamesie said, and a silence fell in which the ticking and the striking of the clocks were very loud.

'It's terrible what people will go to hell for. . .' Mary spoke out of the long silence.

'Change anything you want in that letter,' Ruttledge said as he rose.

'Not a word will be changed. It'll be copied out word for word and sent in the morning.'

Jamesie looked from face to face, unsure and troubled. For a long while, like a painfully held breath, he seemed on the verge of saying something but then quickly reached for his cap and walked Ruttledge out to the lake. The two dogs abandoned their chairs to follow them. The moon was bright and clear above the lake, the line of the path sharp in yellow light. There was a cold wind.

'What if he doesn't heed the letter? He can be as stubborn and thick as my father, God rest him,' Jamesie said.

'You won't hear another word once he reads the letter.'

'Please God,' Jamesie prayed fervently. 'The worst of those old bachelors is that they have nobody to please but themselves and then when they get old nobody wants them and they have to try to get their head in somewhere.'

'We may not be all that much better off when our time comes.'

'Still we have our own house. We haven't to be trying to get in anywhere,' Jamesie said.

They had reached the top of the hill above the lake. 'I think the winter is here,' Ruttledge said, drawing his overcoat tight against the bitter wind.

'It's been here for weeks. You can quit talking.'

At the top of the hill they parted, though Jamesie was pre-pared to accompany him down to the lake. A river of beaten copper ran sparkling from shore to shore in the centre of the lake. On either side of this bright river peppered with pale stars the dark water seethed. Far away the lights of the town glowed in the sky. His own footsteps were loud. When he came to the corner of the lake, the heron rose out of the reeds to flap him lazily round the shore, ghostly in the moonlight. On such a night a man could easily want to run from his own shadow.

There came unceasing rain and wind. Some days the rain was flecked with snow but the lake was always changing, making even the downpours varied. The cattle and sheep were housed. None were calving or lambing or sick. They did not take much tending. Hedges were thinned for firewood during breaks in the rain. There was plenty of time for reading. A few writing commissions came. Trips were made to town, to Luke Henry's bar, to the Thursday market across the border in Enniskillen, to the coal pits in Arigna for trailerloads of low-grade, inexpensive coal. Bill Evans was bundled up like a mummy between the wellingtons and the shiny black sou'wester hat when he came for tea and cigarettes on the way to the lake. If he was hungry he called out for food. On Thursdays he became lord of the bus. Nobody had seen Patrick Ryan for a time though the part of the country and the people he was working for were known.

The burden of putting round the winter disappeared for days in a great flare of excitement, rumour and conjecture. John Quinn had been away for less than a month in his wife's place in Westmeath when he returned home. He had been driven out by the woman's sons. He went there and then to the doctor, the priest, the solicitor, the guards. None of them was interested in his cause. The family was well off and respectable. The doctor examined his bruises and said his injuries weren't serious and wrote him a prescription. The priest advised him to offer it all up as prayers and penance. The local solicitor told him he was far more likely to be sued and prosecuted than to succeed in an action if he insisted in pressing a case. They had been hardworking, decent people who had never been tainted by scandal. The guards took a statement but told him they had no intention of pressing charges as it was purely a civil matter.

The wife had gone to live with one of her sons. John Quinn's few possessions had been dumped on the street.

In Longford he broke the journey to go to another doctor and to spend the night in the hotel. When he was leaving the next morning, he refused to settle his account and ordered them to send his bill to his solicitor. There was a serious law case pending and the solicitor would settle everything, he informed the hotel.

He went to the solicitor to try to sue his wife and was presented with the hotel bill. None of the several solicitors he approached would touch the case. Then he caused a stir in the mart by turning up to bid for several cattle, eventually buying a bull calf though his land was let on the eleven months.

'That little calf won't be taking a bladeen of grass away from the decent man that's looking after the land till next summer and he'll be a little interest to myself over the winter now that I'm back again among good friends and neighbours.'

In this mill of rumour and conjecture John Quinn was not slow to speak for himself. He walked into Luke Henry's bar when it was full at the end of a late-night Saturday shopping and stood at the counter, a wronged man nursing a careful bottle of stout, declaring how happy he was to be back again among good neighbours.

'I have put the whole matter in the hands of my solicitor and am expecting proper redress through the courts,' he said to anybody who would listen. 'In the meantime I have taken to writing ladies again. This time we can have no blessing of church but we'll have our own blessing and the blessing of good neighbours which may turn out even luckier.'

Some managed to remain wonderfully straight-faced. Others assured him how glad they were to see him home and that he shouldn't blame himself in any respect whatsoever. Nobody in the wide world could have done more or tried harder to rescue what turned out to be a sinking ship. In fact, when everything was considered fully and turned over, he had been a veritable martyr to the cause. Extending out from John Quinn, the net of hypocrisy and lies had become as consistent as truth, encircling him.

Johnny wrote that he completely understood what a bad move it would be for him to think of coming home. He had been in a low mood when he wrote and was thinking of writing back to them even before he got their letter. In the short time since then everything had more or less fallen into place and was now completely alphabetical. When he told Mister Singh that Ford had made him redundant and he would have to look for a cheaper room or move to another part of London where light work was obtainable, Mister Sing wouldn't hear. Recently Mister Singh had bought a terrace of Victorian houses overlooking the Heath that ran into Epping Forest and was turning them into apartments for professional and business people – doctors, nurses, accountants, secretaries, a different class entirely to the Fusiliers.

Johnny was to be a sort of porter or Mister Singh's stand-in. He would keep the stairs and landings polished and clean and he would do light repairs when anything went wrong in the apartments. In return, he would have a small weekly wage and a rent-free flat in the basement. When he totted it all up one evening before going out to the Prince of Wales, he reckoned he would be better off money-wise at the end of the week than he was in the very best days on the line at Ford's. He was staying put until he went up as per usual to the Connors in Birmingham for Christmas and was then moving to Leytonstone as soon as he got back after the Christmas. Everything seemed to have worked out perfectly alphabetical.

'It couldn't have been planned better,' Ruttledge said as he handed back the letter. It was written with care and it brought a small world to life.

'It's great,' Mary said, her eyes gleaming. 'He fell on his feet. The poor fella deserved some bit of luck in England.'

'That letter you wrote worked,' Jamesie said.

'It worked powerfully,' Mary said. 'It couldn't have worked any better.'

'Johnny thinks the world of Mister Singh,' Jamesie said. 'And Mister Singh stood by him in the end.'

For many years now, Jim had been pressing his parents to come and spend Christmas in Dublin.

'He'd look nice in Dublin,' Mary used to joke.

'There's be much worse there already,' Jamesie would counter happily. 'You don't have to worry.'

After many hesitations and changes of mind, Jamesie and Mary decided to go to Dublin for Christmas. The Ruttledges would look after the animals and the place while they were away. The letter they received from Johnny was decisive in their going.

The gaiety of spirit grew as Christmas approached. Holly with rich red berries and trailing ivy was picked from the hedges to decorate rooms. Nets of many-coloured small electric lights were draped over Christmas trees and winked from porches. Mary made a plum pudding and baked a Christmas cake to take to Dublin.

At the Saturday market, Jamesie examined crates of live turkeys and finally bought a pair, a small turkey to give as a Christmas present to the Ruttledges and a huge bird to take to Dublin. In return, the Ruttledges gave a bottle of eighteen-year-old White Powers they got from a bar in Enniskillen, a leftover from the time when prosperous bars matured and bottled their own whiskey. The dark whiskey had a slight taste of port from the cask and looked beautiful in the clear glass of the unlabelled bottle.

In the town a great-lighted crib was erected outside the church. The shops were all bright with lights and holly and streamers and tinsel. Alone among all the bars and shops Jimmy Joe McKiernan flew a tricolour in a two-fingered salute to the two detectives across the road in the alleyway –

or to the town in general, which was so complacently celebrating Christmas, with the business of the country still unfinished.

In the little square near the cattle mart and shallow river the market traders erected their stalls around the statue of the harpist. In the evenings, with the street lamps on and the shops bustling and busy, it was moving to watch the families traipsing between the windows, the children in the shadow of their parents, stopping every so often to meet and greet friends and neighbours.

All the bars had a lighted Christmas tree and holly and looped strings of tinsel. Pages were pinned up beside the dart boards, on which lines could be purchased for the Christmas raffle, with prizes of a goose and a turkey, hampers of ham and whiskey and port and gin. Regular customers were served a Christmas round of drinks on the house. In all this feast of Christmas there were some shops that were almost empty, the assistants or owners looking out on the busy street to the passers-by who were all shopping elsewhere; and there were people wandering the town who had no people to meet, who did not want to be alone and were not noticed.

Ruttledge left Jamesie and Mary to the early morning train. They were going to Dublin for the whole week of Christmas. Though he arrived early at the house they were already waiting, their suitcases and parcels on the doorsteps, the two dogs crying in their house, the key in the outside of the door ready to be locked, the brown hens shut in their house within the netting wire.

'Put yourselves to no trouble,' Jamesie raised his hand in a gesture that meant Ruttledge was free to do whatever he wanted to do about the place while they were absent.

Among all the bags and parcels on their doorstep there was only one medium-sized suitcase with their own belongings and clothes. Everything else was presents, the plucked turkey, the plum pudding, even the rare bottle of White Powers.

'We'll taste it in Dublin. Too good for us. No good for us here on our own.'

Since they went to Dublin for their son's wedding seventeen years ago, a single night hadn't been spent away from the house. There was about them a spiritual quality, as if they were going forth as supplicants or communicants rather than to the small diesel train that would take them to Dublin in a couple of hours.

'The poor fellas,' Mary said of the protesting dogs as they drove away. 'They don't like to be closed in. They know full well that something is happening.' Then she withdrew into herself, but Jamesie named every house they passed, not with his usual fierce interest but as if it were a recitation of prayer, until it began to irritate Mary. 'You'd think it was to America he was going.'

'Or to heaven,' Ruttledge said.

'Much more likely the other place.'

After getting the tickets they waited with the rest of the passengers on the white gravel of the platform though the potbellied stove in the waiting room was red. There was a lighted Christmas tree in the opposite corner. Not many people were going to Dublin. They could see down a whole mile of track. In a field across the tracks an old horse and a few cows were eating hay together.

'Have you heard from Johnny?' Ruttledge asked as they waited.

'We had a card,' Mary said. 'The poor fella even put in a note for us to have a Christmas drink on him.'

'He's away to Birmingham to the Connors,' Jamesie said. 'He's in great fettle. After Christmas he takes up in his new place.'

'Will Patrick Ryan stay away or will he be home at Christmas?'

'He'll be home,' Jamesie answered with total confidence. 'On Christmas day he goes to the Harneys in Boyle. They come for him in a car. They're cousins but I hear they are sick enough of the whole performance. Every Christmas starts off all right but then he has to try to put the whole house under him. That's Patrick.'

'They'll come for him all the same,' Mary said sharply.

'They'll come. It's just one day. They're not going to stop now.'

'I might wander up to the house to see how he is or if he's there,' Ruttledge said.

'You'll see a choice house if you do,' Mary said. For the first time that morning she laughed. 'All modern comforts and appliances.'

The signal fell at the end of the platform and the snub nose of the little diesel train came into view far down the tracks. The young stationmaster locked the ticket office and walked down the platform towards the signal box. He was carrying a white hoop and nodded and smiled at the passengers he knew.

'He didn't even notice us,' Jamesie joked to hide his excitement, all his attention fixed on the approaching train.

The train drew in, and with a few nervous words they were gone.

On Christmas Eve, Kate had some last-minute shopping. Ruttledge said he would go with her to the town and call on the Shah. It was late. He dropped her under the tricolour flying over Jimmy Joe McKiernan's and drove slowly through the stars and crowns and trees and streamers and the chaotic parking of the town. The crib was floodlit on the steps of the church and the windows were ablaze with light for Midnight Mass. For this night anyhow, its modern ugliness had disappeared and it resembled a great lighted ship set to sail out of the solid middle of the town into all that surrounds our life. There was a white star above the entrance of the Central Hotel encircled by beads of coloured lights. When he reached the Shah's domain, suddenly all was in darkness except for the street lamps. The scrapyard and big sheds were closed and there wasn't a light or Christmas decoration in sight. The big light above the door of the station house was on and the light of televisions came through the windows of the cottages. As he approached the station house, the door suddenly opened and was held open while his uncle said goodbye to Father Conroy. When the door closed, the priest and Ruttledge stood face to face.

'This is a surprise,' Ruttledge said as they shook hands.

'There's nothing wrong,' the priest said. 'Every Christmas I come to the house to hear his Confession. We must be doing it for four or five years now.'

'You gave him Absolution?'

'And Communion,' the priest responded with equal lightness. 'You'll find him white as the driven snow.'

'A happy Christmas.'

'Many happy returns.'

When Ruttledge rang the bell, his uncle was plainly surprised to have a second caller and didn't open the door until he recognized the voice.

'You're some boy hauling our poor priest in from the country to hear your confession instead of going down to the church like everybody else,' Ruttledge said.

'You met the man,' he responded defensively. 'By all accounts you don't bother him too much yourself.'

'The man is overworked with people like you.'

'That'll do you now,' he began to shake with laughter. 'It's more than you do anyhow and that poor man you met going out needs a lock of pounds from time to time like everybody else.' He was enjoying the display of the power that could draw the priest to his house for an individual confession. He wanted Ruttledge to delay. He swung open his liquor cabinet to display a formidable array of bottles. 'You might as well have something now that it's Christmas.'

Ruttledge shook his head. 'Kate will be waiting. I just dropped in to say we'll not be eating till around four tomorrow. But come out whenever suits you. We'll be there all along.'

'Will it be all right to bring Himself?' he indicated the sheepdog stretched in front of the hot fire.

'Of course. Doesn't he come every Christmas?'

The dog rose from the fire and looking first at his master trotted over to Ruttledge to be petted.

'He knows. He makes no mistake, I'm telling you. He knows,' he said triumphantly.

'I find it hard to believe it is Christmas Day and that there are just the two of us,' Kate said when they rose in the morning. 'When I was little all my aunts and uncles and their families used to gather at my dear grandfather's house. The best part of Christmas Day was the morning when we drove to church, knowing that the long morning was ahead of us – the presents under the tree, the traditional lunch. Cousins, servants, an adored German shepherd, my grandmother's cats, all of us milling around during drinks, taking stock of the presents; then the solemn prayer before the feast began. I was usually asked to sing "God Bless America", my grandfather's eyes misting at the sight of little Kate singing. After that, it was downhill all the way. The old resentments and antagonisms surfaced, barely kept in check by my grandfather's Edwardian presence.'

'What would he think to see you here this Christmas morning?'

'He would be appalled. He never travelled outside America and thought it vulgar for people to go abroad since everything that anybody could want was in the greatest country on earth. He never forgave my mother for marrying an Englishman.'

'The greatest country in Ireland was always the world to come.'

'And all we have is the day.'

'We better make the most of it,' Ruttledge kissed her lightly as they rose.

He tended his own cattle and sheep. The work was pleasure. All the animals were healthy and the tasks took up little more than an hour. Then he walked round the lake to Jamesie's, taking a bottle of whiskey. The heron rose lazily out of the reeds. Wildfowl scattered from the reeds to gather out in the middle of the lake. The two swans were fishing close to their old high nest in the thick reeds. The first bell for Mass came over the water but no cars could be heard starting up between the bells. Everyone had attended Midnight Mass and was still sleeping. At the house he was met by the furious barking of the closeted dogs, the expectant clucking of the hens, the lowing of the old cow. The brown hens were loosed and fed, then the excited dogs. The cowhouse had been recently whitewashed inside and out and the stone walls were a soft, glowing white. The two doors were painted bright red. Inside, the four cows were tied with chains to posts, their calves loose in a big wooden pen made from straight branches of ash taken from the hedge. Most of the bark had peeled or was worn away and the timber was so smooth it shone in places and was cool and polished to the hand. To the excited bawling of the calves, he fed each cow a measure of crushed oats from a sack on a raised stand, watered them and fed them the hay he had baled in summer. The bales had the sweet smell of hay saved without rain. With a graip and brush he quickly cleaned the house before letting out the calves to their suck. Despite Jamesie's manly protestation that he had no interest in the cows other than the money they brought in, they were all placid and used to being handled. When the work was done and he had returned the calves to their pen, the brown hens and the dogs to their houses, he stood for a while on the street while a clock struck the hour from within the house: the whole place and everything about it was plain and beautiful. He then took the bottle of Powers, which he had left beside the pot of geraniums on the windowsill, and walked quickly towards the lake to see if Patrick Ryan was at home this Christmas morning.

The road he climbed from the lake was no longer passable

other than on foot. Parts of it had been torn away by floods and never resurfaced. A rusted iron gate stood between two thick round stone piers but the entrance was choked with fuchsia and sally. There was a fresh gash in the ground where the gate had been pushed open and there were recent footprints. The whole street was grass-grown. Beside the door was a small pile of tins and bottles and plastic bags and milk cartons. Both the house and sheds were iron-roofed and solid but they hadn't been touched by paint or whitewashed in years. Beyond the house, the old hayshed had been torn down in a storm. A mangled sheet of iron hung from an iron post like a dispirited brown flag. It was to this house Patrick Ryan had moved when he allowed the house he had grown up in to fall.

There was no answer to Ruttledge's knock and call. The door was unlocked. Inside, the room mustn't have changed in fifty or so years. It hadn't changed since Ruttledge first saw it ten or fifteen years before, the brown dresser, the settlebed, the iron crook above the open hearth, the horse harness hanging between the religious pictures on the wall – the smiling Virgin, the blood-drip from the Crown of Thorns – all faded now with damp spots underneath the glass, the cheapness moving, since it too had been touched and held in depths of time. In the small window the stone walls were at least four feet thick. The naked electric bulb that hung from the ceiling answered to the switch. By the fireplace was a bale of peat briquettes and in the centre of the floor was a pile of dry branches. A brand-new red Bushman was thrown among the branches and here and there on the floor were little piles of sawdust. A bowl of sugar, unwashed cups, milk, part of a loaf, a sardine tin, a plate with eggshells, a half-full bottle of Powers, a bar of soap, butter, an empty packet of Silk Cut, red apples, a pot of marmalade, salt, matches, a brown jug, an open newspaper, a transistor radio, an alarm clock littered the table. In stark contrast, one small corner of the room was spare and neat. An iron rested on an ironing board. Two perfectly ironed white shirts were hung beside a pressed dark suit. A pair of fine black leather shoes **that** had been polished till they shone sat on a chair.

Ruttledge called again and was answered by an indefinite sound from the upper room. When he pushed open the door he saw a big iron bed with broken brass bells piled high with clothes and overcoats in a corner of the room. The only sign of a human presence in this mound of clothes was a nose, straight and sharp as a blade.

'What do you want?' The nose was joined to the rest of Patrick Ryan's handsome head.

'Nothing.'

'What brought you, then?'

'To see how you were. Christmas.'

'Christmas brings out the eejit in everybody,' he said and suddenly swung out of the bed. Except for a shirt of rough material that fell to his hips he was naked. The strong body could have been the body of a younger man. This good-looking, vigorous man had lived all his life around the lake where nothing could be concealed, and he had never shown any sexual interest in another. 'I don't have to even countenance that job,' he joked once to Ruttledge. 'John Quinn has agreed to do my share.'

'We'll have to get up that shed one of these days, lad,' he said as he lifted a pair of trousers from the floor and pulled them on.

The alarm clock started up in the lower room as he was pulling on his socks. 'Will you turn that clock off, lad?'

The old blue alarm clock was dancing on the table and he lifted it before turning off the alarm. He moved the bottle of Powers he had brought in beside the half-full bottle of whiskey on the crowded table and waited. When Patrick Ryan came down to the room he was wearing loose shoes and an old brown sweater and was running his fingers through his thick grey hair. 'You'll have a drink, lad.'

'No thanks, Patrick, it's too early.'

'It's Christmas,' he said, and noticed the bottle of Powers.

213

'What the fuck is this?'

'A bottle I brought for Christmas.'

'You'll have to have a drink, then, lad.'

'It's too early.'

'What do you want poisoning me for with what you won't drink yourself?'

'I drink plenty . . . too much sometimes.'

'We all drink too much, lad. Would you see if you could get a bit of a fire started to see if we can make anything of this Christmas Day?'

With the Bushman Ruttledge sawed the dried branches. Using a fire-lighter he soon had a bright fire going under the black kettle on the crook. While they waited for the kettle to boil, Patrick Ryan ate the red apples and a few slices of buttered bread with a mug of milk into which he tipped a splash of whiskey. 'Are you happy, lad?' he demanded.

Ruttledge had added turf briquettes to the fire and was looking silently into the flames.

'I'm not unhappy,' he answered, surprised.

'What does that mean?'

'I'm not over the moon. I have health, for the time being, enough money, no immediate worries. That, I believe, is about as good as it gets. Are *you* happy?'

'I am in fuck. There are times I don't know who I am from one minute to the next. That's why I always liked the acting. You are someone else and always know what you are doing and why.'

He wanted boiling water not for tea or coffee but in order to shave and wash. He shaved with a yellow plastic razor in an old mirror he got from the dresser. Then he dressed in the pressed suit and ironed white shirt and brushed the thick head of hair.

'You wouldn't think of getting an electric kettle? It'd be very handy,' Ruttledge said.

'No, lad. I'm not here often enough and the fire is no trouble and heats the place.'

'You heard that Mary and Jamesie have gone to Dublin for Christmas?'

'I heard.' Patrick laughed, mimicking Jamesie's inarticulate wonderment. 'Crowds, you see . . . creatures in thousands . . . all shapes . . . lights . . . buses.'

'And Johnny was made redundant at Ford's but then sort of fell on his feet. He is going to caretake a block of flats.'

'I heard,' he said with unusual grimness. 'Was it you wrote the letter for them?'

'No,' Ruttledge lied. 'We talked about it. It would have been bad for everybody had he come home. It's great how it all worked out.'

'Alphabetical,' he said sharply as he stared at Ruttledge, and then knotted his red silk tie and pulled on the jacket of the dark suit. He would not have looked out of place in the foyer of a great hotel. 'Here. Take this back with you,' he tried to get Ruttledge to take back the bottle of Powers he had brought.

'No. Leave it. We'll have a drink for Christmas from the other bottle.'

'That makes more sense, lad.'

Two measures were poured and the glasses raised to 'A Happy Christmas'.

'I'm going to the Harneys above in Boyle for Christmas. I go to them every Christmas Day.' He told Ruttledge what he already knew. 'I'll bring them your bottle. What goes round comes round. The car could be arriving at the corner of the lake for me any minute now.' He slipped the bottle together with a small package wrapped in Christmas paper into a plastic carrier bag and then put in his shoes. He wore wellingtons to walk the rutted and torn path to the lake. 'You see the wife and family,' he gestured towards his small herd of cattle which was sheltering under whitethorns on the far hill.

'They seem to be doing all right. They have a big run,' Ruttledge said carefully.

'I often come at night with whoever I happen to be working for. I get them to drive me and we throw them a bale,' he said somewhat defensively. 'I suppose no more than ourselves, lad, it doesn't make all that much differ whether they live or die.'

What do we have without life? What does love become but care? Ruttledge thought in opposition but did not speak.

At the lake, Patrick Ryan changed out of the wellingtons into the pair of black shoes and hid the wellingtons upside down in thick blackthorns. Beyond the reeds, a car was already waiting at the corner of the lake. 'I go to entertain them in their own houses,' he said as he walked towards the waiting car, carrying the plastic bag.

The Shah rolled up to the porch at his usual Sunday time with the sheepdog in the front seat that Christmas Day and they ate at four. Kate put out a tablecloth of embroidered linen and lit two candles in silver candlesticks. The black cat with the white paws sat high on the back of an armchair, surveying the sheepdog's movements with a wary eye. The small roast turkey was carved in the kitchen and placed on a large white oval platter. The meal began with leek soup. There was a dry white and red wine and to their surprise the Shah asked for a glass of sweet white wine. There was little conversation. As with heavy people who can move with lightness on a dance floor, the Shah ate with great delicacy. His enjoyment was palpable and it was as much a pleasure to be part of as lively speech. Not until the plum pudding and cream arrived did he relax and ease back.

'I hope four o'clock wasn't too late for you to eat,' Kate said. 'It's well past your usual time at the Central.'

'Myself and that woman went to Second Mass instead of First and had a late breakfast in the hotel. Both of us were fasting.'

He sighed with pleasure; then the talk turned to the sale and transfer of the business. The final papers had been agreed and were expected to be ready for signature as soon as the offices opened after the holidays.

'Will he be able for it though?' he asked several times.

'Anyhow you're sitting pretty no matter what happens,' Ruttledge said.

'You can swear,' he said. He produced a few cigars and offered one to Kate.

'I'd love to but it'd be the same as if I never stopped.'

'They're good. I was given them by a traveller.' He left two big cigars on the table. 'They'll be there for the other man. He won't have any trouble.'

Ruttledge drank a brandy while the Shah smoked the cigar. Then the Shah called the sheepdog, rose and left without abruptness or awkwardness. They watched from the porch as the headlights turned on the water and went slowly out along the shore.

'He probably has another call to make. He could be on his way to see Monica.'

'I never guessed he'd become such a dear presence.'

'That's what happens,' Ruttledge said, looking away.

Late in the evening a loud rapping sounded on the glass of the porch. It was Bill Evans. He was wearing shoes, and in his Mass clothes he looked well. He rested the heavy blackthorn stick against the side of the rocking chair. He wanted brandy. Downing the glass quickly, he demanded another. Ruttledge gave him three glasses, each time pouring a smaller measure, and then refused him any more. When he was leaving, he was given the two cigars and he tried to light the wrong end. Kate cut and lit the cigar for him. He watched her impatiently and when he took it started smoking furiously. Ruttledge walked him all the way up the hill in case he would fall.

'How do you feel now?' he asked when they were close to the house. In the darkness he could only see the outline of his shape and the red glow of the cigar.

'God, I feel lovely. Couldn't feel better. A very happy Christmas to yourself.'

'And a happy Christmas yourself.'

The days were quiet. They did not feel particularly quiet or happy but through them ran the sense, like an underground river, that there would come a time when these days would be looked back on as happiness, all that life could give of contentment and peace. They would cross the lake together in the morning, let out the hens, loose and feed the pair of dogs, clean out and feed the cows, let the calves to their suck. Each morning the mule came to the little gate beside the pond and bared his teeth as he was thrown hay. As Kate was staying to make some sketches, the dogs did not have to be put back in the house and the brown hens could pick about in the dirt inside the netting wire. The place fascinated her and she was using their absence to work near the house undisturbed.

Because they were so bounded, the days of Christmas slipped by quickly. In the evenings they put down a fire in Jamesie and Mary's yellowed Stanley to keep the dampness out and the house warm for their return, and wound the clocks. No two clocks were the same or told the same time but all were running. Each one had its separate presence and charm.

A few visitors called to the house. The Ruttledges spent an evening with Monica and her children. The Shah had visited her late on Christmas Day, bringing many presents.

On some days Bill Evans called twice to the house. When the brandy was no longer forthcoming, he took tea and cake and cigarettes without a murmur. The bus to the Home had been suspended for the week of Christmas. He was anxious that the trips might not resume once Christmas was over; what was once given could be taken back in the same mysterious way it had come.

'It's going to be a normal Thursday next week,' he predicted after the Thursday of Christmas had passed. 'The bus will be back.' The words highlighted his anxiety.

'Jamesie will be back from Dublin by then as well.'

'Begod he will. He'll have lots to tell,' he remarked without a flicker of interest.

Jamesie and Mary were returning on the early afternoon train from Dublin. Ruttledge dropped Kate at their gate on his way to the station. She was putting a fire down and bringing flowers to the house, a sheaf of red and yellow chrysanthemums.

The Christmas decorations were still up in the waiting room of the station. In the late evening light the green metal bridge that crossed the tracks glistened with raindrops from a recent shower. The rails were wet. Across the track the few cattle and the one horse sheltered under a thick whitethorn hedge at the far end of the field.

As soon as the small train drew in, he saw Jamesie's head in the window of one of the doors, his great hand grappling inexpertly with the outside handle. Next he saw Mary's face, smiling over her husband's shoulder. When the door was opened and they stepped down on the gravel, Jamesie swung his suitcase away when Ruttledge went to take it from his hand.

'No. There's nothing in it. It's as light as a feather.'

Mary kissed Ruttledge warmly but Jamesie hardly felt the hand he gave. They both looked exhausted and walked to the car without a word.

'How are they all in Dublin?'

'Great. Couldn't be better. They were all asking after you and Kate.'

'That was nice. You must have had a great Christmas.'

There was an uncertain silence until Mary said dismissively, with careful nonchalance, 'It was all right. What does anything do but go by.'

'It was topping,' Jamesie echoed. 'There wasn't a single thing that could be faulted.'

'There was a big crowd for Christmas Day,' Mary said. 'Her father and mother were there as well.'

'The old father was no joke,' Jamesie said. 'He was a retired old bank manager but a sharp whippersnapper and you'd be surprised at all he could drink.'

'You don't have far to look to tell what you were interested in,' Mary said.

The low cheer that greeted the remark was a return to his old self. All his attention was fixed on the houses and fields and turns of the road they passed. He did not call out any of the names. He did not ask to stop at Luke's or anywhere as they drove through the town. In bits and pieces their Christmas in Dublin came out. Mary had spent all the time in the house except for a shopping expedition she made to the Christmas sales with Lucy and the children. The children had been the best part. Jamesie had met Jim's boss and people he worked with in the city.

'They were high up like Jim . . . important . . . clever . . . no daws anyway. The clevers are always plain. No big shows or blows. I was able to talk to them all.'

'Jim said he was a big hit. You could take him anywhere,' Mary said with pride. 'He was always well able to swing the lies.'

'I had nothing to do but be myself,' he said 'What else was any of us doing?'

'I'm sure there was some shaping and pretending as well.'

'They adored Mary,' Jamesie raised his great hand. 'The children adore the ground she walks on.'

'I got on all right. I think I passed. But it was too long,' she said as if in correction of the praise, adding, 'No house is big enough for two women. This fella was wild to be away as well. You know what he said when he saw the train was coming into Longford? "If the frigging thing breaks down now we'll be able to walk home from here."'

'It was all right,' Jamesie said in an artificial voice he used when he was too impressed with the subject matter of his own speech. 'Jim did his level best to show us as good a time as any old pair can be showed. It doesn't take long to see everything you want to see in a city. There are too many people. After a while they all start to go by in a blur. If we were ever to go again we'd not go for more than a day or two.'

The light had dimmed to a half-light. The driving was difficult because of the shadows, but when they came in sight of the lake there was light enough to show the brilliance of the two swans riding out beyond the reeds but not the wildfowl. The huge bare trees stood out on the far shore as the headlights travelled weakly over the road. Not a word was spoken, even when the car turned away from the lake and began the climb to the house. As soon as they drove in on the street they saw the nape of the woman's neck leaning across the lighted square of the window and then her face turned sharply towards the sound of the car.

'Kate is here!'

There were shouts and kisses and handshakes and laughter. 'You're welcome home!' 'It's great to be home. We missed you, Kate.'

Jamesie demanded that they have a whiskey straight away but Ruttledge insisted that he see the animals first. He looked at them intensely for a few moments. They all recognized him and the old cow looed her recognition. Then he snapped the light off.

'They were far too well done. They'd nearly order you around. A touch of hardship would do them a world of good.'

The dogs were with Kate in the house when the car pulled up and Mary had hardly been able to move with the frenzy of their welcome. 'The poor fellas. The poor fellas,' she kept saying over and over. 'What did you do at all? They've missed us too,' she laughed.

Now they were seated in their chairs. Kate had a good fire going. The aluminium kettle was boiling. There was a big plate of sandwiches. They had hot whiskeys with cloves and lemon and sugar. More quietly, they talked of Dublin and the children and the parents and their stay. The presents they received were taken out and displayed: a headscarf of blue silk with the print of a medieval church, and a box of hand-made scented soaps – 'Maybe they don't think I wash enough' – a thick woollen sweater and a bottle of Black Bush for Jamesie. They stood gazing at the presents as if they held all goodwill, all generosity.

'The poor children even saved,' Mary said.

'They're as good . . . as good . . . as good, pure toppers,' Jamesie said, and taking off his jacket he pulled on the sweater. It took persuasion to make Mary wear the silk headscarf.

'They'll be great talk at Mass when you march up to the front seat with that scarf on your head,' Jamesie said.

By now they were truly home but they were so visibly tiring that the Ruttledges rose to leave, despite their protestations that it was far, far too early in the evening to even think of leaving yet.

A few days after Christmas, Ruttledge witnessed the signing over of the Shah's business to Frank Dolan in the solicitor's office.

The offices were in a plain Victorian house in the middle of the town. Brown photos of the main street taken many years before, when horse and bicycle were the means of transport, hung on the walls of the waiting room beside the diplomas. 'Changes,' the Shah remarked stonily.

'Nothing but change,' Ruttledge echoed, but Frank Dolan did not speak at all.

There were no other people waiting and in a few minutes a girl led them up narrow stairs and showed them into an office. The solicitor rose from behind a heavy mahogany desk to welcome the Shah warmly and then shook hands with the two other men, motioning them towards the leather armchairs. He wore a well-cut suit and his greying hair was parted in the centre. The agreement was read and assented to. Frank Dolan handed over his cheque and was given a receipt. All the papers were initialled and signed. The only unusual thing, outside the solicitor's friendliness and charm which seemed to extend beyond the merely professional, was that the two principals never addressed a word to one another throughout. Out in the street together they still did-n't speak. Ruttledge took Frank Dolan's hand and wished him all the luck in the world.

'Thanks. Thanks for all the trouble. Thanks for every-thing,' Frank Dolan said in an emotional voice.

'It was no trouble. It was nothing.'

The Shah stood solidly on the pavement, without a word or movement, as inscrutable as a statue of Buddha.

'Thanks,' Frank repeated again and walked to his old car without another word or look. He walked slowly and natu-rally, as if any possible acknowledgement of the Shah's pres-ence in the day was unimaginable, and his very separateness was as impressive as the Shah's own. The car had already been turned around and he did not wave or look either way as he drove towards the scrapyard and the old railway sheds, all of which he now owned.

'Whether he makes it or not I doubt if he'll ever come to look the part,' the Shah said as he watched the old Toyota drive away.

'The two of you are never going to kill one another with talk,' Ruttledge remarked.

'You wouldn't know where to begin,' the Shah said. 'You could be taking your life in your hands.'

The weeks following Christmas were mild and damp. Then the storms came, breaking branches, uprooting small trees in the hedges, lathering the road round the shore with foam. Between the storms they had precious days of frost when the light was dry and clear and sounds carried. Thin ice glittered along the shore and clinked and chimed when there was any movement on the water.

In all these weathers Bill Evans went every day to the lake. Jamesie counted the twenty-six times he had to set down the buckets and rest on the steep climb between the lake and the top of the hill and he imitated the sideways, crab-like gait and the way he blew on his hands and folded them into the long black sleeves and wrung them against his breast.

They had never seen Bill Evans in better spirits. He was often condescending, as he smoked and ate and took tea in his huge wellingtons and roped black crombie and the shiny sou'wester tied beneath his chin, and talked of the bus and Michael Pat the driver and all that travelled on the bus and how they would nearly cause any normal enough person to laugh. He was no longer living from moment to moment, from blow to blow, pleasure to pleasure, refusing to look forward or back: he was now living these bus rides on Thursday in the mind as well. The seeds of calamity were sown.

On a Thursday in February, with the rain pouring down, he came to the porch holding on to the two buckets instead of leaving them in the fuchsias at the gate. He would have carried them into the house except for the narrowness of the porch door.

'Bring them into the house if you want, Bill, but they'll come to no harm in the rain.' Kate saw at once that there was something very wrong.

'I was stopped,' he cried out as he entered the porch.

'Stopped from what?'

'Stopped from going on the bus.'

'Why?' She had never see him break down before or weep, the small choked cries of a child.

'I was stopped,' he repeated, tears slipping down his face, catching in the deep lines.

She made tea, adding biscuits and fruitcake to the plate of buttered bread and jam. He drank the tea but he wasn't able to eat. 'Somebody or something must have stopped you or did the bus not come?' she asked.

'They stopped me,' he admitted reluctantly.

'Why did they do that?'

'They stopped me,' he cried out and rose. 'Did he leave any fags?'

She gave him the ration of cigarettes from a mug on a shelf above the stove and walked him to the door. She watched him lift the two buckets outside the porch and go in the heavy rain towards the open gate and down past the fuchsias towards the lake.

'We'll have to do something. You'll have to go to the house and confront them,' Kate said when Ruttledge returned.

A cold, appraising look came over his face that she normally liked but now felt uncomfortable with. 'Why?' he asked.

'You know well that I'd be no good.'

'Neither of us would. We'd only make matters worse.'

'We'll have to do something. It means the world to him. It was like looking at somebody who has lost everything.'

'The only person with power in this case is the priest.'

'Why don't you go to him? The two of you get on well together.'

'I'll go to him tonight.'

The church was in darkness but there was a light above the door of the presbytery. It was a strange place to have built this church and presbytery, far from any human habitation. Its natural place should have been beside the bars and post office and school and the old monastery at Shruhaun. The sound of trees waving in the darkness and the steady rain increased the sense of night and isolation. Ruttledge let himself in through the small gate beside the sacristy and rang the bell. The hall lights came on immediately. The priest appeared glad to see him, inviting him in. He was wearing a heavy black pullover and an open-necked shirt. Newspapers and bills and letters and a few books were scattered about the large oval table in the sitting room. A coal fire burned brightly in the grate. The rest of the furniture was old and dark and comfortable and must have served many undemanding masters.

'We haven't met since Christmas Eve,' Ruttledge remarked.

'If everybody paid me as well as that man I'd never stop calling to the houses. Will you have tea or something stronger?'

Ruttledge asked for tea. The cups and tea bags stood on a silver tray on a dark mahogany sideboard with an electric kettle. The priest made tea, offered biscuits, but he himself drank only warm water.

'I should state my business,' Ruttledge said. 'You know Bill Evans?'

'I know all my parishioners,' he answered.

'For some time now the bus has been coming to the house on Thursday and taking him into the Home.'

'I know that.'

'It's been his one great pleasure. The whole week is spent looking forward to Thursday. Now he has been stopped. I came to see if you could get him back on the bus.'

'Who stopped him?'

'They stopped him, as far as I know.'

'Why would they? It's not costing them anything.'

'I'm not sure I want to know. They may miss him for drawing water, for the various jobs he does about the house. They may have even come to resent the pleasure he gets from those Thursdays.'

The priest continued looking at Ruttledge after he had spoken and then turned away to take tongs and arrange coals on the fire. 'They don't know it yet – and naturally *he* doesn't know – but his days out there by the lake are numbered,' he said. 'A housing development has already begun in the town to provide small apartments for the elderly, for people still able to manage on their own but in need of help. All of it is state-funded. I'm on the board and our friend is one of the first names on the housing list. We are going to call the development *Trathnona*. What do you think of the name?'

'The evening of life,' Ruttledge translated for his own ears. 'Somehow it doesn't sound so bad in English. Next stop: night. I think it's pretty awful.'

'I thought you might say that,' the priest laughed. 'They could call it Bundoran as far as I'm concerned, as long as it serves its purpose and the deserving people get the accommodation. We have quite a few Fenians on the board and they thought the name both patriotic and appropriate.'

'I'm sure it doesn't matter. Not many will know what *Trathnona* means. In time it'll just become another name.'

'I don't care. Bill Evans and two other homeboys are on the list. When the development is completed he'll get one of the houses.'

'He'll be in heaven,' Ruttledge said.

The conversation moved to the cattle both men kept, the price of cattle and the animals they intended to take out and sell in the mart on Monaghan Day. John Quinn's name came up. The priest smiled but was slow to judge. 'He's been consoling himself with a few ladies. He takes them up to the front seat at Sunday Mass and sometimes to the empty church where they light candles at Our Lady's shrine. At a distance it is a most touching and romantic ceremony. If I'm around he always introduces them.'

From there the talk turned surprisingly to the priest's own faith. He spoke with warmth of his mother and his father, who had been a farmer and small cattle dealer. 'They believed and brought me into life. What was good enough for them will do for me. That is all the reason I need. When my father was dying he said that if he were given an opportunity to start life all over again he'd take it without a thought. I doubt if I could go that far. Once is more than enough.'

'It would be wrong to say I envy you,' Ruttledge said.

'Live and let live is what I say,' the old priest said. 'The man above in Longford will never see it that way. Those Northerners want to bulldoze everybody into their own view.'

'We are not short of people like that down here, either,' Ruttledge said.

The evening had flown.

'I'll drive up your way tomorrow to see what I can do but I'll not call. It would look a bit obvious. I'll drop in with whatever news I have later.'

'Would you like to come and eat something with us then?'

'No,' he said firmly. 'I'll call to let you know what happened.'

The next day they saw his car climb past the gate to the house. He was a poor driver and drove slowly, his eyes fixed resolutely on the road. They thought he must have spent a long time at the house because they did not hear the car go back down towards the lake. The next day Bill Evans was as distraught as ever. He had seen the priest call but couldn't imagine that the call had anything to do with him. A couple of days later the priest came to tell them the matter had been settled but he would not delay as he had a sick call to make, and on the next Thursday morning Bill Evans was back on the bus sitting beside Michael Pat in the front seat. When he called on his way to the lake the next day, he told of all the help he gave Michael Pat and spoke as if they had never missed a day.

Monaghan Day was the biggest mart of the year and was held on the last Thursday in February. By now it had grown so large that it extended to the Friday and Saturday, and there were years like this year when it entered March. All the big buyers and dealers came to Monaghan Day. Because of the number of dealers, the prices to be had were generally higher than at any other time of the year. In talk in the bars around Monaghan Day some argued that the name derived from the time Monaghan buyers came to the fairs at the end of winter to buy young cattle for shipping to Scotland. More asserted that the name went much further back to the time of the faction fights, when a famous family of fighters called the Monaghans were kings of the early spring fair, with their lead-filled ash plants. Great crowds gathered to watch these fights. On one Monaghan Day the fighters had to be smuggled out of the town, hidden in cartloads of oat sheaves, after a local man had been killed in a fight. A few others declared it had nothing to do with either Monaghan, other than in the heads of ravellers and romancers who had neither knowledge nor religion: it was not Monaghan Day but Manachan Day, after Saint Manachan, who founded the old abbey and whose feast day falls on the 25th February. A great deal many more swore that they couldn't care less if it was the fair of Timbuktu as long as plenty of buyers came and the prices were high.

Jamesie took an inordinate pride in his few young cattle, and bucket-fed and currycombed and groomed them for Monaghan Day. Patrick Ryan had two young cattle still running with their mothers and he came with Jamesie to the house one morning. The three men separated Patrick's calves – they were at least yearlings – and took them over to Jamesie's in Ruttledge's trailer. They were wild, unused to any handling, and were housed with great difficulty.

'Racehorses,' Jamesie laughed. Patrick Ryan was unperturbed throughout and made jokes and was in great good humour. He planned to be in town on Monaghan Day. He was living with a rich family in Carrick, putting in bathrooms in houses bought to rent, and they would drive him to the mart on the day.

Mary was delighted to see Patrick again and he grew more handsome in the warmth of her affection. They all had a whiskey together, to the ticking and the irregular strikings of the clocks, while arranging to meet up with Patrick outside the main ring before the bidding began at noon. Then Ruttledge left. They had much to talk about together and the talk would flow more freely in his absence.

On the evening before Monaghan Day, Jamesie and Ruttledge loaded the cattle into the trailer and ran them into the mart. The grounds around the mart were relatively empty and it was easy to back the trailer in between the gates. They made three runs. Because of their wildness, they had to make an extra run to bring Patrick's cattle in.

'A most hopeless man,' Jamesie sang as he gloated over the sleekness of his own cattle set beside Patrick's rough beasts. 'As clever, as clever a man as ever walked these parts but no care, no care in the world.'

'Do you think he'll turn up tomorrow?'

'Don't you worry. He'll turn up. With all that excitement and show and a world of strangers, our Patrick will not be found missing.'

The great wastegrounds around the mart were deserted except for the cars and tractors bringing in cattle early. Plastic bags shone gaudily where they were caught in the ragged line of whitethorns that marked the boundary on a high mound. The powerful arc lamps were on and men were testing and oiling gates and spreading bales of straw. In the low-ceilinged office lit by naked bulbs, a woman wrote down their names and addresses and handed them the white paper discs with their numbers. They then drove the cattle from the holding pen into the narrow chutes. On a concrete walk above the shoots an attendant in a blue cloth coat checked each ear-tag against the cattle cards, and with a dab from a big pot of glue fixed the pale numbered discs to their backs.

'Good luck tomorrow,' he said as he bound their green cards with a rubber band and placed them with other cards in a big cardboard box. They separated the bulls and heifers and closed them in pens beside the sale rings and left them hay and water for the night.

'They'll never see the fields around the lake again,' Jamesie repeated.

In the near-empty mart the small early herds looked forlorn under the glare of the arc lamps in the rows of tubular steel, all of them lowing plaintively, their breaths showing in the cold air.

Jamesie didn't want to go for a drink to Luke's or any other bar. He was too tense but would never admit to such feelings. Tomorrow all the pride and care for his animals would be tested against the prices they would fetch. When they reached the lake he insisted on getting out of the car at his gate and walking all the way on his own to the house in the darkness. 'Haven't I done it thousands and thousands of times?'

He was waiting at the corner of the lake the next morning. So many trucks and cars and tractors were drawn up along the sides of the road on the outskirts of town that they decided to abandon the car and walk. It was as if a great show or circus had come to town, except no flags were flying other than the lone tricolour outside Jimmy Joe McKiernan's. At the mart gates, horns were hooting and men were getting out of lorries and shouting and swearing as they waited to get out and in. Every square yard of the wasteground round the mart was filled.

The traders had already set out their stalls. Chain saws were displayed on a long trestle table beneath a canvas tent that bulged and flapped. From the open back of a van a man was selling animal medicines, sprays and drenches and large cans of disinfectant, sticks of caustic for removing horns, bone-handled knives with curved blades for dressing hooves. One whole side of a covered lorry was open. They had grease guns, tins of oil, top links for tractors, chains, pulleys, blue bales of rope. Close by was a van selling wellingtons, work boots, rainwear, overalls. Elsewhere, shovels, spades, forks, hedge knives, axes, picks were displayed leaning against the side of a van. All kinds of tool handles stood in barrels. Every stall was drawing its own small crowd.

Their cattle were safe in their pens but now other cattle were packed in among them so that they didn't have space to move or lie. All the other pens were similarly filled and it was like a breathing sea of cattle under the steel girders and the lamps and the spluttering loudspeakers. A group of judges accompanied by a crowd moved along the pens reserved for the cattle competing for prizes in the different breeds. They paused and discussed and sometimes looked again before handing out the red and blue and yellow rosettes to a sudden sharp burst of clapping from the crowd.

Then they moved on quickly to the next stall where the same process was repeated. The names of the winners in each section and the overall winner, the champion of Monaghan Day, were broadcast on the crackling, echoing loudspeakers to further applause, followed by a warning that the sale was commencing shortly. When the loudspeakers went dead, the lowing and bellowing and shouting, sliding of hooves, the clanging of gates resumed.

Jamesie entered both pens to quickly groom and freshen the appearance of his animals, but Ruttledge thought the grooming would have little effect. In his mind the cattle were already gone. The buyers were moving among the pens. They were easy to pick out, as they wore hats and ties and suits protected by cloth overcoats with large square pockets, and they wore the red cattlemen's boots laced high. Some carried bamboo canes like military batons. The signs were good if they paused outside the pens, and even better if they prodded or felt the cattle, and better still if they noted down their numbers.

Jamesie and Ruttledge didn't have to meet Patrick Ryan until the commencement of the sale and went to the restaurant and had mugs of tea at the counter. Some men who had come distances were already eating dinners or big sandwiches at the Formica-topped tables on the rough concrete floor. In the kitchen behind the counter, women with their hair gathered up in pink plastic hats were busy rushing about as they prepared the hundreds of meals they would be serving till late into the night. While they were at the counter another announcement that the sale was about to begin spluttered over the loudspeakers but not until they heard the unmistakable sound of the actual bidding did they leave for the ring. Patrick was already there. In a dark suit and white shirt and tie he looked more like one of the dealers than any of the farmers gathered around the ring.

'Patrick. You're shining,' Jamesie held out his great hand.

'The two of yous are a sight for sore eyes,' he said with

perfect poise in the middle of the jostling and pushing in the crush around the ring. 'If you didn't leave your manners behind today you'd be walked on.'

'We never had much in the first place,' Jamesie responded, delighted.

'Did ye get my poor steers in or did they take to the hedges?'

'In no time they'll be coming under the hammer. They look so good we were nearly putting them in for the prizes,' Jamesie said.

'Would you like to see them, Patrick?' Ruttledge enquired. 'The pen is nearhand.'

'I'll see them soon enough,' he laughed agreeably.

The initial bidding was slow. The cattle entered the ring through a weighing cage, the hands of the scale swinging wildly around the big white face before settling on the number of kilos the animal weighed. The assistant to the auctioneer then chalked up the animal's number and weight on the back of a board and then swung it round to face the ring. None of the first six cattle to enter the ring was sold. There was much of the actor in the auctioneer; he bantered and traded insults with the tanglers, to the amusement of the crowd packing the barriers and sitting in the high stand above the ring.

'This is a fucken disaster,' he shouted down.

Then, to further laughter and cheering, he rolled his sleeves up as if getting ready to fight. 'We might as well all go home and go to bed,' he shouted, and the shouts and the answering jeers and laughter crackled and spluttered out from the loudspeakers.

'You'll have a great time riding Molly,' was shouted back and cheered to the roof, while the auctioneer pretended to be shocked, which increased the cheering. 'Nobody ever does the like of that in this part of the country,' he shouted nonchalantly back, which was received with wild hooting and cheering and wolf-whistles.

Suddenly, a dramatic hush fell. The big dealers were taking their places around the ring and on the steps of the stand. The banter ended. There was a deadly silence as the bids rose quickly: 'Who'll give me four hundred? – 420, 430, 440, 460, 70, 80. Who'll give me five hundred? On my right – 505, 510, 520, 510. All done,' the auctioneer leaned to the caller in the box below the auctioneer's seat. They held a brief discussion. 'Not enough. He wants a little more. Who'll give me 520, 515, 510. I have to my left 510, any more, who'll give me more?' The price didn't advance, and he looked to the seller again, who nodded. 'On the mart – 510, 515, 520, 540, 550, 555, 65, 70, 75, 80, 580 pounds. All done. All done.' He looked round at all the bidders moving slowly from face to face. 'Sold! Five hundred and eighty pounds!' bringing the hammer down.

Once started, the selling went very quickly. The auctioneer's voice took on the incantation of prayer; it was the rhythm and repetition that indicated its simple purpose more than any words or numbers. After the first dozen or so sales, a murmur of approval went round the ring. The prices were good, more than good, and all the indications were that it was going to be a great Monaghan Day.

Jamesie's face expressed his relief instantly but he was too tense to speak or rub his hands in satisfaction. Already Patrick Ryan had wandered away to another part of the ring and was talking with other people. Ruttledge and Jamesie decided to separate. Ruttledge was to go to the other ring and sell the heifers. They couldn't risk staying together because they couldn't be sure which would come on the market first. On his way between the rings he passed Father Conroy, who nodded recognition but did not pause or speak. Close to him was his old acolyte, the church sacristan, Jimmy Lynch. The priest had made no attempt at disguise and was wearing his white collar with old clerical clothes. He was absorbed and separate. There were many there who knew him but once they saw his face they turned aside. Care was needed passing between the rings, and a number of times Ruttledge had to climb on gates and the rungs of pens to avoid the rush of milling, frightened cattle being moved between the rings and the pens.

As soon as he reached the heifer ring, he saw from the chalked numbers that he hadn't come too early, and he recognized his own cattle in one of the holding pens. They did not look distressed. By now, they were probably numbed. As their numbers drew close, the selling seemed to race. Ruttledge watched the big hands of the scale until it came to rest when the first animal entered the cage, and waited to see that it tallied with the number chalked on the board before entering the box. Through the little window he was able to look out at the buyers crowding round the ring and packing the stand. Like prayers, the bids were called out, and when they slowed to a stop the auctioneer leaned down. 'What do you think yourself?' he found himself asking, despite the fact that he knew the auctioneer would not want to take responsibility. The auctioneer went round the ring again. The bids rose a little higher. The next time he looked his way he nodded vigorously to sell.

'On the mart – slowly.' The bidding rose quickly and when the auctioneer brought down the hammer, he turned towards the box and nodded his satisfaction with the price. What followed was over in an instant. He was being handed the sales' slips and another man was taking his place in the box. At other marts he had seen old farmers leaving the box looking as dazed and befuddled as he felt. A man clapped him on the shoulder and brought a smiling, friendly face up close. 'Those were great prices. They were nice cattle!'

'Are you buying or selling yourself?'

'Selling but it'll be hours yet till I'm on.'

'Good luck. The mart is good.'

'Thanks . . . as long as it keeps up,' the man said fervently.

On his way back, a look at the sales' slips confirmed that Jamesie had got the higher prices. In the crowd round the ring he found Jamesie and Patrick back together again. He handed them the slips. Jamesie's huge hands were shaking.

'The prices are good but Jamesie got the best prices.'

'Jamesie is always winning,' Patrick Ryan winked. 'He must have the best, best cattle in, in, in the whole of Ireland.'

'Not the worst anyhow,' Jamesie sang out, ignoring the play. 'The prices are so close that there's hardly a whit of difference.'

The bidding had slowed around the bullock ring as previous withdrawals were rerun again, to the auctioneer's obvious impatience.

'Tanglers trying their cattle,' Jamesie said.

Then the bidding quickened. They saw their cattle being driven into the holding pens next to the weighing cage. The number chalked up on the board was only two numbers away from their numbers. Because of the good prices the heifers went for, Jamesie insisted superstitiously that Ruttledge sell the bullocks as well. Patrick Ryan didn't want to go near the box. 'Sell them no matter what you get. Sell them if you get anything. Sell them to hell. They are not coming home.'

Ruttledge was calmer now. He saw his own animal enter the ring, its weight chalked up on the board, and watched the coded signals of the dealers as they bid, the bids translated into the rhythmic exhortation of the auctioneer. When the bidding slowed and the auctioneer leaned towards him, he nodded to him to complete the sale. There were a few shouted insults about racehorses and 'age is venerable' when Patrick Ryan's steers entered the ring. At first the bidding was much lower than for the other cattle but once they were put on the mart there was sharp competition and they went for a higher price than anybody had expected. The two men were delighted and they were being congratulated all round when Ruttledge rejoined them.

'Do you want to stay around for a while or will we head off?' Ruttledge asked.

'We'll go,' Jamesie said with feeling. 'I hate the mart. We'll go.'

'We'll go in the name of God. We'll go like good Christians,' Patrick Ryan laughed.

Slowly they untangled themselves from the crush of men around the ring and reached the wide passageway between the pens. At a distant pen they saw the priest and his sacristan looking at cattle.

'You'd think he'd go and get someone else to sell the cattle for him. It doesn't look the thing to see him in his black gear in the middle of the mart,' Patrick Ryan said.

'I'd have no fault with poor Father Conroy. He's as good, as plain a priest as ever came about,' Jamesie said.

'If his black gear hasn't a place in the cattle mart, it hasn't a place anywhere else either. It either belongs to life or it doesn't,' Ruttledge said.

'Everything has its place, lad. Even you should know that,' Patrick Ryan said.

'Shots, shots!' Jamesie warned gently.

'They had this whole place abulling with religion once. People were afraid to wipe their arses with grass in case it was a sin.'

'They'd be better off with hay,' Jamesie said while nudging Ruttledge to stay silent. Because of the crowds filling the sidewalks they had to thread their way through the town. Patrick Ryan started to chew the side of his mouth, a sure sign he was in foul humour, but it changed quickly as soon as people greeted him. Their progress through the town was slow. Jamesie and Ruttledge paused several times and waited while Patrick delighted in the chance meetings. They did not mind. They had the whole day.

'Don't go against Patrick in anything to do with religion or politics or we'll be sick all day listening to lectures,' Jamesie warned during one of the waits, and Ruttledge nodded agreement.

There were three detectives instead of the usual two in

the alleyway across from Jimmy Joe McKiernan's bar. The door of the bar was wedged open to let in air. Men stood shoulder to packed shoulder outside the counter of the narrow bar as far back as the eye could follow, spilling out into the wide yard at the back. The hubbub of the voices was intense.

'They're getting surer of themselves. They think their day will be soon here,' Patrick Ryan said.

'They honoured themselves at Enniskillen. How many innocent people did they kill and maim?' Ruttledge said.

Jamesie stretched out his boot to press hard on Ruttledge's, reminding him to be silent.

For the first time that year the cabbage man was outside Luke Henry's bar. The doors of the van were open, on view the neat rows of plants – Early York, Flat Dutch and Curly – tied in bundles with yellow binder twine.

'Me old comrade,' Jamesie took hold of his arm. 'The winter is over.'

The man was wearing overalls and his pleasant round face under a cloth cap was smiling. 'The plants are ready for spring, whatever about the weather,' he said self-effacingly. 'You wouldn't think of coming back to chance it with the potatoes again?'

'No, not on a bet,' Jamesie put his hand out with finality. 'Too old. Finished. No use.'

'You wouldn't try me out?' Patrick Ryan asked roguishly.

'There's only the one Jamesie,' the cabbage man said. 'They pegged away the mould when they made Jamesie.'

Jamesie cheered and everybody laughed. All three men bought a bundle of Early York. As Jamesie continued chatting, Patrick and Ruttledge entered the bar.

'He could be there an hour yet. He's a pure child,' Patrick said.

The bar was crowded. Many greeted them. Because of the high prices, there was great praise for this Monaghan Day, and there was unusual good humour. Patrick insisted on ordering the first round and buying three whiskeys to have with the three pints.

'Too much. Too much. Too much,' he heard Jamesie's voice like a measuring echo, and raised his glass in no more than a ritual protest. 'Good man, Patrick. You have a heavy hand but may you live for ever and never die in want,' Jamesie raised the glass of whiskey disapprovingly when he joined them but drank it with a flourish, buoyed by his chat with the cabbage man.

'You're flying, Jamesie,' Patrick countered defensively.

'Never even tried it, Patrick,' he said after finishing the whiskey, before taking a long satisfying drink from the pint.

'The same again, Mary, when you have the time,' Jamesie called softly to one of the girls serving behind the counter. He may have disapproved of Patrick's heavy hand but was determined not to be outdone.

Already, there was an air of holiday in the bar and both Patrick and Jamesie were drawing shouts and waves of recognition. Drinks would soon start to flow their way. Ruttledge told Jamesie he had messages to do about the town before slipping away unnoticed.

He walked slowly through the crowded town, with cars parked everywhere and passing traffic blowing angrily as it made a slow, tortuous way through. A few people greeted him and he returned their greetings but most people were just faces. In a little alcove by the bridge across the shallow river was the bronze statue of the harper bent over his harp. All the bars were full, the small shops crowded. There were displays in windows. He had great affection for the town but knew it came from long acquaintance and association. No two houses were alike in the long, wide, winding main street. People had come in from the country and mountain and put down a new house next to the last built house without any thought other than to shelter together and survive and trade. To prosper was such a distant dream that it was both dangerous and unlucky to even contemplate. A stream of people came and went from the Central Hotel. They were better dressed and more prosperous than the people in the bars. The Shah would have long since eaten and left. Soon, Ruttledge reached the edge of the town and found himself looking across at the small kingdom. The square was full of packed vehicles, lorries and tractors and trailers as well as cars, and he had to move closer than he wanted to see across to the sheds. Monaghan Day had brought them much business as well. People were continually going and coming and standing about in small groups at the entrance to the sheds. The big iron gates to the scrapyard were open and several people were moving about searching among the scrap. The old gardener, Jimmy Murray, had been conscripted for the day and stood on guard in his porkpie hat outside the gates.

As a child, Ruttledge used to travel on the train with his mother to this town. The low-grade Arigna coal the train burned during the war gave so little power that on the steepest hills the passengers had to dismount from the carriages and walk to the top of the slope where they climbed aboard again. In his mind he could see the white railway gates clearly, the high white signal box, the three stunted fir trees beside the rails, the big hose that extended from the water tank and hung like an elephant's trunk over the entrance to the boiler shed. For a moment, the old living railway station stood there so vividly in his mind, like an oil painting of great depth, that the substantial square looked deranged. Nobody could ever have imagined that the little station, then the hub of the town, would become this half-wasteland with the Shah lord of it all. Unease had brought Ruttledge to this edge of town. Ever since the sale he had been afraid his uncle could be riding for a fall. He had relinquished power without relinquishing place and was as vulnerable as a child to loss of face. The business was Frank Dolan's now.

He walked very slowly back. The traffic was more chaotic now, the horns blowing wildly, the doors of lorries open while their drivers went in search of whatever was blocking the way, which must have been even more frustrating still since it was nothing less than the whole disordered town. Several of the lorries were full of cattle coming from the mart and their lowing added to the pandemonium. Ruttledge met a few people he knew. The small shops were all busy. The pleasure was in walking among the human excitement and eagerness of the market. The cabbage man and his van were still parked outside Luke's. He returned a friendly wave to Ruttledge's. Only a few bundles of plants remained unsold.

The bar was more crowded than when he left. Jamesie was sitting in a corner with other small farmers, comparing sales' slips and descriptions of the animals they had sold. As always with Jamesie, he was using his hands to block out the descriptions. Patrick Ryan was with the Molloys, a family of contractors who owned and worked heavy machinery for whom he had often built and repaired houses and sheds. As soon as he entered the bar, Patrick detached himself from the Molloys and joined Ruttledge. Patrick's face was flushed but he was rock-steady and coldly charming. 'You have been so long away you must have bought the town,' he chided. 'You'll have a large brandy.'

'It'd kill me,' Ruttledge said, and shook his head to the girl's silent enquiry. 'I'll have a pint of stout. And besides it's my round and I have to drive.'

'What the fuck matter whose round it is? – all we are on is a day out of our lives. We'll never be round again,' Patrick said belligerently and insisted on paying for the pint.

'It doesn't matter. We are as well to try to keep it middling straight,' Ruttledge said, and ordered a large brandy for Patrick and a pint of stout for Jamesie, who was still absorbed in discussion.

'We'll have to get that shed up of yours before the summer, lad,' Patrick Ryan said. 'It's just been going on for far too long.'

'You know there's no rush. There's nothing depending on it,' Ruttledge said easily, used to the dialogue.

Patrick went on to say how sick he was of working for the country, of travelling from house to house and listening to all their wants. A man would want six hands to keep all of them happy. The material for the roof for his own house had been bought and stored away for more than twenty years and it was time the house was re-roofed and lived in again, he said. Sick to his arse he was of travelling, he would settle down on his own fields among the neighbours and a few cattle until the hearse came.

Luke Henry must have been preparing food and drink since the early morning. Now he sat with arms folded on a high stool inside the counter, leaning back against the shelves that rose high above him, glinting with amber and blue and pale lights from the rows of bottles. The red wig failed to hide the grey of his hair along the sides and at the back. The expression on his face was kindly and contented as he watched the young people he had hired for the day go about their work. Occasionally, with great charm, he rose from the stool to lean across the counter to an old customer who wasn't receiving attention or to greet or say goodbye to someone entering or leaving. His movements were slow but precise; they had been refined by practice to their essentials. Then he slipped back again into repose on the stool.

'Me old comrade.'

Ruttledge suddenly felt a heavy blow on his shoulder, and before he turned he knew that his friend was well under the weather.

'We are having a great day,' Jamesie said and Ruttledge handed him the pint he had brought.

'It's only starting,' Patrick Ryan said, but Jamesie didn't rise to the bait. He was too tired.

There was no attempt to buy another round. Ruttledge said he could drink no more and drive. He would prefer to head for home and Jamesie said he would leave as well.

'God hates a coward,' Patrick Ryan, who had no intention of leaving, reminded him playfully.

'He lives to fight another day,' Jamesie said absently and made his way to say goodbye to the people he had been talking with. There were many promises they would meet again before too long. It had been a great Monaghan Day.

'A pure child,' Patrick Ryan repeated as he and Ruttledge waited.

'Are you sure you don't want to be left to the house?'

'Unlike yourself there's nobody waiting up for me, lad. I have several clients lined up to see in the town yet. It'll be night before I leave.'

'You have somewhere to stay?' Ruttledge enquired, and Patrick Ryan flushed a deeper red.

'Did you ever yet see the actor that wasn't able to find a bed?' he responded sharply, and all trace of drink and tiredness fell from his handsome features. 'If you did, lad, you were looking at one that wasn't any good.'

'I was just asking,' Ruttledge said.

Out on the street Jamesie was uncertain on his feet but soon steadied purposefully. On none of the faces that came and went beneath the lights did he make a single comment. They passed the three detectives in the alleyway across from Jimmy Joe McKiernan's without a word. Once outside the street lamps, it was dark but the cattle mart blazed with a white light. Huge lorries continued to pass in and out. The auctioneers droning out the bids over the crackling loudspeakers sounded more than ever like prayers.

'God bless us,' Jamesie said when they saw the number of trucks and trailers still in the grounds. 'There are poor souls who won't be out of there before daylight.'

'We had a good day and got good prices,' Ruttledge said when they reached the car. Many of the cars and tractors parked ahead of them had already left. There was space to turn without going back into the mart or the town.

'We had a famous day and got famous prices,' Jamesie said. 'Even Patrick got good prices,' he laughed.

They drove in silence towards the lake. The pale reeds and

a sweep of water showed in the headlights but the rest of the lake was dark under a dark sky. Jamesie nodded off but woke and looked around him when the car swung in the open gate and started to climb towards the house.

'We're home already.'

The street was dark except for the yellow square of the small window that was as calm and beautiful as if it were the light of a vigil. Hearing the car and footsteps and voices, the cows tied up in the byre started lowing for their calves. Mary and Ruttledge kissed but as their lips touched she looked critically at Jamesie. The room was warm, the door of the firebox open on a blazing fire of turf and logs, the pair of dogs lying passively in two armchairs on either side of the empty chair in which Mary had been sitting, the book she was reading turned face downwards. The white terrier bared his teeth as Jamesie reached down to uproot him from the chair and left snarling loudly. Mary scolded Jamesie for his drinking but it was no more than ritual scolding and she had difficulty holding the stern expression. Jamesie handed her the sale slips proudly. She read them greedily, praising the prices, and was particularly pleased that Patrick Ryan got such good prices. 'I thought poor Patrick would get nothing for those greyhounds.'

'They had the age,' Jamesie said. 'There was nothing wrong with them except they weren't fed.'

Mary poured Ruttledge a whiskey but was sparing with Jamesie's measure. When he protested, she poured a few drops more but he was already too tired and happy to notice how little she added.

'He always has to go and make a meal of things. He'll be even worse when Johnny comes home,' she complained.

'Some of these ladies are far too precise,' he protested. 'They'd have you clipped and circumcised before you'd notice.'

Mary made a hot whiskey for herself. Then she removed a damp cloth from a platter with a border of white and blue flowers on which small squares of ham and chicken sandwiches were sprinkled with sprigs of parsley. Before she sat down again she refilled the kettle with fresh water and set the aluminium teapot to warm on the chimney box.

'The year'll start to fly soon,' Jamesie said tiredly as they ate and drank. 'In a few days the Lent will be in and before you'd find it'll be Patrick's Day and Easter. Everything will have started to grow. It's all going to be very interesting.'

The cycle of lambing had started. The lights were left on all night in the lambing shed; and they rose every two or three hours. The tiredness turned into muted satisfaction when all the ewes came safe.

Jamesie crossed the lake to look at the new lambs. He was incredulous when told that Bill Evans would soon be on his way to a house of his own in the town.

'What good will it do him? He'll be lost. He's been too long the way he is.'

'He'll have a life of his own,' Kate said.

'None of us has a life of our own,' he answered dismissively.

'At least he won't be abused,' she said.

'Dogs and cats around the lake were treated far better. Those people could have no luck.'

'I don't think luck has much to do with it. They could be as lucky as anybody. The bad go with the good, in and out the same revolving doors,' Ruttledge said.

'If there's a God above they could have no luck. And look at them now!' Jamesie said. 'They had no luck.'

Ruttledge went into town one evening to see what was really happening at the railway sheds. As cover he took in a broken drive shaft of a mower to be welded. On his way through the town he discovered it was Ash Wednesday. To his surprise not many were wearing ash. He remembered when everybody in this town would have worn the mark of earth on their foreheads, and if they had failed to attend church would have thumbed their own foreheads in secret with the wetted ash of burned newspapers. The Shah's forehead was marked with ash when he found him under the arch of the main shed. The sheep dog was by his side. They seemed delighted to see him.

'I think we can put a spot on it all right,' he said after examining the drive shaft.

'I see you didn't neglect your duty,' Ruttledge observed the mark of ash on his forehead.

'That'll do you now,' he laughed. 'That woman down in the hotel wanted to go to Mass and I got the job done as well. She said a while ago that she'd like to see you if you were in.'

'About what?'

'She didn't say. She wouldn't be likely to tell me.'

'How is Frank doing?'

'He hasn't hit any rocks but I suppose it's a bit early in the day yet,' he declared.

'How do you feel since the changeover?'

'Great. Should have got out sooner. It was a big responsibility to be carrying around,' he said importantly.

The conversation was interrupted by customers a number of times and by the ringing of the telephone in the tiny office. The Shah seemed to greet and serve each customer with much greater friendliness than when the business was his. 'You'll have to see the boss about that,' he would say whenever there was a question about price, and direct them to Frank Dolan, who was working somewhere deep within the sheds.

He took up the drive shaft and turned it round a number of times as he examined the break and got out the small welder and the shield. The blue light of the welder was blinding and Ruttledge went in search of Frank Dolan, picking his way among the half-dismantled skeleton of trunks and engines and all kinds of machinery.

Far back in the shed he found him sorting small parts and placing them on shelves within an arched alcove that must have served some similar purpose in the time of the trains.

He explained meticulously that he was reorganizing the storage of the spare parts so that they could be more easily found and also gradually reducing and dismantling much of what was piled in the scrapyard.

'I take it you'll not be employing young people,' Ruttledge said. The only answer Frank Dolan gave to the gentle thrust was a broad quick smile.

'How do you find Himself since the changeover?' Ruttledge asked.

'I don't know how I'd have managed without him. He couldn't have done more.' His voice was emotional, the gratitude showing clearly.

'Then everything is going well?'

'So far anyhow,' Frank Dolan said, and the talk moved to other inconsequential things.

When he returned to the forecourt the Shah had changed out of his work clothes and was waiting to go to the hotel. With his shoe he pointed out the welded drive shaft lying on the ground. 'I'd say it's not too bad,' he said with pride as Ruttledge examined the neat and skilful welding.

'It looks like new.'

'You never can tell for sure with the old drive shafts till they are working,' he said. He cleared his throat: 'I was on the phone to that woman down in the hotel while you were talking to that man. They're expecting both of us.'

As they were leaving, Frank Dolan appeared silently in the forecourt and the sheepdog went to sit by his side. On the way to the hotel the drive shaft was dropped into the boot of the car. In off the square a new development of tiny houses was being completed. The houses all had front gardens and walls and gates. A raw concrete mixer stood in the middle of the road into the small cul-de sac.

'It's for old people,' the Shah said dismissively. 'They're calling it some Irish name.'

'That must be *Trathnona*. Do you know what it means?'

'Something silly I'd suppose.'

'*Trathnona* means evening.'

'That's rubbing it in all right.'

'Bill Evans is getting one of the houses,' Ruttledge said.

'They'll be made up when they get him in the town. It's about time ye were brought up to date out there at the lake and those buckets pensioned off.'

The receptionist behind the horseshoe reception desk in the Central greeted them warmly. 'Susan,' the Shah spoke her name softly as they passed into the empty dining room. Three places were laid on the raised table in the alcove. As soon as they were seated the chef came from the kitchen in his tall chef's hat to shake Ruttledge's hand and tell them what was on the evening menu. They both had mushroom soup and the Shah had an enormous plate of vegetables with the wild salmon, but Ruttledge only wanted a green salad with the salmon. The Shah had ice cream and sherry trifle; Ruttledge had no dessert, and refused the wine or stout or whiskey that was pressed. Mrs Maguire joined the table. She, too, chose wild salmon with a green salad.

'I don't know how the two of yous eat that stuff,' the Shah remarked about their salads but otherwise was silent in the enjoyment of the food. Ruttledge recalled that the last time they had met was at the reception for John Quinn's wedding.

'A good boy,' the Shah shook. 'A warrior.'

'The marriage, I believe, hasn't gone too well,' Mrs Maguire said.

'She got some sense in the finish. She left that lakeside residence after a week,' the Shah said.

'Then he went for a while to her place in Westmeath but now he's home again,' Ruttledge added.

'They ran him,' the Shah said succinctly.

'I have no quarrel with John,' Mrs Maguire said. 'The family all stay here when they come home from England in the summer. They are charming and have got on wonderfully well in the world.' It was clear Mrs Maguire was closing the subject down and when the Shah remarked, 'Often people like John Quinn have the best children,' it was pursued no further.

'How did you find things up at the centre of the world?' Mrs Maguire asked Ruttledge in a voice that betrayed the purpose of the meeting. Its source was the same anxiety that had brought about his own visit.

'That'll do you now. There are worse places,' the Shah said defensively.

Ruttledge looked from face to face before he spoke. This man and woman were very close. Every Sunday and holy day they drove to Mass together, every day he had his meals in the hotel. There were many married couples who were not so close. 'How do you settle with the hotel?' Ruttledge had asked his uncle once. He had never seen money changing hands. 'That woman needs a lock of pounds like everybody else from time to time and she tells me.'

From similar backgrounds they had risen in the town without ever quite belonging; both of them remained outsiders; neither had the interest or desire to join the bridge or golf club or any of the other circles in which people of their standing moved; both were too intelligent and independent to want to belong where they were ill-at-ease or at a disadvantage: their culture was that of the church and the family.

'What particular things had you in mind?' Ruttledge enquired carefully.

'How do you find Frank, the business, the whole place?' she asked plainly.

'Amazingly enough – exactly the same. Nothing has changed or seems likely to change. This man appears to be working harder than ever. Frank appears grateful and happy.'

'You'd want to give him a bit of a push when he's starting out. You wouldn't want to lie on him at this stage,' the Shah said.

'Of course he'll never be the man the first man was,' Mrs Maguire said, and it brought the release of laughter.

'That'll do both of yous, now,' he shook happily, wiping his eyes with his fists.

'I was very worried when he first brought up the idea,' Ruttledge said. 'Even Kate didn't like to see him retiring or the place changing hands.'

'He told me,' she said. 'I was worried. We were all very worried.'

'There wasn't a bit of need,' the Shah said confidently.

'You can never be sure with people. Once they get the reins into their hands you don't know what way they'll drive.'

'When money and power are involved people can change very quickly. I've seen it happen too often,' she said.

'I imagine you'd think twice of handing everything over to your children,' Ruttledge said, and saw at once that he had blundered.

'More than twice,' she said, looking straight ahead.

'Anyhow this man was determined from the very beginning and it seems it couldn't have turned out better,' Ruttledge said. 'My only fear is that he's doing too much.'

'He's trying to hold on to his job,' she said, looking at his ash-marked forehead with pure affection.

'That'll do you now. That'll do yous all.' He shook with pure pleasure and rubbed his eyes with his fists.

The fields long sodden with rain hardened in the drying winds. Small flowers started to appear on banks and ditches and in the shelter of the hedges. Around Mary's old house by the lake, with the ash tree growing in the middle of the living room, hundreds of daffodils and scattered narcissi met the spring again with beauty. Birds bearing twigs in their beaks looped through the air. The brooding swan resumed her seat on the high throne in the middle of the reeds. The otter paths between the lakes grew more beaten. In shallows along the shore the water rippled with the life of spawning pike and bream: in the turmoil their dark fins showed above the water and the white of their bellies flashed when they rolled. The lambs were now out with their mothers on the grass, hopping as if they had mechanical springs in their tiny hooves, sometimes leapfrogging one another. Jamesie helped Ruttledge harness the old horse plough to the tractor and guided the handles as they turned sods and tore up ground at both houses for spring planting. Jamesie had been in the bars of Shruhaun on Patrick's Day and complained that people with big bunches of shamrocks in their coats who had been off drink for Lent were footless. The fruit trees were fertilized and pruned. Flowers were planted out. The bees were making cleansing flights from the hives and gathering pollen. Out on a bare rock, in the middle of the drinking pool by the house, the black cat sat as studious as a scholar amid all the spawn and stirring of the pool as she waited to scoop up with one white paw any amorous frog that rose too close to the rock.

Easter morning came clear. There was no wind on the lake. There was also a great stillness. When the bells rang out for Mass, the strokes trembling on the water, they had the entire Easter world to themselves.

'On such an Easter morning, as we were setting out for Mass, we were always shown the sun: Look how the molten globe and all the glittering rays are dancing. The whole of heaven is dancing in its joy that Christ has risen.'

They heard Jamesie's racket out at the gate and his hand rattling the glass of the porch before he entered the house. 'Christ has risen and God is good and Pat is earning,' he shouted out as he walked into the big room where they were sitting. 'Take a break. Have a Kit-Kat.'

'Jamesie,' they said. 'You are welcome, very welcome.'

In his Sunday suit he was shining and handsome. On the lapel of the dark suit was pinned an Easter lily.

'Kate,' he held out his hand. She pretended to be afraid to trust her hand to such strength.

'God hates a coward, Kate,' he demanded, and she took his hand.

Not until she cried, 'Easy there, Jamesie,' did he release his gently tightening grip with a low cry of triumph. 'You are one of God's troopers, Kate. Mister Ruttledge,' he bowed solemnly.

'Mister Murphy.'

'No misters here,' he cried. 'No misters in this part of the world. Nothing but broken-down gentlemen.'

'There are no misters in this house either. He that is down can fear no fall.'

'Why don't you go to Mass, then, if you're that low?'

'I thought you didn't support the men of violence?' Ruttledge fastened on the Easter lily pinned to Jamesie's lapel, abandoning the game they had word perfect by now.

'I support them all,' he thrust out his hand. 'They were collecting outside the church gate today. They'll be gathering soon to march from the Monument to Shruhaun. I shake hands with them all. You never know who is going to come out on top.'

'Would you like a whiskey?' Kate smiled, returning to the game.

'Now you're getting down to business, Kate, but you should know by now that "wilya" is a very bad word.'

'Why?'

'Look at yer man,' he pointed to where Ruttledge was taking glasses and a bottle of Powers from the cupboard and running water into a brown jug.

'I'm slow,' she said laughingly, not quite able or willing to hold the straight face the play demanded.

'You're not one bit slow, Kate. You just weren't brought up here. You nearly have to be born into a place to know what's going on and what to do.'

'He wasn't brought up here.'

'Not too far off, near enough to know. He wasn't at school but he met the scholars,' he raised his glass and cheered to greet the perfect ending to the play.

There was a long silence in which they drank.

'Did you hear the cuckoo yet?' he asked.

'No. Not yet.'

'You're very slack,' he said with pleasure. 'I heard her three days ago, at ten past six in the alders on Moroney's Hill, and twice yesterday.'

'How come you are the first to hear the cuckoo every year?'

'I'm a sleepy fox. That's the why.'

In the lull the sound of distant drumming entered the stillness of the house. After a few seconds the drumming broke off as abruptly as it began.

'They're gathering on Glasdrum. In a while they'll march from the Monument to the graves in Shruhaun. I remember the ambush as if it was yesterday,' he said reflectively. 'I was planting potatoes with my father on the hill. The sods had been turned and harted. I was dropping the splits in the holes my father made. They were dusted with lime. There was nearly always a cold blast on that hill.

'We saw them coming up through the bog in single file with the guns, and sloping on up towards Glasdrum under cover of the hedge this side of the river. They were all very young. Some of them were not much more than boys, God bless us all. They were planning to take cover in the ditches and to ambush the tender coming from Shruhaun as soon as it got to the top of Glasdrum.

'They walked straight into a trap. The Tans had got word, and a machine gun was set up. I never heard the sound before or since: a tinny sort of rat-tat-tat.

'Mulvey's red bullock got hit in the eye with one of the first rounds and staggered in circles round the field for hours, bellowing. The poor fellas didn't stand an earthly. Those that were able did their best to escape. All of them were wounded. They tried to hide as soon as they got as far as the bog.

'They were followed down with bloodhounds. There was an officer with a revolver and twelve or fourteen men with rifles. As soon as the bloodhounds sniffed out a man, the officer blew a whistle for one of the soldiers. There was never more than the one shot. None of them put up a fight. They had ditched their guns on the way down. Some of the guns were found later.

'We were in full view and had only to look down. My father warned me not to be looking and to go on dropping the splits as if nothing was happening, but you couldn't but look. They could have seen us plain as well but they never looked our way. We could have been a cow or a horse for all the notice they took.

'We ran out of splits. We stopped all the holes and scuffled the ridges and then my father said he'd chance it to the house for a fresh bag.

'Oh my father was strong in those days. He thought nothing of rising at daylight and he'd have an acre of meadow cut with the scythe before the sun was over Moroney's Hill. I saw him walk the eighteen miles to buy a young horse at the fair in Swanlinbar and he'd have walked the same eighteen miles home if he hadn't bought the horse. He never spoke much. He was ignorant and thick and believed in nothing but work and having his own way in everything, but we never went hungry. My poor mother was like a wren or a robin flitting to his every beck and call. The likes of him wouldn't be tolerated nowadays. They'd be hammered!' He drove his fist into his palm in emphasis and resentment. 'They'd have every right to be hammered.'

'Wasn't your mother afraid to be in the house?'

'She was cutting the splits and Johnny was helping. They heard the shooting and weren't sure what it was but knew better than to open the door. They could tell my father's step on the street when he came for the splits. What could they have done anyhow if it wasn't his step?'

'You went on planting?'

'What else could we do? If we ran or hid they might think we were spies. All the time we could hear the bawling and roaring of Mulvey's red bullock as he went round in circles. After a long while they headed back for Glasdrum without ever coming near us, two men dragging a corpse between them by an arm. The men that lay wounded on Glasdrum they didn't shoot. All were brought to Carrick in the lorry. I often think of that line of young men filing up through the bog towards Glasdrum in the morning and the terrible changes a few short hours can bring.

'Not until we quit setting for the day and it was close to dark did we venture down into the bog. You'd swear to God nothing had happened. There wasn't even a spent shell. Then from a clump of sallies hanging out over the river we heard, "Hel-lo . . . Hel-lo . . . Hel-lo" in a half-whisper as if the caller was half-afraid to be heard.' Jamesie laughed as he tried to capture the tension in the call between the need to be heard and the fear of being heard.

'We went to run away. In the near darkness we thought it could be a ghost of one of the dead men. He had heard our voices and knew we were children. "Hel-lo . . . hel-lo . . . hel-lo . . . hel-lo," he was calling out as hard as he was able. It was Big Bernie Reynolds in the middle of the clump of sallies out in the river. His head was just above the water. He had got into the river further up and worked his way down till he reached his depth. That's how the bloodhounds lost his trail. They also said that the coldness of the water saved him by stopping his bleeding. Somehow he wedged himself in the middle of the sallies so that he wouldn't drown if he passed out. He was very weak. My father got him out of the river by running a rope beneath his arms. We had to run and tackle the pony. For all my father's strength, it put him to the pin of his collar to get Big Bernie lifted on to the cart.

'We had Big Bernie for several weeks up in the loft behind the pony's harness. The priest came and the doctor. We used a ladder. I often held the lantern while Doctor Dolan changed the bandages.

'Hel-lo . . . hel-lo . . . hel-lo,' Jamesie called out suddenly, no longer rendering the plea or call faithfully, but turning it into the high cry of a bird calling out of the depths of the bog.

'The houses on the mountain were raided but luckily not one of the houses round Glasdrum was touched. If they had come and looked in the loft we were gonners. Big Bernie never spoke much. I used bring him his food and drink and take and empty his pot. He hardly ever said a word. My father gave out the rosary at night but he never answered down any of the prayers. Maybe he was afraid there could be somebody out on the street listening. As soon as he was fit to be moved they came for him at night with a sidecar.

'Then they came for poor Sinclair, the Protestant, nine fields away. The Sinclairs were quiet and hardworking and they kept to themselves like all the Protestants. They knew as much about the ambush as we knew.

'Sinclair's wife met them when they came to the back door. She thought they were calling about a mare they had advertised in the *Observer* that week and pointed them to the byre where Taylor was milking. They shot him like a dog beneath the cows and said he had confessed before he was shot. Oh, we are a beautiful people, Kate. They shot him because somebody had to be made to pay and poor Sinclair was a Protestant and the nearest to hand. All the houses around were raided the next day. They searched the loft and threw down the pony's harness but found nothing.

'Never, never, never did Big Bernie Reynolds come back once to the house to as much as say thanks, and we could have lost our lives while he was there. We never, never had as much as a word from the night they took him away on the sidecar till this very day and we are not likely to hear now unless he rises out of the ground.

'After the war he grew rich in the town. He was on every committee in the county. As he got old he used often sit outside his shop on a warm day. Do you think he'd ever recognize us as we passed?'

'Couldn't you have stopped and reminded him? People often forget and are glad to be reminded.'

'I'd be very apt,' he said scornfully. 'He knew where we

lived. Would you forget if you were pulled out of the river and hid and fed in a loft for weeks? We didn't mind. You wouldn't leave a cat or a dog in the river, never mind a wounded man. In the spring and sometimes when it's not spring I often see myself and my father planting potatoes on the hill and that line of young men coming up through the bog and think of the changes a short hour can bring. And that's life!' he called out.

'And it is everything,' Kate said slowly.

'I don't see queues gathering down in Shruhaun trying to get out. They have started to march.' He was listening again intently. The drumming was constant.

'Wouldn't it be more fitting if they had a talking dummy calling out *Hel-lo* every minute or so instead of the stone soldier?'

'They'd not stand for that,' he said.

'Wouldn't it be better than the little stone soldier looking down the hill with his gun?'

'They have left the Monument,' he said. 'There's no way even you, Kate, could get Hel-lo out of a stone.'

'All you would have to do is put a long-running tape in the head that would call out Hel-lo every so often.'

'They'd not stand for it. They'd think you were making fun of them.'

'But isn't it closer to what happened?'

'It wouldn't make any differ. These are serious people. They would shoot you. God, but you'd love to be behind the ditch when the tourists get out of their cars with the cameras and to see their faces when the statue says *Hel-lo*. It'd be nearly worth doing it just to see their faces.' He laughed and drank slowly what remained in his glass. 'I'll never forget the first Hel-lo. There was a terrible gap between the "Hel-" and the "Low". The poor fucker was afraid he'd be heard and afraid of his arse he'd not be heard. Now it's a monument and an Easter march. The dead can be turned into anything,' he said almost in wonderment.

'Why don't we go?' Ruttledge said.

When they came to the lake, Jamesie said, 'Lord bless us, not a soul in sight on this shore. There were Sundays when this shore was black with people. There were some awful poor innocent people going then. They'd believe anything and were easily pleased. Now nothing but the divers and the swans.'

There were primroses and violets on the banks of the lane and the dark leaf of the wild strawberry, dandelion in flower and little vetches. It was too early to scent the wild mint but they could see its rough leaves crawling along the edges of the gravel. The drumming was closer. They could hear the fifes and tin whistles. Jamesie lifted his bicycle from the hedge and cycled alongside. They hurried. When they reached the main road there was nobody else waiting. A Garda squad car had come round the turn. A colour party followed. They wore black shoes and pants, white shirts, black ties and gloves, black berets and dark glasses. Out in front a lone marcher bore the tricolour. In threes the others marched. They carried placards with slogans and photos of Pearse, McDermott and Sands on green, white and gold backgrounds. The effect was somehow sinister and cheap. A small crowd followed the band. A few were local activists but most were from the North. In the middle of the crowd, Jimmy Joe McKiernan walked quietly, the head of the Provisionals, North and South, with power over all who marched. A second Garda squad car followed at a discreet distance.

'One thing you can say about Jimmy Joe is that he never pushes himself out in front,' Jamesie said with approval.

'They'll probably be putting up another statue to him one of these years,' Ruttledge said.

'In jail, out of jail, pulled in for questioning at all hours, watched night and day by the detectives from the Special Branch. Since he was a boy he's been with them and nothing much was ever happening. It must have been a pure godsend when the North blew up.'

'Have any of the marchers any idea of what really happened at Glasdrum?'

'Not a clue. They're not from here and weren't born then. Jimmy Joe is the only one who knows, and he doesn't care. All he cares about is turning it around into a bigger thing. That's why they'd never stand for your shouting dummy. It's in the other direction they want to go.'

'What's that?' Ruttledge asked.

'Big show. Big blow. Importance.'

When the second squad car passed, a small group came into view standing outside the cottage on the corner farther down the road. They had been watching the march and were now waving to the Ruttledges and Jamesie to join them. Patrick Ryan was there and Big Mick Madden, an old antagonist of Jamesie's who owned the cottage. With them were three teenage boys.

'Leave them to hell. We'll stay as we are,' Jamesie said, but it was too late. The Ruttledges were already moving down the road. He didn't want to be seen as the one who turned back.

Big Mick Madden was powerfully built. When young he had gone to work in factories and on building sites in England and had come home in his forties on his father's death. A good melodeon player, he had made money playing in bars and at weddings until drink forced him to give up both music and drinking. While aggressive and boastful, he was also engagingly boyish. The cottage was the traditional three rooms, neat and whitewashed, the door and window frames painted red. Grey sheets of asbestos had replaced the thatch. He embraced Kate and shook hands warmly with Ruttledge but turned at once on Jamesie.

'Have you heard the cuckoo yet?' he demanded.

'Ye can hear nothing out here along the road,' Jamesie countered defensively. 'Your ears are deafened with cars and trucks.'

'Deafened,' Big Mick repeated derisively. 'Elsewhere they

are putting men on the moon and flying to the stars and here we have clients with their ears to the ground trying to be first to hear the cuckoo!'

'Not a great class of bird to be listening for either,' Patrick Ryan added. 'Laying eggs in other men's nests, pushing the rightful eggs out, tricking the poor birds into drawing and carrying, and all he contributes is a song, "Cuck-oo . . . Cuck-oo . . . Cuck-oo . . ."'

'Out in the world they are putting men on the moon and here we have old blows trying to be first to hear the cuckoo,' Big Mick repeated.

'I listen for the cuckoo every year,' Kate said.

'Don't be standing up for him, Kate,' Big Mick warned. 'Give him an inch and the frigger will build nests in your ears.'

'I listen to the cuckoo and call out "Cuckoo" so that people can hear him before their time,' Patrick Ryan said, and gave a passable imitation of the clear call.

'Good man, Patrick,' Big Mick Madden warmed. 'Pack those old blowers and dukers with lies.'

'No, I'd not be fooled. I'd know full well,' Jamesie said dismissively. It was his only contribution.

Ordinarily so nimble and playful, he could not function in the face of such aggression and contented himself with pulling faces for the three youths. Soon he had them laughing at his dumb show behind Mick Madden's back. At first, Mick thought the boys were laughing with him, and this increased the vigour of his abuse, but gradually he grew suspicious and would suddenly whirl round in vain attempts to catch Jamesie in the act.

'We better be making tracks,' Ruttledge said after a time. Patrick Ryan had plainly enjoyed the meeting and the confrontation and made promises as they parted to be around shortly to visit them all. The boys waved shyly and Big Mick hurled a few parting insults after Jamesie with plain enjoyment.

'I never hear. I'm like water and the duck,' Jamesie raised his hand resignedly. 'That Madden is unseemly,' he said as they turned down towards the lake. 'If he had manners he could still be going into bars and houses and have company and a drink or two but he had always to go and do the gulpen. Now he can go nowhere. He has to skulk in the house on his own, driving those young boys wild with talk of all the black women he rode in England. He rode nothing either here or in England. He'd be afraid of his arse.'

'He's still a fine-looking man,' Kate said.

'These fellas are all afraid, Kate. They'll talk plenty and then turn back. They'd sicken your face.'

'At least John Quinn isn't afraid,' Ruttledge said lightly by way of change.

'They say John Quinn never went with women when he was in England the time the first wife was alive. He worked all the hours he could get his hands on, sending every penny home. You can never tell with people,' Jamesie pondered soberly.

They had drawn close to the water. Jamesie stopped suddenly and raised his hand. All the way from the old abbey and graveyard in Shruhaun floated the melancholy notes of a bugler.

'And that was Him who was married to Her,' he said when the distant bugle notes died. He did not move for a long time as he listened, and then climbed on his bicycle and turned round to bow low. 'I have decided, I have decided after serious deliberation that I never liked yous anyhow.'

The sun was now high above the lake. There wasn't a wisp of cloud. Everywhere the water sparkled. A child could easily believe that the whole of heaven was dancing.

The cows calved safely and were out on grass with their calves. A single late ewe that could not open was lost with her lamb. They had taken the lamb from her, broken and dead, and she died of shock before morning. She and her lamb were their only loss.

Monica came to tell them that she was going to marry again. They were glad and wished her happiness and it was arranged that she would bring Peter Monaghan to the house for an evening.

'I wanted you to know before his lordship hears. God knows what he'll say when he hears,' she smiled in her self-depreciating way. 'What I was most worried about was the children, but they seem to have got used to Peter though they were very cool to begin with. We met in the church choir. I'm sure when the poor Shah hears he'll begin to lose his faith in churches.'

It is not always true that people repeat their first sexual choice endlessly. On the surface Peter Monaghan could not have been more different to the hard-drinking, extroverted popular businessman Monica had first loved and married. He was attentive, even diffident, drank little and was in thrall to Monica. What he shared with Paddy Joe and Monica was that, like them, he was intelligent. The evening she brought him to the Ruttledges went well and another evening was arranged at Monica's house.

'It looks as if there's going to be a wedding,' the Shah announced ponderously the following Sunday, his hand on the sheepdog's head.

'What wedding?' Kate enquired.

'Monica,' he cleared his throat. 'You might well have known. She's going to the river again. You'd think one round of the course and four children would be enough for the silly frigger.'

'Who's the fortunate man?'

'Some poor harmless gom of a teacher. He'll get his eyes opened. She was well able for poor Paddy Joe and the size of him and his large Crested Tens. "There's not many of your size walking around," the doctor told him,' and at the very recollection of the doctor's warning to his old adversary, he started to rock with amusement and to shout at the dog 'Who's the boss?' which set the dog barking. 'I could see

262

well what she was up to when we were in that hotel by the ocean in Donegal. Her father's side of the house were all silly in that direction. Daft sexy friggers.'

'Monica is an attractive, intelligent woman,' Kate said carefully. 'If she has found someone she's happy with she'll have a better life than bringing up four children on her own. I hope they'll both be happy.'

'They're welcome to it,' he said vigorously, as if offering poison.

The plum trees blossomed, then the apple came and the white brilliance of the pear tree. May came in wet and windy. The rich green of the grass in the shelter of the hedges travelled out over the whole fields. Weeds had to be pulled from the ridges, the vegetable garden turned and weeded. Foxgloves appeared on the banks of the lane and the scent of the wild mint was stronger along the shore. Each night the black cat took to leaving the house before it was closed and returned soundlessly or noisily with her prey through the open window in the early light. All the hives were working. The spaces between the branches of the trees along the shore filled with leaves and were now a great broken wall of green. In the clear spaces through which the water showed it looked like sky, until the eye travelled to the farther shore.

When the lambing was long over, Kate came on a ewe, a late lamb of the year before, not much more than a lamb herself, with a new lamb that was completely black. She had been checking the sheep and had come up with the worst of all counts: there was one missing. She listened for cries or bleating but there were none. The leaves stirred in a hum of insects and loud birds. A frenzy of gulls came from the lake. Crows were squabbling somewhere else, blackbirds set up derisory rackets in the whitethorns. She searched along the drains and hedges in growing anxiety at each empty field. She was about to turn back to the house for help when she came on the young ewe high on a bank in a small clearing between briar and whitethorn. She was chewing away in contentment and watchfulness, the perfectly formed black lamb by her side. The ewe put her face momentarily down to check the lamb's scent and then looked possessively back at Kate. The place the ewe had found on the bank was both a sun trap and a sheltered lawn. They were a picture of happiness.

Not until evening did the young ewe leave the safety of the bank, but she stayed clear of the flock for another day. The little black lamb and the ewe were always together and a little apart from the flock.

An evening after rain Ruttledge ran the whole flock into the shed for an overdue dosing. With the dosing pack and a can of green aerosol spray he went through them quickly, even impatiently, as his clothes were soaking from the wet wool. When he let them back out into the fields there were the usual cries of the separated lambs and mothers searching for one another, but one ewe continued to cry and came right up to the bars of the gate after the rest had all found one another. As soon as he recognized her as the ewe with the late lamb he caught his breath and started to curse. After searching here and there, he found the lamb lifeless in the straw of the shed. The small lamb had been knocked in the milling about as he seized the ewes and trampled underfoot.

'I have bad news. The black lamb is dead.'

'What happened?' She went still.

'I dosed them for fluke. I was late and in a hurry. I didn't think how small the lamb was. I should have thought.'

'It wasn't your fault.'

'Nine times out of ten he would have been all right. It was bad luck he fell. I could have picked him out and put him safe.'

'That's easy to know now.'

'At least it was a male. We couldn't have kept the lamb.'

In the silence they could hear the loud calling of the mother at the back of the house.

'One good thing. They are not like us. She'll have completely forgotten him in another day. Tomorrow it will be as if he never existed.'

In spite of the knowledge that it was indulgent and waste-ful, they were not able to ward off a lowering cloud. It was as if the black lamb reached back to other feelings of loss and disappointment and gathered them into an ache that was out of all proportion to the small loss.

Jamesie came without knocking, calling out softly, 'All work, no play – finding it much easier; take a break.' He was halfway across the room to the big armchair beneath the window with his head held low when he stopped. 'What's up?' he asked.

'We had a bit of bad luck.'

'What sort?'

'There was a late black lamb,' they said.

'You can quit that,' he said. 'These things happen. Anybody with livestock is going to have deadstock. There's no use dwelling. You have to put all these things behind you. Otherwise you might as well throw it all up now and admit that you're no good.'

As he spoke, the black lamb became an instant of beauty, safe by the side of the young ewe on the bank in the sun, and was gone. The beauty of that instant in the sun could only be kept now in the mind.

Jamesie himself had come to the house on a troubling errand of his own. In earlier years Jim and Lucy and the chil-dren had often visited the Ruttledges but in more recent years the visits had ceased. This had come about naturally, without incident or unpleasantness, in the ebb and flow of human relations: standing invitations had remained in place without being taken up by either side.

Now Jim and the family were coming from Dublin at the weekend. The child Margaret had seen Ruttledge cooking steaks on the iron grill the Shah had made for the old fire-place in the front room. They wanted to know if they could come over to the house and if Ruttledge would cook meat on the fire. Jamesie was so unsettled that he rose to leave even as he made the request. Ruttledge forced him back down into the chair by the shoulders.

'We'll have a feast.'

'Too much. Too much,' he protested.

'It'd be better if they can come on Saturday. The Shah is always here on Sunday.'

'They can come either day. It makes no differ. They are coming for the whole weekend and are staying in the Central. The house is too small.'

They talked of the pleasant times they all had together when the children were small, and he grew easier. They walked him down to the lake. As the heron rose to lead him out along the shore, out of pride he protested again. 'I didn't want to ask but Mary said "Have they ever refused you anything?" That's all the more reason not to ask, I told her. It's Lucy that wants to come over. Jim wouldn't care. It's she that wants it more than the children.'

'What does it matter who wants. Isn't it a great excuse? We'll have a feast. It'll be as good as Johnny coming from England. Unless we hear differently we'll expect you all at two o'clock on Saturday.'

'Too much. Too much,' he protested.

'You were like an angel coming today,' Kate said. 'I was a bit down.'

'No good, Kate. No good and I thought you didn't believe,' he countered sharply.

'There are lay angels,' she said.

'No wings. Can't fly,' he called out as he cycled after the disappearing heron.

Ruttledge recognized Bill Evans's loud knocking on the porch but not his step or walk. There was no sound of the stick on the floor, no swishing from the big wellingtons. When he reached the doorway he stood transformed. He had a new haircut, was cleanly and expertly shaven. He was wearing a fine new wool suit, a white shirt, a dark tie with white spots, and new black shoes that creaked.

'You're shining.'

'Not too bad anyhow,' he grinned as he shuffled towards the white rocking chair.

The sharp features were refined by hardship, but the eyes had learned nothing, not seeing any further than what they looked at.

'I've never seen you better. Where did you get all the finery?'

'In the town,' he answered readily. 'Father Conroy got them. I'm leaving yous. I'm going to the town to live.'

'How did that come about?'

'Father Conroy,' he said.

Automatically, Ruttledge reached for the small ration of cigarettes, set the kettle to boil and got sweet cake from a tin.

'Have you nothing better than tea today?'

'You're right, Bill. It's a special day. There's whiskey and brandy.'

'Brandy,' he said.

He had already lit one of the cigarettes and was inhaling slow deep breaths, releasing each breath haltingly. Ruttledge poured a careful measure of brandy. Bill Evans downed it in a single gulp and demanded more. Another small measure was poured and a token measure poured into a second glass. 'That's all, Bill,' Ruttledge said firmly. 'We can't have you staggering around when the priest calls.'

'I'll be topping,' he argued.

'I hope you'll be very happy in the town,' Ruttledge raised his own glass.

'Good luck, Joe. And may you never go without.'

'What do you think you'll do in the town?'

'I'll do lots,' he said, and then a stubborn look crossed his face. He would say no more.

'What's happened to your old clothes?'

'They're above in the house.'

'Will you be taking them with you?'

'No,' he laughed. 'You're getting as newsy as Jamesie.'

'Will you come back out to see us at all?' Ruttledge asked as he walked him to the gate.

'I'll not,' he laughed again as if the very idea was ridiculous. 'Everything is in the town.'

'Don't forget to say goodbye to the missus for me,' Bill Evans said when they reached the alder tree.

'She'll be sorry to have missed you,' Ruttledge said. 'I'll not say goodbye to you myself as I'm sure to see you in the town.'

'Don't forget the fags when you come.'

'I'll not forget.'

In his new shoes and clothes he walked slowly and never looked back. The branches along the lake had long become intertwined overhead, and as they were now in full leaf the lane had turned into a green tunnel shot through with points of light. From time to time, in his slow walk uphill through this green shade, he stood and rested as if he was still carrying the buckets.

In the evening the priest's car drove past the porch and turned under the unfinished shed to roll back down to a stop outside the porch door. Ruttledge went at once to greet him. Inside, he accepted a chair but would not take tea or coffee.

'Is Herself away?' he asked.

'No. She's outside somewhere.'

They talked of grass and the weather and cattle.

'Of course I saw you on Monaghan Day,' Ruttledge said. 'I heard you got great prices.'

'Prices were never as high since,' he said. 'I made the mistake of buying in some that day,' and he went on to explain how he had seen Ruttledge but had a rule never to greet anybody in the mart or he would spend his whole day greeting and speaking. 'There are people in the parish who complain that I shouldn't be in the mart at all. They'd turn you into some sort of doleful statue if they could.'

'What do you think of that?'

'It's obvious what I think,' he said bluntly. 'I suppose you know or guess the errand I'm on?'

'He was down here a few hours ago, all dressed up, and told me you'd bought him the clothes.'

'I didn't buy them for him. I got help in that,' the priest said with surprising distaste. 'I did pay for them but not with my own money.'

'I hope he'll be happy in the town,' Ruttledge said.

'We all hope he'll be happy,' he said with a hint of aggression as he rose. 'Whether he will or not is another matter. Sometimes I think it may be better to let these mistakes run their course. Attempting to rectify them at a late stage may bring in more trouble than leaving them alone. We shall see.'

'I'm glad he's having his chance no matter what happens,' Ruttledge said. 'What else did any of us have?'

The priest looked at Ruttledge in plain disagreement but was unwilling to argue or to linger. 'I'm not going to be very welcome up there. They are losing quite a bit of money, the State pays them every week as well as their man.'

'I doubt if I'd be any support,' Ruttledge smiled grimly.

'None.'

'What are they going to do for water?'

'Can't they make it?' the priest said without humour as he turned away.

Preparations were made for the Saturday. The house was scrubbed and aired, shopping done in the town, the best steaks bought, heads of lettuce picked from the glass house. The iron grill was cleaned and set in place between the bars of the grate. The vases around the house were filled with fresh flowers. In the centre of the table was a bowl of white roses. A bottle of red wine was opened.

They came in a new white station wagon. Soon after two o'clock it moved through the spaces between the big trees along the shore. The sun was blinding on the glass when it turned in at the alder tree. They were all dressed for a big occasion. Mary had a natural elegance no matter what she wore and was in her Mass clothes. Lucy wore a shawl of white lace over a blue silk dress and white shoes. Jim's blue shirt was open-necked and he was wearing a soft brown wool jacket with slacks. The four children were dressed in the fashionable shirts and denim and trainers of their age, but they appeared strangely downcast and grave.

'You're welcome. It's great you were all able to come.'

'You are great to have us. Are you sure you won't change your mind now that you see the crowd? They were all mad to come.' The Ruttledges knew at once that there was something wrong, and waited.

Jamesie was missing and before they had time to enquire they saw him slumped in the front seat of the station wagon, his head on his chest, dead to the world.

'We didn't know whether to leave him in the house or bring him with us. Mother said you wouldn't mind,' Jim explained.

'Bad luck to him,' Mary added. 'He went to the village on the excuse of getting messages. In the end Jim had to go looking for him. That's the way he came home.'

'Granda always has to be that bit different,' Lucy said tentatively.

'I think I've only seen him like that once. The Christmas he bought turkeys in the town,' Ruttledge said.

'Then you've never seen him when Johnny comes home. He's this way every year they come from the station,' Mary said.

'What will we do?'

'Leave him there to hell,' she said. 'He'll only fall in the fire or something if we bring him in.'

They trooped dolefully into the house. The house was praised, Lucy praising it excessively. She and Jim had a glass of chilled white wine. The children had lemonade.

'I suppose we might as well join him,' Mary said sourly when Kate offered to make her a light hot whiskey, knowing she disliked the taste of wine.

Ruttledge lit a fire beneath the grill with seasoned oak.

They gathered to watch it blaze, the shadows leaping on the white walls, and soon the room was full of the charcoal smell mixed with the faint tang of the oak. Smelling the meat, the black cat came into the room to cry and rub her fur against the children's legs. They were excited by the fire, and when it died to a red bed of glowing embers Ruttledge got them to help him put the pieces of meat on the grill and gave them plates to hold and other small tasks.

'Our friend hasn't moved,' Jim remarked from the window. 'He's still sleeping the sleep of the just.'

'That was all so simple, so perfect, so beautiful,' Lucy said as they moved from the front room to the table. All the children asked for second helpings. Everything was praised many times over and yet reflected in the excessive praise was a pall. He who would have been such fun and life were he in the room was a stronger presence by his absence.

'He made a great impression on everybody he met in Dublin at Christmas. People are always asking after him,' Lucy said as if it was a source of wonderment.

'I suppose they weren't used to the like of him. What's strange is always wonderful. They wouldn't be too impressed if they saw him now,' Mary tried to make light of the uncertain praise.

'What Lucy says is true. Tom Murray, the secretary of the department, talked several times of making an excursion down to see him in his own place,' Jim said quietly. 'He got on with everybody. He didn't care who they were. You'd think he knew them all his life.' He spoke with an affection that reached back to his parents and was generally hidden. With it came a quiet courtesy, deepened by reserve. It was too early yet to tell how the grandchildren would turn out but they looked alert and interesting. They would not have to undergo the uprooting and transplantation of their father. In them the old learned strengths could show up in a new way.

'Granda won't know what he missed,' Lucy said cheerfully as she helped remove the plates at the end of the main course. 'That was wonderful, Kate. We have been looking forward to this all week.'

'I've never tasted steaks as good,' Jim said.

'It's the butcher,' Ruttledge said.

Ruttledge knew that Jamesie would have dreaded the formality of the meal and its slow ceremony. When the cake and cheese and ice cream were brought in, he stole out to the station wagon by the back of the house. Jamesie sat slumped as before in the front seat. Ruttledge opened the door gently and put his hand on his shoulder. 'What have you done to yourself, my old friend?'

Slowly Jamesie opened his eyes and looked at him out of a great distance of tiredness or sleep or stupor, and then shut them. Ruttledge pressed his shoulder and closed the door as softly as it had been opened.

'How is he?' Mary asked sharply when he returned, not fooled by the use of the back door.

'He's still asleep but he's all right.'

'You didn't talk to him?' she asked sharply, as if they might have conspired together.

'No, but I could see he's not sick or anything much wrong with him.'

'Bad luck to him,' she said. 'I don't know why he had to go and get ossified this day above all days. He'll be the very same the day Johnny comes home. Anything he can't face . . .' she said, and left the sentence unfinished to enter more completely into her own thought.

'Granda has always to be that bit different but I suppose he's entitled to it after all these years,' Lucy repeated.

'Entitled my arse,' Mary said vigorously.

'Now, Mother,' Jim said.

His absence had become more of a presence and served to hurry the meal to a close.

'We can't thank you enough.'

'It was lovely to have you all.'

'You'll have to come to us in Dublin the next time. There's

plenty of room. He'll be able to look after the place while you're away. It's a good job he can do something right.'

'We'd love to go.'

While the goodbyes, the embraces, the words of farewell were being said, Margaret suddenly burst into tears. Her father placed an understanding hand on her head, which only worsened the sobbing. She was joined by her sister and younger brother. The eldest boy James alone did not cry but his face was pale. The adults all made faces and hurried silently into the big station wagon where Jamesie sat without movement.

The Ruttledges saw Johnny resting in the shade of the alder tree at the gate, leaning heavily on the girl's bicycle, looking exhausted after the steep climb from the lake. He did not see them though they were only a few yards away. When he straightened, passing his hand over the hair flattened across his forehead, they went towards him. 'You're welcome home, Johnny.'

'It's great to be home. Great to see yous all and to see yous all so well.'

His suit was worsted blue. He wore a red tie with a white shirt. The bottoms of his trousers were gathered neatly in with bicycle clips. His shoes were polished but dimmed with a light coating of dust from the dry road. He leaned the bicycle against the wall of the porch and paused on his way into the house to look up at the shed.

'Patrick mustn't have been back since last summer?'

'He still talks about finishing but we haven't seen much of him lately. He's been working here and there all over the country.'

'That's Patrick,' he said.

'It's been a big year for you, Johnny,' Ruttledge said as he got out the bottle of rum and found the blackcurrant cordial far back in a cupboard of the press, while Johnny lit a cigarette, striking a match expertly on the sole of his shoe.

'A big year. Ford gave me the golden handshake. Yet it all worked out in the end more or less alphabetical. Jamesie and Mary across the lake were as good as gold as was Jim in Dublin. They all did their level best to get me to throw up England altogether and come home for good. I was tempted,' he said, tapping the ash of the cigarette on a small saucer Kate put on the arm of the chair. 'I was tempted at first but the more I thought about it the more I saw it wouldn't work out. People get set in their ways. They can't manage to fit in together any more. Once you get used to London, a place like the lake gets very backward. You are too far from everything. Jamesie and Mary, God bless them, came to see it that way as well. Without a car it would have been hopeless. You'd be stuck there in front of the alders on Moroney's Hill facing the small river and the bog. It was a great thing to know all the same that in a tight corner you were still wanted by your own. Who else can you turn to in the end but your own flesh and blood?'

He was moving in his blindness, as if he was speaking for multitudes.

'Then Mister Singh got to know and from then on I was more or less on the pig's back. I have as much in my back pocket now at the end of the week than even in the best days when I was on the line at Ford's.'

Kate made a plate of sandwiches. Johnny said he would prefer tea to another rum and black and they all had mugs of tea poured from the big red teapot.

'What is your new place like?'

'A row of old Victorian mansions facing the Forest that Mister Singh bought and turned into flats. They are nearly all professional people in the flats – men and women, you don't ask questions. They come and they go. I have my own entrance in the basement, central heating, bathroom, phone, TV, everything laid on.'

'Do you have much to do?'

'There's enough to keep you busy. Clever and all as these

people are, some don't know how to change a light bulb or a fuse. You name it. They do it. Most things that go wrong I can fix. If it's something serious I call Mister Singh.

'Days I go for a bit of a walk in the Forest. You'd miss having a dog. There's a pond at Snaresbrook where you can watch the ducks and the swans. They're pure tame. At night I go down to the Hitchcock Hotel. A Mike Furlong from Mayo, who made his money in the building game, owns the Hitchcock. We get on the best. Mike often puts up a drink for me in the Hitchcock. Mister Singh has me do all the short lets. I haven't made a mistake yet. Touch wood. Mister Singh drives a Bentley now. Before I left he gave me a rise and said how hard it is to find anybody steady and reliable these days.'

'It sounds as if everything has worked out well.'

'You could say it went all more or less to plan,' he agreed emphatically, lighting another cigarette. 'A thing about all those old buildings is the soundproofing though all the flats are carpeted. Over the basement this darkie has a long-lease flat. He speaks several languages and works as a translator. He's tall and thin and good-looking enough, with close fuzzy hair, in or around forty, though it's hard to tell with darkies. His English is very posh and he nearly always wears his Oxford scarf in case you'd make any mistake. He leaves John Quinn in the pure shade as far as whore-mastering is concerned. He can be gone for weeks or days at a time but when he's there women come and go as if there's no tomorrow. They're all white. I have never seen him with a black woman. Because of the poor soundproofing, lying there in the dark you can hear the whole performance as good as if you were in the room. There's one you could set yer alarm clock to her "Oh My God," at three in the morning. They come in their own cars or taxis. He never meets them but you should see the show when they leave. I never tire watching. You'd be in stitches. The performance never changes, from woman to woman, or with the same woman from one week to the next. Oh they are all ages, from their twenties to around forty or fifty. At weekends they generally stay the whole night and leave when it's well into the day, and that's when you get to see the whole show.'

Johnny appeared to grow younger as he rose from the chair, shaking away years of tiredness, and with a delicate movement of the hands suggested a flicking of a long scarf back across his shoulder. He walked with extreme slowness, his arm encircling an imagined waist so tightly that it made all movement difficult, pausing every few short steps to gaze soulfully into the other's eyes. At the point of parting he enfolded the woman in a long embrace, then held her at arms' length, to suffer the more what he was losing and, as if unable to endure this parting, enfolded her again to draw some solace from the last unbearable embrace. Then he stood, flicking the Oxford scarf back across his shoulder, looking after the departing car or taxi as if he was supporting the weight of the loss of all life, all love, all beauty.

Johnny suddenly drew himself erect, clicked his heels smartly together and bowed low with a sweep of his arm. The Ruttledges' applause was not feigned.

'Patrick Ryan would do it far better,' Johnny said modestly. 'But I tell you that darkie is some cowboy. He's some comedian, I tell you.'

'It couldn't be better,' Kate said.

'You'd think some of them would catch on?'

'They just lap it up,' he said.

'Do you get to speak with him at all?' Ruttledge asked.

'No. I never get to speak with him unless there's something wrong in the flat and he makes it clear he wants you out as soon as ever possible. He'd walk away to the window or stand and open a book. No. He'd hardly even have the time of day for Mister Singh. I'm dirt but I don't care. What is he but a man? He can be taken out of the air like a bird if you had the mind. Anyhow he doesn't seem to have any men friends.'

'He probably hasn't the time.'

'We were putting the trailer on the car when you came,' Ruttledge explained. 'I have to run in for a few things before the town closes. Would you be interested in the jaunt?'

'I wouldn't mind. It'd put round a few hours. What about the bicycle?'

'We can hop it in the trailer. That's no trouble.'

'That's great. I was puffed after the cycle round the shore.'

They drove in silence, Johnny folded back into the comfort of the car seat. He did not look around, not at the reeds along the shore, the summer breezes rippling the surface of the lake like shoals, the green brilliance of the leaves of the wild cherry amid the common foliage; not the wildfowl or the few swans or the heron flapping out of the reeds to lead them out before swinging loftily aside and then wheeling lazily around. He was folded back into himself as into tiredness or night.

At the gate he barely protested when Ruttledge jumped from the car, lifted the bicycle from the trailer and placed it behind one of the round stone piers.

'I should have done that,' he said.

'You're on your holidays. I'm used to the trailer. What's Jamesie doing today?'

'Down in the bog, I think. He's never in the house. You should hear the dressing down Mary gave him when we came from the train. She said he disgraced the children when they went over to your place. Jim told me about it as well when he met me at the airport.'

'He disgraced nobody but I was surprised.'

'When we come from the train he always gets that way. He's highly strung. He watches everything like a hawk and you don't notice generally.'

'Why did he go off the rails? Usually he's wonderful when the children are there.'

'In some ways he was always a sort of a mystery man,' Johnny said, tiring of the subject.

When they left the narrow tarred lanes, the car picked up

speed and Johnny sat up in the seat: he knew the names of all the houses they passed.

'You know more about the houses and people than I do.'

. 'I was old when I left. Half strangers sometimes know more about a place than the people who live there.'

'Do you regret having left?'

'Many times over. The whole country was leaving then and I passed no heed. I didn't even have to leave like most of the rest. You don't get reruns in life like you do in a play. There's no turning back now anyhow,' he smiled.

There were so many cars outside the healer's house that they had to stop to allow a truck to pass.

'Seventh son of a seventh son. At least he's doing great business. Do you think the cure works?' Johnny asked.

'Many are cancer patients who have tried doctors and hospitals and have nowhere else to turn. He blesses them and tells them what they want to hear. Maybe that in itself does good. The mind is a strange place. Who knows?'

Ruttledge told him that Bill Evans was no longer drawing water from the lake and had gone to live in a small house in the town.

'Our dogs were treated better,' Johnny approved tiredly, but wasn't interested further. He didn't look up as they passed the cattle mart or at the two detectives in the alley-way across from Jimmy Joe McKiernan's bar. At the cream-ery he sat smoking in the car while Ruttledge loaded the trailer with bags of meal and fertilizer.

'Would you like to go to Luke Henry's? We could have a drink and it'd be a comfortable place to wait while I get the rest of the things before the shops close.'

'No better place. No decenter man than Luke. It was the one call we didn't make on the way from the train. I'd like to see Luke again.'

They found a place to park across the street from the bar. The bar itself was empty, Luke sitting on a high stool behind the counter, his back turned to the door, looking at the television high in the corner. It took him a long time to recognize Johnny, with the help of clues Ruttledge provided. Then he reached his hand across the counter.

'Welcome home, Johnny. Welcome as the flowers in June.'

'Great to be home, Luke. Great to see everybody so well.'

They ordered rum with blackcurrant and a glass of stout but Luke pushed the banknote away that Johnny proffered. 'It's on the house. Welcome home, Johnny. Welcome home from England.'

'I have a few things to get around the town. I won't be long,' Ruttledge explained, intending to leave Johnny chatting comfortably with Luke. To his surprise, Johnny followed him out into the evening street.

'Wouldn't you be more comfortable in at the bar?'

'I'd sooner tag along. We'll come back together.'

The shops would soon be closing. The street was quick with last-minute bustle. In the first shop Johnny stood glued to Ruttledge like a shadow. No one recognized him. Silently, Johnny waited at the checkout until the basket was checked through. On the longer walk to the next shop he started falling behind.

'A bit out of puff,' he apologized, wiping his forehead with his sleeve. The colour of his face had drained to leave an ugly tinge of blue in the paleness.

'Are you sure you're all right?'

'Just that small bit out of puff.'

Some of the shops were letting down shutters.

'Wouldn't you be more comfortable sitting across in Luke's than rushing around the town?'

'There's no chance you'd leave me, Joe? You wouldn't forget to collect me?' he asked in a childlike voice.

'Lord bless us, Johnny. I have never left anybody in the town yet,' Ruttledge was so amazed that he reached out and put his arm round his shoulders. 'I'll come back when the shopping is done and we'll have a quiet drink together at Luke's before heading home. We can have several. It's not every week of the year we get you home.'

They put the purchases in the car and crossed to Luke's. Though the phrasing of the fear was mild, there was no mistaking the anxiety in the eyes, the terror of being abandoned in what had suddenly become a strange place. Because of the suddenness of their exit, Luke looked up enquiringly as they entered, but he was too good a barman to show surprise. He just moved their two glasses solicitously closer on the counter. There was now a number of drinkers in the bar and three shop assistants were playing a game of darts in the far corner, keeping the scores in chalk on the small blackboard. Sitting at the counter, Johnny seemed to revive and recover his ease after a few sips of rum. Ruttledge ordered another round. He decided to put off the remaining purchases to another time.

'You wouldn't mind, lads, if I had a throw?' Johnny asked the dart players when they came to the counter for drinks during a break in the game.

'Not at all. Fire away. We've just been fooling around,' they said, and gave him a set of darts with red plastic fins.

'I'll probably hit nothing. One of the summers I was home I took up the gun again. I could hit nothing.'

He flexed his wrists as he felt the weight and balance of the darts and took a few very casual practice throws before taking his place on the mat. Because he was a stranger, the whole bar went silent with attention as he threw. Magically, easily, each dart flew true. There was polite applause. Pleased and a little flustered, Johnny gathered the darts and offered them back to the boys but they insisted he throw again. For several minutes he threw and each throw went home. Only a single throw was missed and that by no more than the thickness of a wire. When he finally handed back the darts and took his place beside Ruttledge at the counter there was warm applause around the bar.

'It was the best I ever saw,' Luke seized his hand.

'It's as good as on TV,' the players affirmed.

Johnny insisted on buying another round and they drank in the glow of his success.

'I don't understand it. I don't think I ever threw as well playing for the Prince of Wales. I was sure I'd hit nothing. I haven't lifted a dart in months.'

'It couldn't have come back if it wasn't already there,' Luke reassured him.

'The gun was there once but when I lifted it again it was gone. It's a mystery. I doubt if I could throw that well again to save my life.'

It was time to leave. By now the whole bar had come to trace who Johnny was and where he came from and something of his history.

'I'll not say goodbye since I'll expect to be in again before I head back across the pond,' Johnny said to Luke.

'You'll have to come and play a proper game though you'll shame us all,' one of the dart players said. 'If you were staying and we had you on the team we'd be able to beat the rest of the town good-looking.'

'The next time I might hit nothing,' he replied modestly. 'Thanks, Luke.'

'Thanks yerselves,' Luke said as he gathered in their glasses, and they were followed out by a chorus of 'Good luck!' and 'Safe Journey! and 'Don't take to the hedges!'

Johnny was completely revived and needed no guiding to the car and trailer. Except for the bars the town was closed and had the same sense of closure and emptiness as beaches and public gardens at the end of the day.

'Your uncle is still going good?' Johnny enquired politely as they drove out of town.

'Still the same. Dines in the Central. He has sold the business to Frank Dolan but it just goes on the same as ever. You'd think it had never changed hands.'

'He must be a very rich man now. Everybody said he was crazy at the time when he went and bought the old railway.'

'He has more now than he needs. There's only so much you can do with the day.'

'It may be the whole show,' Johnny agreed.

They had left the main road and entered the green lanes, whitethorns brushing the windscreen and filtering down the light. Because of the narrowness, they drove slowly and blew the horn loudly at every turn.

'Patrick Ryan will be sure to be around when he hears you are home. Maybe we could all go into Luke's together some evening and make a night of it,' Ruttledge said.

'That'd be great. Luke's is a very friendly place. He was always decent,' Johnny said.

After the green enclosures of the lanes, the lake met them with space and light. A red sun was low in the sky.

'All I have to do is hop the bike on the trailer and run you up to the house,' Ruttledge said when they reached the gate.

'No. They'd think I was going soft,' Johnny said firmly. 'I'll just get the bicycle from behind the pier and dawdle up at my ease. I have the whole evening.'

They both got out of the car. The engine was left running.

'Are you certain now?' Ruttledge enquired a last time as Johnny took the bicycle.

'No,' he said adamantly. 'We had a most wonderful evening. It helped put round the whole day. It's all A-one. Everything now is completely alphabetical.'

While Ruttledge was unloading the trailer he looked from time to time across the lake. Johnny was climbing the hill slowly, pausing many times, a small dark figure on the pale pass shadowed by the whitethorns. When at last he reached the brow of the hill, he stood for a long time leaning on the bicycle. All he had to do from there was freewheel down to the house. Behind him on Moroney's Hill there shivered a pure sky that was turning pale as ash as the sun went down.

Within the house, Ruttledge told of Johnny's fear of being abandoned in the town and then his triumph in Luke's as each arrow flew true.

'The visit was disturbing,' Kate said.

'Because of his confusion?'

'That and because he doesn't look well.'

'What I'd like this evening is some wine,' Ruttledge said.

The table was laid, a single candle lit, the curtains not drawn. As they ate and drank and talked, the huge shapes of the trees around the house gradually entered the room in the flickering half-light, and the room went out, as if in a dream, to include the trees and the fields and the glowing deep light of the sky. In this soft light the room seemed to grow enormous and everything to fill with repose.

A wild battering on the doors and windows, as if a storm had sprung up on the lake, woke them out of deep sleep. The house was shaking. They looked at one another in alarm and then heard a voice shouting out through all the pounding and battering. Pulling on clothes, Ruttledge ran towards the noise. Outside the glass porch Jamesie stood clear as day in the full moon above the lake. His huge hand was open and beating flatly on the glass while his other hand was shaking the locked door. The glass shook in the heavy frames as if about to shatter.

'Johnny's dead. Johnny's dead. Johnny's dead,' he was calling out. 'Johnny's dead,' he continued calling out when Ruttledge opened the door.

'He can't be. I left him at the lake gate . . .'

'Dead. Had the priest and the doctor. Dead.'

'I can hardly believe. I'm sorry.'

'Dead before nine. Me and Mary were down in the bog. She left his tea ready but saw him come in on the street with the bicycle and went up from the bog to make his tea. She said he was in topping form and spoke of yourself and Kate and the great time he had in the town. When she left him he was watching Mickey Mouse on the TV. He always liked those cartoons. Twice we saw him come out on the street when we were in the bog. He stood as if he was looking across at the alders on Moroney's Hill. Mary was the first to leave the bog and heard a sort of a moan when she got near the house and found him slumped sideways. When he didn't answer she shouted down to the bog. When I got to the house he was still able to talk but it was all ravelled. The priest said he wasn't fully gone at the time he was anointed. The doctor said the heart just gave out and it could have happened at any time.'

Jamesie spoke very quickly and his disarray and shock were obvious but there was a finished feel to the account, as if it had been given a number of times already.

'I'm very sorry.' Ruttledge offered his hand and winced at the fierceness of the clasp. 'I wanted to leave him all the way up to the house but he wouldn't hear. He insisted on walking.'

'I know. He told it all to Mary when she was getting his tea. He had a great appetite after the town and lately he's only been picking at his plate.'

'I'm sorry, Jamesie,' Kate joined them in the porch. 'Will you come in and take something?'

'No. No. We have several houses to call to yet,' and it was only then Ruttledge noticed the small car waiting discreetly beyond the alder at the gate.

'Is there anything we can do to help?'

'Not a thing. Nothing. We can't find Patrick Ryan anywhere. Nobody seems to know where he's been working or gone. Some even said he could be gone to Dublin to do work for the Reynolds that have houses there.'

'We'll be over as soon as we get dressed. Is there anything we can bring?'

'No. No. Everything's got. Take your time.'

The moon was so bright, the night so clear, that the headlights of the small car showed weakly in the spaces between the trees as it crawled out around the shore.

They decided to walk. Wildfowl took fright as soon as they turned round the shore and clattered out towards where flocks of birds were clustered like dark fruit in the middle of the lake. The trees stood like huge sentinels along the shore, casting long shadows back on the moonlit grass. Here and there a barely perceptible night breeze stirred the still water, and stretches appeared like furrows of beaten silver under the moon. The heron had been disturbed by the car and did not rise until they were far out along the shore, and was ghostly as it lifted lazily towards the moon before turning back the way they had come.

'The last thing he said to me was here,' Ruttledge spoke when they reached the open gate: '"Everything is now completely alphabetical."'

'It surely was. Somewhere between Y and Z.'

The small street was filled with cars. Beyond the netting wire the iron posts of the empty hayshed stood out in the moonlight, as did the whitewashed outhouses. The henhouse was closed. Rectangles of light lay on the street from the small window and the open door. The living room was full of people. All the clocks had been stopped. The long inner room was open and several cardboard boxes rested on the oval table. The chairs had been taken from the room and filled the small living room. The door to the lower room was closed.

'Poor Johnny,' Mary clasped their hands. Her face was filled with a strange serenity, as if she had been transported by the shock and excitement of the death to a more spiritual place.

As they shook hands and took their place among the mourners, the muted voices all around them were agreeing: 'I know it's sad but when you think about it maybe it was all for the better. He wasn't old. No family. What had he to head back to? Nobody related next or near. Sad as it is, when you think about it, it could not have happened any better if it had been planned. Of course it would have been better if it had never happened – but sooner or later none of us can escape that – God help us all,' and there was a palpable sense of satisfaction that they stood safely and solidly outside all that their words agreed.

The small car that had waited outside the gate beyond the

alder tree returned with Jamesie. He was very agitated. The muted voices stopped as he went up to Ruttledge.

'We sent out word far and wide and can find no trace of Patrick. Nobody appears to know where he's gone.'

'Why is it so necessary to find Patrick?'

'He always lays the body out!'

Jamesie looked anxiously around. The house was full and though it was now well after midnight people were still coming to the house. The cardboard boxes on the oval table were full of food and drink. By custom, nothing could be offered until the corpse was laid out and viewed.

'I'll lay Johnny out,' Ruttledge offered.

'Will you be able?' Jamesie searched his face. The house went silent.

'I worked in hospitals when I was a student.' Ruttledge tried to hide his own anxiety.

'Do you think . . .?' Jamesie was uncertain.

'I'm sure, especially if I can get any help.'

'I'll help,' a man volunteered, Tom Kelly, a neighbour Ruttledge knew slightly. He worked as a hairdresser in Dublin, was home visiting his mother, and had accompanied her to the house.

'You'll need a glass first,' Jamesie said, and poured each man a glass of whiskey and waited until they drank it down as if it was essential for facing into such a task. He handed Ruttledge a flat cardboard box. 'Jimmy Joe McKiernan said everything is there.'

Mary poured a basin of steaming water. She had towels, scissors, a sponge, a razor, a pair of white starched sheets, a pillowslip. She and Jamesie led the two men down into the closed lower room. Johnny lay on the bed in his shirt and trousers. His feet were bare.

'Poor Johnny,' Mary said dreamily before moving to leave the room.

Jamesie stood by her shoulder but did not speak. He was strained and taut.

'If there's anything you want, just knock hard on the door and Jamesie will come down,' Mary said.

'Is there cotton wool?' Ruttledge asked.

The flat box contained a large bag of cotton wool, a white habit, rosary beads, a bar of soap, a disposable razor. Jamesie closed the door firmly as he and Mary left the room.

'We'll have to get off the clothes.'

For a moment, as he held the still warm flesh in his hand, he thought of themselves in the busy evening street of a few hours ago, all the darts flying true from this now lifeless hand. It did not take an ambush to bring about such quick and irrecoverable change.

By lifting the hips, the trousers were pulled free. There was a wallet, coins, a penknife, a comb, a bunch of keys, betting slips, rosary beads in a small worn purse. With more difficulty they drew the strong thick arms out of the shirt-sleeves and pulled the shirt loose. The long cotton under-shirt was more difficult still. The body was heavy and surprisingly loose.

'Cut it off.'

'Wouldn't it be better to do like the shirt?'

'It's too tight.' Ruttledge handed Tom Kelly the pair of scissors and when he looked doubtful added, 'He won't need it any more.'

'There's no earthly edge on these scissors. You can never get scissors with an edge in the country. They use them for everything,' Tom Kelly complained.

When at last he got the incision made, the cotton tore easily. They did likewise with the underpants. The only thing that remained on the body was a large silver digital watch, the red numerals pulsing out the seconds like a mechanical heart eerily alive in the stillness.

'He won't need that any more either,' the hairdresser removed the watch, but it continued to pulse in the glass ashtray until it distracted Ruttledge, and he turned it face down. He then noticed and removed his hearing-aid.

They closed the ears and the nostrils with the cotton wool, and when they turned him over to close the rectum, dentures fell from his mouth. The rectum absorbed almost all the cotton wool. The act was as intimate and warm as the act of sex. The innate sacredness of each single life stood out more starkly in death than in the whole of its natural life. To see him naked was also to know what his character and clothes had disguised – the wonderful physical specimen he had been. That perfect co-ordination of hand and eye that had caused so many wildfowl to fall like stones from the air had been no accident. That hand, too, had now fallen.

'We'd be better to lift him down to the floor.'

'Are you sure?'

'We'll have more room and we have to make the bed.'

In the sheet they lifted him from the bed. Tom Kelly shaved him with quick firm professional strokes and nicked the line of the sideburns level with the closed eyes while Ruttledge washed and dried the body.

'Does he need a quick trim?'

'Whatever you think.'

Taking a comb and complaining all the time about the scissors, Tom Kelly trimmed and combed the hair. When they were almost finished, the door burst open. By throwing himself against the door Ruttledge managed to shut it again before it swung wide. Profuse apologies came from the other side of the door. They noticed a large old-fashioned key in the lock and turned the key.

'It would have been terrible if he was seen like this on the floor.'

'We should have noticed the key in the first place.'

'It's locked now anyhow.'

They changed the sheet and the pillowslip. Very carefully they lifted the great weight back on to the bed. They arranged his feet and took the habit. It was a glowing white, a cloth breastplate with long sleeves, four white ribbons. The cuffs and breastplate were embroidered with gold thread.

They eased the hands and arms into the sleeves, lifted the back to secure the breastplate by tying the ribbons.

'They skimp on everything these days,' Tom Kelly complained. 'There was a time when every dead person was given a full habit.'

'It makes it easier for us. Nobody will know the difference. What'll we do about the beads?'

'We'll give him his own beads.'

Tom Kelly took the beads from the small purse and twined them through his fingers before arranging his hands on the breastplate. They then drew up the sheet and placed the hands on the fold. One eye had opened and was closed gently again.

'We are almost through.'

'All we have to do is get the mouth right.'

Tom Kelly fixed the dentures in place. With cotton wool he moulded the mouth and face into shape slowly and with meticulous care.

'It looks perfect,' Ruttledge said, but as he spoke a final press caused the dentures to fall loose. This occurred a number of times: all would look in place and then come undone through striving for too much perfection.

'I can hear people getting restless.'

'Mark you well my words,' Tom Kelly answered. 'Everything we have done will be remarked upon. Everything we have done will be well gone over.'

The whole slow process began again. There was no doubting the growing impatience and restlessness beyond the door for the wake to begin.

'If you don't get it done this time I'm taking over,' Ruttledge said.

Possibly because of this extra pressure the face became undone more quickly.

'Don't you worry,' Tom Kelly said angrily as he gave up his place. 'We will all have our critics. We will have our critics.'

By using more cotton wool and striving for less, Ruttledge got the dentures in place and the mouth to hold shape.

'I had it far better than that several times.'

'I know.'

'The cheeks bulge.'

'They'll have to do. Can't you hear?'

'You may not know it but mark my words our work will be well gone over. We will have our critics. We could be the talk of the country yet,' Tom Kelly said.

'I'll take the blame. You'll be in Dublin.'

'Whether we like it or not we could be scourged,' Tom Kelly said so anxiously that Ruttledge pressed his shoulder in reassurance.

'You did great. We did our best. We couldn't keep at it for ever.'

'Maybe it isn't too bad, then. We could still pass muster,' he replied doubtfully.

The clothes and waste were stuffed in a plastic bag and hid in the wardrobe with the flat cardboard box. The door was unlocked, the basin of water removed. Jamesie and Mary came down to the room. They stood in silence for a long time looking at the face.

'He's beautiful,' Mary said and reached across to touch the pale forehead.

'He's perfect. Patrick couldn't have done it a whit better,' Jamesie said emotionally.

'I had no idea he was such a fine figure of a man,' Ruttledge said.

'Stronger than me, stronger than my father, far stronger than me the best day ever I was,' Jamesie said.

A row of chairs was arranged around the walls of the room. A bedside table was draped with a white cloth and two candles were placed in brass candlesticks and lit. A huge vase of flowers was set in the windowsill.

One by one each person came and took their leave and stood or knelt. Old men and women sat on the chairs along the wall. The Rosary was said, a woman leading the prayers, the swelling responses given back as one voice.

Huge platters of sandwiches were handed around, whiskey, beer, stout, sherry, port, lemonade. Tea was poured from the large aluminium kettle. The murmurs of speech grew louder and more confident. At first all the talk was of the dead man but then it wandered to their own interests and cares. Some who smoked dropped their cigarette ends down the necks of empty beer or stout bottles, where they hissed like trapped wasps. People wandered out into the night and the moonlight. Jokes began and laughter.

'If we couldn't have a laugh or two we might as well go and lie down ourselves.'

Morning was beginning to thin the moonlight on the street when Patrick Ryan appeared in the doorway without warning, and stood there, a silent dark-suited apparition. The white shirt shone, the black tie neatly knotted; he was clean-shaven, the thick silver hair brushed.

'I'm sorry. Sorry.'

'We know, Patrick. We know. We were looking for you everywhere.'

'I heard. Word was brought. I had to dress.'

With the same slow steps he went down to the room, made the sign of the cross, stood for a long time gazing at the dead man before touching the hands and the forehead in a slow, stern leave-taking.

The loud talk and the laughter his entrance had quelled rose again. Patrick made an impatient movement when he returned from the room but the talk and noise could not be stilled a second time. When offered sandwiches, he made a dismissive gesture, as if what had happened was too momentous to be bartered for the small coinages of food and drink, but he accepted the large whiskey Jamesie poured as if he was absent and the hand that gripped the glass was not his own.

'Who laid him out?' he demanded.

'I did,' Ruttledge said.

'I might have known.'

'I told you,' Tom Kelly whispered. 'Our critics have landed.'

'I couldn't care less.'

With a peremptory wave of the hand, Patrick Ryan indicated that he wished to see Ruttledge alone outside the house. They stood by the lighted window and could see through the bowl of flowers to the lighted candles and the white stillness of the bed.

'Why didn't you wait for me, lad? Were you that greedy to get stuck in?'

'Nobody could find you,' Ruttledge said patiently. 'They looked everywhere. They couldn't wait any longer.'

'They might have known that important word would have always got to me,' he said.

'They didn't know. Someone said you could even be in Dublin. They thought the funeral would be over before you got word.'

'I suppose it was that molly of a hairdresser who helped you botch the job.'

'Tom Kelly gave great help. Any faults were mine,' Ruttledge said.

'It was some face to give a poor man leaving the world,' he complained bitterly. 'Some face to give him for his appearance in the next.'

'People seem pleased enough.'

'People know nothing, lad. All they want is to be riding and filling their gullets. But there are people who know. The trades know. I know. Anyhow it's matterless now, lad. It's done,' he said as if growing impatient of his own thought. 'I'll be over to your place next week. We'll finish that shed. It's been standing there making a show of both of us for far too long.'

People were no longer coming to the house and many were beginning to leave. Only those intending to keep watch into the day remained. Kate indicated that she was ready to leave. They took their leave of the dead man. With the watchers on the chairs around the walls and the whiteness of the linen and the flowers and the candles, the small room looked beautiful in the stillness of the ceremony. Ruttledge looked at the face carefully and did not think, in spite of all that Patrick said, that it could have been improved greatly. Jamesie and Mary insisted on walking them all the way to the lake. After the warmth of the house, their own tiredness met them in the coldness of the morning breeze from the lake. The moon had paled and the grey light was now on everything.

'Are you sure you should be coming all this distance?'

'It's an excuse to get out and draw breath. We'll be in there long enough. Anyhow, everything went great.'

'Patrick Ryan wasn't too pleased with our work,' Ruttledge said.

'You can quit about Patrick. Everybody knows Patrick,' Jamesie said. 'If the Lord God came down out of heaven he still wouldn't manage to please Patrick. Everybody, everybody said that Johnny looked just beautiful.'

'No matter what they say, Jamesie here is the best of the whole lot of them, Patrick included,' Mary said, her eyes shining.

'Jamesie is special,' Kate smiled agreement.

'Maybe I wasn't the worst of them anyhow,' he said carefully. 'We should start digging the grave about noon.'

'What tools do you want me to bring?'

'There'll be lots of tools but bring, bring the sharp steel spade and that good pick and the crowbar.'

'Do you think will Jimmy Joe McKiernan come with the hearse or will he send one of his men?'

'I'd say one of his men but you'd never know with Jimmy Joe. There's probably too much politics and trouble going on for Jimmy Joe to come, though it was Jimmy Joe himself who handed me the box and the habit.'

'Kate here was a great help,' Mary praised as they embraced above the lake.

'I did very little. It was a privilege to be with you.'

'The children aren't coming. They hardly knew Johnny

but Jim and Lucy are coming from Dublin in the morning,' Jamesie informed them as they parted.

'We'll see you soon.'

'Please God.'

As they descended the hill, they walked into the white morning mist that obscured and made ghostly the shapes of the trees along the shore. Hidden in the mist, wildfowl were shrieking and chattering wildly out in the centre of the lake. At the corner the old grey-suited heron rose and flapped lazily ahead before disappearing into the white mist. They were too full of tiredness and reflection to talk.

'What was it like preparing the body?' Kate asked finally as they were climbing towards their own house.

'I'm not sure except I am very glad to have done it. It made death and the fear of death more natural, more ordinary. What did you do?'

'Made tea, poured drinks, helped Mary make sandwiches. Did you ever see anything like that entrance?'

Ruttledge shook in silent laughter that was a thinner, paler version of his uncle's. 'Sergeant Death appeared and found he had arrived too late.'

As they climbed the hill to their own house he decided not to tell her yet that Patrick Ryan was coming the following week to complete the building of the shed.

Big Mick Madden joined Jamesie and Patrick Ryan and Ruttledge in the digging of the grave. They had to search for the family plot amid the headstones and long grass out from the monastery walls, and found it marked with a rusted iron cross in a rusted circle a blacksmith had made. Some of the marks the hammer made on the iron still showed on the rust. Once the long grass was cleared, Patrick Ryan measured the grave with a tape and marked the corners with small pegs. All four men who had watched the march from the Monument to the graves of Shruhaun on Easter Sunday began to dig. Outside the graveyard wall the priest's cattle grazed on the grass-grown ruins of the ancient settlement. They were sleek and fat from the rich grass, many calves resting with their mothers on the uneven ground. The grave sank quickly at first, but as it deepened the pace slowed: it was no longer possible to swing the pick, and each slow inch had to be scraped out with the crowbar and steel spade. They worked turn and turn about and began to talk more. Around them the bees moved about on the red and white clover and small yellow flowers. The occasional motor or lorry passed in a cloud of white dust. Away across the lakes and the bogs, the mountains stood in a distant haze of blue. As they worked, the shadow of the monastery walls drew closer to the open grave.

'This place was swarming with monks once. They had big disputes over books. They used to raise welts on one another,' Patrick Ryan asserted.

'The likes of us would be just slaves,' Big Mick Madden said. 'They ruled the countryside from here. If we stepped out of line they'd gather a crowd for a quick trial on the shore and we'd be rowed out into the middle of the lake with a stone around our necks.'

'It's all at peace now,' Ruttledge said, looking about at the traces of the streets and huts and the buildings that could be traced through the lines and indentations on the short grass where the cattle lay.

'You wouldn't know, lad,' Patrick Ryan argued. 'It's just more covered up. The crowd in charge are cleverer these days. They have to be. People have more information now about what goes on.'

They reached pieces of rotted board, bones, a skull.

Jamesie gathered the bones into a plastic bag. 'My mother was buried on the village side of the grave. If my turn is next it looks as if I'll be going down to my old father.'

'God rest the dead.'

'Rest in peace.'

'Amen.'

'My old boy is fixed over there.' Big Mick Madden pointed out another iron cross within an iron circle close by, slightly more elaborate than Jamesie's family cross; the outer arms of the cross were shaped and beaten into a suggestion of rose petals. 'It took him two whole days to die.'

All the antagonism he held towards Jamesie had disappeared.

'I remember it well,' Patrick Ryan said. 'Big John, your father, was a huge man, at least twenty stone, and wouldn't harm a child. A big crowd gathered round the house. I was there both evenings. Between every breath he drew he'd say, "It's a huar," as if he was labouring hard. After each loud rattling breath you'd hear, "It's a hu-ar," and every time "It's a huar" came out, the crowd used to burst out laughing. Poor people were easily entertained then.'

'I remember,' Big Mick said. 'I remember it well. I got home from England the night that he died.'

Suddenly the steel spade hit the rock. They could dig no further. As they were scraping the rock clean, the graveyard gate opened and John Quinn came towards them with a spade on his shoulder.

'We might have known,' Patrick Ryan laughed as John Quinn approached. 'You'd want to be out early to best John Quinn. Arriving too late to get in the way of work but in plenty of time for the free drinks in the village.'

'I heard but I heard too late. I was very sorry to hear about poor Johnny, the best shot this part of the country ever saw or ever will see,' John Quinn said as he shook Jamesie's hand. 'I was very sorry.'

'I know that, John. I know that well.'

'Look what we have gone and done!' Patrick Ryan shouted out, and John Quinn's arrival was lost in the dramatic cry.

'I marked the grave out wrong. I kind of knew as soon as we saw the bones. We have put the head where the feet should go. We have widened the wrong fucken end.'

They then widened the other end of the grave. Even John

Quinn helped and they teased him about his women as they worked. He was flattered by the teasing and responded with an earthy zest in which the singsonging cajolery was mixed with cunning and boastfulness.

When they were gathering the tools to go to the village for the customary gravediggers' drinks, Ruttledge asked Patrick Ryan, 'Does it make a great difference that his head lies in the west?'

'It makes every difference, lad, or it makes no difference.'

'In what way?'

'You should know, lad,' he said, enjoying such full possession of the graveyard that even John Quinn's presence went unheeded. 'You went to school long enough by all accounts to know.'

'The world is full of things I don't know,' Ruttledge said.

'He sleeps with his head in the west . . . so that when he wakes he may face the rising sun.' Looking from face to face and drawing himself to his full height, Patrick Ryan stretched his arm dramatically towards the east. 'We look to the resurrection of the dead.'

The shadow from the abbey now stretched beyond the open grave, but the rose-window in the west pulsed with light, sending out wave after wave of carved shapes of light towards that part of the sky where the sun would rise.

'You never lost it, Patrick,' Jamesie said, while Ruttledge bowed his head.

'Begod now, even with good neighbours all around you and everybody getting on well together and helping one another in the end, it'd nearly make you start to think,' John Quinn said.

That evening the Ruttledges drove round the shore so that their car could accompany the hearse. Already there were several cars along the far shore, and they parked the car behind a line of cars and walked to the house. Once they reached the hill they were amazed by the number of cars parked in the fields all the way along the pass.

'I've never seen such a gathering,' Kate said.

'Jamesie and Mary are very well liked everywhere. It's not because of Johnny. He's been too long away.'

At the gate to the house they met sudden consternation. The glass and polished chrome of the hearse waited outside the gate. Cars were backing out to allow the hearse to enter the small street and turn. Because of the panic there was much erratic reversing and revving of engines and clouds of smoke and loud, confusing directions. Jimmy Joe McKiernan climbed from the hearse and stood in the lane observing the panic in detached, silent amusement. Though he wore a black suit and white shirt and black tie he still managed to appear casually dressed, quiet and anonymous; he had caused the panic by arriving an hour too early for the removal. Seeing the Ruttledges, Jamesie came toward them in high excitement.

'Jimmy Joe himself has come. He thought the removal was at six instead of seven.'

'He'll just have to wait,' Ruttledge said.

When the cars had been cleared, the hearse moved very slowly down to the house past the privet hedge and the big rhubarb leaves and the beds of scallions and parsley in the small side garden. The mule came to the iron gate to inspect the hearse as it passed. The brown hens, used to all the traffic by now, went on pecking in the dirt as the long shining hearse turned, pausing to cast a yellow eye studiously on the scene before returning their attention again to the dirt.

'We were looking for you as soon as we saw Jimmy Joe come early,' Jamesie said excitedly. 'We want you to keep him above in the room till it's time to leave.'

'I'm no friend of Jimmy Joe or his movement. You must know that,' Ruttledge protested.

'Doesn't matter. You'll be able to talk to him. We can't have him down with everybody.'

'What about yourself or Jim?'

'No, no,' he said quickly. 'We're wanted below.'

298

'Patrick Ryan is your man,' Ruttledge said in desperate inspiration. 'There's nothing Patrick Ryan would like better than entertaining Jimmy Joe McKiernan.'

'No, no. Patrick would want too much ground. He's too bloody bold,' Jamesie said adamantly. 'Jimmy Joe would be sick listening. It's not much to ask. You'll be well able. Tell him, Kate.'

'I'm out of it, Jamesie.'

'It's not much. You'll be well able. There'll be whiskey and glasses and everything you'll want.'

Ruttledge saw that he would have to refuse stubbornly or agree, and he wasn't going to refuse Jamesie on this day.

They were put in the upper room. A tray with a full bottle of Powers and a big jug of water and lemonade and glasses were placed on the table at the foot of the bed. The pendulums of the four big clocks on the walls were still. The two men had not been alone together and had not spoken other than the daily courtesies whenever they met in passing since Jimmy Joe had sold them the farm above the lake all those years before. They had met in passing many times, especially in bars, where Jimmy Joe sold *An Phoblacht*. There were a few who bought it out of active sympathy, and more still, like Jamesie, out of a desire to please and keep all sides happy. There were also a few like Ruttledge who refused to buy the newspaper because they disapproved of violence and the aims of that violence. Jimmy Joe had always stood courteously indifferent in the face of acceptance or rejection. If the newspaper was taken he would hand the paper over and accept the coins with a smile or an inclination of the head; and if refused he would acknowledge the refusal with the same slight bow and turn silently away.

'I made the mistake of thinking the removal was due at the church at six,' he was the first to break the silence after the door had been firmly shut on them both and they had shaken hands.

'They think you too important to sit below and for some

reason or another I have been appointed to look after you,' Ruttledge explained apologetically.

'I'm used to people looking after me,' he responded with grim humour. 'A lot has happened since I sold you that place across the lake.'

'More to you than to me,' Ruttledge said as he offered whiskey.

There were the explosions in towns he had been linked to, kidnappings, the making and carrying of bombs, murders, maimings, interrogations, executions, the years in Long Kesh; it was a source of some surprise – but finally none – that such a man should be declining the whiskey so courteously. Easier still to imagine him on hunger strike and proceeding to the final self-effacement with a quiet, unbreakable resolve. Others he would use pitilessly as tools.

'I gave it up. I used to enjoy it once but was meeting too many people and was too much in the way of it. I don't even miss it now,' he explained.

'Would you like water or lemonade or a cup of tea?'

'I'm quite happy without anything.'

After a long silence, Ruttledge asked, 'It must have been hard in Long Kesh?' more out of courtesy in the face of the silence than any desire to know.

'It was no holiday camp,' he answered.

He had led a breakout in which his arm was broken but insisted on continuing when others wanted him to turn back. The escape and his part in that escape had been made into a ballad that was often sung at gatherings.

'They thought you'd be too busy to come yourself. They were expecting someone else to come with the hearse.'

'I often have to get a man but I find it a relief to get out among people when I can,' he said with a watchful authority in a conversation that had become more halting and difficult. In the many silences, the talk and laughter, and words of welcome and condolence, entered the room with the clink of glasses from other parts of the small house. The street was now filled with people and loud with a murmur of voices and the occasional laugh and then the constant sound of shoes changing position on the gravel or walking to or from the house.

'They are enjoying themselves,' Ruttledge reflected during one of the long silences, but Jimmy Joe McKiernan made no response.

'What do you do over there on that place of yours?' Jimmy Joe asked.

'The usual: a few cattle, sheep . . .'

'You can hardly make it into a living?'

'We would probably just get by if we had to – we don't need much – but I get outside work as well,' Ruttledge said.

'What work?'

'Writing work.'

'Is that hard?'

'Hard enough. Being out and about in the fields is much more pleasant.'

'Would the birds and the quiet over there be useful to that kind of work?'

'No.' It was Ruttledge's turn to smile grimly. 'The quiet and the birds are no use.'

'What are you doing over there, then?'

'You mean I should live closer to my markets? It is where we live, a place like any other. You asked me about the birds as well that first day you showed us the place.'

'I don't remember,' he said agreeably. 'I'm told your uncle still visits you regularly.'

'He's been coming every Sunday since we moved here.'

'I like the Shah. He doesn't support us very much but he doesn't stand in our way either. He takes life easy.'

Gradually, the talk moved into the easier waters of personalities and finally how the dead man had come home every summer since he had first left the place for England. So easy were these neutral waters that Ruttledge was fully expecting them to see the hour out when Jimmy Joe

McKiernan took him by surprise by asking, 'You don't seem to have any interest in our cause?'

'No,' Ruttledge said. 'I don't like violence.'

'You don't believe in freedom, then?'

'Our country *is* free.'

'A part of it is not free.'

'That is a matter for that other part. I don't think it's any of our business.'

'I think differently. I believe it is all our business.'

Ruttledge knew that as he was neither a follower nor a leader he must look useless or worse than useless to this man of commitment and action. As far as Jimmy Joe was concerned he might as well be listening to the birds like an eejit on the far side of the lake, and he made no further attempt at speech.

'Do you have the time? My time is plainly untrustworthy,' Jimmy Joe said with his quiet, disarming charm out of the held silence.

'We could be making a start,' Ruttledge said when he looked at his watch.

'We might as well be showing ourselves, then,' Jimmy Joe McKiernan said.

Ruttledge opened the door and stood aside. When Jimmy Joe entered the lower room there was a distinct hush. Patrick Ryan came towards him quickly, his face wreathed in effusive recognition. As soon as Jimmy Joe realized Ruttledge wasn't following, he disengaged himself from Patrick and turned back to thank Ruttledge for his company. Patrick Ryan then accompanied Jimmy Joe out to the hearse to carry in the coffin. The house quietly emptied. The door was closed. A woman started to call out the Our Father, and the Hail Mary was taken up by the thronged street until it swelled out to the people standing as far back as the cars parked in the fields.

Jamesie and Jim and Patrick Ryan manoeuvred the coffin out through the narrow doorway to the hearse with Jimmy Joe McKiernan directing and helping. Mary and Lucy followed arm in arm behind. Nobody cried out in grief or anger. Jamesie's face was taut and strained but only Mary was visibly upset. Patrick Ryan climbed into the hearse and sat like a stern, implacable god beside Jimmy Joe. It would have been customary for Jamesie to ride with the corpse on the last journey: he must have given his place up to Patrick. The hearse moved slowly out from the house. The mule was no longer at the gate but grazing far back in the field. People walked behind the hearse, thinning as soon as they reached their cars. The line of cars was still coming down the hill from the house when the hearse stopped at the corner of the lake where, on Sundays long ago during the shooting season, the guns used to gather. Once it moved on, it quickly gathered speed. The Ruttledges' car was one of the last to join the procession, and at the corner of the lake they turned in round the shore instead of continuing on to the church.

A few days after the funeral the Ruttledges drove round the lake in the late evening to see how Jamesie and Mary were and if they wanted anything. At the corner of the lake they stopped the car in amazement. A telephone pole had been set down in the middle of the wild cherries and a line of poles stretched all the way out towards the main road. Some months previously the telephone company had offered to connect each house in the country for the same fee, no matter how remote it was, and nearly everybody around the lake had agreed to the offer. After all the talk and final agreement it was still a shock to see the substantial creosoted poles in place.

The street in front of the house was empty, the brown hens pecking away behind the netting wire, the pair of dogs barking the car to the open door.

Within, the house was altered. The clocks had been removed from the walls and were spread everywhere on beds and tables and chairs. The shapes of the clocks were distinct and pale where they had hung on the walls: without them the walls looked impoverished and plain.

'The place is a mess. I don't even know if I can invite you in,' Mary said as they embraced.

'The little clockmaker was here all day. We couldn't get some of them to start after the funeral so we thought we'd get them all looked at. Severals of them haven't been telling the right time in years,' Jamesie said in a rush of words.

'He's cleaned and oiled them. He'll adjust them tomorrow when they go back on the walls. He says some are near enough to antiques and worth money and there's nothing much wrong with any of them.'

'Like ourselves,' Jamesie said.

'Do you think for a minute anybody would give money for you?' Mary said.

'Lots of money. Because I'm a topper,' he argued. 'That's what Tom Casey told everybody after he married Ellen, who was a bicycle and ease and comfort to the whole country. "Was I as good as the rest of them?" he asked her after he had performed on their wedding night. "You were a topper," she told him. "You were the very best."'

'He'd disgrace you but I suppose we are used to him by now,' Mary said.

'Did you see the telephone poles?' Ruttledge asked.

'Saw them, saw them early this morning,' he stretched out his great hand. 'They all went up today. They have machines, diggers, everything. It'll be all done in a matter of weeks. The men are from Cork. Everybody has a telephone in Cork. They have no work there now and were sent here. They go home at weekends on a bus and think this is a lovely part of the country.'

'So it is,' Kate said.

'Since everything is askew with the clocks, why don't we take a run into the town,' Ruttledge suggested. 'We'll come round another evening when the clocks are back on the walls.'

They were both plainly glad to leave the house.

'You can't twist or sit or turn with the clocks. It's great to get out.'

As she was locking the door Mary paused. 'Poor Johnny's gone. It's almost as if he never was.'

'Jim flew over to London in the aeroplane to get his things,' Jamesie explained. 'There wasn't much. The flat was in the basement and smaller than he said. Jim said it was a nice part of London. The flats were big but not all that posh.'

'Did he meet Mister Singh or anybody that knew Johnny?'

'No. No. He saw no one,' Mary said. 'He wrote a note for Mister Singh and pinned it on the door. Johnny had a will made. We were all surprised. He left everything to the children. Most of what he got from Ford's was still left.'

'That was very good of him,' Kate said.

'Johnny was always very precise when it came to himself,' Jamesie said.

'Poor Patrick took it very hard. He never quits about the acting and the plays and how on Sundays when everybody was blazing away all Johnny had to do was to raise his gun for the bird to fall,' Mary said.

'Patrick has his shite,' Jamesie said. 'Patrick had no more value on Johnny while he lived than he had on anybody else that's plain and ordinary.'

'Maybe Johnny has become big and strange for him now that he's gone,' Ruttledge said.

As they passed the new line of telephone poles, Jamesie counted them silently. 'Fourteen in the one day. In no time at all they'll be up.' They drove past the closed mart, past the two detectives standing in the alleyway across from Jimmy Joe McKiernan's, the church, Luke Henry's bar. As they were approaching the Central, Jamesie, who was leaning forward in an intensity of watching, called out, 'Hold your horses. Stop. Look,' and Ruttledge drew in along the sidewalk.

The Shah had just come out of the hotel and his round, heavy figure was making its satisfied way towards the station house, a knotted white plastic bag in his hand. At the same time the sheepdog emerged from the sheds and made his way across the square to the place where the white railway gates used to close. The sheepdog sat and waited there with its beautiful head raised. When they met, the words could practically be heard in the rhythm of the petting and endearment before the dog was handed the white plastic bag. The sheepdog walked proudly ahead with the bag but paused every now and then to wait with wagging tail as they went together towards the station house.

As they turned the car, Ruttledge pointed out the new street of tiny houses in off the square that was *Trathnona* and Jamesie rolled down the car window in order to get a clearer view.

'You'd love to go in to see what the set-up is like, how he's getting along,' he said.

'What good would that do? It's none of your business,' Mary said.

'He's probably watching TV like the rest of the country. *Blind Date* could be on,' Ruttledge said.

'No. It only comes on on a Saturday,' he answered.

In the bar, Luke Henry shook Jamesie's and Mary's hands in formal sympathy. They spoke of Johnny's last evening in the bar and how well he had thrown.

The darts with the red plastic fins were arranged in groups of three on the face of the dart board. They had two drinks in the bar and left long before the late-night drinkers were due.

Jamesie and Mary insisted on walking all the way to the house and were set down at the corner of the lake. An evening was arranged for the Ruttledges to come round when all the clocks would be back on the walls and when everything would be back to normal again.

The arranged evening came clear. The telephone poles now extended round the lake. They were surprised when the dogs didn't meet them at the gate and even more surprised to find the clockmaker's car on the street and the door closed.

The car was a small, modified car with a disabled person's sign. They entered the house after knocking. Inside, all the clocks were back on the walls and striking. The clockmaker was laboriously manoeuvring himself into place with an aluminium crutch along the edge of a table to make adjustments to the clock beside the unlit stove. Jamesie stood close by but made no attempt to help because of the clockmaker's pride. He had a beautiful, sensitive face with dark hair and an emotional smile. 'That'll do for now,' he said studiously when he made the adjustments, and swinging himself free of the table with surprising quickness he was soon in the armchair. Mary poured tea.

'I think that's all we can do for now. I'll be back this day week to see how they are doing.' He had a precise, careful way of speaking.

'You were great,' Mary praised. 'It's great to have the house near normal again.'

Suddenly several clocks struck the half-hour together but the clockmaker held up a spoon for silence and smiled a knowing smile when a clock struck late. 'I knew that boy wasn't right but we'll know more next week,' he smiled winningly. 'I think there's another one as well.'

'This man here sold John Quinn his wife's wedding ring,' Jamesie said as if he could contain this news no longer.

'I sell jewellery,' the clockmaker said in his precise way. 'A lot of people know about me by now. They come to the house. John Quinn came with his wife-to-be to buy her wedding ring. The ring was a thin gold band and cost a hundred pounds. They tried several rings and that was the ring she wanted. He paid in cash.'

'Wait. There's more,' Jamesie said.

'A few days after they ran him out of Westmeath he was back at the house with the wedding ring,' the clockmaker said disapprovingly. 'He wanted his money back for the ring.'

'She probably threw it at him,' Mary said.

'If she didn't you can be sure he asked for it back,' Jamesie added.

'In all my time I've never had a wedding ring returned. I told him it wasn't done, but he still wanted his money. To be rid of him, after making sure it was the right ring, I offered him fifty pounds. "We'll split the difference," he said. I raised the fifty to sixty pounds and told him he could take it or leave it and he took the sixty pounds. I thought it'd be the last I'd see of him.'

'Wait!' Jamesie raised his hand.

'Only last week he was back. We were all in bed but he kept knocking till my brother went and opened the door. I told Michael on no account to let him into the house and to make him wait outside. What he wanted was to tell me that he had bought a calf with the sixty pounds and sold the calf that very night in the mart for a hundred and thirty. The ring had done better on the calf than on the woman. "Could the news not have waited till morning?" I asked. He said he wouldn't be able to sleep till he'd told me how well the ring had done.'

'John was back winning. That's all he wanted people to know,' Jamesie said. 'That's all he cared or thought about.'

'I'll just wait till the clocks strike. It'll be nine in a few minutes,' the clockmaker said.

All the clocks throughout the house, magically, seemed to strike the hour together until, with a knowing smile, the clockmaker waited until one of them struck up on its own a few seconds after the others, and then one other. Then all the clocks continued ticking away quietly again.

The clockmaker smiled and made a note on the back of an envelope and gave it to Mary to keep. 'I'll be back this day week. It shouldn't take long then and we'll have all the boys striking together for sure.'

Jamesie and Mary saw him out to the car, Jamesie carrying his small tool box. They stayed with him while he stowed away his crutches and levered himself in behind the wheel and drove away. Jamesie was first to return to the house, Mary closing in her brown hens for the night.

'That little man is great. He can nearly make the clocks talk. We thought he'd be finished with them by now but he's most particular. All his people were decent and gave him great seeing to. He didn't let it go to waste,' he said as he went and took a fresh bottle of Powers from its brown paper bag in the press.

'I suppose he has the bottle of whiskey out already,' Mary teased him when she returned, but no one this evening wanted more than a ritual glass.

'John Quinn is still winning,' Jamesie said as they drank, and reached across, pretending to be about to eject the terrier from the armchair. The terrier stripped his teeth at the sight of the great hovering hand, and then Jamesie took his hand away.

'If someone is winning, then someone else is losing,' Kate said.

'What are *we* doing?' Mary asked.

'Standing put while going past,' Ruttledge laughed.

'You should have been a priest.'

'I nearly was,' Ruttledge said.

'Sleepy fox,' Jamesie cried out instinctively. 'Two arms and both of them as long as one another.'

'Did you ever hear such rambling?' Mary said as all the clocks struck ten, and then they waited until the two struck late. 'Do you think will he ever be able to get them right?'

'If the little man isn't able – nobody will.'

'I suppose they should be sold or thrown out and new clocks bought but they'll be kept for our time,' Jamesie said superstitiously.

'They'd have a tale to tell if they could speak,' Mary said.

'Wise. No daws. Never got into trouble,' Jamesie said. 'All they said was tick-tock. Tick-tock. Pass no heed. Tick-tock. Say no bad. Tick-tock. Turn a blind eye. Tick-tock. Get into no trouble. Tick-tock. Put the hand over. Tick-tock. Don't press too hard. Tick-tock. Ask why not but never why. Cleverer than the wisest that ever tried.' He cheered, but grumbled when no one wanted a second whiskey, and capped and put away the bottle without tipping a measure into his own glass. 'Ye are no good. There was people going once who wouldn't be afraid.'

They walked out into the clear night. The hens clucked on their roosts in the small house. The path was clear, winding round by the edges of the fields. The pair of dogs that had clung jealously to their chairs all through the evening now started to hunt birds in the whitethorn hedges, their impatient barking answered by the alarmed racket of blackbirds they had disturbed. The two women lagged behind the men. Jamesie was silent as they walked.

'Do you think is there an afterlife?' His question startled Ruttledge because it was so uncharacteristic.

'No. I don't believe there is but I have no way of knowing.'

'You mean we're just like dog or cat or a cow or a leaf – that when we are dead we are just dead?'

'More or less,' Ruttledge answered carefully. 'I don't know from what source life comes, other than out of nature, or for what purpose. I suppose it's not unreasonable to think that we go back into whatever meaning we came from. Why do you ask?'

'I've been thinking about it a lot since Johnny went.'

'What do you think?'

'I think if there's a hell and heaven that one or other or both of the places are going to be vastly overcrowded,' he said with surprising heaviness. Even his walk and tone had changed.

'I suspect hell and heaven and purgatory – even eternity – all come from our experience of life and may have nothing to do with anything else once we cross to the other side,' Ruttledge said briskly, anxious to hide his affectionate amusement at Jamesie's display of weight and gravity – he who was so important because of his wondrous lightness.

'At the same time you wouldn't want to leave yourself too caught out in case you found there was something there

310

when you *did* cross over,' Jamesie said doubtfully. 'They complain that poor Father Conroy is very hard on money but he did everything, everything a person could ever do for Johnny. He was in the house less than an hour after we found him slumped in the chair, gave him the last sacraments, received him in the Church, said the funeral Mass and preached a most beautiful – most beautiful sermon. In the sermon he said that Johnny belonged to a whole generation of Irish people who had been forced into England to earn their bread. In Johnny's case he was wrong but he was right in the case of nearly every other person that left from around. While there were some who prospered and did well there were others who experienced great hardship and there were many that fell by the wayside. These people forced into England through no fault of their own were often looked down on – most unjustly looked down upon – by some whose only good was that they managed to remain at home with little cause to look down on anybody. It's always the meanest and poorest sorts who have the need to look down. Everybody said it was a mighty sermon and longer than he gave for the TD's mother. At the grave he blessed the coffin and said the prayers. And do you know how much he charged for all that?'

'I haven't an idea. A hundred pounds?'

'Twenty pounds. "Give me twenty pounds, Jamesie." They say he's hard on money and I had to nearly beat him to get him to take forty pounds.'

'Less than John Quinn got back for his second-hand wedding ring.'

'John Quinn's a living sight but Father Conroy is as good a priest as could be got anywhere. You can go to him any hour of the day or night and never be run and he'd leave no man poor. Those that complain have their shite and have no reason.'

'I like him too,' Ruttledge said.

'Then you should go to Mass,' Jamesie whispered mockingly.

There was a new moon above the lake, a pale crescent. The night was so still that the lake reflected the sky and looked as deep. A huddle of wildfowl was gathered at the centre. The two swans were feeding close to the shore. High overhead, the lights of a passing aeroplane pulsed like hearts in the sky.

'You can't see sight or light of your house with the way the trees along the shore have grown,' Jamesie said and turned towards Patrick Ryan's hill, which looked ragged even in this soft light, with such deep satisfaction that the pleasure could be heard in his voice. 'Isn't Patrick Ryan the most hopeless man? The poor cattle alone and fending for themselves on that big hill and Patrick astray all over the country. I may not have travelled far but I know the whole world,' he said with a wide sweep of his arm.

'You do know the whole world,' Ruttledge said. 'And you have been my sweet guide.'

Jamesie paused, and then turned quickly away: 'I wasn't the worst anyhow,' he said.

As Kate and Mary drew close they embraced, and the Ruttledges went quickly down towards the lake. When they were close to the gate, they heard a call or a cry from the hill and turned around. Jamesie and Mary stood framed in the light.

'Kate,' Jamesie was calling.

'Jamesie,' she called back and waited.

'Hel-lo. Hel-lo. Hel-lo. Hel-lo,' he called over the lake in the high cry of a bird mocking them out over the depths of the bog. They heard coughing and scolding and laughter as Mary, and then Jamesie, disappeared from the sky.

No heron rose out of the reeds where the new telephone pole stood in the middle of the wild cherries to lead them in round the shore. The night and the lake had not the bright metallic beauty of the night Johnny had died: the shapes of the great trees were softer and brooded even deeper in their mysteries. The water was silent, except for the chattering of

the wildfowl, the night air sweet with the scents of the ripening meadows, thyme and clover and meadowsweet, wild
woodbine high in the whitethorns mixed with the scent of
the wild mint crawling along the gravel on the edge of the
water.

When they turned the corner to climb towards the house,
Kate cried out in fear. Patrick Ryan stood between the narrow high banks of the lane exactly as he had appeared in the
doorway on the night of the wake, the white shirt and face
and silver hair glowing. Everything else was black and
merged with the night.

'You gave her a terrible fright. Why didn't you show yourself?' Ruttledge demanded.

'I was on my way,' he said coldly. 'Ye weren't talking. I
was above at the house. Nothing was locked, neither car nor
shed nor house. I thought ye might be out in the fields and
waited.'

'We were across in Jamesie's.'

'I know. I heard him yodelling a few minutes back above
the lake. He'll never get sense. Already you'd think Johnny
had never died.'

'Do you want to come back with us?' Kate asked. The invi-
tation surprised Ruttledge. Her voice was calm.

'No. I was up there long enough. It's time I was heading
for the Tomb,' he dismissed the offer impatiently. 'I'm going
to be there all summer. We're going to finish that building.
One good thing about the house and place being open to the
world is that I was able to go around and check up on what
we'll need. I left the list on the table. It's propped against a
jug, but all that is matterless now. Bring the list with you
anyhow in case we forget something in the morning. Meet
me with the car and the trailer at the corner of the lake at
nine. We'll head for the town and get everything we need. It
takes a hard jolt now and then to learn us that we'll not be in
it for ever. Tomorrow we'll make a start, in the name of the
Lord, and we'll not quit until that whole cathedral of a shed

is finished,' he said in the same ringing, confident tone that had ordered Johnny's head to lie to the west in Shruhaun so that when he rose with all the faithful he would face the rising sun.

'There's no great need or rush with the shed, Patrick,' Kate said uncertainly, surprised by her own forwardness. 'Maybe it could be left there for another summer in deference to Johnny?'

He stood amazed but did not speak. The chatter of the wildfowl out on the lake was loud in the strain of the silence. With slow economy of movement he turned his back on Kate and spoke to Ruttledge, slowly and carefully. 'You must do what you have to do, lad. Meet me at nine at the corner of the lake with the car and trailer if you want. It's completely matterless whether you turn up or not. If you don't turn up I have plenty of places to go to. I'll go and entertain them all in their own houses.'

Then he was gone, walking slowly round the shore in the half-light.

The Ruttledges did not speak as they climbed the hill.

'What are you going to do?' Kate asked as they passed beneath the alder tree.

'I'm not sure,' he said. 'We can talk it through. We don't have to decide on anything till morning.'

At the porch, before entering the house, they both turned to look back across the lake, even though they knew that both Jamesie and Mary had long since disappeared from the sky.